A HUGE PANORAMIC NOVEL OF AN
ENGLISH GIRL—RAISED IN A
CHINESE HOUSEHOLD—

Pat Barr's unusual, perceptive, and erotic
novel tells a spellbinding story of the clash
of cultures...of an English girl brought
face to face with the oldest existing
civilisation in the world...

It takes the reader into the very heart of a
Chinese household with its formalities, its
emphasis on beauty and style...and its
cruelties to the 'ugly foreigner' with her
hideous unbound feet and curious coloured
hair...

When Alice finally returned to the world of
European China—the world of
missionaries and the Treaty Ports, she
found herself a misfit. Nothing had
prepared her for life as a Victorian middle-
class girl for in her heart she was totally
Chinese...

'Seized in a murderous outbreak of
xenophobia in Tientsing, a missionary's
pubescent daughter becomes a mandarin's
responsive concubine...and has serious
problems of adjustment when she
eventually rejoins her own prim
kind...The gulfs between East and West
are exhaustively charted and the teeming
picture of the treaty ports in the late 1880s
is fascinatingly detailed...'

Observer

Chinese Alice

Pat Barr

CORGI BOOKS

A DIVISION OF TRANSWORLD PUBLISHERS LTD

CHINESE ALICE

A CORGI BOOK   0   552   11962   8

Originally published in Great Britain by Secker & Warburg Ltd.

PRINTING HISTORY
Secker & Warburg edition published 1981
Corgi edition published 1982

Copyright © Pat Barr 1981

Conditions of sale
1. This book is sold subject to the condition that it shall not, by
way of trade *or otherwise*, be lent, re-sold, hired out or otherwise
circulated without the publisher's prior consent in any form of
binding or cover other than that in which it is published *and
without a similar condition including this condition being imposed
on the subsequent purchaser.*
2. This book is sold subject to the Standard Conditions of Sale of
Net Books and may not be re-sold in the U.K. below the net
price fixed by the publishers for the book.

This book is set in Highland 9½ on 10 pt.

Corgi Books are published by Transworld Publishers Ltd.,
Century House, 61–63 Uxbridge Road, Ealing, London, W5 5SA

Made and printed in Great Britain by Cox & Wyman Ltd.,
Reading

In memory of my dear Father and Mother

Lines from Chinese Poems by Arthur Waley are quoted by permission of George Allen & Unwin Ltd.

Part One

1

Thomas Greenwood stood at the door of the chapel with a pistol in his hand. He looked anxiously along the street which was so deserted that it made him more uneasy. Usually, at this time of day, the shops along it—selling cordage, netting, fish-baskets for use on the boats in the nearby Tientsin harbour—were filled with customers. But this afternoon's emptiness was unnerving, especially when, in the distance, there was a great deal of noise. He could hear gongs beating, temple-bells clanging, wheels grinding, the shuffle of many feet and above all the sound of a multitude of threatening voices pitched at an ominous and sullen rumble.

Suddenly, two pistol shots cracked in quick succession and the noise of the crowd rose to a shrieking crescendo. Thomas examined his pistol; his hand was shaking; he had never fired such a weapon in his life. Gingerly he stroked the trigger, wondering if he could ever squeeze it, knowing that he might have to, astounded that matters could have reached such a sorry pass. But gradually they had and it was too late to escape. Now the matter was out of his hands and in God's.

He waited, but there was no further sound of firing, so, laying his weapon on a stool in the porch, he walked slowly down the centre of his humble chapel to the table at the end on which stood a silver cross. The only other furniture was some rickety benches on the hard earth floor, a lectern and a picture of the Crucifixion. He looked at it.

"It is nothing," he murmured, "to die... There is a green hill far away," and paused. For it was not the green hill of Calvary that filled his vision but one little more than a hillock and covered with English wild flowers.

It was springtime, and he, Mother, Father, his brother Robert and baby Sarah had gone for a picnic into the country just outside the city of Norwich where they lived, because it was his birthday. Twelve he must have been, the same age as his little Alice was now. And, after the picnic, he and Robert had run to the top of the little hill and rolled down the other side shouting for joy, and he smelled again the young crushed grass, saw the sun tippling around him as he tumbled over, heard the larks high in the blue sky and his mother calling, "Thomas, Robert, whatever are you doing? And in your best suits, stop it at once!" And there she stood on the hill's crest in a bright dress of sprigged muslin looking down at them, vexed, but smiling a little in spite of it.

No Calvary, just a green hill in Norfolk so many years ago. The intensely sweet pleasure of that long-forgotten day pierced him with such agony that he gasped as he stood in the chapel of the Church Missionary Society in a side street of the port of Tientsin, China, on the afternoon of 21st June 1870. If I could just see that hill once more, hear those larks, I would die gladly and with gratitude, he vowed silently. But in his secret self he guessed he never would. He was about to pray for a broader courage to meet the present circumstances when his wife Eliza came rushing in from their living quarters behind the chapel.

"Thomas, there you are! What is happening? Are things worse? Tan-sho has just arrived with the most dreadful tale, something about the French, as far as I can make out, but he's so upset I could hardly understand... Come..."

He hurried to the parlour, where Alice, his daughter, stood white-faced.

"Oh, Father, what shall we do? Tan-sho says the people have just killed two Frenchmen, right in the middle of town. Can it be true, do you think?"

Alice's grasp of Chinese was good for her age; moreover Tan-sho always took time to make her understand him, for he had become rather fond of this quaint foreign child with her large greenish eyes, her merry laugh, her spirit of independence and vitality that was very unlike the obedient passivity of his own granddaughters. Thomas looked straight at the man, an elderly basket-maker and one of his most loyal converts.

"If Tan-sho says that, then it must be so, my little one. Frenchmen eh? I heard shots a while ago . . . But come over here, my man," and he drew Tan-sho aside so that the others should not hear.

It was as bad as Thomas had feared, and he was alarmed, though not unduly surprised to learn that the French Catholic missionaries had provoked this situation, for they had, in his view, been behaving quite reprehensibly. Two years ago they had built a large, pretentious cathedral in the town's centre, on the site of a former temple, and had taken into their new orphanage so many sick Chinese children who soon died that the place had developed a sinister reputation as a disease-ridden death-trap.

Apparently, Tan-sho told him, matters had come to a head that afternoon when the French Consul had visited the Chinese magistrate's *yamen* to demand protection for some Catholic missionaries who had recently been severely harassed by the local populace. The Consul, a choleric man, had evidently lost his temper entirely and stupidly fired a pistol at the magistrate. The bullet had missed its target; nevertheless, on leaving the *yamen*, the Consul and his assistant had been literally torn to pieces by an enraged mob outside.

Frank, the youngest Greenwood, who had been pretending to read while trying to hear Tan-sho's story, jumped up restlessly and opened the back door. "Phew—it's hot in here, I'm going into the yard."

"You stay inside, Frank," Eliza said sharply, but joined him in the doorway. There, they both heard it—an active, swelling sound rather like the sea on a choppy unpredictable day, but, unlike the sea which was glittering in its usual place a few miles away at the mouth of the River Peiho, this sound was coming nearer, and occasionally, above the general swell, Frank heard wild hoots of fury.

"They're coming this way, Father." He tried to sound matter-of-fact and manly for his ten years. "Do you think we should lock the back gate?"

"Or should we leave, Thomas? Go away at once—perhaps to the Consulate? It would be safer there surely?" Eliza appealed. She had had lovely clear blue eyes when he had married her and her hair had been as fair and curly as Frank's was now. But she had been a missionary's wife for nearly twenty years since then, and now her hair was scraped back in a lacklustre bun, her eyes dimmed and red-rimmed from so many years of witnessing the heathen ways of the Chinese and their almost total rejection of the Word of the Lord.

"I don't think there's time to leave, my dear—and we can't go by cart because the mule is lamed, remember." He paused irresolutely, listening, as they all were, to the threatening sounds.

The trouble was that Thomas hated the idea of seeking protection from that odious young whippersnapper of a Consul, Mr Waters, who, having spent less than three years in China, thought he knew everything about it. "Tientsin is a potential trouble-spot, a hot-bed of crude xenophobia," he had grandly informed Thomas soon after his arrival. "This is where we and the French negotiated the new treaties that the Chinese dislike so much you know—and we had troops here till '63 which always arouses resentment. Still, it's a pity we don't have any here now, in my view."

Thomas had curtly explained that, as he and his wife had first come to China in 1852, he was indeed aware of the treaties that the British and French had forced upon the country in 1858. However, he did not agree that the generally touchy situation in Tientsin could be improved by stationing a regiment there; far better to allay the people's natural fears by spreading the peaceful message of the Gospel among them.

But, in spite of the efforts of Thomas and missionaries of other denominations working in the district, hostility against them had recently intensified and vile propaganda had been circulating. He remembered with sick incredulity the translation of an anti-Christian pamphlet that Mr Waters had shown him only the week before. It was entitled "The Foreign Devils worship the Incarnation of the Pig they call Jesus." Jesus, Thomas read, "... was very licentious by nature. As soon as a woman heard his Pig's grunts, her clothes unfastened of themselves and she would let him satisfy his lust. The followers of the Pig therefore exhort the people to worship him, making use of this as a pretext for satisfying their own unnatural desires..." The pamphlet concluded: "Those missionaries who have committed a thousand times ten thousand malicious acts, who have castrated boys, removed foetuses from pregnant women, gouged out people's eyes and cut off women's nipples—do you think that the gods will permit themselves to be taken in by their wickedness?"

"You see what we're up against?" Waters had waved the document in his face almost triumphantly. "Can you wonder at the people being hostile towards you when they read this sort of filth? That's why I'm asking you to be very circumspect and not go preaching where you're not wanted and not keep so-called converts in your house, as the Catholics do in their orphanage. They'll have every foreigner in the town slaughtered if we're not careful—for what common Chinese rabble can distinguish between a Catholic and a Protestant, or a consul and a missionary come to that—in the middle of a riot?"

Obviously Waters had been frightened, but Thomas had been too deeply outraged by the pamphlet to feel any fear and he had stormed from the Consulate after saying that, with eighteen years of Chinese experience behind him, he knew better than to adopt the Catholics' ill-advised tactics and that he was not about to take orders from Her Majesty's Consul on how to conduct the mighty work to which God had called him. Brave words at the time, but now his heart quailed a little as it occurred to him that many of the ignorant people who had just killed the Frenchmen and were even now moving towards his Mission had actually heard and probably believed propaganda of that sort.

"Perhaps you are right, Eliza, I must swallow my pride—we will go to the Consulate immediately, on foot if we can avoid the mob. I'll see which way they're heading." He hurried to the back gate, Alice and Frank clinging to his arms, for he was a big man with an air of reassurance and they felt safer at his side.

"What's that smell?" Alice sniffed. Accustomed as she was from birth to the numerous, generally unsavoury odours of a Chinese town, this was something different. "Burning—something nasty?" She looked at him doubtfully.

He too sniffed; it was a sickly, deadly smell and it evoked a vivid memory for him. On the way Home on leave several years ago, he had visited his brother Robert, stationed with the Indian Army at Calcutta. Robert had taken him to see the funeral pyres lit beside the River Hooghley; mound upon mound of smouldering human flesh. He locked the gate quickly and hurried the children back inside; his face had gone chalky, as Eliza noticed.

"What is it, Thomas?"

"They're burning something ever so nasty," Alice volunteered.

"I'm afraid some buildings must have been set on fire," he began.

"Look, I can see the smoke...there..." Frank pointed

11

excitedly over the yard wall to a thick black column that was billowing from the direction of the town centre only a few streets away.

"Quickly, children, run to your bedroom and put some clothes in this," Eliza handed them a calico bag. Thomas, taking another, went to his desk, and, with a feeling of disbelief, threw in his Bible, prayerbook, purse, mission accounts, bundles of letters from Home. As he did so he felt his guilt growing: here he was, suddenly faced with what was perhaps the greatest challenge of his dedicated life, and yet he was bundling together his paltry possessions and fleeing to save his skin just like any small-town merchant with no more idea of salvation than a beast of the field. He should be in the chapel beside the Cross, uplifted by the chance to make a sacrifice of his humble life, inspiring his family to accept God's will for them all.

He stood helplessly as his wife rummaged through the desk drawers. "William's picture? Wherever is it? Upstairs? The frame broke and we put it by to mend..." Their eldest son, William, was ensconced in an English boarding-school and, at that moment, Eliza thanked God for it. Usually William's absence was the hardest burden she had to bear, for he had been born during their early years in China when she was still resilient and full of hope, and he had never caused any trouble. She had lost a daughter in infancy, and then had come Alice and Frank, who were such a boisterous handful that they often made her feel tired and old, though she was not yet forty. She ran upstairs in search of her son's picture, and suddenly stopped.

"Thomas," she called, "what about Wo-wo?" Thomas dropped his half-filled bag feeling obscurely relieved. How could he have forgotten Wo-wo till now, he thought with shame? Wo-wo was an old woman now; when they had come to Tientsin six years ago she had been their first true convert and they had called her Wo-wo as a joke because that was how her name sounded in the unfamiliar local dialect. For the past four years she had lived in the Mission, faithfully and cheerfully sweeping the chapel and polishing the cross every week, handing out prayer leaflets at the door with a wrinkly smile of welcome, bouncing her favourite young Frank on her knee and giving him sugar plums. But for the last few months, she had been visibly failing; her screwed-up little hoofs of feet, bound into deformity from childhood, would no longer support her considerable weight even as far as the chapel, to which Thomas carried her every Sunday.

She was upstairs in the box-room now, peacefully dozing the warm afternoon away as usual, undisturbed and unknowing.

"Wo-wo," Thomas said helplessly to Tan-sho, who had been sitting watching their preparations for departure with a quizzical, bewildered look. "We can't leave Wo-wo, and I couldn't possibly carry her far and the mule is lamed..." Tan-sho nodded as if he had realised this long before. Thomas put the contents of his bag back into their customary places. Eliza joined him.

"We cannot leave her to the mercy of the mob," he said. "You know what they do to converts. The way is made plain. God will protect us, darling."

She nodded. "It's not so much us, it's the children."

Thomas's mind seared with pain as he thought of Alice, his favourite child, so young, vulnerable, alive; the way she jerked her long hair back from her face when she was reading. It was soft-brown and glinted like ripe nuts in the sun just as his own had when he was a lad in Norfolk. How could he not make every effort to save her—at whatever cost to himself, his pride, even to helpless Wo-wo?

"Alice, Frank, come down, we're not going," Eliza was calling them. "We can't possibly leave Wo-wo, can we dears? We'll be alright, Father says so."

At that moment they heard loud banging and calling at the back gate. Tan-sho jumped up. "I'm sure that's my son's voice... Let him in please, Mr Greenwood, he may have news."

Thomas hurriedly unlocked the gate and Tan-sho's son rushed in, his face terror-stricken. He grabbed his father's arm and began dragging him away, shouting in his rough, dock-side accent. Tan-sho pulled back, his skinny old legs, swathed in thin cotton, visibly shaking.

"He says the Catholic cathedral and orphanage are all a-blaze, Mr Greenwood—and the people threw the nuns and priests into the streets and stripped them, and they—oh, may the Lord preserve us all—then he says they cut off the women's breasts and the men's genitals and threw the poor creatures back into the flames to burn. Can you imagine such terrible things? But my son speaks true and he says I must flee with him at once and he'll hide me for I'm a known Christian. He has done a filial deed in coming here, Mr Greenwood, for it's dangerous to be seen anywhere near a Mission, he says. Oh I don't know... Mr Greenwood, dear pastor, what shall I do?"

"You must go at once, Tan-sho, and may God protect you."

Thomas raised his hand in blessing, then caught up with the son at the gate. "Tell me, my man, is it possible for my family to get to the British Consulate without being attacked, do you think?"

"Not a chance," he shrugged. "You'll have to hide here and hope for the best. I've never seen such savagery as is going on, it's quite terrible. No one seems able to control the rioters, can't you hear that noise?"

And indeed the noise of the mob was perceptibly closer now, and mingled with it the crackle of flames, the thud of timbers falling, smells of burning cloth and that sick-sweet odour which was worst of all. The children ran up, Alice clutching a book, Frank a painted wooden horse. "Look at the flames now, Father, they're getting nearer. Will they spread to our chapel?"

"Oh, Father," Alice ran into his arms and buried her face against his chest. "Can't we go away from here at once? I'm frightened—there's a whole crowd gathered at the end of the street, you can see them from the other window. Wo-wo's awake and she says they may come for us and we should go quickly. She doesn't mind, she wants us to. . . ."

Eliza put her arm on Frank's shoulders. "Oh let us pray, children, let us pray for deliverance. Surely, Thomas, the people won't harm us? It is the Catholics who've caused this dreadful trouble. . . . Surely it is only they who are being punished for their misguidedness? But, oh the punishment. . . terrible indeed are the ways of the living God and we must all quail before his righteous anger. Let us go to the chapel and pray together." She shepherded the children inside and Thomas went to reconnoitre again.

"Yes," he said gravely, when he returned. "There is indeed a mob coming towards us. I fear it is unwise to go to the chapel, my dear—they're bound to make for it first. I think we must all be very brave and hide quietly in Wo-wo's room which is the least likely place."

He took his Bible from the desk and handed his wife the prayerbook she'd carried on their wedding day. "Alice," he asked sternly, "where is your *Child's Garden of Prayers?*"

"I don't know, Father, but I've got *Alice in Wonderland* instead."

"And I've got Dobbin," Frank patted his horse. "He's not frightened."

"Surely not 'instead' Alice?" Thomas smiled gently, but there was no time for theological corrections. As they ran

14

upstairs, they could hear feet pounding nearer and, to Thomas's dismay, they seemed to be converging on every side. Wo-wo had managed to stagger to the door of her room, her round face screwed into an anxious ball.

"In here—you must hide here—they are shouting such terrible things outside, terrible. Frank, my poor little one. Come to Wo-wo, she'll protect you." She engulfed the trembling child in her stout arms and said over his head, "Get into the store-cupboard behind my bed, Mr Greenwood. I shall stay in the bed and say you have all escaped. They will believe me, I pray they will, if God is good."

Thomas marvelled at the true Christian strength that had come upon her, it was deeper and firmer than he had understood. He thanked God for it and was proud.

"But you—what will they do, Wo-wo, if they find you here?" Eliza cried, as a hail of stones and mud came clattering over the wall into the yard.

"They will not harm me, I am an old woman. And if they do—I am still an old woman, is that not so, Mr Greenwood?" He bowed his head humbly.

"But I shall face them with you, Wo-wo. Eliza, you and the children must hide . . ."

"If you are seen, the people will know your family is here," Wo-wo said simply. "You would never leave them."

"No . . . I suppose . . ."

Another shower of stones landed and they heard the gate breaking as people crashed against it. The burned air vibrated to the sounds of yells, thumps, hoots and shrills of bamboo whistles.

"Quick children, in. . . ." Eliza and Thomas shifted Wo-wo's bed and slid open the cupboard door behind. Thomas kissed the top of Alice's head. "Come, dear, don't look so alarmed. You'll be safe in there—and think of the story you can tell William—about the day when we all had to hide in the cupboard among the jams and pickles!"

Suddenly two more pistol shots cracked in the distance and Eliza jumped, "Oh Thomas, perhaps that's the troops or the Chinese guards coming to save us?"

"Let us pray so, my dear . . . but my pistol? Oh where is it? I had it earlier this afternoon . . . If the worst comes I must defend you all. Oh, where on earth did I . . . ?" He looked round wildly, suddenly very distraught, for he had earlier comforted himself with the secret vow that he would shoot them all and himself last rather than they should suffer the same fate as the Catholics. And now his pistol. How could he have been so careless? A lack of organisation and fore-thought had bedevilled him all his life, and that it should do so at this most crucial juncture of all was inexcusable.

"Get into the cupboard, Eliza," he bundled her in. "And Wo-wo, you sit on the bed...I can't...I believe I left it in the porch..."

He flew down the stairs, aware of the din of the multitude on every side; the whole of the orderly little world which he, his family and their few faithful converts had painstakingly built was crashing round his head. He pelted up the chapel to the porch and grabbed the weapon from the stool where he had left it. Just as he did so there was a tremendous crash against the chapel door, it splintered like matchwood and a large battering ram came thrusting through. He turned to run, but the faces peering through the hole had seen him.

"There's a child-eater! There's one of the goat-farts! Get him, take his piglet progeny and tear out their livers!"

Thomas stopped, brandished his weapon at the leering faces and fired into the door above their heads. He could not...thou shalt not kill. He turned his back on them just for a second and looked at the silver cross on the chapel table. A beam of late afternoon sun, in which danced the dust of all these disturbances, shone upon it from the lattice above, and he knew then with absolute certainty that his hour had come. He had been right; he would never again see the green Norfolk countryside of his childhood. If only they would kill him, just him, there and go away. "O merciful God, take me and spare the others, my young ones," he prayed aloud. "I am ready to die for Thy Sake, O Lord."

The leaders of the mob were nearly through the door and Thomas faced them again, his pistol steady and straight at them. They were armed with wooden pikes, swords and bat-tered shields. It is medieval, Thomas thought; these are me-dieval people and they will have me for a martyr. There was a pause of confrontation which was, for Thomas, an agony of indecision through which he could not think fast enough. Should he fire? Or should he save the remaining bullets for his family? How many bullets did the pistol hold?

Then he heard Eliza's voice behind him screaming, "Thomas, Thomas my beloved. You shan't die alone, I can't bear it. Thomas, don't fire at them—we will die here to-gether." And she rushed to him, obsessed with the vision of their joint martyrdom.

"No," he barked. "Go back—back to the children, woman." He pushed her behind him.

She clutched at him blindly, then obediently ran away to the living quarters and he tried to cover her retreat. But the interruption had broken his small threat of defiance and the crowd came pouring through the broken door, hooting derisively. They were a motley, ragged collection—casual fishermen, labourers and loafers—and they brandished sticks and spiked truncheons, while two carried poles tipped with pitch. Thomas knew what those were for.

At the door of Wo-wo's room they fell on him; he could not bring himself to fire the pistol after all and it was torn from his grasp. As he went down before them he heard his children's piercing screams and Alice's cry of agonised disbelief, "Father, Father, help...help...!" One of the leaders had a sword, rather rusty, but sharp enough to hack three times through Thomas' neck. The blood spouted in a thick red jet and the head thumped along the floor. Alice saw her father's eyes roll away.

Hands grabbed at her—Mother's and Wo-wo's—shielding her and Frank against the wall. There were thuds, grunts, cries and a rivulet of bright red creeping towards her and Mother screaming, "Thomas, Thomas, Thomas" over and over again. Then she was torn from Wo-wo's arms and saw her mother, her face covered with blood, sprawling across her father's headless body, and Wo-wo thrown roughly upon the bed where she lay, wailing helplessly and praying for death.

"We're to take the children alive," said the man with the sword. "There's one who wants to taste the piglets' livers," he guffawed and aimed a kick at Eliza. "As for the women, leave them to burn where they are, it's getting too hot for comfort in here."

And indeed the room was beginning to fill with smoke from the fires that had been lit in the chapel below, where the prayer-benches were crackling merrily. Suddenly came the distant sound of rifle fire and the men looked uneasy.

"Let's go, it might be the *yamen* guards," the leader growled as he poked about the room, disappointed at the lack of worthwhile loot.

"Or the barbarians landed from the sea," said his comrade, as he swung screaming Frank under his arm. A stringy fellow smelling abominably of sweat, blood and ashes similarly caught up Alice and they clattered down the stairs and out of the back gate where a covered mule-cart waited. The children were thrown inside, two men leaped aboard and the vehicle rattled away towards the town boundaries.

For the remainder of that dire day and through the night the children were jolted along inside the stuffy cart, so stunned with horror that they simply sat, clutching each other and sobbing. Once during the night they halted, the mules were fed, the men drank tea; the children were offered nothing and were too sick to ask.

Frank whispered, "Did you see—Father and Mother?"

"Yes, they killed Father..." she began to weep bitterly again.

"But not Mother, she was alive and so was Wo-wo. They'll send soldiers to rescue us." He squeezed her hand, neither of them daring to remember the sight of the burning chapel, the way flames were shooting up towards the room where Mother and Wo-wo lay.

At dawn, hands shook them roughly; the cart had stopped and light shone through the awning. Guards pushed them down into a courtyard, ropes were thrown halter-fashion round their necks and they were led off like convicts. "The master says he wants their eyes and livers on a plate," one sniggered to a stable-boy as they passed. Alice, who partly understood the words, decided to make no further effort to understand anything. They found themselves immured inside a dim, airless room. Light, sneaking through a high barred opening, told them roughly about day and night, but of how many they soon lost track. Twice a day they ate rice and gruel; at night they drifted through nightmares of such terror that they often woke each other with their screams and cries. In the middle of one such night two different guards marched in and dragged them outside. Alice whimpered and clung to Frank. "Our last hour has come," she thought, "soon I shall see my Father in Heaven," and clasped hands for a prayer which, in her panic, she could not remember. Instead they were thrown into another cart, with a shutter fixed at the back, reaching almost to the floor. One of the men jumped inside, the other on the shafts, the driver cracked his whip, whistled "Hi, yeh ho" and the mules plodded off.

During the next numberless number of days and nights they became very used to those sounds of the muleteer's whistle, the rumble of the ancient cart, its smells of dust and dung, how wind, rain and sun filtered through the awning. One guard had the habit of hissing disgustedly through his few teeth whenever he looked at them, so they called him

Old Hisser; the other, a jollier fellow, passed the time chatting to a succession of drivers about the state of the roads, the prices of crops. But neither of them would talk to the children, except to bark occasional orders.

"Where are you taking us?" Alice sometimes popped the question unexpectedly, hoping to catch them unawares, but the men simply shook their heads. Frank, remembering early geography lessons, guessed they were heading south; Alice thought Hong Kong lay there and hoped it was their destination. It soon became clear that the cart's shutter was to prevent them from being seen, for they were only allowed out at night—to exercise a little and eat a sparse meal. At such times it was hopeless to guess where they were. Sometimes empty plains stretched as far as they could see, or hill tracks wound away to an infinity of dark mountains; sometimes moonlight glinted on a silver thread of river or wet paddies; they heard owls hoot, dogs bark from distant settlements and, once or twice, unknown beasts roar and growl from the hills and the guards mutter uneasily.

Apart from their nightly respite, their view was confined to the patch of ground beneath the moving cart: pebbles, stones, rocks, white, beige, grey; earth dry and dusty, brown and damp, treacly-black and thick; wisps and tufts of yellowing grass; near habitations it was more interesting—scraps of peel, eggshells, excreta, chicken-bones and broken shards for the wheels to churn over. But it all went on forever.

Sometimes, sitting with her chin in hand gazing at this low-level landscape, Alice wondered if she had been killed with Father after all. Surely she had seen this same stony track a hundred times before? Perhaps she had entered those eternal circles of purgatory of which she had heard and which would lead her to Heaven after a thousand years of journeying? But no; it was still the earth, the familiar night sky, the real sun beating on the cart-awning. But how could any country, even China, be so huge and never reach an end of land? Surely they must be somewhere near the South Pole by now? By whatever time of day or month it was.

Eventually they came to a watery region where rain drummed on the awning and the animals' hooves sploshed and squelched. That night stars were reflected in vast stretches of water near the track, flocks of disturbed wild fowl clacked in the marshes and the children decided they were approaching the sea. But, at dusk of the next day, they saw in the direction where they thought the sea would be, the distant lights of a city. The guards pointed at it with unusual animation, and the friendlier of the two put his hands wide apart, then close together and grinned.

"He means we're nearly there," Frank guessed.

"Wherever 'there' is..." Alice's heart thumped in alarm. Later the cart halted and there came the sounds of people arguing; when they moved on, occasional flickers of light showed that the ground below was paved, while strong smells of habitations, people and open drains wafted to them. Again the cart stopped, again men shouted; hinges creaked and they passed through a gate that was slammed behind them. They were pushed out into a courtyard, more imposing than the one they had left so long ago, and with lanterns swinging at its corner eaves—but just another Chinese courtyard nevertheless.

Frank grabbed his sister's hand, "I thought we'd be out of China now, but we're not."

A group of men, obviously surprised by their arrival, stood nearby, one shone a lantern in their faces and laughed jeeringly, the others crowded for a closer look. Alice leaned wearily against the cartwheel, wishing now that they could just go trundling along forever inside rather than face the unknown hazards of this alien place. After an interval, Old Hisser led them inside a shadowy pillared hall. In its centre stood a lacquer table and high-backed chairs. On one of them sat a dignified Chinese, wearing a loose robe, looking sleepy and peevish. Old Hisser bowed low and handed him a scroll. The man studied it, looked at the children over its top, reread it. Then he gave a deep sigh, came round the table and, twisting his fingers into Frank's hair, tugged hard.

"Ow!" Frank yelped. The man smiled faintly, then gave instructions in an unfamiliar dialect to a servant who ushered them out, down long passages to the back of the house.

"You should have asked him where we are and who he was," Frank said accusingly as they trotted behind the bobbing lantern.

"All very well for you to say that, but I couldn't think of the right words, and he looked so stern and important. I thought he might be like that Queen in *Alice in Wonderland*, do you remember? If you said the wrong thing, she'd shout, 'Off with her head.'"

Aunt Sarah, Father's sister in England, had sent Alice a copy of that newly popular story last Christmas, saying every little girl called Alice should have one. Alice had read the story a dozen times, and now wished desperately for it.

"Scaredy-cat!" Frank taunted; then had a terrible memory of a certain blood-stained sword.

"Well, why don't you learn Chinese yourself instead of telling me what to say?" Alice countered.

"So I will—now we're still in China," he retorted grandly as they crossed a small courtyard.

A servant unlocked a door, pushed them through, threw two quilts on the floor inside and disappeared. The room was dark and empty—at least of people, though there were scuffles in the corners.

"Mice?" Frank suggested.

"Rats," Alice shuddered.

A great weariness swamped them and they lay down close together for comfort between the quilts and fell into exhausted slumber. As they slept, several rats, in pursuit of their customary nocturnal activities, ran over them, but they did not stir.

Grey light filtered through the door. Alice woke abruptly with a sense of dawn and a shift of relief from the nightmares that had, as usual, haunted her sleep. She stood up, aching from the rigours of the journey, and looked round. They were in a store-room filled with sealed boxes, sacks of herbs, maize, shreds of dried ginger and peppers, jars of sesame seed oil and red-bean paste, piles of broken utensils, baskets and sieves. The combined smells were quite pleasant, both fusty and sharp, but although she was very hungry, she could find nothing edible. She chewed a leathery scrap of ginger and spat it out in disgust.

Cautiously she opened the door. In a small empty courtyard, rain dripped steadily from the eaves of the dilapidated thatch atop the buildings on all sides. The centre was a mess of mud and pebbles through which many feet had tramped; the branches of the one straggly willow tree growing there were bent with the tears of the rain. An early clatter of pots began in the building opposite; beyond a wide gate in the far corner came the snort of pigs, the cluck of fowls.

Behind her, Frank stirred. "Is it morning?"

"Yes, but there's no one around."

"I'm hungry." He inspected the sacks in his turn.

"There's nothing to eat—that dried stuff tastes horrid, I've tried."

He joined her in the doorway. "Why don't we try to escape before they all get up? That gate must lead somewhere."

"But I can hear people across there..."

"They're a long way off. Come on..." Boldly he scurried to the gate, heaving at the heavy latch. "We're locked in." He looked back at his sister in panic. "Will they leave us here to starve? I'm so hungry."

"Of course not—I can smell cooking. I expect it's our breakfast."

The cooking of the first day's meal for the entire household of the Chu was indeed going forward and as there were many mouths to feed, it was a lengthy process. On account of seniority and gender, the mouth with top priority belonged to Grandfather Chu, who was enjoying an unmolested retirement in his own apartments. In his private courtyard stood lions on lacquer bases and huge pots of golden-coin and tousled-dog chrysanthemums; plum and cherry trees bloomed in their season and from their branches on balmy days swung cages of brilliant song-birds. The next most important mouth to fill belonged to Chu Lung-kuang, "Dragon-Brightness", Grandfather's eldest son, a deputy-governor of the interior province of Hunan and functioning head of the house now that his father had reached an honourable old age. It was he who had briefly inspected the children the night before.

Waiting without impatience for the arrival of the most important breakfast in the senior women's apartments known as "fragrant" was Yun-hwei, the Deputy-Governor's first official wife. Her name, which meant Hidden Glory, was appropriate, though no one gave it much thought. Twenty-five years before, when just seventeen, she had been carried to the Chu residence in a closed bridal chair and had but seldom left since. In the course of the uneventful years, she had borne her husband seven children; two had died in infancy; two boys and three girls survived. Gradually and increasingly since her childbearing had ended, she had become withdrawn, any glory she had once possessed being hidden from others and neglected by herself.

The eldest daughter of the house, invariably known by the affectionate family name of Tamao, "Big Puss", and her husband, Weng, had spent the night in their apartments on the east side, where they would breakfast together the next morning. Along the passage, Lung-kuang's secondary wife, Red Jasmine, who could never wear the red skirt of official recognition, offered morning gruel to her baby daughter, who cried because it was too hot. In the room opposite, Vegetable Aunt, Hidden Glory's sister, fretted at the crying and jabbed a needle into her embroidery. She was a childless widow who had forsworn the eating of meat when her young husband

22

died; but she looked forward to the morning gruel nevertheless, and was impatient because, as usual, she was outranked in order of breakfast precedence.

There were, however, many lower in the household's hierarchy: the younger children of the family, their tutors and personal servants; scribes and secretaries, messengers and guards, cooks and gardeners, gatekeepers and seamstresses, grooms and chairbearers, fowl- and pig-keepers, skivvies, slaves and enfeebled old retainers, an idiot boy, a rag picker and a scavenger—all of these were sustained by the Chu kitchens and were never disappointed. But the portions diminished in size and quality according to rank, so the two barbarian children, lowliest of the lowly, eventually received for breakfast a bowl of much-watered gruel topped with the scrapings from the pot of last night's stewed vegetables.

"I can't eat it," Frank wailed. "It looks so horrid I'll be sick."

Alice set her teeth. "We'll have to eat it—they won't give us anything else. It will warm you up. Food always does, even cold—so Mama used to say."

As they slurped dismally at the sloppy mush, a man in a neat dark robe came in, followed by Old Hisser. It was Weng who, before his marriage, had twice visited Canton where he had seen barbarians walking about, so he knew just what they looked like.

"Ha, real barbarians," he said knowledgeably. "Yellow hair on the boy, you perceive, and the girl—very odd eyes. How old are you?" he asked Alice, who, in her anxiety, understood nothing.

"I thought you said she spoke the tongue?" He turned on Old Hisser in annoyance.

"Only a little, sir, and a very ignorant way of speaking."

Weng tried again in precise Mandarin and Alice stumbled, "Twelve—I think." For perhaps she had had another birthday without even knowing?

"And the boy—your brother?"

"Yes. He's ten."

Frank tugged Alice's sleeve. "Tell him we're hungry." Alice tried to summon the word. "Food," she blurted.

"Did they eat?" Weng asked one of the cooks who had come over to inspect the barbarians. "Yes? Then never mind. They look sufficiently fat. Barbarians eat too much and their food is unwholesome, too much animal fat. See they get enough to keep well. They're only children—younger than they look."

Weng strode off, disappointed at the extent of the barbarians' ignorance. If he wanted to learn anything useful from them they would have to know more Chinese—but probably they were to die. He must find out.

The cook left lounging in the doorway was joined by other servants. "Just look at them," he jeered. "What disgustingly big feet she has—and their skins are pink as piglets."

"And his hair—like old yellow goat's wool!" A groom tugged Frank's curls hard.

"Stop it, stop it!" Frank beat his hands away and squared his chubby body into a fighting posture. The servants cackled merrily, pleased at this show of defiance.

The cook reached forward, rapped Frank's knuckles smartly with a wooden spoon. "I've heard foreign devils have holes in their chests so you can put poles right through them and carry them strung up like hogs... Let's see if this one has!" He hit Frank hard on the chest. "No hole!" They all guffawed, while Frank, bellowing tearfully, lunged at his tormentor.

Alice pulled him away. "Frank, don't—he's too strong. He'll only hurt you more... Beasts, leave us alone!"

Then they heard footsteps approaching and, as the servants slipped unobtrusively away, Weng reappeared, accompanied by his wife, and two children, Han-li, Younger Son, and Hung-mei, familiarly known as Mei, Younger Daughter.

"Why, they're squaring for a fight," Han-li laughed. "Look at him, isn't his hair funny, and his eyes?" He danced round Frank, waving his fists.

"Leave them alone, Younger Brother, they're only frightened."

Han-li giggled. "What, of me?" That was a novel and pleasant idea. Under-sized, and not very robust and with a bullying elder brother, Han-li felt fright much more often than he inspired it. He was the same age as Frank, and the practice of those military arts at which Eldest Brother Han-fei excelled and to which he was just being initiated seemed rough and difficult. That very morning he had been fetched out at dawn for exercise round the field and had first dropped his bow and then fallen from his horse and twice been called a bumble-fisted milk-sop. His legs were still trembling from the experience, so it was good to flail his arms and see the fear in the barbarians' faces.

"Ah, yi, yi, let's beat the filthy foreign devils," Han-li yelled and Frank, recognising the dread term, shrank back.

"Oh stop that noise, no fighting indoors," Tamao ordered.

She went up to Alice and they inspected each other with mutual interest. Tamao was her father's favourite daughter and she was reasonably happy in her marriage; for a mere woman, therefore, her position was enviable and she thanked the gods daily for it. "Ask what her name is, you say she understands a little," she said to Weng.

"A-li-chi...ree-woo," they repeated the strange syllables among themselves, amused at their oddity. Tamao pointed at the boy. "Frank" was equally impossible.

"Also Greenwood," Alice added desperately.

"Ah, the same name—brother and sister," Weng explained importantly.

They all nodded solemnly at this point of understanding. Then Frank ran to pick up a green-painted box in the corner. "See—green wood."

Alice laughed. "You know, I never thought of it like that before."

"Nor did I, till now."

"Box?" Mei, entering the game, pointed to another container.

"No—green," Alice pointed to some herbs.

"Whatever does that mean?" Mei pouted. "She must be half-witted. I thought she was explaining her name."

"Barbarians are all half-witted," Han-li chanted.

Alice went up to Weng and pointed at the green button on his tunic collar.

"Ha," Weng smiled. "Jade—that's the name."

"Green Jade," added Tamao. "That's what they meant—green box, green herb."

"Green-Jade, that's not a proper boy's name," Han-li jeered at Frank.

"Perhaps that's only part of it," suggested Mei, for they all had three names apiece.

"You will remember the words of Li-chi," Tamao turned to her husband. "'Uncut Jade cannot be turned into a serviceable vessel. So men untaught can never know the proprieties.'"

"Just so—Uncut Jades. That is most appropriate."

The moment of communication had passed. Alice sensed that the name they had settled on was both incorrect and derogatory. She shivered; not even her own name anymore.

"She looks cold," Hung-mei fingered Alice's grubby frock. "And she doesn't smell nice either."

"Barbarians all stink like rotten cabbage," her brother announced. He wrinkled his nose. "Phew!"

25

"They must wash, and I'll send over some bits of old clothing." Tamao turned to a servant.

"Aren't they going to be killed then?" Han-li asked Weng.

"I don't think just yet anyway. A letter came with them last night. After your father read it, he ordered them put in here. Perhaps I'll find out more later."

Speaking of Lung-kuang, Weng was always uncertain, mindful of his insecure position in his wife's household. In the normal way, he should not have been living there, but disasters beyond the normal had befallen his own family. Eight years before, soon after he was betrothed, his father and elder brother had both been killed fighting against the rebel Taipings during the battle for Nanking. His mother had died soon after, from shock it was said.

So, when Weng and Tamao married they had stayed in the Chu residence. It was a temporary measure that had drifted into permanence and suited everyone except Han-fei, Eldest Son, who disliked having a male senior in age but inferior in standing competing for his father's good opinion. For Weng was astute and scholarly and made himself very useful to his father-in-law. Yet, aware of Han-fei's jealousy and superior status, he never felt secure and sometimes dreamed of taking his wife and their first-born son to Canton and making his own way, as a few of his contemporaries had. But generations of innate conservatism held him back; better to entrench himself where he had taken root; there was much truth in the old adage that those who run after kites trip over straws.

On the strength of his Canton visits and his vague aspirations, Weng was the acknowledged authority on any peripheral "barbarian matters" that affected the household and so he wanted to learn what he could from the children. Obviously, he thought, picking his way back over the muddy courtyard, they would be of no use to him dead. Moreover he had heard that the barbarians' military might was practically limitless and their directing of it quite inexplicable. He quailed at the vision of a phalanx of fully-armed Western soldiers storming into this city of Changsha, the Hunanese capital, and blowing it sky-high simply to revenge the killing of two pathetic scraps of Uncut Jade. Clearly then it was in the interest of himself and the family to keep the foreign devils alive. But, as he robed himself for the day's business, he sighed, knowing that the main opponent of this endeavour would, as usual, be Han-fei.

"Eldest Brother—come and see the barbarian monsters!

They're so peculiar and they smell awful..." Excitedly Han-li dragged at his brother's coat as he returned home in the afternoon of that same wet day. "You've heard about them? They came late last night."

"Yes, Father told me. They're no more important than diseased pigs," Han-fei shook off his brother's enthusiasm. "I'll see them after I've seen Mother."

Han-fei didn't like his routine altered. At the end of every day he took tea in his mother's apartments—his visits were always the high point of her day, sometimes of his.

Han-li dropped back disappointed. "Well, let me come when you go. I want to see them again."

"Aren't they going to be killed?"

"Weng doesn't seem to think so."

"Huh—what does he know about it?" Han-fei shook the rain off his head violently and threw his wet cloak to a servant. "Ugh—it's raining as though a tub had overturned. Too bad for riding even." Han-li nodded, secretly glad.

In his mother's apartments, Han-fei made the customary salutations to her and Vegetable Aunt, received the customary tray of tea and dough-cakes.

"Too wet for riding," Mother said. "A pity, Younger Son needs the practice."

"He does indeed," Han-fei grinned. "He dropped his bow *and* fell off his horse this morning!"

"He's not sturdy for his years," said Aunt in extenuation, for Han-li was her favourite.

"Have you seen the foreign-devil children?" Han-fei inquired.

Mother shook her head in disgust, fixing her attention on her youngest daughter, Hsiao-ping, "Little Piece", who was stolidly rolling a hank of twine.

Aunt said, "No—and I don't want to. Han-li says they've got light eyes and big noses and smell bad—faugh! Why doesn't the respected Father have them done away with at once?"

"I don't know, I've not talked to him yet."

"Why were they brought here, that's what I can't understand?" asked Aunt querulously. "We've not had any barbarian troubles here before... Mother thinks it must be something to do with that nutty old firebrand Lung-pao, Third Uncle."

Lung-pao was the younger brother of that elderly grandfather who was happily pottering through his declining years

27

in the flower-filled courtyard. Lung-pao, even if he lived to such a ripe age, would be incapable of pottering. The Chus had not seen him for years, but his bellicose deeds were a family legend, for he had spent most of his eventful life fighting losing battles against the barbarians.

He had been one of the young defenders on the walls of Canton nearly thirty years before when British forces had assaulted the city and forced trading agreements upon his people. And had then watched helplessly when the foreign-devil soldiers proceeded upstream and ruthlessly looted the city of Chinkiang, while hundreds of its inhabitants committed suicide by burning or throwing themselves into wells. Later, as a full commander, he had seen his eldest son and many of his foot-soldiers mown down before the European siege guns that had been brought upriver from Tientsin to storm the forty-feet-high walls of Peking itself, capital of the Celestial Empire. For the last few years, Lung-pao, retired from his military career, sour and ageing with the sense of continuous defeat, had been a deputy salt-commissioner in Tientsin, nursing an abiding, obsessive hatred for the Westerners who were invading and humiliating the glorious Middle Kingdom of his ancestors.

"I thought he'd quietened down at last?" Hang-fei signalled for more tea.

"There was trouble in Tientsin a while ago, Father told Weng," Mother replied. "Some child-eating barbarians were killed by our people and their religious places burned."

"If there were any anti-foreign riots going on near Lung-pao he'd be involved," Aunt affirmed. "You know how he feels. Weng put two and two together and decided that's what happened—apparently the devil-children come from Tientsin."

"Weng's always making five out of two and two," Han-fei retorted. "I'll see Father myself and get the full story. But I suppose I'll look at them first. Where are they?"

"In one of the kitchen courtyard store-rooms."

"Are they boys?"

"One boy, one girl." Aunt replied. "Tamao says the boy is about Younger Son's age, but looks older. They're always too big."

Han-fei tapped his youngest sister on the nose teasingly. "You're not too big, are you, tiny Little Piece? We come in the right sizes, don't we?" He chuckled and went off towards the kitchens, calling for a lantern, as the damp twilight was thickening to darkness.

For the Greenwoods, the day had been one of misery and fear. Earlier, a servant had brought ice-cold washing water, a couple of frayed tunics, padded leggings and straw sandals; later bowls of rice and pickled cabbage had appeared. They ate in defeated silence, huddled on the mats.

"We should have sprinkled some herbs on to make it taste better," Alice remarked with forced cheeriness. "We'll remember next time."

"Next time! How long do you think we'll be here then? Mama must come and rescue us soon."

Frank had been saying that, with decreasing conviction, every day since their capture. Alice had always replied that, yes, Mama would come as soon as she was well enough—blocking from her mind that frail and bleeding body on the floor—but that, in any case, William would surely come. Six years her senior, William was certainly capable of charging across uncharted China to rescue them single-handed. She thought about him now, as she had last seen him when he had left for England two years before—solemn and swallowing hard as he bade farewell and ran up the gangplank of the *China Cloud* that would land him in Southampton three months later.

"If only William were here, he'd know what to do."

Frank tried to look elder brotherly. "He'd try and escape at once." He got up and looked round. Rain still poured from the courtyard eaves and into the spreading pool round the stunted willow; wisps of charcoal smoke from the kitchens melted into the indeterminate twilight.

"There's no one about."

"But where would we go?"

"Out of that gate. We can climb over even if it's still locked. I can hear animals on the other side, it must lead somewhere."

"But if they catch us escaping they may do even worse things..."

"They won't. Anyway, how are Mama and William going to find us, shut in here? We've got to get out and meet them." It was transparently plain to Frank that the longed-for figures could be no more than a few miles away by now, on the other side of that gate.

Alice said doubtfully, "Perhaps you're right. We'll try as soon as it gets dark."

For a while they listened nervously to the splash of rain, moan of wind, occasional chatter of distant voices; certainly they seemed to have been quite forgotten. "Come on, it's almost dark—let's go, don't be such a sissy!" Frank tugged at her.

She jumped up indignantly. "I'm not." He crept off and reached for the gate's latch which still would not lift. In the gloom he discerned notches in the wooden post and, using them, managed to clamber up, straddling the gate and peering down the further side. Dim clucking bundles were moving in the mire; whitish porcine shapes snuffled and grunted. "Come on—it's all clear," he whispered.

Alice started after him, then stopped, heart pounding— a swinging light had suddenly appeared in a doorway opposite, a figure behind it. "Frank," she screamed, "there's someone coming—get down, come back—quick."

He turned, saw the light, froze to the gate-top. Han-fei glimpsed Alice first, lunged and grabbed her by the hair. "Where d'you think you're going? A little foreign devil, isn't it?" He shook her head back and forth.

"Frank—jump and run!" she shouted desperately.

He took a deep breath and leaped into the dark on the gate's far side, landing with a great splosh in the mire. Hens and ducks scattered squawking, a goose flapped its wings and hissed. He scrambled up panic-stricken, careered forward into a large, evil-smelling beast that knocked him back into the filth and began to snuffle his face.

"Help me—Alice, Mama, Wo-wo, help me!" he bellowed. The rays of a bobbing lantern lit up the beady eyes of hens, the sinister close glint of piggy ones. Han-fei and a fowl-keeper converged on him as he lay sobbing.

"That'll teach 'em to try any tricks." Han-fei, yelling with laughter, dragged him up by the hair and beat him across the back. "Just the place for a barbarian—wallowing in the dung of the farmyard, that's what Third Uncle would say!"

"I suppose he was trying to escape?" The keeper was deferential.

"Looks like it." Han-fei jerked Frank's head back and held up the lantern. "What a sight! Not only a foreign devil but one covered with shit! He's got yellow hair, what you can see of it . . . Well, back he comes, I suppose." He marched Frank back by the scruff of the neck to the store-room, where Alice cowered in a corner. "Son of a foreign-turtle! That's for thinking you could get away from us!" He kicked the boy inside and went to the kitchens, calling for water to wash, just as Han-li ran up.

"What was all that noise? Have you seen the barbarians?"

"They were trying to escape just as I got here—the boy

jumped into the farmyard, but I soon collared him." Han-fei held up his hands, grinning. "I've always heard barbarians are filthy beasts—they're covered in shit!"

Han-li giggled. "He was in the mire then?"

"Yes, and a pig was at him—what a sight! Father will be home now and I'm going to find out about them. Might as well throw them back to the swine, if you ask me."

Han-fei strolled off and Han-li, about to follow, heard a strange noise across the courtyard. Creeping towards it, he recognised the universal cry of anguish, fear and hopelessness that welled from the dark store-room. It was a very human noise, but in the circumstances there was something eerie about it. He paused, fearful, then opened the door and held up a light. The children were huddled together on the floor in a dirty, damp and trembling heap. Frank shrieked as the light flickered over him.

"They'll kill us now we've tried to escape... Oh, Mama, Mama, come quickly... please come..."

Alice muttered, "O merciful Father, save us, O God in Heaven protect us." She tried to recall the pictures she had seen of righteous boys and girls wearing golden haloes and nightdresses as they walked calmly towards some bloody martyrdom, but her courage was not up to it. "Please don't kill us," she clasped her hands beseechingly. "We're not even grown up yet."

Han-li understood the look though not the words, and his desire to torment them further abated. "It's nothing to do with me, you're only barbarians," he muttered, backing away to the safe lights of the kitchen.

"They sound like caterwauling wild cats, don't they?" remarked a servant as he passed. "Nothing but beasts they are."

Reluctantly Han-li went to his room where books for evening study were laid ready. From the third of Mencius' seven volumes from which he had to learn long passages by heart, he read: "The feeling of compassion—that is benevolence; the feeling of reverence—that is propriety; the feeling of discrimination between right and wrong—that is wisdom. Benevolence, righteousness, propriety and wisdom are not instilled into us from without, they are part of our very being. Only we give them no thought. Hence the saying, 'You can have them for the asking, or lose them through neglect.'"

Han-li had never considered the real meaning of these words, but now he re-read them carefully. Impulsively he jumped up—he would tell Eldest Sister about the barbarians, she always knew what was best. Tamao was painting her face for the evening; she wore a robe of green satin embroidered with red flowers, and the jet coils of her hair, decked with jewelled pins, shone in the lamplight.

"Did you know," Han-li blurted, "that Eldest Brother caught the boy barbarian in the farmyard trying to escape?"

"The serving woman just told me," she replied calmly. In such normally uneventful households any news travelled fast.

Han-li took a sugar plum from a bowl. "They're making a terrible noise now—and they're absolutely filthy."

"The Uncut Jades?"

"Yes, I think they're ever so frightened and cold out there, in the dark..." He hesitated, not wanting in the least to appear milksoppish.

"Did Elder Brother knock them about then? Weng doesn't want them to die just yet."

"I don't know, but they're certainly howling loud enough..."

She sighed and summoned a servant, ordering that the barbarians should be given washing water, warm gruel and a candle. "Does that satisfy you? This morning you thought it was fun to see them so terrified."

He shrugged away her teasing. "I thought they might die, that's all, and there'd be no fun in that, would there? I just saw Elder Brother go in to see Father about them."

Tamao looked annoyed for Father had not yet consulted her husband on the matter. She turned on Han-li. "It's near suppertime. Why aren't you at your studies? Get along now and if Eldest Brother has left Father, let me know."

As he passed Father's room he heard Han-fei's voice and grinned—know-all Weng would not like that, discussing the barbarians without seeking his expert advice on the subject!

Behind the closed door, father and son had exchanged the usual pleasantries and Han-fei now concluded his account of the barbarians' attempted escape with, "So—shall I throw them back to the swine, Father? No point in keeping them alive any longer surely?"

"I have to for the time being. A letter came with them from that scoundrel Lung-pao in Tientsin..." Lung-kuang paused to light his pipe. "Why couldn't the old fool stick to his salt-taxing? But no—still full of the red peppers that one. So he and his younger son, Cheng-ta, remember him?—got involved in the latest anti-foreign riots there. Now, he says, the foreigners have sent in troops to seek out the instigators, so he'll be for it. But the worst thing is—Cheng-ta's being held as a suspect by the authorities."

"You mean our authorities?"

"Yes, they're very careful not to offend the foreign devils in the treaty ports these days. Lung-pao says he had the barbarian children sent to him as he intended to cut out their eyes and livers and dispatch them on a plate to the barbarian consul—a typically scatter-brained idea, not very subtle, I must say. Anyway, before he could do so, he heard of his son's arrest, so he kept them in his summer residence for possible exchange as hostages. But now he's under suspicion himself, which is why he's sent them here secretly. No formal charges have yet been made, so I have to keep them till I hear more. What a mess!"

"When did all this happen?"

"The letter was written late in the seventh moon and took nearly two moons to get here. I've sent a letter back asking for news and agreeing to keep them alive till I hear." He sighed. "Why for all the gods can't Third Uncle retire quietly like Father?"

Lung-kuang's father had always been a peaceable man who, in his time, had enjoyed the ceremonials of his office, hunting, chess and women and was now content with his song-birds and chrysanthemums. Lung-kuang took after him, being also content to stay in the province of his birth, performing his duties reasonably and keeping his household in peace. But there was a bellicose volatile streak in many Hunanese who were not called "the red peppers of the Empire" for nothing. Lung-pao had it in abundance, so, to some extent, did Han-fei.

Han-fei jumped up with an oath. "But why should Third Uncle lump this barbarian filth on us—faugh! Slaughter 'em and be done with it, I say. It's no business of ours."

Father shook his head. "Third Uncle's son is in danger. What can I do? It will be expensive and tricky to get Cheng-ta off the hook—he's obviously guilty. So we must await developments. Then you can kill them if you like—if they are not to be ransomed."

Han-fei clumped about moodily. "I'll have them publicly executed in the marketplace...And what does Grandfather say? It's his brother causing all this trouble."

"I haven't told him yet. Father is too old for such matters. He is to be left in harmonious peace; it is his privilege. Come, it's time for supper, no more of this unpleasantness. And don't spread this matter about, Eldest Son, it is best kept quiet. The barbarians have spies everywhere and they even travel to the remotest provinces disguised as men of religion, I've been told, in order to learn the secrets of our country's greatness. Faugh! What despicable tricks they play."

"They'll never reach Hunan, never," Han-fei said confidently. "They'd be slaughtered to a man if they set foot on our soil."

"Many Sons of Han have vowed that. But it has not always been so. The barbarians are wily and persuasive and have much power and wealth."

"You are only repeating what Weng says," Han-fei muttered jealously. "Remember rather the words of Mencius, 'I have heard of barbarians being converted to the institutions of China, but never of men being converted by barbarians.'"

"Power and wealth are strong weapons for conversion nevertheless," his father retorted sharply. "And as for Son-in-Law—he uses his brain to better purpose than you do often ... Enough, it is time to eat."

News, which travelled faster than seeds in the wind within the closed circles of Chinese domestic life, moved but sluggishly from one region of the vast Empire to another. Three moons waxed and waned and nothing further was heard of subsequent events in distant Tientsin. During those moons, Alice was later to say, she shed nearly her whole life's supply of tears—pools of them, enough to swim in or drown a dodo, if she had been in Wonderland. But the kitchen courtyard that was their prison produced no wonders and few comforts.

They were fed, but were usually hungry; they were sheltered, but usually chilled; they were given nothing whatever to do. And that, to Alice, seemed very odd, for her childhood till then had been crammed with things to do, to be, to learn. Yet now she was in a world where no one cared whether she knew when Queen Elizabeth lived, her eight times table, the words of the twenty-third psalm—or whether she washed her hair, mended her dress, cleaned her teeth.

The only person to evince the slightest interest in them was Weng, the "green-button man" they called him. Sometimes he would come and stare at them curiously without either warmth or distaste. And he would question Alice in slow Mandarin: How big was her country? How was it governed? Why had her family come to China? Alice struggled to reply, but the questions were difficult. Once she tried to explain that the Chinese were heathens and God had sent her father to save their souls. But Weng only barked a curt laugh and went away in disgust.

In the absence of other diversions, the children noted

every trivial happening in their immediate surroundings. Each dawn they woke to the sound of cocks crowing and the shouts of the farm-boys belabouring the animals with sticks as they herded them for the morning feed. Then sleepy-eyed kitchen servants came to piss, hawk and pick their teeth in the yard, and throughout the day there was a continuous bustle: the slicing of turnips and cabbages for pickling; the pounding of beans into curd, the stringing of mushrooms and peppers, the preserving of eggs in salt and lime; the cutting up of fowls and fish for drying—all the processes that would keep the large household in food during the coldest season.

For soon it was truly winter. The stunted willow was hung about with the damp straw raincloaks of the bearers and the frayed baskets piled at its base rotted in the wet. Whenever the sun briefly shone, padded quilts were put to dry on bamboo poles and the servants' babies came out to play— and to stare in alarm at the foreign devils, whom they were forbidden to approach. Ice formed on the thatch eaves and the servants, bundled up like rag dolls, skittered across the yard carrying portable stoves filled with glowing embers; cold winds blew the last leaves from the willow and smoke into the cooks' eyes so that they swore with more than usual violence. And after dark the house closed in upon itself and the children were quite alone.

From early waking to final sleeping the focus of their attention was the farm-gate, through which, they daily assured each other, their rescuers must eventually come charging. In her cheerful moments, Alice could imagine the scene vividly: William and Mama to the fore, backed by a regiment of cheering British redcoats, carrying flags and beaming as she flew into Mama's arms. The scene was similar to the brightly painted pictures of the Relief of Lucknow that Uncle Robert from India had shown her when he had visited Tientsin the previous year. Having inspired the original scenario, Robert too became part of it—a handsome, dashing figure, commander in charge of the advancing soldiers—for, as he had been in the Lucknow siege, he was bound to be experienced in rescue operations of the sort required.

And the farm-gate did sometimes open; but only farm-boys came through, carrying eggs, doomed fowls, animal carcasses for the kitchens. One, a gangly lad called Spots on account of his smallpox-marked face, seldom passed without a ribald comment. One morning he advanced and swung a squawking fowl in their faces.

35

"Look at the barbarian runts!" he shouted. "Never mind, ducky, they won't get a taste of you! It's the scrapings of the swill-pots for the likes of them!"

Worse than Spots' taunts was the sustained bullying from the cook One-Eye who had first hit Frank. One-Eye had had his other one rubbed out with quicklime as a punishment for pilfering and his face was set in a permanent leer of remembered agony; his queue was greasy and coated with bits of food as if he stirred the soup with it and his hands, coarse and pudgy for a Chinese, frequently cuffed the devil-children—just because they existed. They hid at the sound of his voice and his misshapen countenance figured prominently in Alice's next-to-worst nightmares; the worst still centring on that dreadful day in Tientsin.

One-Eye was their worst enemy and they had no friend. The nearest was Kau, a hefty girl who beat mats, scrubbed floors, bundled rubbish for the scavengers. She belonged to the Miao tribe of the Far Western provinces and was despised as an "aboriginal" by all true-born Sons of Han. Her feet were unworthy of being bound, her hands not clean enough to handle food and her body belonged to the household. She was a slave and had been since her birth fourteen years before.

Recently, Kau's mother had died and the girl was now as much an unloved outcast as the barbarian children. She accepted her condition stoically, moving lumpishly about her tasks when the other servants were about. When they were not, she would dart with surprising speed to the barrels of dried fish against the wall and hide some scraps in her sleeves—for the starveling yellowish kitten with no tail that curled on her quilt each night and was her only friend. When Alice first spotted her doing this, Kau put a hand to her mouth in a gesture of secrecy and Alice smiled—establishing an outcasts' bond between them. Soon after, Kau produced two balls of dirty brown sugar for the children and, a few evenings later, a whole handful of delicious nuts.

It was about the same time the following evening that the children again heard steps outside the store-room. "I hope it's Kau with more nuts," Frank said with nervous optimism as the door slid open and the slave came in, followed by Han-li and Hung-mei.

The day after the Chu children had first seen Alice and Frank, Father had issued orders that the barbarians were not to be visited or talked about, for it was a matter best kept quiet. Lung-kuang wanted no part of it and whether they were eventually killed or ransomed it would do him no good. He did not share his uncle's brand of hysterical xenophobia, but he did not want to be labelled a Western sympathiser. And things were changing, the present state of the nation was so uncertain under the rule of the incompetent and oppressive Manchus, that it was wise to hold one's fire, not to be seen jumping in any direction. Better, therefore, for the untoward presence of barbarians in his house to be forgotten.

Indeed, the Deputy-Governor himself, often absent on provincial inspection tours, usually did forget, but his family's younger members did not. "Are the Uncut Jades still there?" they would ask the kitchen servants. "Do they still cry? Can they speak properly yet?" But despite their curiosity, Father's instructions had been obeyed—until that evening. That evening Kau had been in the act of stealing a few of Han-li's favourite sugar plums from the study-room bowl when Han-li ran in, followed by his sister.

"What are you doing?" he yelled. "Abo child of a bastard mother—I'll tell the cook about you!"

"No—please don't, he'll beat me!" she pleaded in the rough mixture of Miao and Hunanese he could hardly understand.

"Beat you, you say. You deserve a good hiding—cursed thief!"

"I wasn't stealing them for myself."

"Not for you? Who for then?" Mei asked curiously.

"For the barbarians. They're always hungry."

"Are they?" she looked uneasy. "Let's be quiet about it, Younger Brother. Don't tell Cook."

He whistled through his teeth. "Alright . . . They're still in the store-room?"

Kau nodded and Mei shivered, "It must be awfully cold there now."

"Do they still look as funny?" Han-li asked.

"I suppose so—funny coloured eyes, green like the grass."

"Green you say? Blue as our Nanking vase, I thought," Mei contradicted.

"Pink as pigs," her brother teased. "Bright pinky-red eyes like a hare's in the dark, they have."

"No they don't . . . Don't be silly."

"Let's go and peep at the pink-eyed ones," he challenged. "Father's away and no one will know. You can take us, Kau, as a punishment for stealing."

"Let's take a few plums, anyway." Mei snatched a handful as they went off to the kitchen.

Inside the store the five of them looked at each other in silence.

"Their eyes aren't pink—I knew they weren't," Mei said.

"They're not as big as I thought," Han-li remarked uncertainly. And indeed their recent hardships had shrunken them and they were whey-faced. Mei stepped forward. "Here, take these plums, Uncut Jades."

"They might be poisoned," Alice whispered.

"Don't care . . ." Frank mumbled, his mouth already full of sugary sweetness. Alice stuffed her mouth also.

"They're still greedy," Han-li jeered.

"Just hungry," his sister corrected.

"They look as if they might die soon," Han-li remarked neutrally. "And Father doesn't want that to happen, so Weng says."

"He's probably forgotten about them. Shall we tell Weng how poorly they look?"

"But we're not supposed to have seen them. You won't tell on us, will you, Kau?"

"No, I shan't," she replied spiritedly. "I feel sorry for them—I'd rather be me than a barbarian. Why don't you slip me a little food for them sometimes? It would be easy for you—who have so much. They could die of starvation because no one noticed." And it would well suit Kau, the slave-born, to share a secret with the children of the house.

"Good idea." Mei turned back to Alice and Frank who sat in mute anxiety.

"I wish we could talk to them." Han-li was exasperated. "Father won't tell us anything. Where are your parents—father and mother?" he bawled. Alice began to snivel and Han-li sighed. "Oh she's such a cry-baby. It's no use, they can't understand a proper language. Come along, Younger Sister, I'm supposed to be studying."

From the door, Mei gave Alice a sweet smile: "Don't cry. You'll be alright. We'll send you some bits of extra food."

The Greenwoods spent an uneasy night wondering what new deprivations might result from this unexpected visit, for nothing seemed productive of good anymore. But, to their delight, Kau brought them two dough-cakes in the morning and, in the evening, scraps of meat spooned from some good soup to which the taste still clung, a tantalising reminder of food's deliciousness. Undoubtedly the offerings came from the girl with the kind smile and it was comforting to think that someone in that noisy, uncaring household was concerned for their welfare.

"Let's include her in our prayers tonight," Alice suggested as they knelt, just before the candle guttered, and prayed—for deliverance from captivity, for the soul of their father and the lives of Mama, William, Uncle Robert and Wo-wo—and, from then on, for the girl with the smile, that she might be rescued from her heathen state. And the efficacy of at least one prayer was apparent, for food-offerings continued to arrive, usually grubby, having been concealed about Kau's person, but just enough to dull the edge of hunger that had previously gnawed them.

Then, one fine morning, it seemed for a few glorious moments as if their most fervent prayer was to be answered. They were sitting listlessly on the mats as usual, when a most unusual uproar began in the farmyard beyond the gate. Pigs squealed, goats bleated, ducks, hens and geese squawked; sticks thwacked, wheels creaked, men shouted. The children ran out to look.

"Oh, what do you think is happening? Could it be . . . could it . . ." Alice was starry with hope.

"It must be them . . . it must . . . Mama . . . William . . . we're in here!" Frank rushed to the gate and peered through its chinks. "I'm going to climb up and see if they're in sight. . . ."

But Alice shook her head, light draining from her eyes. For two servants sitting against the wall slicing vegetables with their nails were paying no heed to the noise, which they certainly would had it been caused by the arrival of a regiment of foreign soldiers.

"What's the boy-devil shouting about, I wonder?" asked one. "Perhaps he thinks he's next for the knife."

"About time he was—I don't know what the Honourable Head is thinking of, keeping them still, eating our food for nothing," the other replied.

"Stop, silly," Alice called. "Don't climb up, it's nothing to do with us. Look, no one's bothering."

Frank looked and came leadenly back as one servant honked at him, "Watch out, barbarian runt, or they'll cut your throat too while they're at it."

For a while the sounds beyond the gate continued and the children glued their eyes on it, just daring to hope. Then it opened and farm-boys came through, copiously splashed with blood, carrying bundles of dead fowls, carcasses of goats and pigs.

"So that's all it was," Frank said in a small voice. "Killing animals."

"It must be a special occasion to be having all that meat at one time."

And certainly something untoward was afoot. The next day glowing piles of oranges, pomegranates and pomeloes were dumped along the courtyard walls, old women hobbled in with branches of pine, red berries and bunches of white narcissus. From the house interior came sounds of vigorous sweeping, banging of mats, sluicing of floors. That afternoon three servants staggered into the courtyard with long lacquer boxes from which they took scrolls of red silk, coloured paper lanterns and decorations shaped like birds, lions and dragons. As they shook the dust from them, Alice cried, "I know what it is—Chinese New Year coming, when they decorate their houses and have feasts, remember?"

"Of course, that's it—so Christmas is over then, and we didn't even know about it?" Frank added forlornly.

"That's right—their New Year is in February, I think."

"Last Christmas I got that painted horse, Dobbin, do you remember? Father had it made specially for me by the carpenter in Orchid Street... I still had him that day when..." His eyes filled with tears and the bright colours of the New Year decorations blurred together.

"Yes—and for me he made that little rocking chair, and there was *Alice in Wonderland*, I had it with me when..."

"And I got a toy drum and a whistle..."

"And you put your foot through the drum a few days later and Mama was ever so cross..."

Alice dabbed her eyes. "It's no use crying. Perhaps we'll get some extra food—the kind girl is bound to bring us something special." She squeezed Frank's shoulders, thinking, as she often did, that being two years older it was her duty to be brave.

Preparations for the festival continued for several days. Strips of red paper were hung from the farm-gate, the eaves and kitchen lintels. Delicious odours wafted from the huge iron pans on the kitchen's plastered brick stoves; above the largest was hung the picture of the Kitchen God and dishes of candied sweetmeats were set before him as offerings for the household's prosperity in the coming year. Mei, her hair specially dressed in a more grown-up fashion, sang as she hobbled about in new embroidered shoes that fitted snugly round her tiny bound feet. Even Kau laughed aloud as she trailed paper streamers across the yard for the kitten to chase.

"Look, he's grinning at you," Alice said, coming to join in the fun. "I read a story about a cat who grinned—he was called a Cheshire cat and kept disappearing, leaving just his grin behind." Kau looked puzzled. Alice grabbed the kitten. "Has he got a name?"

"Only 'cat'."

"Then let's call him Cheshire, please!"

"I don't mind. Call him what you like."

Alice hugged the docile ball of fur. "Cheshire, Cheshire— now you've got a lovely name!"

On New Year's Eve there was the customary feast in the large ancestral hall in front of the house to which all relatives of the Chus were invited. Servants dashed about with piles of food, pots of tea, jars of wine; beyond the courtyard walls bells tolled merrily, firecrackers rattled, gongs banged; smells of incense, burned powder, perfumes and boiled crabs hung in the air. After the feast, family and servants gathered in the hall to celebrate the passing of the old year. Only the foreign children remained outside in the store-room, totally forgotten, without food or light.

"I'm ever so hungry." Frank sniffed forlornly at the appetising smells.

"So am I. I can't think why we haven't got our meal—not even anything."

"Everyone seems to have gone away—I don't think there's anyone in the kitchen."

"Let's look," suggested Alice, goaded by hunger. "We might find something to eat." They crept across to the kitchen which for the only time in the year was empty of people— but, oh, the food, succulent, left-over panfuls of it: barbecued pork ribs, fried prawns, livers in sour-sweet sauces, golden-brown dumplings, bowls of beancurd, morsels of roast ducks and geese, persimmons, preserved peaches, raisins, spiced almonds. For a moment they stood round-eyed, then fell to recklessly, cramming their mouths.

"We should take some away instead of eating it here," Alice mumbled.

"Yerp..." Frank was munching busily.

Suddenly they heard steps along the passage. "Run, quick!" Alice gasped. But it was too late—One-Eye lurched into view and, though reeling from a quantity of New Year wine, saw them at once.

"Barbarian scum! Filthy beasts—stealing our food were you! I'll get you for this—you leavings from the piss-pots, you see if I don't." He grabbed a meat cleaver from the wall and made to bring it down with full force on Frank's head. The boy ducked under his arm and went flying up the passage, screaming wildly. Alice tried to dodge too as One-Eye raised the cleaver again and smashed it towards her face. She twisted away, but the blade caught her as it fell and blood gushed from a deep nick in her cheek. As he made to grab her, he slipped on the greasy floor, while Alice fled up the passage, holding her cheek and screaming in her turn.

"Whatever's that noise?" whispered the head cook irritably. He was standing just inside the great hall with the other male servants, holding a cup of wine and a piece of preserved ginger. The world was warm and lovely, lights from the red and yellow lanterns on the beams danced merrily and there was the continuous rustle of silk gowns as people, flushed and smiling, bowed to each other in formal greeting—for another year had just been ushered in.

The cook went into the passage to investigate and Alice ran sobbing into his arms, her face covered with blood. She closed her eyes, half-fainting from pain and terror as he carried her over to the women's group in the far corner of the hall. There was a buzz of voices, red lights blobbed blurrily above her, then the faces of the kind girl and the woman who had first visited her. Someone tied a piece of dirty rag spread with black paste over the wound and gave her a cup of tea, which she sipped gratefully.

"How did it happen, Eldest Sister?" asked Mei quietly.

"The cook says old One-Eye found them in the kitchen stealing food and went for them with a cleaver. He was drunk, I suppose."

"Poor things, I quite forgot—I mean, I suppose no one remembered to feed them tonight?"

By this time the gathering was about to disperse, for another day of pleasure lay ahead. "Where's the boy?" asked Tamao. "They'd better go back to the store." They found Frank outside, weak and trembling, for he'd been violently sick and lost the best meal he had had for many a day.

"Oh, they can't go back there tonight, Eldest Sister—it's so cold and she's still bleeding and they're both ill!" Mei pleaded. "After all, it is the New Year."

Tamao smiled, affected by the general bonhomie. "Oh alright, as long as Father doesn't know—let them sleep inside."

She issued instructions to the chief cook who was also in genial mood, having received much praise that evening for the excellency of his culinary endeavours. Not unkindly, he took the two barbarians and led them off, putting Frank above the stables with the farm-boys and Alice in the attic with the junior domestics. And so it was that New Year's Eve 1871, when the Year of the Tiger came in, was the first of many nights that the Greenwoods spent actually inside the residence of Deputy-Governor Chu.

2

As the sun rose reluctantly on that New Year's Day, Deputy-Governor Lung-kuang reached for the soft thigh of Red Jasmine and stroked it languidly. It was a dalliance he seldom indulged in at that hour when so many official duties awaited attention; but today there was time before the rituals of feasting began. Red Jasmine responded eagerly for she had sensed a waning of his ardour since the recent birth of her daughter. She began to touch him knowingly and he relaxed; the fumes of last night's wine clogged any urgent desire, but he drew her nearer nevertheless.

Steps thudded along the passages and a humble voice piped outside, "Please excuse this interruption at such an hour, my lord, but the matter is of vital importance, I'm told." Lung-kuang merely growled. "A letter has just come from Tientsin. It's been long delayed en route, but its contents are most urgent apparently. The messenger insisted I inform you at once."

"Am I to have no peace, no enjoyment in this life? How dare you disturb me so early on this first day of the year when even the lowliest skivvy in my house is still a-bed?"

"Pay no attention," Red Jasmine whispered hopefully.

But his small desire had evaporated; he lay scowling at the bed-curtains.

"Tientsin—must be that scatty old pepper Lung-pao. Blast his eyeballs! But he's Third Uncle . . . Bring the letter here!"

Red Jasmine sighed and drew the padded red coverlet round her whilst Lung-kuang called for tea. He snatched the letter-roll from the servant who waited while he read. He looked up.

"Tell my secretary to come at once, I must write a reply. And root out those barbarian whelps, they are to be sent back."

Red Jasmine handed him tea. "That letter has taken a whole moon longer than it should to reach me," he grumbled sourly. "And now it's probably too late to be of use." She nodded uncomprehendingly, for he did not discuss such matters with her. ". . . And I'll never find out why—the Empire is falling apart, so much slovenliness, broken bridges, roads like quagmires, people failing in their duties. Why should I alone keep to the right way?"

She clucked sympathetically. "You need to take more time for pleasure and recreation indeed, my lord. It is invigorating for body and spirit."

"Ah yes, and when I try you see what happens, even on this most auspicious day? That damned old fool, Third Uncle." He stared moodily into his cup.

There was another knock and Weng came in, bowing apologetically. "Please forgive my intrusion, honourable, but I've just heard about the letter from Tientsin and your order concerning the barbarians . . ."

"Well, I'll explain later, it really is intolerable, on this of all days."

"Indeed yes, but someone has to tell you that the female barbarian has been injured and is now in high fever." Hesitantly Weng explained what had occurred the previous evening, concluding, "But the male is well enough, shall we just send him, or risk the female dying on the way, or delay a few days, or . . . ?"

"Or, or . . ." Lung-kuang groaned. "Even today I have to make decisions. Here, read this—what do you think? Lung-pao says the authorities intend executing his son for his part in that ridiculous Tientsin disturbance and the only hope is to bargain his life for the foreign whelps. But see the date— that letter has taken a thousand and one moons to get here and by my reckoning it's too late to prevent the execution. But I shall be rid of them at least . . . Only if it's not too late and the she-bitch dies on the way . . . only the girl though . . ." He paced up and down.

"The barbarians value their females quite highly," Weng reminded him carefully.

Lung-kuang turned, "Show me this Uncut Sliver—is she bleeding to death? Why do I have drunken cooks in my kitchen, tell me that?"

Soothingly Red Jasmine draped a fur robe over his shoulders and he and his son-in-law went to the attic over the kitchens where the under-servants slept. Alice lay on a string bed with Kau beside her and looked up with unnaturally glittering eyes as the men approached. A wad of dirty blood-stained cloth was clamped over her wounded cheek, the other was hectically flushed.

Lung-kuang stared down. "Fever, yes—the wound going bad, I suppose?"

Weng nodded. "Perhaps I should get the doctor?"

"A doctor—to heal a gobbet of barbarian flesh!"

"But if it is to be redeemed for your cousin..."

Lung-kuang shrugged irritably. "Is she hurt anywhere else, I wonder?" He pulled off the moth-eaten quilt, raised her night-gown and gazed at her hot, damp flesh. "Looks whole enough." He felt her stomach and between her thighs.

"Has she seen the red snows yet?" he asked Kau.

"I don't think so, my lord."

"Presumably female barbarians have the same visitations?"

Weng was nonplussed. "Physically I think they function in the same fashion, yes."

Alice smiled loosely at Lung-kuang, for his hands felt cool and soothing. Through the pitiless throbbing of her head she tried to remember who he was.

"Strange eyes—like a cat's."

Weng grimaced. "Doesn't appeal to me."

"Ah, but you are yet young, with many chambers still unexplored. However," he threw the quilt back over her, "you'd better get the doctor. Ask him her chances for surviving a long winter journey. I've decided they can't go for two days anyway—it would cost a fortune to hire drivers and carts during the Festival."

As he made to leave, Alice grabbed his hand, placed it on her aching forehead. "Are you the doctor? Please tell Mama I'm ill and ask her for tincture of iodine. It's for cuts and it's in the blue bottle in the washroom..."

He disengaged her hand gently. "What an unattractive gibberish they speak. Still, get the doctor—and tell him I won't pay twice his usual fee. All this is not a very auspicious beginning for the New Year, I fear."

For Alice the year certainly began inauspiciously. The doctor came, scraped off the black paste and put on some yellow, felt under her armpits, pronounced she would certainly die within two days unless she took quantities of his infallible medicine made of powdered hartshorn, rhubarb root and dried pigs' testicles. He would return on the morrow, he added gravely, realising the pecuniary advantages of a New Year visit.

Through her delirium Alice heard the distant crackle of firecrackers that sounded horribly like flames; then Mama was bending over her with a blue bottle; then it was Papa, his eyes very sad and faraway; then it was the real Frank, gripping her hand anxiously. The next day the doctor returned and pronounced that, thanks to his powerful mix, she had as much chance as any other fever-ridden patient of surviving a long journey.

As he rose to leave, his bearer lifting his medicine box, Han-fei rushed into the attic shouting, "Doctor—thank the gods you're still here. Come quickly, it's Honourable Old, the Revered Grandfather, he's fallen senseless in the courtyard. Summon all your skills at once..."

After a while, Frank, still crouched by his sister, realised that the racket of New Year revelry had ceased. Han-li and his cousins who had been flying kites in the paddock were told to fold them away and the many visitors who had called with long red cards of felicitations went home early. The servants returned to the attic, sullen and sober; as each candle guttered it was not renewed and a hush of fear descended on everyone. For already the year had begun with the violent spilling of blood, and if now the ancient head of the house should die before the year was set truly on its course, then the portents were ominous indeed. "May the gods give him strength just to live through two more dawns," they whispered to each other.

Lung-kuang, bowing his head in the ancestral hall where the red festive banners still hung, echoed their prayers; if his revered father should resign his last dignity now, then the demons were truly in ascendant. He raised his eyes to the proud row of wooden tablets placed upright before him, each carved with the names and dates of birth and death of his illustrious ancestors. The family had long been respectable, many of its members had laboured diligently to maintain tranquillity in this remote province; only a few years before, two had fallen honourably, fighting the cursed Taipings. They had obeyed the laws, had not ground the noses of the poor

47

further into the mire; he himself had remained close to his ancestral tree and, banyan-like, taken root in its shade; he had never knowingly behaved unfilially towards his revered father. Why then should the soul of the most elderly be threatening to depart at this inauspicious moment? But, yeh, yeh, old age is like a candle in the wind, easily blown out...

As the incense sticks spluttered in the gathering dusk, his wife and eldest son joined his vigil, their faces equally anxious. No one spoke, but, beyond the gates, the sounds of revelry went on unabated, making the nearer silence heavier. In the hour before midnight a cock crowed loudly from the farmyard and they all quivered, for such a sound at such an hour was a sure sign of approaching death.

Shortly after, at the very beginning of the festival's last day, Lung-kuang was summoned that his presence might facilitate the passing of the spirit from his father's body. White-robed priests from the city's largest temple came to chant prayers for the soul's safe deliverance and in the chill dawn the voices of the household's womenfolk were raised in lament. Lung-kuang and Han-fei went into the main courtyard where they threw coins in the well and returned with bowls of water with which to wash the corpse.

"Frank, is that you?" Alice whispered to the huddled shape beside her. "I've had so many frightening dreams."

He smiled sleepily. "Oh thank goodness, Alice, you're better—you're talking sense again. You had such a fever from that dreadful cut."

"Did I?" She felt the bandage gingerly. "It still hurts. But where are we?"

"In the servants' attic, they brought you here. But now Kau says someone important in the house has died—can you hear the praying?"

They listened to the distant wails of mourning that flowed in sad waves along the dim passageways. Alice shivered, "It's ghostly—a sort of heathen chant I suppose. Oh Frank, I'm so tired..." And, burying her head to hide the melancholy sound, she fell into a heavy, dreamless slumber.

The lamentations continued until noon when a few relatives arrived, still flushed and flatulent with rich festal fare. They were shown into the ancestral hall already hung with white funereal lanterns to replace the red, its floor strewn with the ashes of wads of paper money that had been burned in reverence. There, Grandfather's cleansed body, a piece of silver under its tongue, was laid inside a coffin made of valuable wood brought from Szechuan several years ago for just this occasion. Workmen arrived to seal and varnish it carefully and place it before the ancestral tablets until burial day. Only after this was satisfactorily completed did the weary Lung-kuang and his wife rise stiffly from their knees and withdraw.

Lung-kuang ate supper alone in his apartment, the rich viands cloying tastelessly in his mouth as he remembered the harmless foibles of his father's later years. At the end of every summer Father and four servants used to carry all his caged birds into the hills beyond the city so that they should see the colours of autumn and gain strength to sing throughout the winter, as Father put it. The cages were hung in the trees and Father would stroll about and drink a little wine while the birds sang.

It was near those same hills, Lung-kuang suddenly recalled, that the whole family once went for the Festival of Field-Ploughing. He was a mere lad at the time, and Father, being chief magistrate, was required to break the first clod ceremoniously. The weather had been spring-like, and the people picnicking on the slopes and watching the ceremony had laughed a little at Father, who, encumbered with his stiff, official robes, had struggled ineptly with the recalcitrant plough. But the laughter was good-natured and Father had borne it in good part, for he was a kindly man.

"Yeh, yeh," Lung-kuang sighed aloud, for that was many moons ago, and now the man was dead. Poor Father, better to be a turtle wagging your tail in the mud than to be dead. But perhaps his soul was now a bird in Paradise, flying free, and Lung-kuang began to wonder what should be done with all those beautiful birds of his—the pairs of silver and gold pheasants, the chirpy grey and yellow thrushes and the songster larks, the "Hundred Spirit Birds", Father called them. And the lovely wicker cages, porcelain feeding-bowls, ivory wands shaped like branches for them to sit on. Then he shook himself impatiently, these were mere trivialities; he had to think of his new position as undisputed head of the house and of arrangements for the funeral.

Distant relatives must be summoned from afar and firstly, of course, Father's only remaining brother, Third Uncle... Lung-kuang swore loudly as he then remembered the previous day's news from Tientsin. What to do now? He would have to send news of his father's death along with the barbarian whelps. He long afterwards remembered that he was actually cursing his firebrand uncle and equally hot-headed cousin when the knock came on the door.

"Another messenger has come with great speed from Tientsin, sir." The servant handed him a scroll with an unfamiliar seal and Lung-kuang's fingers shook as he broke it open. His forebodings were well-founded: he was informed that his nephew had been executed as an instigator of the murders of foreign god-preachers the previous summer and his head exposed to public view. Worse yet—Third Uncle, utterly crushed by this final humiliation had retired to his summer residence and drunk the official poison cup two days later.

Lung-kuang groaned and staggered to a chair, his knees buckling. The demise of his revered father, news of his uncle's and cousin's death all in the first three days of the Year of the Tiger before it was properly set upon its course. This indeed was beyond all reason; in some unknown way he had deeply offended the gods and clearly the coming year must be one of mourning and austerity. He sat for a long while, hands folded inside his sleeves. Tomorrow he would call in the soothsayers to advise him on the form of his public piety; personally his course was plain and, as he was in his middle years and overwrought with the cares of office, not entirely unpleasant.

The following day, after news of the fresh disasters had been broken to the family, he formally outlined his intentions to Han-fei and Weng.

"I intend to hand in my seals of office for the rest of this year," he announced to their bowed heads. "Immediately after the ancient's burial I shall retire to the rural residence at Hang-hsien. It is plain that we have offended, that we must walk quietly and carefully through all the days of the Tiger. Eldest Son, your marriage must be postponed until next year, which I pray will be more auspicious. In my absence you will manage any urgent affairs, Eldest Daughter will order the household. It will give you time to stabilise yourself, for you have yet to learn the exercise of the three universal moral qualities—wisdom, compassion and courage. There is to be no commotion, no untoward going forth in any direction. Is that understood?"

Han-fei nodded stonily, though the news of the marriage postponement delighted him. He had never set eyes on his future bride, but he had heard that she was a specially "Dull Thorn" whose only lustre came from being the eldest daughter of a wealthy land-owner in the province. "Yes, Father, there'll be no violence, even in sport. And I'll endeavour to pass Grade Two of the military exercises."

"And not only those—remember what I've often told you, 'the silkworm spins silk, the bee gathers honey'; if men neglect their book-learning they are inferior to brutes."

Weng smiled. "And you can rely on me to preserve harmony in the house, Father-in-law, as is fitting...But may I ask, what is to be done with the young barbarians? Presumably they are of no further use as hostages?"

Han-fei growled. "I'll have them quietly disposed of..."

His father was sharp. "No. I've just said, no more violence. The infant year is already sufficiently blood-stained. Let them loose, I suppose, to find their way back to their own people."

"The difficulty is," Weng began softly, "that if they did manage to get back, they'd tell the barbarian authorities how we held them prisoner. It might lead to new trouble."

"Well, what do you propose then?" Lung-kuang knew that Weng's specially courteous patience foreshadowed some plan.

"Might they remain here? At least until they've been completely forgotten by the outside? Eventually I'm sure I can learn some useful 'barbarian matters' from them, and they could earn their keep meanwhile. The boy is strong and the girl seems to know more because she's older—and growing up fast." He glanced meaningfully at Lung-kuang who nodded dismissively.

"Alright, do as you think best—put them both to menial work and don't bother me about them."

The sun glinted on the golden flanks of the carp as they occasionally rose to the surface of the circular pond in the women's courtyard. The little splashing swirls of their movements, the cooing of doves on the tiled roof and the scrape of Alice's broom on the flagstones were the only sounds to break the quiet of the long, still summer afternoon. Alice had been sweeping those same flagstones every day for months.

In early spring, when she had first begun, she had listened to the windbells tinkling wildly in the fresh winds and watched the arrival of the swallows that nested in the eaves of the verandah where the bells were hung. Soon the gardeners filled with peonies, marigolds and tiger lilies the glazed porcelain vases that stood on tripods along the paved walks. Alice cleaned the vases regularly, especially the one patterned with pink and lavender tracery of petals, clouds and dragonflies. It bore an inscription which, Hung-mei told her, meant "The flower opens. Lo! Another year." Alice liked that. When the early summer rains came, she often stood in the shelter of the servants' verandah watching the drops plop and splatter on the flat leaves of the lotuses in the pond or nestle into the spotted throats of orchids hung in baskets near the windbells. Now the rain had ceased and the mid-summer heats begun; but otherwise all went on in the same quiet fashion.

Because of the household's state of continued mourning, the usual seasonal festivals were scarcely observed, few visitors came and the occupants seldom left. Only Han-fei, chafing at the bit of too much serenity, often went hunting in the western mountains with a group of vigorous young bloods. He cared little for his father's untended duties and it was Weng who managed things with mild circumspection. The even tenor of his rule had only recently been disturbed by the outrageous behaviour of one of Han-fei's cronies who, after an evening of drinking in the house, had formed the habit of sneaking along to Red Jasmine's apartment for more intimate revels. The inadvertent discovery of this irregular union had roused Weng to unusual fury. Han-fei prudently denied all knowledge of it, but the young man was forbidden to enter the house again, and, after consultation with the absent Lung-kuang, Red Jasmine was sent packing to her parents' village with her baby.

The woman's distressed wails of departure had destroyed the peace of the previous afternoon and Eldest Daughter Tamao was thinking of them as she came down the verandah steps into the courtyard. She was attended by servants carrying her first-born son, a bamboo chair and books, and she balanced with more than usual care on her maid's arm, for her new pregnancy had recently been confirmed. Looking very warm and ripe in her embroidered robe, she sank under the shade of a magnolia tree with a contented sigh and began to wonder idly about the fate of Red Jasmine's baby in these unfortunate circumstances. And who, she also wondered, would Father choose instead? She hoped it would be a young and tractable girl, for unofficial wives could cause a lot of dissension if they got above themselves, as Red Jasmine had.

Languidly she took up her favourite volume of the Book of Songs and read again Wu-ti's charming ditty:

"At the time when blossoms fall from the cherry tree,
On a day when orioles flitted from bough to bough,
You said you must stop because your horse was tired,
I said I must go, because my silkworms were hungry."

Tamao smiled and looked up, aware that Alice's sweeping had stopped. The little barbarian had dropped her broom and was bending over the pond. She reached far out over the water's surface, then stood up and raised her arm. From her opened palm a purple and crimson butterfly flew, cavorted against the blue sky for a moment, flicking moisture from its wings, then sailed away, higher and higher over the roof tiles towards the distant hills. Alice watched it go and, with a sigh, bent to pick up her broom.

Tamao called softly. "Come here, Uncut Jade."

Alice came shyly. She was clad in the faded cotton tunic and baggy trousers, the bound-cloth shoes of the servant class; her hair, plastered with crude gum, was covered by a grubby kerchief; her tanned, roughened face and hands were not clean.

"Why did you rescue that butterfly?"

"It had settled on a lotus leaf and might have drowned. Was it wrong then?"

"On the contrary—your good deed for the day. We believe that departed spirits sometimes inhabit butterflies just after they die—so we try to take care of them. Li-po has a poem about it somewhere... I'll see..."

As she looked through one book, Alice picked up another. "Oh, I wish I could read this. I can speak and understand most things now but I can't read a word." She looked appealing. "You're teaching Younger Sister to read and write. I suppose you wouldn't... couldn't...?"

"You? But that would be most irregular."

Just then Mei came out with a servant carrying her ink and brushes for the afternoon's study. "Uncut Jade wants to learn to read and write too," Tamao greeted her.

She clapped her hands gleefully. "Oh please let her, Eldest Sister, she'll be even more stupid than I—and I shan't be the dunce anymore. See, look," she grabbed a brush, "that's jade—*yu*. Half your name that character. You didn't know that, little barbarian?"

"No, but I do now," Alice replied grimly. "And I'll soon learn more, if you'll let me."

"But you must keep up with your other work, or the other servants will grumble and there'll be discord," Tamao warned.

"I will, I promise. You see, when I was in my other life, before I came here, I had to learn all the time—but now there's nothing much to think about. It doesn't seem right somehow."

"I taught you how to embroider my tunics," Mei said.

"But I'm not as good as you at it."

"Well, you won't be as good at this either." She grabbed her writing-brush defensively and Tamao smiled, realising that some competition would be good for her light-minded sister.

"Alright, show her some easy characters, Mei, it's good practice for you. But it must stop when Vegetable Aunt comes back with Father and Mother. She thinks educating a girl at all is like sowing corn in another man's field—as for educating a barbarian girl... well..."

For Alice it meant that the days took on a shape beyond the diurnal routine of sweeping, polishing, scrubbing, with nothing to look forward to except the evening meal and the hours of oblivion in the attic with the other domestics. There were so many houseservants that Alice was not overworked and was too small for the nastiest chores like collecting the rubbish bins and swilling the chamber pots that fell to the lot of strong-limbed Kau. But there was not much fun in it and before the reading lessons began Alice used often to stand at the inner gate wondering whether to make a bolt for it. But where to? How could she possibly survive as a penniless, friendless barbarian in a city of generally hostile people? So she waited, comforting herself with memories of the moral tales she had heard of young girls who lived in bondage and were eventually released to wider horizons. It seemed a fairly common female fate and one day she and Frank would be fully grown-up and run away together.

She saw little of her brother, for he worked in the farmyard beyond the outer gate, mucking out the pigs, swilling the stables, chopping corn stalks and churning bran for animal food. His clothes were always filthy and he stank of manure, but he was reasonably happy—especially in the evenings when he and the other lads were let loose in the paddock to kick about balls made of blown-up pigs' bladders. He had become friendly with "Spots", the duck boy, and sometimes he would sneak Alice a fresh egg or some wild raspberries picked in the boundary thicket.

"I'm learning to read and write Chinese," she told him smugly at their next encounter. "I'm starting with the Three Character Classic."

"Are you? Whatever for? Here...." He popped a berry in her mouth. "You can speak better than I can now."

"But writing's different."

"Too much like school for me!"

54

"Father always said you were lazy."

"I'm not—I just like learning different things. Younger Brother's teaching me to throw the javelin and now I'm better than he is."

"And I'm much cleverer than Younger Sister," she snorted, "but they still call us stupid barbarians because we're British and I suppose they always will."

Frank rubbed his dirty nose. "Do you remember, Uncle Robert used to say the British are the strongest country in the world?"

"Yes—but it's hard to believe, the way they despise us here."

"Oh well, it could be worse, at least I don't have to learn Latin and stuff."

"You would think that! Give me another berry and I must go, or they'll say I don't work hard enough and the lessons will stop."

But Alice saw to it that they did not. She always finished her chores in time for the afternoon study and, in the precious leisure hour after supper, when the day-long click of the weaving looms and the stirring of the cooking pots eventually ceased, she squatted in a corner of the kitchen courtyard practising the characters. Apart from an occasional cuff from One-Eye the cook, no one paid her much heed anymore; but her round eyes, unbound feet and stumbling speech all doomed her to remain, like Kau, a permanent outcast. Outnumbered, the two of them presented a united front, sleeping beside each other in the draughtiest corner of the attic guarding each other's small possessions, managing, between them, to keep scraggy Cheshire fed. Lulled into a sense of timelessness by the monotony of these days, Alice was vaguely alarmed one morning to hear the servants discussing preparations for the imminent return of the house's head, who was planning to resume his official duties and then celebrate the passing of the bad old year and the coming of a more propitious one.

"And to start the Year of the Rabbit really well I must produce another healthy boy," Tamao remarked as she, Mei and Alice sat together in her room that afternoon. "So I shan't be doing anymore teaching for a while."

"Because of him inside you?" Alice asked tentatively. She had heard mutterings to that effect when one of the servants had recently given birth.

"Of course, of course, haven't you noticed her swollen belly, you silly Sliver of Uncut?" Mei roared with laughter.

"Here—look!" She untied the sashes of her sister's voluminous gown. "See—in about a moon it will pop out between her legs and it hurts ever so much, doesn't it, Eldest Sister? You screamed and screamed last time. Feel it..." she placed Alice's hand on the hard mound covered by a white undergarment.

"Do you mind it hurting so?" Alice asked fearfully.

"Oh no—it's not for very long and you soon forget because the baby is so beautiful." Tamao spooned tranquilly at some rose-jelly specially made for the pregnant.

Mei giggled. "Perhaps barbarian babies pop out from somewhere else, do you think?"

Alice sniffed. "My Mama told me years ago that people found them under gooseberry bushes—but I guessed that was a fairy story."

Mei cackled. "Gooseberry bushes—heh, heh. I'd like to see a man sticking his thing into a gooseberry bush!"

"What do you mean?" Alice felt uncomfortable.

"With his Stalk—why, you look as puzzled as a pig in the weeds! You mean you don't know about *that*?"

Tamao took pity on her. "Well, Uncut, the man pokes it up the woman's hole—which we have between our legs, and he leaves a seed there which grows into a baby inside your belly, see?"

"Yes, sort of..." Though, having seen the boys' stalks when they were urinating or washing, she thought it would be a rather difficult manoeuvre. "Is it nice?" she asked Tamao.

"Being poked? Sometimes it's lovely—if you like your husband and he's kind, like mine."

Alice's cheeks burned, for what she heard gave her shivery thrills of delighted recognition.

"It will happen to you one day, then you'll see how it feels and you'll have babies."

"I wonder what they'll look like?" Mei broke in. "Will they have funny eyes and mud-coloured hair, like Uncut?"

"I suppose that partly depends on the man who takes her." Tamao hauled herself upright. "I must get ready for supper. You two can help each other with the characters if you like, but not a word to Vegetable Aunt, she's returning with Father and Mother."

That night Alice lay sleepless, restless and tense. The last candle guttered out, rats began their nightly scamperings among the smoke-blackened roof-beams and the warm fug created by the charcoal stove and the steaming supper bowls evaporated into dark, harsh cold. On the other side of the partition separating the younger domestics from the older, she heard vague movements; she had often heard them before, but tonight they took on a positive, purposeful rhythm which made her even more restless. What could be going on? She crept across and peeped round the partition. Several servants were asleep in the room, but one candle still burned and in its light Alice saw One-Eye straddled over the half-clad body of a woman, she lying spread open and he thrusting vigorously into her. He had a twisted smile on his face that she had never seen before and his one eye looked quite jolly. As Alice watched, a fist crammed into her mouth to keep herself quiet, the movements increased, the two bodies jerked closer together, came a spasm, a gasp, then silence. Alice crept back to bed, her whole body tingling as she imagined a man of One-Eye's size but much nicer thrusting deep inside the warm damp places between her legs.

The fertile seed which in early summer Weng had implanted inside Tamao was a good one. For the bunches of camellias were still in bloom on the New Year festal tables, the piled bowls of persimmons, oranges and loquats not quite consumed when the midwife was summoned. The birth was easy; it was another boy, and Lung-kuang's face glowed with relief. Now the gods were surely appeased and his policy of quietly withdrawing and waiting for the ill winds to pass elsewhere had undoubtedly paid dividends. The proof was his second grandson, healthy and crinkle-skinned with beamy eyes. Baskets of red-dyed eggs arrived in salutation of his masculinity; he was patted, petted, passed from hand to hand; his "milk name", bestowed a month after his birth, was Custard Apple. Now, Lung-kuang decided, it was safe to arrange the delayed marriage of his eldest son; the appropriate horoscopes were consulted; the go-betweens selected and a date in early April was agreed.

"Have you seen the beautiful presents that are going to the bride's house tomorrow?" Mei asked Alice a few weeks later. Since Custard Apple's birth, Tamao had been too preoccupied to teach them, but in the afternoons, when the vigilant Vegetable Aunt retired to rest, Alice practised her calligraphy in Mei's room, while Mei embroidered the colourful robe she would wear at her brother's wedding.

"Come and see..." Mei led Alice into an adjoining room where a huge camphor-wood trunk stood open on the floor. It was piled high with silks the colour of peaches, lilacs, roses and emeralds, and capes lined with the furs of snow leopards and golden monkeys; there were bundles of hairpins shaped like butterflies and peacocks; agate, pearl and pink crystal earrings, jade and turquoise beads nestling in sandalwood boxes; embroidered and sequinned three-inch-long shoes; a creamy satin robe patterned with chrysanthemums and tiger lilies.

"All that—for her?" Alice touched the satin gingerly with her work-roughened hands.

"It's the custom."

"Why is she called Dull Thorn, it's such an odd name?"

"Oh, her real name is Unimpeachable Splendour—but people say Dull Thorn suits her better. She's wealthy but stupid, you see. Why, they say she can't even make good pickles!"

"And is that necessary?"

"But all well-born daughters should—my pickles are delicious."

Alice smiled, looking again at the trunk. "And will you get presents in return?"

"Oh yes, lots. When she comes to live here she must bring furniture and utensils, bed-hangings and quilts, spices, oils and meats. And when Eldest Brother takes these things to her house, he'll be given a huge feast."

"It sounds such fun." Alice felt suddenly resentful. How awful it was, to be a menial on the outside of everything, eating the scraggiest offal, drinking the sifted leavings of the tea, stroking other people's fine satins. She remembered a scene from an early story book of a London street, with two ragged urchins pressing their noses against a shop window. It was bulging with jars of coloured bonbons and a fur-clad lady inside was buying huge boxes of chocolates. The unfairness of it had stuck in her throat then; now it was much worse, for she felt as ill done by as those beggar children.

"I suppose Dull Thorn will be overjoyed at all these presents?"

"Oh no—she'll weep and wail and beg her parents not to make her leave home. That's the custom."

"The bride isn't supposed to be happy?"

"Oh no—and she'll hate her wedding day because the men guests will all laugh and jeer at her—that's the custom too."

"And Eldest Brother, what does he think?"

"He never mentions it—it's his duty to marry her, that's all. Knowing him, I'm sure he'll enjoy all the eating and drinking."

"And it's the custom for her to live here? So one day when

you marry you'll have to go and live with strangers?"

"Yes," Mei sighed. "And I shan't like it at first. But I've been betrothed for a long time and I'll probably be married in a year or two."

"You—married!" Alice was horrified.

"I'm almost fifteen and it's time for me to be a wife soon and have babies."

Alice picked an ivory comb from the trunk and ran her nail down its teeth. "I'm glad I'm not Dull Thorn after all. It doesn't sound a happy prospect, in spite of this finery."

"Oh she'll get used to it, we women have to, and our family don't treat daughters-in-law as badly as some."

Alice shuddered. "I'm going—it's all too much, Younger Sister. I'll see you tomorrow." She fled away down the passage, in a nameless panic, filled with desperate longing for one of her own kind. Hurrying along the verandah she noticed that the east gate leading to the park was open, and she slipped through, revelling in the full extent of a view which, till then, she had only glimpsed. In the foreground was the paddock, edged with lean-to huts full of sporting equipment; archery butts were spaced at intervals across it. Beyond lay the fine sweep of the park—spotted deer were grazing on the hillocks and the grounds were dotted with small lakes and pavilions sometimes used as tea-houses. The whole was enclosed within a high peak-tiled wall that snaked away over a wooded hill in the distance. Alice's eyes widened, unaccustomed to so much space; she had forgotten how large the world was, how distanced she was from anything truly familiar. She was about to retreat, almost afraid, when a figure appeared from the stables carrying swill. "Frank—it's you, isn't it? Come here."

He came towards her, his hair was drawn back in a stubby queue she noticed, but its dirty-straw colour was still outlandish. "Hello, Uncut Jade, is anything wrong?"

"No . . . well, it's just that we talk so seldom now. You don't enjoy working in the stables like this, do you?"

"It's alright. They don't beat me or call me so many dirty names these days. What about you?"

"Oh—I sweep and clean." They looked at each other awkwardly.

"You look just like a servant." Frank grinned.

"And you like a farm-boy."

"Well I am, I suppose."

"You're not, you're Frank Greenwood, son of a missionary, and don't you forget it! Frank, we don't talk of people coming to rescue us anymore, or even of escaping—but we could, they don't watch us carefully now."

"Well no one is ever coming for us, so what's the point? And where would we escape to?"

"I don't know. Only, sometimes it seems so very foreign here. And I think how horrified Mama would be if she saw us now."

He snorted. "We've been forgotten—so we might as well make the best of it here. Eldest Son's getting married soon, did you know? We've reared some special geese—fat as barrels they are. I'm looking forward to it—Spots says there'll be piles of good grub around."

The day of the wedding dawned grey and chill. This was not particularly propitious, nor was the fact that, owing to exceptionally strong spring gales, no shred of peach blossom remained to adorn the reception hall. But it looked resplendent anyway, hung with red lanterns and banners inscribed with wishes for the harmonious union, immeasurable prosperity and felicitous fruitfulness of the bridal pair. Crowded in a corner of the main courtyard with the other servants that afternoon, Alice thrilled to the shrill blast of pipes, the beat of gong and drum, snap of firecrackers that heralded the bride's arrival.

The main gate was flung open and a long procession came pouring through. In front were the banner-bearers and men armed with staves and truncheons to keep the rabble at bay, then the musicians and grey-robed acolytes from the Temple of the Heavenly Clouds on the hill. Other bearers followed carrying caged mandarin ducks and drakes to symbolise conjugal felicity and lacquer boxes full of the bride's gifts. Bearers of more exalted rank with glittering conical hats carried sedans containing Dull Thorn's relatives and attendants, and behind came eight strong men bowed under huge stone tablets inscribed with the generational names of bride and groom. Then a forest of red silk umbrellas appeared, their tassels joggling in the breeze, and in the midst of them a closed sedan chair, decorated in vermilion and gold, borne aloft by four men.

"Look—she's inside there!" Kau pushed Alice forward excitedly as the chair was set down before the door of the reception hall. Tamao, her eyes cast down, stepped forward and opened the chair, formally bidding the bride set foot in her new home. A small female shape emerged; she was clad in a mantle of crimson brocade with a stiff embroidered skirt below; around her neck hung long strings of pearls, on her head a high jewelled tiara. From its front hung a veil of golden beads so thick that her face was completely hidden. She stood there for a moment, a faceless, doll-like figure shivering slightly with apprehension and Alice's heart went out to her.

Poor Dull Thorn! How dreadful to be brought here like this, to be linked to uncaring, irascible Han-fei, to have to let him do the things that men did to women, to have to live in uncomplaining subjection within this alien household for the rest of her days.

Two servants approached, carefully lifted the stiff, red figure up two red-carpeted steps and over the pan of charcoal that was burning on the hall's threshold to prevent the ingress of any evil influence. Inside the hall, Lung-kuang and his family were waiting to receive her.

"How long will she have to wear that veil over her?" Alice asked Kau as the servants dispersed to their duties.

"The groom goes to her chamber and lifts it up later—it's the first time he sees her closely. And she's not allowed to wear any paint on this day, so he'll see her plain enough." Kau chuckled. "And it'll be quite a shock for him, so I've heard. Then they'll all worship before the ancestors and the marriage will be officially announced. Then comes the feasting—that's the best part. We'll all eat well tonight."

And everyone did eat well, except Dull Thorn herself, who, as custom demanded, partook of no food and sat silent and expressionless as the smells of the delicious viands wafted round her and the guests chewed and sucked appreciatively, crunching last of all at the white-sugar cocks and hens that adorned the tables' centres. The air of the hall was heavy with fumes of warmed wine, smoky candles, spent firecrackers, incense; replete people sat together; the young male guests, flushed and raucous, had gathered round to enjoy the customary teasing of the bride. They were pulling at her dress, grimacing in her face, tweaking her hair.

"I should snuff the candles before you lay her," one shouted at Han-fei.

"And here—make her stand on this," yelled another, inverting a goblet on the table. "Let's see how delicate her golden lilies are!"

The groom, his cheeks hectically glowing, guffawed and tried to propel his bride upward, but she refused to rise, seeming indifferent to the whole proceedings.

"She'll be a stubborn vixen, Han-fei," his neighbour announced. "Not biddable, you can see that. Make her give you some wine at least."

Han-fei thrust a brimming goblet in his wife's hand and leered at her with open mouth waiting for a drink. Dull Thorn leaned forward and Alice, crouched with Kau behind a pillar, saw her face clearly for the first time. It was, as rumour had suggested, flat and dull, the eyes that looked at her new husband were those of a stupid, dumb animal, tinged, just then, with fear. Her hand shook uncontrollably as she held the goblet to his mouth and some of the wine spilled down his embroidered robe. A roar of mirth went up, and someone shouted, "Look at that, the clumsy upcountry clod! —She can't even find the way to your mouth." Han-fei grabbed the goblet and drained it, dabbing his robe angrily.

Attracted by the noise, Lung-kuang went over to them; he too was wine-flushed, but benevolently so, Alice thought. At his suggestion, Dull Thorn rose, bowed low to her husband and went to join the women at the lower table, while the men, half-mocking, burst into a traditional wedding-song:

"My Lord is all a-glow.
In his left hand he holds the reed pipe,
With his right he summons me to make free with him,
Oh, the joy!
My Lord is carefree.
In his left hand he holds the dancing plumes,
With his right he summons me to sport with him,
Oh, the joy!"

Alice seized the diversion to run up and tug at Mei's sleeve. "Let me have some of those lovely sugar-cakes, please, Younger Sister."

"Oh hello, Uncut—isn't it fun?" She was happy and excited. "I'll make sure I don't spill the wine like that on my wedding day. Here you are..." She slipped some cakes into her hand and Alice and Kau carried them to the attic where other servants were lounging about, munching the banquet left-overs and discussing the unimpressive appearance of the bride.

Later that night there was a fresh outburst of shouting and laughing as the male guests accompanied the groom to the door of the bridal chamber. One tried to trip him up while another drew a cord lasso over his shoulders in playful pretence of stopping him. Han-fei roared, butting them with his head like a young bull and thrusting his loins rhythmically towards the closed door.

"You'll need your bellyful of wine to break that one open!" they yelled, pushing him against the door. "Go to it, man, touch the fish, she's all yours!"

He stumbled inside, slamming the door, and the guests departed, calling for lanterns and cloaks, for the night was chill, damp and moonless.

"Ho-ho, the male-rain and the woman-clouds have come down," they said to each other. "A good sign for a merry coupling!"

The aftermath of the wedding went on for days, with much ceremonious coming and going between the houses of bride and groom. Dull Thorn's parents, reported those servants who saw them, were up-country bumpkins like their daughter and they wondered at Lung-kuang for blessing such an alliance, even for the money. As for Dull Thorn, she found little pleasure in her new home. Her mother-in-law simply ignored her, as she did most people; Vegetable Aunt found another target for that constant irascibility which, said Lung-kuang, resulted from the consumption of far too much hot pickled cabbage; and even Tamao's good nature did not extend to the bovine, sullen girl whose embroidery and pickle-making were not up to scratch.

And Mei positively hated her new sister-in-law. "Look at her out there," she said to Alice one summer day as she sat sewing in a verandah-corner. "She's fallen asleep right in the hot sun and her complexion will be a mess. Her paint's melting and she'll look like a wrinkled old crone—the silly bumpkin! I shall be careful not to do things like that when I'm a wife." She turned her pretty face to Alice. "Have you noticed anything different about me?"

"Oh yes—you've got different paint on."

"Yes, it's called Nonchalant Approach. And see—Elder Sister's plucked my eyebrows in the one-day-old-moon style, so...and so..." she traced the arched lines with her slim fingers. "Uncut, you're about my age—it's time you put paint on. You look like a paddy-peasant!"

She held up her mirror teasingly and Alice winced at her weatherbeaten tousled appearance compared to Mei's smooth elegance. "You're right, I do look a fright. Here, let me try some!"

She fetched the make-up box and sat still while Mei, giggling, white-powdered her neck and face, rouged her cheeks, blackened and arched her eyebrows.

"There!" She handed over the mirror. "That's certainly an improvement—it makes your funny eyes look much better!"

Alice was both dismayed and excited by the suddenly older, mask-like face reflected back at her.

"And we'll put some gloss on your hair..." Mei plastered some heavily-scented oil over Alice's hair, drew it back with combs, set off the whole concoction with a pink peony above her ear. "Now you're beginning to look much too pretty for an outside domestic—perhaps Vegetable Aunt will let you come and be my personal servant at last!"

This had been Mei's hope for some time, but Vegetable Aunt was quite determined that no barbarian should ever be granted a position of such intimacy inside the house. Nor did the enhancement of Alice's attractiveness have any effect whatsoever on Aunt's resolve; but, a few days later, it had unforeseen consequences in another quarter.

"Eldest Daughter, are you there?" The commanding tone of the man's voice set up a little flurry among the females passing the afternoon in the women's courtyard as usual. Dull Thorn was dozing in her chair in the sun; Mei was embroidering and keeping an eye on Little Piece, Alice was desultorily cleaning a bronze urn. Lung-kuang strode through the gate looking rather peevish.

"Honourable Father, is there anything wrong?" Mei jumped up.

"Not really—Weng has sent a message to say he's been delayed at Yin-pu with a slight fever. I thought I'd bring the news. Send for tea quickly, little Second Daughter. It is too hot. And ask Tamao to come here."

Cursorily acknowledging Dull Thorn's presence, he slumped in a chair, took a fan from the case at his waist and fanned himself languidly. It *was* too hot. The time of Great Heat always went on too long; one yearned for the first yellowing leaves and the autumnal chrysanthemums, though no one cared as much about them as his Honourable Father had. Fragments of long-ago-learned poetry drifted into his mind:

"Then from the flutes of the forest came a thousand voices.
The colours of autumn are fresh in the wind and rain.
Though the virgins have all gone their way to the yellow graves....
Why is it that paintings still hang on the walls?"

*　　*　　*

Written by the admirable Tu-fu surely? A poem about an abandoned palace? How did it go on...?

"Standing there, even now, under the hanging cliffs.
In dark rooms ghost-green fires are shining..."

Lung-kuang shivered despite the heat and opened his eyes upon the young domestic industriously polishing a courtyard urn. What was the name of that eerily beautiful palace? Jade Flower Palace, that was it. Alice looked up, wondering if she should leave.

"Uncut Jade, come here," he said.

She approached shyly, bowing low.

"I hear that you've been learning the characters with my daughter? How is it that my domestics have the time to read books?"

"I work doubly hard the rest of the time, Honourable, and Eldest Daughter says it helps Younger Daughter to attend." She looked at him, greenish eyes pleading beneath her delicately arched eyebrows.

"What do you read?" he asked curiously, as Mei and a servant appeared with tea.

"The wise ones... the poets."

"Ah, I've just been thinking of a poem, it is by Tu-fu, quite well known. The Jade Flower Palace..." He took the tea. "I cannot remember the end. What is it, Younger Daughter?" Mei hesitated and Alice broke in eagerly.

"All the while singing I am overwhelmed with
    lamentation.
Among these lanes of life disappearing in the
    distance,
Who can make himself eternal?"

"Ah—just so. Melancholy, is it not? You are learning well, it seems." He stared at her firm young body beneath the faded blue tunic.

"She's very clever, Father," Mei said, adding timidly, "Eldest Daughter is feeding little Custard Apple, he is ailing in the heat. Shall I ask her to come?"

"No, I'll go to her in a minute. And now Weng is indisposed and of no use, and while I work myself ragged along these 'lanes of life' my domestics learn to read and write!" He barked a grudging laugh.

"But Uncut isn't an ordinary domestic, Father—she's special and strange. I think it would be much better if she were my personal servant instead of a skivvy. Can she be, please, Father?"

"And what does Vegetable Aunt say?"

"She says no, just because..."

"Then there is no question, I do not meddle in these domestic arrangements." He stood up, looking at Alice crouched before him. "Why you and your brother are still living under my roof, eating my food, I can't imagine."

"But, Honourable, we've no choice. Would you give us permission—and a little money—to go now?"

"Permission? Money? We'll see. Or perhaps I have something else in mind for you." He stuck his fan under her chin, tilting her head for closer inspection. "She paints herself."

"That was my idea," Mei said eagerly. "It makes her look better, doesn't it?"

"Yes, it does." He ran a forefinger down her cheek. "Strange and special you say? Well...we shall see...Now, take me to Eldest Daughter."

Tamao's shaded room smelled of hot babies, milk and vomit and he felt indisposed to linger once he had inquired after the baby's health and told her about Weng. But, as he moved to leave, she held him with, "And you, Father? Are you in good heart? You've had so much work to do since your return and there's been little time for leisure, I think?"

He sighed. "Very little. The incompetency of my subordinates during my absence was beyond belief."

She smiled sweetly at him. "Don't work too hard, Father—do not wait for the almonds till you have no teeth!"

He chuckled. "You are right as usual, daughter. That girl, the barbarian servant, is she virginal?"

Tamao looked up in surprise. "Why...yes...I assume..."

"Well find out, and if her red snows have arrived."

"But, Father, why...?"

"The matter need not concern you, simply send me word."

She stared after him perplexedly as he left; but she did as she was bid and duly sent word the next day to say Uncut Jade was a virgin with the red snows upon her. She remained vaguely puzzled by the matter for several days, till the morning her maid appeared bringing news just whispered to her by the master's body-servant. The Uncut Jade, the ignorant barbarian, with feet the size of boats and eyes like a wild cat, the foreign bitch from the gods knew what monstrous litter, had been summoned to the bedchamber of the head of the house the night before, and was still there.

3

Morning sunlight filtered through the lattice high in the wall of the Deputy-Governor's bedroom; it speckled the matted floor and a black lacquer table edged with golden flowers. Under the red silk quilt Alice lay very tense and still, staring at the light through a gap in the brocaded bed-curtains. Her naked body throbbed with unfamiliar usage, most specially the tender places between her thighs where the man had thrust and thrust. Gingerly she explored the sore region with her fingers, then looked at her hand. He had made her bleed; she remembered the pain of it. Tears rolled from under her closed lids and she wiped them away, leaving smears of blood and rouge on her cheeks. She felt unclean, empty, and she did not know what to do.

The summons of the previous evening had been so unforeseen. And even when the master's body-servant had slapped layers of powder and paint on her face and neck, wrapped her in a blue and orange silk robe and pushed her contemptuously into the master's presence, she had not understood. Then she saw the speculative gleam in his eyes, the way he stroked his small black beard, the large bed in the room's centre with its curtains looped back, and a heave of fear swamped her.

"Oh no, no, no, please let me go away," she begged in

English several times, as the servant took off her robe.

"Leave her leggings on, I don't want to see those monstrous feet," Lung-kuang instructed.

Waiting on the bed, she tried to console herself with the memory of One-Eye and the woman. It had not looked too dreadful; indeed at the time it had excited her. But when Lung-kuang drained his wine-cup, came over and looked down at her with a weary smile, she trembled violently. "Well, little barbarian," he said, "let us explore the golden gully of an Uncut Jade, perhaps it is slightly different." He examined her pubic hair with cool approval. "Yes, growing the right way." She flinched. "There's no need to be afraid," he assured her. "I shall do no more than all men do to womenfolk. It will not hurt you long."

But it did hurt, she had not thought a penis could grow so big. He enjoyed the virginal tightness of her Jade Gate and called for more wine, though he did not get drunk and was not brutal, for it was not in his nature. Eventually, he rolled away and slept; she listened to his heavy breathing for hours, terrified he would awake and go inside her again. But he did not, and soon after dawn, a servant arrived bearing tea and a copper bowl for his washing.

"You can go back to the servants' quarters now," he said shortly, as he left for the business of the day. She intended to obey, but, overcome with exhaustion, finally slept, so that the sunlight through the lattice was noon gold when the servant reappeared, hustled her from the bed and back to the kitchens. That evening, when she and Kau gave Cheshire his nightly feed, Alice whispered the story of her night's adventures. But Kau, unbelieving, cackled with scornful laughter.

"You—with the Most Honourable? What sort of cretin d'you take me for? I know where you were—with Spots. He has a taste for barbarians, see how friendly he is with your brother."

"Spots and me!" Alice sprung up, frightening the cat. "How dare you think I'd share a bed with that swineherd... It was the master, I tell you. Look, there's still paint on my face and this..." She dug into her baggy trousers. "There's blood down there still!"

"There always is, when you're a virgin. Spots could make you bleed as well as the Most Honourable—and did!"

"No, he didn't. It was the master. I was called to his room. There's a red quilt on the bed, and paintings of mountains and lakes on the walls and a writing-on-wood panel that says,

'Because we gaze on flowers, the wine is warmed.' And before he did it to me, he said he was going to explore the golden gully of an Uncut Jade."

Certainly that did not sound like Spots, but Kau remained unconvinced.

"Alright—we'll ask Spots, you'll see!" Alice dragged her up and they went to find Spots who was chopping maize stalks for the pig swill.

Kau jerked his queue. "What were you doing last night?"

"Last night? Sleeping like I do every night—unless I can get my hands on a wench."

"And you didn't last night?"

"No, more's the pity." He leered up at her. "Would you like to try me tonight? I'm free."

"I told you," said Alice triumphantly as they walked away.

"But that doesn't mean it was who you said." Kau was seized with doubt and envy. "Even if it was, that'll be the only time. Men of the master's age like a virgin now and then. So they can break their narrowness apart with pain and see the blood I suppose. It's called deflowering, did you know? Funny sort of flowers!" She snorted. "Anyway, you'll never see the inside of the master's bed again, I can tell you."

And for a while Kau's prediction seemed true. The cooler weather for which Lung-kuang had longed duly arrived; bronze, crimson and yellow chrysanthemums flourished in the courtyard urns and he looked at them gratefully before leaving on his autumnal tours of inspection, taking with him Han-fei, who needed much initiation into the responsibilities of future office. Severe storms and floods hit the northern districts that year; hundreds of fishing rafts, traps and boats were broken up, ruining the livelihood of the lakeside fishermen and trebling the price of fish in the city markets. The common people were disgruntled and hungrier than usual, but it was a recurrent pattern, he told Han-fei; one just had to remain unobtrusive, waiting for a better time.

Yet he found it hard even to imagine the goad of hunger, so extravagantly was he feasted by local officials. Wherever he went, piled dishes of roast pig and succulent river fish garnished with gingers and peppers were put before him, however high the prices. After supper, wine and singing women were available if he so desired. So it was not until he was again home near the year's end that he realised he had neglected to install a replacement for the unlamented Red Jasmine—and remembered the soft young flesh of the green-eyed barbarian.

Alice was called three times to the master's bedroom during the New Year period when the wine flowed freely, and she went feeling both scared and exultant. She had longed to prove Kau wrong, longed to explore further that strange and intimate coming-together. Soon, rumours reached the ears of Hidden Glory, whose lips twisted in pained scorn at the idea of such a grotesque coupling. Tamao, however, took a purely practical view of the matter: it was preferable, in some ways, that Father's occasional lusts were being satisfied by Uncut rather than a potentially disruptive, official concubine. But it was insupportable that the most private intimacies of his bedroom could therefore be circulated among his lowliest domestics. Whatever else, she told her husband, the hierarchies of the house had to be preserved, and she must take steps accordingly.

Father was warming himself by the charcoal stove when Tamao went to his apartment. Shadows of snow fluttered outside the paper windows and wind whistled through their cracked frames. He rubbed his hands together.

"It is cold, is it not? And how is Custard Apple faring?"

"He is much stronger, thank you, Father. Snow suits him better than sun, it seems."

"And Dull Thorn? Is there a pregnancy advancing yet? It is time she started breeding sons...Take some tea, Eldest Daughter... Is anything amiss?"

"No, Father, thank you. I am well contented with my lot, as you know."

"That is good to hear. Women seldom are—the sex that is moulded out of faults." He sighed and they exchanged a few more pleasantries, he waiting, knowing she had come for some purpose. She set down her cup.

"Just a small matter—of little moment, Honourable. Second Sister is growing in years and stature as you know, and she has begged me to allow her a personal servant. Her preference is for the foreign Uncut Jade, which is strange, though she's certainly quicker and more intelligent than the other attic servants. I wonder if this would be agreeable to you?"

"Why bother me with such domestic trifles, do as you wish," he replied imperturbably.

"But it is not an arrangement that would ever be sanctioned by Vegetable Aunt, for the barbarian would then sleep in the women's quarters and handle Second Sister's food."

"Ah..."

"Alternatively, Uncut Jade could be cast from the house, which would please Aunt more."

"Vegetable Aunt does not rule."

"Precisely. But nor do I without your support on occasions."

"Then you have it on this occasion, Daughter. The arrangement sounds satisfactory, and you can tell Aunt so, from me."

"Thank you, Father." She rose and bowed. "I'm sure Second Sister will be most grateful."

Returning to her room, Tamao wondered how long this strange predilection of her father's would last; probably this effort on her part was unnecessary; though he did not usually tire quickly of a woman.

The next day, Alice, ignoring the envious, ribald taunts of her fellow domestics, bundled her few possessions into a ragged goatskin and went to the women's apartments. She would in future know and possess many rooms of varying size and elegance, but few so satisfying as the cubbyhole in the corridor near Mei's apartment. It contained a string bed, a bamboo stool, a strip of matting and a window overlooking the women's courtyard; branches of an almond that would bloom in the spring hung within touching distance.

It was wonderful and Alice did not much care whether she had Hung-mei or Lung-kuang to thank for it, happy to do the bidding of both in return for the pleasures of her new position. No longer had she to sweep the courtyards; instead she dressed Mei's hair, mended her clothes, carried her embroidery, books, writing materials, favourite caged cricket, wherever she wished to go. Mei was occasionally petulant, but never very demanding, for her nature was sunny, and Alice had time to study the characters, watch the blossom unfolding in the courtyard, talk with Tamao, Han-fei and sometimes even with Weng, who spent more time than was customary in social communication with his wife.

That spring, a friend of Weng's returned from Hong Kong and described to him the steamships in the harbour, the high stone buildings and how the foreign devils were pressing inland demanding new trading rights as they came.

"I've been thinking—why do you barbarians pile the rooms of your houses one above the other?" he asked Alice one day, coming upon her in Tamao's room.

"I...I don't really know. But yes, I remember pictures of London, the houses so tall, with stairs going up inside."

"Perhaps it's because you have so little room to spread sideways in your miserably tiny country called England?"

"It's not small surely?" Alice was uncertain.

"Oh but it is—I hear that hundreds, perhaps thousands of Englands could be contained within the borders of our Celestial Empire."

"But we have the British Empire too, and that is huge, Father told me."

"It is a subject of great puzzlement to me that such an insignificant island can control such an Empire, while we Celestials..." He sighed. "It is a question of vessels, weapons and trade, I'm told. We should be learning more 'outward things', we live like frogs in a deep well here."

"But, Honourable Husband," Tamao broke in, "such things are mere conveniences surely? Our imperial power resides in the ancient wisdom, the splendid deeds of our ancestors. The barbarian races are but uncultured savages in comparison."

"But we have our history and our heroes too," Alice protested. "Kings and queens, poets and writers. There's William Shakespeare, and Charles Dickens and a man who wrote about the Greek gods. A Mr Thomas Babington Macaulay who wrote the history of England and all the saints in the Bible..." She tried desperately to remember more, but there was only a jumble of school-book pictures—armour-clad Roman soldiers, Jonah and the Whale, poor Ophelia drifting downstream somewhere—nothing one could easily explain.

Tamao looked contemptuous. "Greek—is that a country near England?"

"Fairly near, I think. On the shores of the Mediterranean." All these untranslatable names fell heavily and Alice was aware of making little progress. "And there's *Alice in Wonderland*," she continued more confidently. "About a little girl who fell down a rabbit-hole where all the animals talked. And she met a turtle who sang a song that began, 'Will you walk a little faster, said the whiting to the snail'..."

"Whoever reads nonsense like that?" Tamao's disdain mounted.

"Children do—it's a children's story really."

Weng looked puzzled. "You mean foreigners write books just for children? How odd! *We* prefer our sons to learn the wisdom of the sages from an early age—it is study enough for a lifetime. No, we don't need your children's books, but we need your knowledge in some directions. It still puzzles

72

me, for instance, how your vessels manage to move so fast against the wind?"

Alice was nonplussed. "Well, they have engines and steam comes out of their funnels..." But she could find no proper way of translating this, so that Mei giggled, saying she had heard that the foreign devils kept tame dragons under their ships to pull them along and the steam you saw was really the smoke from their nostrils.

Lung-kuang asked no such difficult questions of her when she went to his bedroom, for his curiosity about the world beyond the Hunan borders had long since waned. In earlier days he had been an ardent supporter of Tseng Kuo-fan, nicknamed the Python, the vigorous patriot, Confucian scholar, brave general who had led his army of Hunanese braves against the Taiping rebels. Tseng, a Changsha man by birth, used occasionally to return home where he would talk of China's need to have its armies equipped with Western-style weaponry for, he used to say, this was the only means of defence against the barbarians' wily, grabbing games.

But poor old Tseng was dead now and Lung-kuang found he had no time for such abstractions. Did he not have enough to do—arranging and supervising public works contracts, organising fishing taxes and the storing of food supplies against times of famine or drought? No, a man could not spend his entire life trying to improve the naturally inperfect order of things; wiser, when the opportunity arose, to pass a few pleasurable hours dallying in the warm soft country between a woman's thighs.

The barbarian woman, he soon learned, was little different from the many daughters of Han he had known, and her fleshy parts, like theirs, grew rosy and juicy as the inside of a pomegranate at his expert touch. Her breasts were fuller because they had never been bound and her odd eyes, flecked green like a river, grew moist and dreamy as he stirred her Yin. "Let your moonflower essences flow freely from you," he would murmur, as she lay spread wide on the bed, moaning with pleasure at his caresses, watching adoringly as he paused now and then to sip tea or bend to drink from her Jade Fountain.

"Come, it's time for you to bestir yourself," he said on one such night, putting down his pipe. "Now you shall straddle the White Tiger."

She rose obediently above him, varying the speed and

depth of her movements in accordance with his murmured instructions. "Gently and quickly go down so...there and then there on me, now think of a sparrow picking at the rice-grass, so and so..."

"Yes, Honourable." She smiled lovingly at him, her young body attuning easily to any motion he desired. "Is that good?"

"Yes, yes, you are learning well..." He closed his eyes and tightened his muscles, forcing himself back from the brink of expulsion. He was still in good condition for his middle years, he thought complacently. And, correctly performed, these sensual delights were good for a man's circulation, they strengthened his bones and renewed his spirit. "Now then, turn round, let me see your back—like the mounting turtle." She grasped his legs, bending forward feeling his increased size, her whole being concentrated on their point of delicious coming-together.

"Now wait a little, I shall have a rest." She got off obediently, still trembling with desire, and he walked to the window. "There's a full moon tonight."

"Yes, Most Respected." She got up too, came and nuzzled against his belly, caressing his buttocks. "Oh Honourable, how strong and lovely you are!"

He stroked his beard. "You wouldn't find a man like me among your barbarian tribes."

"I'm sure I wouldn't." She snuggled and rubbed against him. "Which position would please you next, Honourable?" For she was now well-versed in the various ways of pleasuring the Jade Stalk.

"I think perhaps we will cleave the cicada." She shivered in tremulous anticipation, took the hard, silk bolster, put it against the bed's edge and spread herself high over it, face downward. She held tight to the coverlet, waiting, gasping with the fullness of him as he gripped her waist and entered her, thrusting slowly, like a carp moving in a pool on a summer's day. As he did so, he watched the lovely moon through the lattice, grimacing slightly at her gasps of pained pleasure. Again, as her essences flowed, he contained himself, but he was tiring, he must not over-indulge.

"Now you must play the flute," he offered his uprightness to her.

Their encounters usually ended thus. She knelt, bent over his crimson bird, nibbling and squeezing with her lips and tongue in the way that pleased him most. He continued to stare at the moon for a while, but with decreasing attention; then, with a little growling grunt, he pushed her head right down. "There—take me there, lick harder..." He held her there for a minute, for his Yang essence was good for her, then he patted her hair. "Bring the cloths and then I must sleep." She wiped him tenderly, then herself and sank into bed beside him, encircled, enchanted, enamoured of his expert lust.

Alice's days came to be dominated by dreams of these musk-scented night encounters. Sick with yearning, she would wait in the passageways hoping for a glimpse of her lover, even though he invariably passed her without a flicker of recognition. In the evenings of that early summer, after she had helped Mei disrobe, she would sit in her cubbyhole looking at the sky and longing for the servant's tap, meaning that the master required her presence. When it came, she dabbed herself with jasmine water, powdered her breasts and neck and hurried to him eagerly; when, as was more often the case, no summons came, she would toss for hours in bed, beset by lush fantasies of past and future intimacies.

It was on one such night that she first distinctly heard the sound. It was a half-suppressed, low moan that went on and on. She shuddered, reminded of Tamao's tale about the evil spirit of a wailing woman with the eyes and teeth of a fox who reputedly haunted the house when trouble was brewing. Unable to sleep, she crept along the passage towards the noise which, she now realised, was a very human cry of distress, emanating from the room of Third Daughter, Little Piece. Candlelight flickered through the room-screen and she peeped in. A nurse was hunched by the child's bed, crooning a dozy chant. Little Piece lay wide-eyed, her small hands helplessly plucking the quilt; her steady wail of sorrow seemed more profoundly hopeless than any seven-year-old mortal could rightly utter.

"Is she ill?" Alice whispered.

"Oh, it's you, Uncut... No, it's just the foot-binding trouble upon her. The first few months are always the worst to bear, poor mite."

Alice shivered and looked pityingly at the child who stared back in a kind of defiant agony.

"There, there, have another sugar plum then, and remember, child, not every night can be a feast of lanterns." The nurse spoke mechanically, giving a plum to Alice also.

"Is she like this every night?"

"No, she's had the new bandages on today, so it's specially bad. I take the old ones off every few days, wash her and then fold the smaller toes under the big one a little more tightly each time—well, they say each bound foot has to cost a bath of tears."

"But it's a slow torture," Alice stared at the suffering child. She had, of course, seen hundreds of bound feet hobbling along awkwardly, deformed hooves concealed by white leggings and embroidered slippers, and she had seen Mei's feet unbound—the grossly swollen ankles and folds of loose skin, the deep cleft across the sole where heel and toes had been forced into unnatural conjunction over the years. But Mei had always treated the matter lightly, as she did most things, dismissing it with her usual, resigned, "But it's the custom." Now, watching Little Piece beginning to undergo the same remorseless process, Alice understood her dreadful, helpless wail—the inevitability of a crippled life. "How long will it go on like this?" she asked.

"Oh, about three or four years only. As I tell Little Piece, look at Number Two Sister, she's alright now."

"But her feet often hurt and she'll never walk normally..."

The nurse shrugged; she was from the lower classes and not bound. "Ah well, no gentleman of rank would marry a big-footed woman."

Little Piece jeered up at Alice. "There you are—no decent man would ever marry an ugly barbarian like you, would they, nurse? 'Cos she'll never have beautiful golden lilies."

"That's right, my pretty blossom—so don't you fret. It's all in a good cause, as they say."

Alice sighed, realising fully for the first time what a prison the house was for its womenfolk. They left it so seldom, and when they did had always to travel in chairs, be supported by attendants and servants. How could all this have become "the custom"? She longed to ask Lung-kuang about it—was he not moved to pity by his daughter's wailings? Did he really find those fleshy, maimed hooves desirable? Yet her own naturalness repulsed him and he never removed her leggings.

"We're all going out of the house soon for a whole long day!" Mei announced to Alice shortly after she'd begun to chafe anew at this sense of perpetual confinement. "It's the Ching-ming Festival—the first suitable season for going into the countryside, so we make a pilgrimage over the hills to our ancestral tombs."

"Oh, let me come with you please," Alice begged.

"Well—alright. It's highly irregular, but with so many of us, people may not notice you. The hairdresser is giving Eldest Sister and me a special hairstyle for the open air, and

76

I must finish my new slippers. You must carry everything proper for me, Uncut—a basket for wild flowers, a cage in case we find more crickets, my Spring-Festival fan, and two umbrellas, one for sun and one for rain, to protect my complexion whatever the weather—but I do hope it's sunny."

And so it was. Ching-ming Festival day glowed cloudlessly with a warm spring breeze that rustled the manes of the ponies waiting in the courtyard and the paper pennons of the banners for the ancestral tombs. The senior members of the family set off first in closed chairs, and Alice watched longingly from behind a pillar as Lung-kuang emerged, wearing a fur-bordered conical hat and a resplendent brocade mantle. He looked so tremendously magisterial; she could scarcely believe that the Crimson Bird which gave her so much pleasure nestled somewhere beneath his finery.

After they had gone, the family's younger members and servants followed in humbler procession led by Han-li riding on horseback. His mount was stringy with buck teeth and sores on its tail, but he was proud of it and so was his groom Frank, who, capitalising on his sister's promotion, had managed to procure the job. Frank's fair hair was concealed by a grubby turban, but his legs, bared to the thighs for running, looked pink and muscular beside the other grooms'.

He grinned when he saw Alice walking demurely behind Mei's chair. "Isn't it exciting? Have you been out before?"

"No, not once since we came in these gates—and I wonder how long ago that was?"

He shrugged. "I don't know. I've been out with Han-li several times. Keep your head down in the streets, or the people shout 'foreign devil' at you."

Outside, Alice duly lowered her head, occasionally glancing at the passersby—vegetable-, fruit- and toy-sellers, carriers of water and firewood; men with carts full of excrement bound for the paddies, other trundling hand-carts stacked with grain, trussed pigs or stones; only a few women were abroad—aged crones selling sweetmeats, scavengers with baskets on their bent backs, ragged girls with pock-marked babies.

When the party reached open country, Alice's spirits soared at the expanses of spring grass, the trill of meadow larks, fresh breezes untainted by city smells. The freshness reminded her of the sea, how she used to walk along the Taku Road near the Tientsin docks—that glittering expanse of water, junks jostling at their moorings, Papa telling her about the flowery meadows and golden cornfields of his Norfolk childhood.

By the time the junior procession reached the ancestral resting-place, the senior Chus had all assembled to bow, clap hands and pray before the tombs on the hillsides. But it was not in the least funereal, Alice thought, watching from a discreet distance. The white banners on the grave mounds flapped as merrily as sails against the blue sky; children, dressed in their colourful best, bounded about the grass and, on the slopes behind, masses of yellow, mauve and crimson azaleas were in bloom. In the far distance loomed a range of forested mountains; its most sacred peak, Mei told her, called Hensha, was guarded by a bird with wings of flame belonging to the God of Fire.

During the afternoon, trays of watermelons, peaches and loquats were passed round and a troupe of wandering musicians played ballads on their bamboo flutes. Even Hidden Glory looked less remote as she sat gazing at the flowering bushes and holding in her gold-ringed, long-nailed hand a silver pipe at which she contentedly puffed. As for Vegetable Aunt, she wore flowers in her hair and, leaning on her cane, cracked nuts and jokes with elderly relatives she had not seen since New Year. When the younger males went off riding, Mei went to pick azaleas, moving slowly among the bushes. "You must choose with care, Uncut," she instructed. "Try to see which way each branch expresses itself, that's what Eldest Sister taught me. We want one colour for each vase and an uneven number of branches—three, five or seven is best."

"Why?" asked Alice, recklessly gathering a multi-coloured armful.

"Because the shapes of the flowers and twigs must form a harmonious whole—and even numbers are unlucky. Isn't that right, Tamao?" she turned to her sister who had just joined them.

"Yes, didn't you know that, Uncut? And why are you here anyway? Keep out of the way of the honourable elderly, they wouldn't like to see a barbarian in their midst on such a day."

"But my brother's here—with Youngest Son's horse."

"Yes, and Weng told him the same. Anyway, Dull Thorn whispered something to me this afternoon—she even smiled—she's podded at last. So we're all adding a prayer today for a first-born son."

Mei clapped her hands. "How exciting! I hope he'll take after Eldest Brother and not have her face—flat and broad as the bottom of an old cooking pot."

Tamao giggled. "So do I. And he'll be an important little personage, first son of the first son..."

Alice looked over at Dull Thorn sitting near her mother-in-law, staring, with her usual passivity, at the grave-mounds which bore none of her family's names. This day of honouring the dead seemed a strange occasion to announce a coming birth. Yet perhaps not, for, in quick painful vision, the whole of life's little cycle compacted before Alice's eyes—the baby growing in the mound of Dull Thorn's belly would as child and then adult probably come here to worship his ancestors when the azaleas bloomed, and be laid to rest in his turn inside another of the hillside mounds. So perhaps, after all, Dull Thorn had chosen auspiciously.

But Senior Daughter-in-Law's advancing pregnancy cast a shadow over the ensuing summer. She became increasingly tearful and petulant and, because of her condition, had now to be humoured. Her younger, equally lumpish sister moved in to attend her, and they made a doleful pair as they tottered round and round the inner courtyard every afternoon, looking at nothing. Dull Thorn developed a craving for boiled pigs' bladders, fishes' brains and bears' paws which she ate in huge quantities, just because they were expensive, in Tamao's opinion. Mei and Little Piece had to keep quiet in her presence and embroider caps and shoes for the coming infant, and Alice helped, having acquired a certain skill. And how soothing it was to sit in the shadow of the orange trees in the hot afternoons, twisting and threading the coloured silks whilst the crickets chirped in their cages and she daydreamed voluptuously of the next night with Lung-kuang.

As the time of the birth approached, Han-fei shunned his wife's presence entirely, but female relatives appeared with coarse red-sugar balls, lichees, mangoes and the flesh of turtles to strengthen her. Her belly strained bulbous and sweaty under its cotton casing as she sat in the verandah chair eating greedily through every offering. But there was never any joy in her deeply-embedded eyes, only a haunting fear that no gift could dislodge. Walking across the courtyard one evening, Alice saw her rotund shape still sitting in the twilight. Dull Thorn was nervously clicking her charm-beads and mumbling plaintively, "Oh may the gods protect me.... Oh I know it will go ill with me...oh, oh..."

Alice hurried away shuddering, but remembered the scene a few weeks later when the sound of Dull Thorn's screams rent through every closed screen of the women's apartments. Unable to bear the noise, Alice crept into Mei's bed and the two clutched close together, rigid with fear as the shrieks intensified and urgent steps hurried along the passageways.

"I didn't think she had it in her to make so much noise," Mei whispered, "she's much worse than Eldest Sister ever was."

"Perhaps she'll die. Women do die having babies. A friend of Mama's did in Tientsin once. Think of trying to push a huge baby out of a small hole—it must be awful."

"Well, all our mothers did or we wouldn't be here." Mei was practical. "So it's no use worrying—and it may be your turn next!"

Alice put her fingers in her ears and shook. Until then, Mei had not referred to her relationship with Lung-kuang and she did not want to think of it in this light.

Dull Thorn's screams continued unabated till the next afternoon when another doctor arrived looking solemn. Silence fell with the dusk, and soon after the news spread rapidly through the waiting household: Dull Thorn's spirit had unfortunately departed from her torn body; the female she had borne was just alive.

As the ritual wails of lamentation went up from the gathered womenfolk, Alice watched a line of white-robed priests arrive from the Temple of Heavenly Clouds chanting obsequies and carrying candles to show the newly-released spirit the way to the land of shades. A chill autumnal wind blew the light flames sideways, scudded clouds across the moon, whipped leaves off the almond tree. Alice murmured:

"The sound of her silk skirt has stopped,
On the marble pavement dust grows.
Her empty room is cold and still.
Fallen leaves are piled against the doors."

She fell silent, with a sense of dispassionate pity for the short, dispirited life of poor Dull Thorn. Was anyone truly mourning her that night?

"Were you sad about Dull Thorn's passing, Honourable?" Alice asked Lung-kuang curiously as they lay together under the red quilt. It had been their first coupling since the death, for all the correct funereal proprieties had naturally been observed, including the two-month period of sexual abstinence for relatives. Tonight, in consequence, Lung-kuang was in a particular enthusiastic and relaxed mood and Alice was emboldened to ask a personal question.

80

"It's a damn-blasted nuisance. I hoped marriage would keep Eldest Son in check a little, he has this peppery Hunanese devil in him. But that woman was useless—a lump of mildewed rice-dough. So there'll have to be another one for him, but it is not proper for at least a year. All that wedding expense and fuss over again and worse yet—the delay in getting a grandson from my first son. There are always women-problems of one kind or another."

"But not from me, Honourable?"

"No," he chuckled and began to fondle her again. "That is the advantage of an unofficial female. How does that feel—like the fluttering of butterflies in you, hey?" He spread her gently, thrust inside her for a while, then withdrew, staring complacently at his still-upright stalk. "See, I'm not quite in need of the bald-chicken potion yet, am I, Uncut?"

"The what, Honourable?"

"Ha—you don't know? Bring me some fresh tea and I'll tell you... Well, there was this aged Prefect, an old old man, but with the lust for women still in him, only he just couldn't keep his stalk up long enough, poor old sod! So he called the doctor who gave him a special potion—black as spiders' bile it was. Well, the old rascal took a dose and lo and behold!—his Jade Stalk positively leaped to attention and went down only to spring up again. And ho, what fun they had for a while, he and his old wife, he gave it to her this way, that way, t'other way, till the poor old duck couldn't sit on a chair or lie on a bed. And, 'oh mercy on us' she cried, 'it's too much, this potion of yours, you should be ashamed of yourself at your age!' But he only spread her again, saying, 'Well, if you don't let me have you, I'll have to fetch some lusty young wench from the village who will.' And at this she picked up the bottle and threw it into the courtyard where it broke.

"Now, there happened to be a fine young cockerel in that yard and he ran right over and drank as much of that potion as he could before it sank into the mud. Then this cock jumped upon the first hen he saw and off he went—in and out, in and out, up and down, fuck, fuck, cluck, cluck... And that cock wouldn't get off his chicken for twelve whole days, and all the while he was at it he kept pecking her head till at last, by the time he did leave her alone, she was bald as a coot—and that's the story of the bald-chicken potion!"

Alice screamed with laughter, "Oh that's a lovely, lovely story, Honourable! I wonder what the stuff was made of?"

"Ah, no one knows—the man who discovered that would be as rich as the Emperor himself. Well, Uncut, let's see what I can do without the potion in me!" They enjoyed the Kingfisher Union and the Turning of the Yellow Dragon together that night, before Lung-kuang eventually spent his Yang essence deep inside her and then slept, his arm heavy across her body.

Safe in the master's bed and with the master in amiable mood, Alice's position seemed secure and the intense delight of her new-found sensuality usually overwhelmed the shadows of shame and guilt that were the legacy of her childhood. Why should she know so clearly that her parents would have been utterly scandalised by her present behaviour, she sometimes wondered? As she wiped the natural juices from her lover, smiled down at his trim, hairless body, lay relaxed by the close feel of him, she could not understand how it could be wrong. But during his frequent absences she was often afraid. Lung-kuang and she were not married, never would be, and so she was living in mortal sin; and even here, in the deepest recesses of heathendom, was not God watching her?

As for Lung-kuang, he took delight in the supple and lively body of his unofficial woman, even though he was slightly ashamed of his perversity in preferring her to a true daughter of Han. In any case he gave the matter little thought, for, in addition to his onerous duties, he and his fellow officials were deeply troubled that winter by rumours that came from the Imperial Capital. Apparently, the young Emperor, the Celestial One, T'ung-chih, had been visited by the heavenly flowers—a euphemism to conceal the dreaded ravages of smallpox—and his death was daily anticipated. An intense struggle for power was going on in the Imperial Court and T'ung-chih's mother, the Empress Dowager, was plotting to dominate whoever became the new Emperor. It might lead to a rebellion against the much hated Manchu regime, it would certainly mean some shift in power, the formation of new alliances. Between the capital and the Empire's distant regions messengers rode secretly back and forth with the latest tidings and the provincial governors were on constant alert.

Thus it was that, on a cold night in late December, at the Time of Winter's Standing, Alice, wakeful in her cubbyhole, heard a disturbance in the main courtyard. Lantern lights bobbed, horses' hooves clattered on the paving, servants' feet padded along the verandahs. She dozed finally, haunted by foreboding, then slept until a servant called her to her duties.

"Didn't you hear people about in the night?" she asked Mei, who sat waiting for her hair to be oiled.

"Come, Uncut, you're late..."

"I'm sorry, Younger Sister, but didn't you..."

The door slid back and Tamao hurried in. "Have you heard the news? Father has been called to Peking."

Alice dropped a comb. "Father...the Honourable. Why? What?"

"The Governor sent messengers during the night—Father is to go to Peking immediately to report on what is happening and who we Hunanese should support. He's about to leave, so you must hurry and bid him farewell—come, Second Sister."

Dread in her heart, Alice hurried to the main courtyard which was all abustle. The men of Lung-kuang's official retinue sat waiting on horseback, their faces muffled against the cold; in their midst was the master's gilded chair, its ill-clad bearers stamping around to keep warm. Breath steamed from the mouths of every man and beast. Frank hurried to her.

"Look at that white horse—isn't he a beauty? Goes like the wind, and Honourable will ride it once they've left the city."

"Oh, will he?" Alice stared miserably at the fine creature, its flowing mane and tail festooned with official green and red ribbons.

"Here he comes," Frank tugged her sleeve as Lung-kuang came outside, saying to Han-fei in a stern voice for all to hear, "And you, Eldest Son, are in sole charge of all household affairs in my absence. Is that understood?"

The son bowed low to hide his shining eyes, while Lung-kuang looked beyond to where servants were loading the carts with baggage and provisions. Stepping into his line of vision, Alice raised her hand in a desperate gesture of farewell. His eyes swept unseeingly over her. "Tell the servants to hurry," he snapped.

Alice long remembered the back view of his rich, brown fur robe as he climbed into the chair without another word. Reins jerked, steeds snorted, as they raised the master aloft, the bearers gave the ritual groan to signify the magnificence of his weight; the gates opened, house-servants bowed low as the chair was carried out and Alice rushed away to hide her tears.

It was not until the squeals of the pigs doomed to supply the New Year's pork again rose from the farmyard that news reached Changsha of the succession to the Dragon Throne of Kuang-hsu, the "Emperor of Glorious Inheritance"—and a puny three-year-old. He was the nephew of the Empress

83

Dowager and she had ruthlessly pushed aside more legitimate claimants so that he should succeed and she could consolidate her behind-the-throne power.

"Now the new Emperor is proclaimed, your Honourable Father will be returning very soon surely?" Alice asked Tamao, on the afternoon of the news' arrival.

"No, I fear not. Weng says he has other business to attend to in the capital on the Governor's behalf and gives no date for his return."

"Oh," Alice bowed her head miserably, and Tamao smiled. "You mustn't let it concern you, Uncut. Men have many women in their lives and they think little about any of us when they're away."

Alice sniffed. "But...I can't...I mean...I'm worried, Tamao because my red snows haven't come for almost three months now. Do you think they'll come back when he does or...?"

"Oh dear, I expect it's a baby. What a nuisance, Uncut, especially with Father away. I don't know what course he'd want us to take..." She looked thoughtful. A half-barbarian whelp would only be an embarrassment; the obvious thing was either to get it aborted now or send the girl away. But is that what Father would wish? And how could she know till he returned, which might be too late? She must consult her husband, and perhaps even Eldest Brother, though she so disapproved of his recent behaviour that she tried to avoid him.

For Han-fei, restrained by neither father nor wife, was thoroughly enjoying the fruits of his new-found mastery over the household. He spent much of his time gambling and wenching in the city's gay quarter and, when the New Year Festival began, filled his apartments with street entertainers, drinking cronies and heavily-painted women, their high coiffures glinting with flowers and jewels. Weng, stiff with angry powerlessness, spent the Festival in the customary fashion with the usual relatives and friends, though Vegetable Aunt was so incensed by Han-fei's behaviour that she became a martyr to hysterical fits. Falling flat on the floor, she unleashed her hair, kicked her tiny feet in the air and screamed till her cheeks were as purple as her favourite pickled cabbage.

"She'll die if she goes on like that," Tamao remarked to her mother. But Hidden Glory only shrugged disdainfully, "It's the Hunanese peppers in her—she's never learned to control herself and never will, at her age."

By the end of the Festival's third day, Han-fei and his companions were fairly besotted with their various indulgences and the floors of the male apartments were littered with chewed bones, spilled wine, nutshells. In the main bedroom, a woman with flowing hair and white-powdered face sat on a cushion playing plaintively on a three-stringed lute; outside it was snowing heavily. Han-fei leaned out of the window, catching flakes on his hot tongue, then surveyed the scene with a bored sigh.

"I'm tired of her and that dismal caterwauling," he announced to his friends. "A man needs something more unusual to rouse his senses by this time."

"How about the outlandish she-devil with jade eyes that your father has tucked away somewhere?" sniggered one.

"Faugh! the barbarian whelp—not on your life!"

"Let's see her anyway. Has she got yellow hairs top and bottom like the male?"

"I don't know—but that reminds me—get the Uncut Sliver," he called to a servant.

Pushed into the room, Alice stood shivering, a tatty goatskin over her night-robe. Han-fei went over, jerking her head up by the hair. "My father's whore—this little dog's fart!"

"I'm not a whore, I'm a proper concubine—and he likes me well enough."

"Oh he does, hey? What revolting taste... Well, I've just heard you're breeding, wench, and he won't like that, I know bloody well. So you can get out of this house, we're not having any little green-eyed devil-monsters running loose here."

"Well done!" His companion raised a cup. "Show a decent respect for the proprieties. I'd roll that rotten egg out of the gates right now if I were you!"

"But Number One Son, please..." She dragged at his sleeve. "Please don't turn me out now—it's your father's child, remember."

He cuffed her across the mouth and threw her from him so violently that she fell backwards. "Out, out, I tell you— you devil-arsed whore."

"But what will the Respected Father say when...?"

"He'll thank me for getting rid of you, you breeder of monsters. And I'll have a pretty wench waiting for him who'll give him a proper son of Han—faugh! Out I say! If you're still in this house of Chu by this time tomorrow, I'll take a knife and cut that sickening grub out of your belly with my

85

own hands—do you understand, foreign-whore?" He thrust his red face contorted with fury towards her; she scrambled up and fled in terror.

There was no hope of Han-fei's relenting, and Weng, the only one who might have interceded on Alice's behalf, refused to risk another confrontation with him over such a trivial matter. Alice's only course, Tamao advised, was to live quietly in the countryside nearby until Father returned, as he might agree to give her a little money.

The next morning, Alice sought out her brother in the farmyard. "Number One Son's thrown me out of the house," she faced him directly. "I've got to leave before nightfall and not come back—oh Frank, help me, whatever shall I do?"

"But why...whatever made him...? Oh Uncut, how dreadful!"

She felt confused and ashamed; it was impossible to explain; she had no idea how much he knew. "He's always hated us, you know that. And I annoyed him yesterday when he and his friends were drunk and he ordered me out. Oh Frank, please come with me! I want so much to find Mama and William, and I don't know how to start."

"Me? Go away from here? But I'm alright, Uncut. And they've forgotten all about us by now, perhaps they're dead."

She looked at him miserably. "Oh Frank, please don't say that, I couldn't bear it. Please come with me, it would be so much easier with two..."

He shuffled his feet in the mud. "But I don't see why I should, Alice, especially now I'm Han-li's groom. We're good friends and he treats me well and I get plenty to eat."

"Well, I'm going to try and reach the nearest treaty port, and get in touch with Mama—and then you'll be sorry you didn't come too, so there!"

"But I shan't know how you get on."

"Frank, if I find them alive, I'll come back for you one day. Then you'd leave, wouldn't you?"

"Yes, I suppose so, but..."

Just then Kau appeared, carrying rubbish. Alice had seen less of the Miao girl since her own elevation in the house, but she had kept her and Cheshire well supplied with delicacies from the well-stocked tables of the women's apartments.

"Kau, come here, did you know that I...?"

"Yes, I've just heard, I'm sorry, Uncut. Where will you go?"

86

"Oh dear, I don't know. If only Frank would..." she looked pleadingly again.

"Why don't you sneak away with Uncut, Kau?" he said impulsively. "You've often said you wanted to return to your mother's tribe in Kweichow, you could go together."

Alice seized on it. "Oh please do, Kau. We could go to your relatives first, they'd take us in surely? Only the other day you said you'd never find a husband in this household."

She smiled. "That's so. I need a Miao man and there aren't any hereabouts. And I'm growing up, and I've been putting a little cash by... Alright, Uncut, I'll come. I was just thinking it would be much worse for me and Cheshire here without you."

"Good old Kau." Frank slapped her shoulder and Alice clasped her hand.

"Oh thank you, thank you Kau. Now we must get ready and remember, Frank—I'll come back some day for you, promise..."

"Alright, Alice, I feel bad about it, but... here wait a minute..."

He rushed off, returning with a little cloth bag. She felt it curiously.

"Money?"

"Just a little and don't ask how I came by it... Well goodbye, Alice, and good luck."

They parted awkwardly, having lost the habit of kissing each other.

"I'll meet you at the north gate when they open it for the scavenger cart," Alice told Kau as they parted.

Early dusk was falling among windswept snow-flurries as the scavenger cart trundled in through the north gate and two wrapped up little figures, each carrying a basket, slipped discreetly out. In the street, Alice paused to look back as the scavenger threw the rubbish aboard. From Kau's basket came a tiny bleat. "Oh Kau, you've not brought Cheshire?"

"I had to, Uncut, no one would look after him now we're gone."

The cat mewed pitifully and Alice shivered. Snow caked her eyelids and she wrapped the moth-eaten fur cloak that had been Mei's parting gift more tightly across her stomach. As the cart creaked away the north gate was slammed shut.

"Which direction shall we take?" Alice asked in a quavering voice.

4

A disintegrating corpse floated out of the thick fog and, borne up by the river's oily waters, jostled against the prow of the trading junk on which Alice sat, as if trying to roll aboard. She shuddered as she watched it, thinking incongruously— you can't come on here, there's no room. "No room, no room"—bizarre echoes of a distant tale drifted back to her. "No room," they cried as Alice approached the Mad Hatter's tea-party. But Alice sat down anyway and later the Hatter recited the poem, "Twinkle, twinkle little bat, How I wonder what you're at, Up above the world so high, like a tea-tray in the sky".

Alice smiled wistfully upwards, hoping for a vision of bats or tea-trays or even stars. But there was no sky, just dense fog pierced only by the crowded masts of the craft moored along the banks of the River Tzu as it went through the town of Shaoyang. Hundreds of "boat families" always lived there, but now their numbers were swelled by vessels waiting for the fog to lift before negotiating the rapids below the town. So tightly jammed together were they that the water between was insufficient to let a corpse sink decently and, as Alice watched, the bloated blob of flesh bobbed helplessly away towards the steps leading up the bank, where three leprous beggars crouched, picking with scaly fingers at a hen's carcass.

She and Kau had managed to buy a passage to Shaoyang, southwest of Changsha, en route to Kweichow. Rivers were the main highways of the region and travel along them, though often perilous and always slow, was cheap—except for unforeseen delays such as fog, which could prove expensive, as she was about to discover. For, as she huddled outside to escape the foetid crowd of humans, dogs and fowls crowded under the junk's canopy, she became aware of a nearby disturbance. A rotund, bald man flanked by two flunkeys with stout staves came stamping down the bank steps. The beggars cowered away, but were given passing thwacks nevertheless. The man thudded aboard the nearest boat shouting, "Mooring dues, how many aboard? Pay up or get out, you litters of water rats!"

"Oh, rot his eyeballs, it's the River Boss," Li-chi, the junkmaster, came running up and pushed Alice inside. "If he counts heads you'll have to pay."

A minute later their craft rocked as Boss jumped aboard and stuck his oily pate through the opening. "Alright, how many here?"

"Just me, the wife and kids," whined Li-chi, holding up a string of cash.

"And who's this?" a flunkey, pushing past, thumped Kau on the shoulder.

"An abo—getting a ride to Kweichow."

"And this?" he leered in Alice's face. "Another abo. Pay up you two—double dues for every passenger and you know it, you gobbet of dog's spittle!"

"I can't pay," Li-chi growled. "They'll have to pay for themselves."

"But we've no money," Alice appealed, which was true for they had paid their last coin to secure their passage.

"Then off the boat and into the debtors' jail—you might discover some cash after a while there." Boss poked her hard and Kau wailed in horror, for she knew about jails.

"Oh not that—anything else. Please, most kind and honourable sir."

Boss considered her, scowling. "You've got a face like the backside of an old goat," he remarked, "But you're young... And this one?" He jerked Alice's head. "Squint as an abo alright, but might do. Alright, if you want to earn your dues in a couple of days, come with me. Or it's the debtors' jail, take your pick. You're not staying here for free."

Alice got together her little bundle of clothes, Kau scooped up Cheshire from behind the stove and they followed Boss along the tow-path to where a dilapidated houseboat was permanently moored just offshore. It squatted eerily in the foggy murk; tatty, unlit paper lanterns hung from its rat-holed roof. Boss strode across the gangplank shouting, "Madame Plum-blossom, here, I've found a couple of wenches."

A tousle-headed woman in a dirty robe and with a heavily painted face peered out. "Ah, Boss," she simpered, "wenches—that's what I'm short of, so long as they're not riddled with the pox like the rest of 'em. Another of mine's gone down with it..."

"And have you the pox?" Boss turned on Kau.

"No," she shouted angrily, "and nor has my friend—we're clean girls."

"But they're abos," Madame sniffed.

Boss scowled. "Can't have everything and perfect golden lilies are hard to find. Their cunts will be the same in the dark and they can't pay their dues. So I take fifty percent of their earnings in lieu, right? You'll need them during the days of the Dragon Festival, the randy lads'll be along then, fog or no fog."

"You're a hard man, Boss, but you're right. Here, you, get inside."

"I'll be back for my cut tomorrow evening and perhaps I'll sample one of your fairy-flowers—the Chinese variety for me please," Boss called as he stamped off.

Inside the dim, low room on the main deck a girl in a soiled pink robe sat silent beside a smoky stove; Madame Plum-blossom lit a lantern and inspected them closely. "Wenches—brought by Boss, that old sack of turds... Abos, the thick one will do in the dark, and this...." She pulled aside Alice's cloak, grasping at her body. "Big tits for a young 'un, but healthy. They'll see me through the festival, I suppose."

Alice looked round in horror, suddenly aware of the grunts and shoves coming from behind a curtain at the room's end. "Kau... does she mean to...?"

"This a brothel-boat and she's the devil-granny," Kau said sullenly.

Alice went very pale and the girl beside the stove drew her gently towards it. "I'm Little Willow... don't worry. Sit down and have some tea."

Alice sank gratefully on the mats, feeling sick. Kau let Cheshire out of his basket and he nestled close, purring amiably. The sounds behind the curtain ceased and a stringy river-coolie, grinning toothlessly and re-arranging his dirty baggy trousers, emerged, nodded at them and clattered off down the gangplank. A dishevelled woman then appeared, a robe partly covering her nudity as she mopped between her thighs with a wad of cloth. "Get me some tea, Little Willow... and what strange bitches have we here?"

It was Kau who explained while Alice sat clutching Cheshire, frozen into a helpless panic. Bowls of steaming noodles arrived, but they stuck in her throat. She had to escape. She thought of the coolie's loose mouth, his gnarled, dirty hands groping at his trousers. Madame Plum-blossom peered through the blinds.

"Huh, this fog's dense enough to blunt any man's lust. We'll get no more customers tonight. So you two abos doss down in there and get your strength up—the Dragon Tower Festival's always good for business and the fishermen come early. If they're wine-sodden, give 'em some chrysanthemum tea first, and if they're old and shrunk up, move yourselves about like a millstone and keep your legs close together when they're inside you." She bustled them into an alcove, taking away the only lantern.

Alice lay tense, waiting till she could hear only the water lapping outside—and the women snoring. "Kau, we can't stay here," she shook her companion awake. "I won't do it—not with filthy low-bred men like that."

Kau grunted. "It's not nice, but what else can we do? What with the fog and the Festival, Li-chi won't be able to move for days and we can't pay our dues. This is better than the debtors' jail, I can tell you."

"I don't care, I just won't." Alice was wrapping on her cloth leggings with trembling fingers.

"But it's only for a little while—then we'd have some cash by us for Kweichow. The men don't hurt if you do what they want..."

"You're staying then?"

"But, Uncut, what can we..." Kau wailed softly as Alice drew her cloak round her, grabbed her bundle and crept out.

On deck she paused in dismay: the gangplank had been lifted and there was a considerable gap of mist-shrouded water between boat and tow-path. When she tried to heave the plank up, it fell from her grasp with a clang, and there came a shout from the nightwatchman in the poop. She took a deep breath, then launched herself outward, realising, even as her feet left the deck, that there was no spring in her. She landed on the verge with a sickening thump; as her feet slipped towards the water she threw herself bodily forward, clutching the grass and lay there panting. As the watchman came running up the deck with a lantern she stumbled away along the path, gasping with fear. Unable to see more than a few inches ahead, she tripped heavily over a mooring rope and simply lay there, spattered with mud, freezing cold and aching with a pain that spread from her lower abdomen. "Oh Mama, William," she sobbed helplessly, "come and help me, whatever can I do?"

She was still lying there, clutching her aching body and crying when she heard Kau's voice calling her. And it was as well she came for, on rising, Alice felt warm blood seeping down her legs. Fortunately, the first hut they came to along the path belonged to the grandmother of Little Willow, who lived there in peaceful retirement with seven hens and three ducks. The old woman, knowing a lot about Madame Plumblossom's establishment and not liking what she knew, offered temporary house-room to the distraught girls. And so, during the three days of the Dragon Tower Festival, Little Willow's grandmother nursed Alice through her miscarriage, while Kau returned stolidly to the brothel-boat to earn money for her keep.

The day after it was over, Alice felt strong enough to get up, to walk out of the hut into one of the first bright mornings of early spring. The fog had completely vanished, washed-yellow light shone on the river waters; the hens and ducks were pecking at the weedy grass and Cheshire was leaping in mad pursuit of the season's young flies. Leaning weakly against the doorpost, Alice was overwhelmed by the joy of life that is sweetest to those who feared losing it and who come upon unexpected human bounty.

"The varmints ain't laying much." The old woman poked about in search of eggs.

"They're too busy finding worms," Alice suggested.

"Heh, heh, greedy pigs." She straightened up smiling, a frugal, kindly soul with a scraped-back knot of thin hair and very cleanly-faded tunic. Cleanliness was a habit with her for she had spent forty years as a washerwoman, and her only indulgence was a nightly pipe of opium. Several times in the last few days, she had offered Alice a few puffs as escape from her misery and it was an experience Alice's young body did not forget.

"Honourable Old," Alice said with a catch in her voice, "Kau says we must leave very soon and I want to say how kind you've been to a sick, homeless barbarian."

"Heh, heh, I had similar trouble myself once. It's one of

women's burdens and only women know how it feels—barbarian or not."

"That's true indeed." Alice felt her flaccid body, glad to feel it belonged to her again, that Lung-kuang's seed had not flourished long enough to begin making its inevitable demands upon her. Just then Kau came running along the towpath shouting, "Uncut, Uncut, get your things and bring Cheshire. Li-chi says the weather's right for the rapids now and we're leaving at once."

On their way to the junk, they passed Madame Plumblossom's brothel, which in the sunshine looked sad and seedy rather than sinister. Alice thought of Little Willow trapped inside, waiting or lying spread under yet another heaving coolie. "Let's hurry," she urged fearfully, "I never want to see that woman again."

"She wasn't so bad, only doing her job and she paid fair as long as you did yours." Alice shivered at Kau's way of looking at it—and at how she had benefited from that way.

Li-chi's junk called the Silver Turtle was fully laden with cassia oil, Hunanese red peppers, lily roots, and bundles of the tough Dragon's Whisker grass grown in the southern districts and used for weaving hats and mats. Its south-westerly route lay down a series of treacherous rapids, across stretches of shallows where fish slid just below the surface and men cast nets to catch them, through deep gorges where the waters were overshadowed by cliffs and whirlpools swirled dangerously round half-submerged rocks.

With nothing to do but enjoy the beauties of the passing scene, Alice began for the first time to relish the freedom she had regained. The ways open to her suddenly seemed limitless, yet she could formulate no plan of action. No one seemed to know how far or in what precise direction the treaty ports lay; no one had ever seen them. Indeed she sometimes doubted the reality of her own memories—of Mama's face framed by an old-fashioned spoon bonnet, of Father in a sombre black suit, of prayerbooks and teacakes on Sundays. Was it possible that, somewhere, such a world still existed? Anyway, the river people assured her that she and Kau were heading vaguely in the direction of the "Island of Fragrant Streams" which positively crawled with foreign devils; so it seemed best to go where the waters took them.

Eventually, as spring warmed into summer, they reached the hill-town of Santu on the River Jung in southern Kweichow—the Precious Province. And to Kau it was precious indeed, for, though she had never seen it, it was where her mother's tribe lived and her stolid face lit up with delighted recognition as they walked into the main square. It was market-day and folk from the nearby hill-villages had come to buy and sell—sacks of maize and peanuts, piles of peaches, musk melons, salted eggs, rolls of coarse cloth and caged hawks and eagles. Itinerant fortune-tellers, barbers, letter-writers waited for custom, and some boy-acrobats were tumbling about, led by a black mountain bear with a brass begging bowl.

By far the most extraordinary sight, in Alice's view, and that which made Kau walk with a new air of jaunty assurance, were the numbers of Miao women like herself. They wore loose blouses, skirts decorated with bands of red and green embroidery and black turbans; heavy bangles and necklaces of silver and beads swung about them and their faces were round, their noses broad. They walked tall and erect on their normal-sized feet, looking bold, even brazen, and they laughed loudly and often as they lifted baskets of farm produce on their sturdy shoulders.

Within minutes Kau had fallen into conversation, using the tongue of her own Black Miao tribe that neither Alice nor the local Chinese understood. It seemed, Kau reported triumphantly, that her mother's ageing brother and family still lived nearby, and so, with her remaining cash, they bought four sesame seed cakes and set off for his house. It stood on the town's edge, up a dirt track; it was of wattle and daub, with a pitted yard for fowls and pigs, a clear stream beside and, beyond, as far as one could see, the magnificent wooded ranges of the Nanling mountains.

Kau went to the door diffidently, with Cheshire in one hand and the cakes in the other; she called and went inside. Alice leaned against the wall feeling apprehensive. After all, even if Kau's uncle were to welcome with open arms the niece he'd never met, he would be unlikely to approve of her outlandish, penniless companion. And if not...what next? But she need not have worried, for the Miao, like most outcast groups, shared a clannish solidarity more generous and certainly more informal than the Chinese.

Kau's grandparents, now dead, had not wanted to sell their daughter into slavery, but there had been an uprising at the time, when the Miao fought against their Manchu masters. They had lost; a period of great hardship and famine followed; it had been a question of survival. Now times were better. The family's sons had worked doggedly, had produced children to work also and bought a little land. It was thus fitting that Kau should return to live among them, marry and bear children for the good of the tribe. They asked little about where or how she had previously lived, for they had no concept of such distant parts, having never ventured more than a few miles beyond Santu. As for Alice, she was a green-eyed stranger from an impossibly far-off place; but she was Kau's friend, not Chinese, young and fit enough to earn her keep and even marry and have green-eyed children in her turn, if she so desired.

So she was given a sleeping-space in the women's room next to Kau and through all the clear bright summer days she worked from cock-crow to sunset with the rest of them— making sandals to sell, baking buckwheat cakes in ashes, gathering eggs and brushwood, shiny green fruits from the wood-oil trees and apricots from the hill orchards.

It was an open-air, free-and-easy life, very different from the cloistered courtyards of the Chu. The young men and women of the neighbouring Miao families worked alongside each other in the fields, harvesting barley, gathering creamy juices from the capsules of the opium poppies. On the frequent festival days, they played tubular pipes, cymbals, drums and danced together, drank strong fruit brandy, smoked opium and later tumbled together on the floors of the hay-lofts.

"I'm going to marry with Bao-nyi before the winter's out," Kau whispered to Alice on the morning after the last summer festival as they walked to the stream, and she grinned gleefully, as she often did these days.

"Oh Kau, I'm so glad. Bao-nyi seems so nice and his name's nice too!" Translated it meant "Hill-Silver" Kau had explained, because he had been the first boy born in a family of five girls—and as rare as silver in the hills.

"And then you and Cheshire will come and live with us in the hut near his home across the river, Hill-Silver agrees... Won't it be fun?"

Alice assented with an appropriate show of enthusiasm, but, as they began washing clothes, her heart secretly sank, for the news made her face the fact that she could never really belong among these peasant people. By mutual consent, she and the young men avoided any close contact; to them, she remained a mysterious alien, and she found them too rough and bawdy when the brandy was in them, and their hands smelled always of manure. For her, there could be no setting up in a hut by a stream with a man of Hill Silver's ilk, and she did not relish the idea of living with Kau like a

95

supernumerary aunt and within close proximity of Hill Silver's five sisters who were reputedly of quarrelsome disposition. So something different had to happen, Alice thought, as she swilled the coloured cloth through the mountain water; and in due course it did.

Autumn came, the distant ranges turned gold and then brown; mists hung low in the valleys throughout the day and rain beat the country tracks into a reddish mire that spattered the young women's long skirts as they walked to market one morning to sell the last of the season's walnuts and sun-dried apricots. Kau and her two cousins were singing as they came towards the square—about a one-legged mountain imp who, if he met you in a lonely place, demanded three silver pieces. If you had none, he wound the three branches of his arms around you and squeezed... Alice was lagging behind, feeling left out, when an elderly Chinese woman rushed up and grabbed her arm.

"You—you're the barbarian wench, aren't you? A real foreign-devil, not one of them abos? Am I right?"

"Yes, I'm a foreigner from across the waters originally, not an abo."

"Good, good," she pushed forward the man behind her. "This is my son, Fu-to, he's a boatman just come from Tushan. Listen to him—you must go there at once!" The man tugged his queue nervously.

"It's like this, woman. There's a barbarian—a huge male foreign-devil, lying in an inn there, very ill, and he keeps shouting for one of his own kind. He's offered a reward to anyone who'll bring him another barbarian before he yields up his spirit—if he's got one."

"And my son was telling me this, and I suddenly remembered what I'd heard about you. So there you are—go quickly, woman, there's money in it."

Alice hesitated, "And for your son?"

"Yes of course. But the man's very ill and he's one of your own kind too. Tushan isn't far—my son will get you there in his boat before dark." Alice nodded. The words "one of your own kind" left her no option; it had been long since she had seen such a one.

Kau lent her a shawl against the river's chill and she and the cousins saw her off, waving cheerily and telling her to come back with a crock of barbarian gold.

Twilight and a soft drizzle were falling by the time the yellowish lights of Tushan appeared along the river bank and Fu-to pointed out a long wooden building with its verandahs overhanging the water—it was, he said, the Inn of the Five-Tiger Pass where the barbarian lay. On reaching the inn, its landlord confirmed Fu-to's story, adding that the barbarian was failing fast and causing the devil of a nuisance with his ravings every night.

"He'd have been out on his ear days ago," he snarled, "except that he can afford to pay for my best room—the Mandarin's room—so he has money still about him." His eyes gleamed and so did Fu-to's as he urged her forward.

"Go in and see him, and don't forget it was I, Fu-to the boatman, who brought you and I'm entitled to my reward."

The man lay on a bed against a boarded partition-wall, his feet sticking out below a dirty quilt. Barbarian feet, Alice thought—so very large, long, bony. His face also looked large and skeletal thin with a stubble of reddish beard and red-rimmed eyes that opened at her approach.

"Good evening," Alice faltered over words so long unused. "Can you speak English?"

He focused on her a distressed and fearful glare. "I am English," and there was a hint of pride in it.

"So am I."

"You? You don't look it."

She glared back. "I've been living away from my family for years—that's why I'm wearing these Miao clothes. They don't belong to me—I suppose." She plucked them uneasily, not having thought that before.

He tried raising himself on an elbow but failed. "I didn't mean to offend you," he offered weakly, and then, "What are you doing here?" they both said simultaneously, and smiled at each other.

"I've come south from the Tibetan foothills," he explained wearily. "Trying to reach Hong Kong. I was with the Tor-rington-Graham expedition, did you hear of it? All dead ex-cept me—and I'm on my last legs. We were exploring, map-ping territory, got roughed up by tribesmen..." His voice had faded to a whisper and she bent close to hear. "Then we all got this accursed fever—don't come too near, it's probably contagious, kills you off... Have you any quinine? Opium?"

"Quinine, no... But I could get opium, it's plentiful around here. The Chinese sent for me to come, they said you were very ill and wanted to see one of your own kind."

Forgetting his earlier warning, he grabbed her wrist and drew her down to him. "Yes, there's one thing you must do for me—a dying man—one of your own countrymen..." He stared past her, as if seeing what she could not. "Me—

97

dying... And I thought it would be in some worthwhile place if it did happen—a mountain top perhaps, or some lovely green valley, not this stinking hell-hole... But can I trust you? What's your name?"

"Alice—Greenwood. My father was a missionary, but he was killed in Tientsin years ago, that's why I'm here now."

It was a vast, totally illogical leap; the man paused, decided he was too weak to attempt it, said merely, "My name's Stewart Carr... A missionary's daughter, hey? So you should be honest."

"Of course I am. I don't tell lies."

"I didn't exactly mean that. Here, give me more of that tea, young lady. I must collect my thoughts..." He mopped his brow. "It's this fever. I keep floating away, not seeing you properly, not remembering what I've said. How old are you?"

"Seventeen—I think."

"You're not *sure?*"

"I've been living in a Chinese house for years and their time isn't the same. I was captured when I was twelve, that I do know."

He stared at her bewildered; it was too much for his mind. "You must tell me all about it sometime, Alice Greenwood. But first there's something important I must tell you, in case anything happens. This fever can carry a man off in a night, that's how poor old Tommy Graham went..." He sipped the tea. "Mountain fever, dries you up inside. Can I count on you?"

He gripped her again and she looked with aversion at his grasping fingers. "Yes you can. I told you. I'm English and my father taught me always to keep my word." Yet that was years ago; now even the sound of such a promise sounded odd. "Keep a word..." Was it even correct?

Stewart Carr seemed to think so, for he went on, "Good—now then, what is it? Oh yes—the loot. Listen carefully, Miss, the landlord of this place is a rogue, they're all robbers, these bloody Chinks... smile to your face and fleece you behind your back."

"Not always," Alice was indignant. "I've lived with them, and they never stole from me."

"Well you speak their lingo and... Oh dear, ache, ache, ache all over. Now what was...? Oh yes, where I've hidden the loot. You see that tin trunk against the wall? Well, it's underneath—in the earth under the mats. I dug a hole when I first came, it's in a box."

"But what is this loot?"

"Jewels, ornaments and stuff... worth a helluva lot. And the Chinks'll rob me of every mortal bauble if they find it."

"Where did you get it?" Alice prised his fingers from her wrist. "If you want me to help, you'd better not give me your fever."

"Yes, you must... Where did I...?" He looked vague, then remembered. "Years ago it was, from the Summer Palace in Peking. I was a young subaltern then—God, those were the days—pounding into Peking with the five thousand, hey? Eighteen-sixty, I wasn't much older than you are now..."

"So you were there when the British and French burned and looted the Summer Palace. My father told me about it—he said it was scandalous."

"Oh that—war's war. Anyway, the French froggies got the best of the pickings. But I was lucky and was there in time for some of the left-overs. I've sold a piece now and then to keep going, always got a good price..."

"But what do you want me to do?" Darkness had fallen, the gloomy room smelled ominously of sickness unto death and Alice was finding it all very distasteful. From the courtyard came the cackle of fowls being driven into shelter, which reminded her that, as yet, she had no bed for the night.

"It's Flossie, my little sister. Our parents were killed in the Mutiny when she was a baby and she lives in Calcutta with an aunt. God, I'm afraid I'll never see Flossie again... haven't seen her for years... should have made more effort..." He stared miserably into space.

"I'm sorry, Mr Carr, truly I am. But let's look at the bright side. You'll probably recover. I'll bring a good doctor to you tomorrow." She went to light the candle on the table; by its flickering light his gaunt face looked even more deathly.

"A Chink doc? Kill or cure, hey?" He tried to laugh, but only breathed more shallowly. "But if I don't recover, Alice Greenwood, I want you to get that loot away from these thieves here. Take it back to Hong Kong, will you? You can sell a piece, anything, to pay for the journey, you don't look as if you're very well-heeled. And you can keep another piece too, as a reward. But the rest must get back to Flossie. She's an orphan with no money of her own. I've always held on to the best pieces meaning her to have them, you understand? Can I trust you, Alice?" He tried to grasp her hand again. "Swear to me you'll do it—as if we had a Bible. Your father was a missionary, so you must be an honourable English girl, though a pretty rum one, I must say. You'll keep your word, won't you? Swear now—it'll be well worth your while. The key of the loot box is under my pillow—and in the trunk you'll find a roll of cash."

She took it out. "I have no money at all. This will have to pay for my night here and the boatman—he's claiming the reward for bringing you a barbarian."

"Oh alright, use it how you like... I can't think straight anymore." He moaned restlessly. "Only please don't double-cross me, Alice... and tomorrow..."

The door was flung open and the landlord strode in carrying a lantern. "So, what's wrong with the barbarian?"

"A mountain fever he says. Is there a good doctor in town? He'll pay, I promise."

"So, he's still well-loaded, is he?" he leered. "Well he owes me a pretty penny for his keep already. Who's that for?" He swung the light on the cash in Alice's hand.

"Some for the boatman, some for you." She tried to conceal the full extent of the roll up her sleeve. "I want to stay here tonight and get the doctor tomorrow."

"Alright—being as you can pay, even if you are an abo woman." He held the lantern over Carr, who had fallen into a feverish doze. "Looks a goner to me."

"Let him sleep now," Alice wiped his forehead gently. "He's exhausted. Mr Carr, I'll come back tomorrow—and I won't forget what you've told me, I promise."

He groaned inarticulately as she left. Fu-to was waiting outside and she gave him half the cash-roll.

"Do you want to go back to Santu with me?" He was suddenly eager for her custom.

"I'll see, I have to look after the barbarian first."

"Well, I'll be here till the day after tomorrow," he said as he shuffled off.

In a bare, chill room overlooking the river Alice spent a restless night, for the rushing of the waters below echoed through her troubled dreams, and several times she woke uneasily, thinking she heard the distant cries of the sick man. But she could not make herself find out, and eventually, pulling the quilt tight over her head, she slept deep and late. The sun was high when she woke and went in search of the landlord, whom she found in the courtyard, peering through a pair of field-glasses at a duck and chuckling. Their expensive leather case dangled incongruously over his dirty tunic, the strap clamped across his thick queue.

"Where did you get those?" she asked with foreboding.

"From the barbarian's box of course. He died in the night."

"Oh no—poor Mr Carr, he kept saying he'd die." She stared at him numbly.

"Well when people say that they usually do—the spirit gives up the ghost." He focused the glasses on her and chuckled again. "Makes your face look even more rum . . . That man owed me money, so I shall keep these and the other strange things in his box."

"You won't keep everything," she said hotly.

"Who's going to stop me, you?"

"He told me yesterday that I was to take possession of his things if he died."

He leered. "Most of them have already been taken possession of."

She pushed past him and into Carr's room. Flies were buzzing round the shape on the bed, its head covered with the quilt so that the bony legs stuck out yet further. In awful fascination, Alice touched one toe; flesh still and chill. She took a deep breath and lifted the quilt. His eyes, thank goodness, were closed, and his cheeks, hollowed with fever before, had completely caved in; alive he had been in his late thirties, now he looked as ageless as any other death's head.

"I'm sorry, Mr Carr," she whispered, "but you'd want me to . . ." She lifted the head, took the key from under the pillow and thrust it in her pocket. The tin trunk had already been well rifled; its remaining contents were some travel-stained clothes, an empty brandy flask and a battered letter-case. She opened it: a British passport for Stewart Carr; two old letters posted in Worthing, England; yellowed newspaper cuttings about the setting off of the intrepid Torrington-Graham expedition; a sepia-faded photograph of a girl sitting on a swing on a lawn, on its back the one scrawled word "Flossie". There was also a vellum envelope and inside that—oh joy— a map of China and a small bar of silver that the thieves had missed. She put the things aside and cautiously began to move the trunk from its significant place on the floor.

The door opened and the landlord came in accompanied by an official from the local *yamen*. "I've reported the death to the proper authorities," the latter explained importantly. "The body is now to be removed and a report made to the magistrate in Kweiyang."

Two coolies came in with a litter; they dumped the lank body on it, its white legs sticking out straight over the end, for Stewart Carr was several inches taller than most Chinese.

"I'm sure not all his possessions are here." Alice looked resolutely at the official. "There was a pair of field-glasses for instance..."

He stared back at her. "You're an abo, aren't you? Are you proposing to make a charge of theft? If so, you must come to the *yamen* and see the deputy-magistrate. He'd be interested to know who you are, for a start."

She hesitated. "Well, I realise of course that Mr Carr had been well attended here during his illness."

"Carr? Is that his name?" The official halted the coolies at the door, and studied the dead man's face.

"Yes—Stewart Carr, and these are his papers." She handed him the letter-case.

"And that?" He indicated the envelope.

"Oh—just a plan. Surely I can keep it? It's in English and of no use to you." She handed the map over, holding on to the envelope with the silver inside.

He stared at it upside down, grunted, gave it back to her. Another coolie picked up the trunk.

"Well, do you wish to make a formal charge about the contents of this box?" he challenged.

"No..." Alice tried to peer under it; the matting below looked undisturbed. "But please let me keep his personal letters and a picture."

The official blew out his cheeks. "No. Everything must go to the *yamen*; reports must be made. You are not a relative?"

"No, but..."

"Well, come on then," the landlord grumbled at the door. "I've a rich merchant from Yunnan arriving any minute and he always takes this Mandarin's room—so out of here, abo woman."

She stood nonplussed. "Someone in here... tonight?"

"Yes of course, I run a popular establishment and it's always full of silk traders going east at this time of year."

"But how long will the merchant want this room?"

"How do I know? He's a good customer, stays several days in Tushan every season, the longer the better..." He hustled her to the door and she had no choice but follow the official, the body of Stewart Carr and his trunk outside.

At the inn-entrance, the official beckoned her: "So who are you? Have you travelling papers? What are you doing here?"

She extemporised rapidly. "I was travelling through Santu to join my brother who's a missionary. They told me about

Mr Carr and begged me come to him. I left my papers behind in the rush."

It sounded very unlikely; on the other hand he did not want any awkward questions asked about the dead barbarian's possessions. Much better for all concerned if she just disappeared.

"My honourable chief is absent today," he said heavily. "But if you're still here tomorrow, he'll want to see you—and your papers."

"Yes. I understand." They looked at each other; his eyes were blank. He climbed into his chair and, with a flourish, bade the bearers lift it.

As she stood there considering the implications of that exchange, the main gate opened and a fat man on a fat horse followed by a string of mountain ponies tramped into the courtyard. The landlord rushed out, bowing profusely.

"Oh you are most welcome, honourable sir. How fortunate I am to see you again. The Mandarin's room has been pining for your presence..."

Alice slipped away to her room, took out the map, the silver bar, the key to the loot box and stared at them. What was to be done? The first priority was to get more cash, and fortunately, she discovered, the exchange rate for silver in the Tushan market was high. Her first purchases were a pair of Chinese-style trousers, a padded tunic, an over-jacket, a covered basket to put them in. Then she went to the river bank and asked Fu-to to wait for her there until tomorrow.

By the time she returned to the inn, other merchants had arrived and the courtyard was full of coolies carrying baggage, unladen mules and ponies rolling happily in the dust, servants carrying bags of fodder and bowls of soup. Eventually she found the landlord.

"If I cannot have the Mandarin's room tonight, at least give me the one next door. The hole I had last night is filthy and the noise of the waters kept me awake."

"You, faugh! An abo woman in one of my best rooms!"

"I'm not an abo, I'm a foreign barbarian woman as you know, and I have money to pay." She produced a large roll of cash from her basket.

He caught a passing servant by the queue. "Take this abo... this barbarian woman to the room there, next to the Mandarin's."

Ensconced in her comparatively grand apartment which boasted a stool and a lantern as well as a bed, Alice applied her eye to one of many gaps in the board partition between her and her neighbour. The fat Yunnanese merchant was slurping a steaming plate of stew and she noted with dismay that rolls of silks were piled against the wall where the trunk had rested. She sighed in frustration; there seemed nothing to do but wait. As darkness fell and she again heard the fowls cackling in the courtyard, she pondered the sad story of Stewart Carr. If only she had talked more to him, given him more comfort, and above all, if only she had taken that loot away while the going was good.

Hearing voices, Alice again applied her eye to the gap; three other merchants had arrived and the talk was about prices—of silks and mulberries, of white wax, furs and opium, of cart-hire and inns. Soon they gathered round the table under the lantern for a prolonged gambling session. Coins and dice clinked merrily, the men cracked melon seeds, spat, called for wine, roared with laughter when one of them lost a newly won pile of cash. Alice watched impatiently; how could she possibly get into that room unseen that night? But if she was still here tomorrow, the *yamen* official would surely track her down.

There was a knock on the next door and three musicians appeared to entertain the guests. One carried a stringed lute, another a flute, the third a hand-drum; two singing-girls with heavily painted faces accompanied them. The music twanged, while girls swayed slowly round the room singing in high falsetto voices. The older looked absurdly plump and motherly for her role, but the younger had a natural grace and her eyes glinted teasingly at the men.

"Let's hear just her," shouted the Yunnanese. "What's your name, my pretty poll?"

"Golden Persimmon, honourable sir." She folded her hands in her drooping sleeves and sang:

"How sweet this branch of jasmine flower,
On the morning of the day t'was dropped in my house.
I'll wear it myself, yet not out of doors,
But will match it with others to make myself glad."

The men applauded, poured more wine while Golden Persimmon sang again and again by popular request and the Yunnanese watched her with heavy attentiveness. At length, the leader ended the performance explaining that other guests waited to hear their melodies. As Golden Persimmon handed round a silken bag for tips, the merchant caught her by the neck and whispered to her, while the other men guffawed bawdily, and the leader, bowing low, said, "Her musical gifts are needed for the moment sir, perhaps later there will be a chance to explore her other treasures."

The merchant released her. "As you will—let her sing for her supper instead."

The merchants gathered round the table again, but the heart had gone from their game and the visitors soon departed. The Yunnanese's servant brought his master a chamberpot and washing water. The merchant bolted the door, scratched his belly and crotch, oiled his queue, picked his teeth, blew out the lantern, got into bed. Alice waited a little, then, wearing her new Chinese clothes, tiptoed into the passage and knocked on his door.

"Sir, Honourable sir, I've a message for you."

He opened it. Keeping her face concealed, she said, "From Golden Persimmon, sir. She will accommodate you now, if you desire. But you must go to her for it's not the usual practice. Down the passage, across the courtyard, take the small passage on the left and through the gate."

"Huh, that sounds better, wait a minute, wench."

"I'll see you there, sir."

As he went to don his cloak, she slipped back into her dark room and soon had the satisfaction of hearing him leave. She rushed into her room, threw aside the rolls of silk and folded back the matting. It was easy to see where a patch of earth had been recently disturbed. Hurriedly, she dug below the surface and lifted out a small square box of inlaid wood. She jammed back the earth and the matting, hearing a distant shout as she did so. As steps thudded along the passage, she threw the silks back in place and scurried to her own room.

"T'was a trick, I tell you," the Yunnanese was shouting at his servant, "and now I'll bet a turtle for a tortoise I've been robbed blind. You lazy sod, why don't you keep watch, blast you? That girl was a thieves' moll, I'll raise the roof if..." Alice listened as he and the servant checked their untouched stores of silver, silks, opium and cash.

"I must have been too fast for them," the Yunnanese grunted at last. "I'm not a man to be hoodwinked for long. I soon smelled a rat. Still, I'll have it out with that slimy toad of a landlord in the morning," she heard him muttering to himself as he again got into bed, the servant now instructed to sleep outside his door.

Only when she heard them both snoring did she dare light her lantern, and, with shaking fingers, unlock the box. The loot: two bejewelled gold hairpins, one long pearl and rose quartz necklace with ruby clasp, two porcelain perfume bottles with carved jade stoppers, a gold ring set with amber, a silver opium-holder shaped like a walnut, and a little ivory box studded with turquoise. She opened its lid and jumped, for a tinny tune sprang from its inside, a sweet and merry waltz, so totally unexpected. The ladies of the Peking court, it seemed, had a passion for foreign musical boxes. She played the tune, waltzing a little round the treasures spread out before her, then she scooped them back in the box and slept with it cradled in her arms.

Next morning early, dressed again in her Miao clothes, she paid the landlord and hurried away before the Yunnanese had slept off his disturbed night. A while later, huddled on the deck of Fu-to's boat, she grinned to herself as they passed the Inn of the Five Tiger Pass and heard the shouts of coolies loading animals in the courtyards. How furious that fat merchant would be if he knew what treasures had lain within his grasp!

Getting out the map, she muttered the unfamiliar English words to herself; it looked a very long way to Hong Kong, and it seemed better to continue on this same river, the Jung, to Jungen in Kwangsi. But first she would return to Kau and her family—or would she? It would be dishonest not to tell Kau of her "crock of barbarian gold"; but then those happy-go-lucky Miaos would expect her to share it with them as generously as they had shared their smaller bounty with her. They would eat, drink and smoke it all away; she could just imagine the merrymaking at Kau's wedding. But then . . . how would she get to Hong Kong? She watched the clear waters of the Jung sliding by and all her instincts told her not to return to the Miao again. She went up to Fu-to, who was poling along whistling through his teeth in the boatman's fashion. "I want you to take me straight through Santu and across the Kwangsi border to Jungen. How much will it cost?"

At Jungen three days later, Alice exchanged the gold hairpins for silver and bought silks for Fu-to to take to Kau as a wedding present, and then, dressed in her Chinese clothes, the loot-box concealed in her farm-basket, she set her face determinedly to the south. The journey took a long time for it lay across sparsely populated country. Winter closed in and as the weather worsened boatmen and carters were increasingly reluctant to travel far, even for good money. Not that

Alice felt any sense of urgency, for she had only the vaguest idea of what lay ahead, and was uneasily aware that no one, anywhere, was expecting her arrival.

Indeed, as her destination approached, her rate of progress noticeably slackened and she was happy to pass a prolonged New Year with a friendly family of boat people. But eventually, on a bright, blustery day of early spring, she boarded a vessel of the Hong Kong, Canton & Macao Steamship Company that carried her across the stretch of open sea to the Island of Fragrant Streams or, as its barbarian inhabitants called it, Hong Kong.

Jostled down the gangplank with the rest of the Chinese passengers, Alice walked along Queen's Road in a daze, staring up at the clock tower, the church on the hill, the tall rows of shipping, consulate and mercantile offices with various national flags flying from their balconies. And there was the Union Jack, gracing a very imposing building indeed, standing back from the road behind a wall. Rickshaw men were sprawled against it, waiting for custom, and a large barbarian in red and black uniform stood in the guardbox. She went up to him.

"May I go in please?"

He looked down at her small figure, clad in baggy trousers, grubby tunic, carrying an up-country basket, and grinned. "Why?"

"Because I'm British and my name is Miss Alice Greenwood. I want to see an official."

His grin broadened. "Oh yes—and my name's Mr Disraeli!"

She looked puzzled. "But, Mr Disraeli . . . I really am British, you can see I'm not Chinese."

"What a caution! Do you realise this is Her Majesty's courthouse? I've seen the likes of you before, wench, little bit of the old half and half's been going on, hey?"

Again she did not understand and, in desperation, drew a roll of cash from her basket. "See here—I've money, if you'll let me . . ."

With a roar he pounced forward, giving her a thwack that sent her sprawling into the gutter. She sat there looking at him for a second, then burst into tears. The watching rickshaw coolies cackled with laughter.

"Scram, you little varmit—scarper—or you'll feel a real genuine British boot up your backside." He advanced threateningly; she scrambled up and fled sobbing. She ran and ran, away from the Queen's Road and the large buildings into the narrow streets of what the Queen's Road residents called "the native quarter".

Exhausted, she sat down at a food-stall, ordered a bowl of noodles, began to dry her eyes and clean the mud from her clothes.

"Had a fall, did you? Never mind—every day can't be a feast of lanterns." It was the cheery voice of the coolie next to her.

"Yes...I..." Alice sniffed. "I'm better now." The noodles came and as she ate she studied his kindly face. "Do you pull people about in that little cart? I saw them on the big road near the sea."

He stared at her. "Little cart? It's a rickshaw of course."

"I've never seen one," she said doubtfully. "I don't remember them."

He shook his head in amazement. "You've not been long in Hong Kong then—I've been pulling fat old barbarians about in them for the past five years."

"So you'd know if there's a Church Missionary Society here?"

"'Course there is—up the Victoria Road."

So Alice's first-ever rickshaw ride ended at a wide gateway, with an imposing stone house looming in front of her. "That's it, girl," said the rickshaw-coolie. She paid him and walked to the door. "Church Missionary Society. Hong Kong Director: Mr G. Penfold" announced the brass plate at its side. She pulled the bell-rope and a black-suited Englishman appeared.

"What do you want, missee?"

"I've come to see the director, Mr Penfold." Alice summoned the last of her reserves.

"You? Do you have an appointment? Who are you?"

She swallowed hard. "My name's Alice Greenwood. My father was a missionary of the Society, which is why I've come here. He was killed at Tientsin years ago and...I've been away ever since..."

He looked puzzled. "You're not a native, no. Well, wait here a moment, missee."

She leaned against the doorpost, her legs had turned to water and her heart thumped wildly. If he does not let me in, she thought, I will lie down on the mat and scream and scream..."Who are you?" the question echoed in her mind..."Who are you?" said the Caterpillar, and Alice replied, "I hardly know sir, just at present—at least I know who I *was* but..."

The man returned. "You are to step this way, please. Someone will see you soon."

She walked tentatively into the hall and the door was shut behind her.

5

Jimmy Callum, cub reporter from the *China Mail* was looking eagerly at Alice, pencil poised.

"So, Miss Greenwood," he framed his last question of the interview carefully, for the young lady was obviously ill-at-ease, "now you've told me the exciting story of your captivity and your brave escape—I'm sure my readers would be most interested to know what you find most surprising and different about the civilisation to which you've now returned?"

She hesitated cautiously, mindful of readers who would hang on her every word. "Well—yes, it is different. Last evening Mr and Mrs Penfold took me for my first carriage drive along the Bund, and everything seemed so large and solidly made—the tall buildings, the macadamed roads, the ships in the harbour. And English people—especially the men—look very large too. I said to Mrs Penfold that it was like Alice, you know—in Wonderland—who kept swallowing drinks that made her different sizes. Well, Hong Kong makes me feel very small."

Grand, he thought, framing the headline in his mind: "Alice returns from a Chinese Wonderland to Hong Kong."

"And, you know it's a great surprise to find Hong Kong actually here. You see, in Hunan, it's hard to believe such a place could exist in the same country."

"You know, Miss Greenwood, I've never thought of it like that, never..." Jimmy Callum shut his notebook with a snap that sounded almost irreverent in the Penfolds' drawing-room. Alice rose, but stiffly, for the root cause of her unease was physical. Early that morning, Mrs. Penfold had insisted on taking her to a dress shop in Robinson Road where she had been fitted into what her hostess termed "proper clothes". The boned stays, tight-waisted jacket-bodice, apron overskirt, stockings and button shoes which Alice now wore were, she had been assured, of the light-weight summer variety, but she felt extremely constricted and uncomfortable and more conscious of her body outline than ever in her life before.

She felt herself blushing as the reporter shook her hand almost reverently, casting admiring eyes on her shaped bosom. "It's been a real pleasure to meet you, Miss Greenwood. And I think you are quite a little heroine, I do honestly."

Her modest disclaimer was interrupted by Mr Penfold who bustled in waving a piece of paper. "Alice—here it is—a message from the Consulate. They've checked their files and it is as I thought, your mother, the former Mrs Eliza Greenwood, remarried four years ago, and her present husband is a Mr Edward Blake of the China Inland Mission. They are normally resident in Mukden, Manchuria. And listen to this, my dear girl, about a year after the marriage your mother gave birth to twins—so you now have a new brother and sister, as well as a stepfather!"

Alice sat down quickly and so did Jimmy Callum, who reopened his notebook and scribbled furiously. "And finally," said Mr Penfold, waiting for Jimmy to catch up, "...I sent a messenger to the China Inland Mission here and they tell me that your mother, whose health is rather precarious, is at this very moment recuperating her strength in Chefoo with the babies. So you'll be able to see her very soon, my dear."

"Oh, I can hardly believe it—she's alive and still here in China—oh, that's so wonderful! But...but I thought she'd have been too old?"

"To have more babies you mean?" he smiled. "She was under forty when your poor father was martyred—and mothers tend to look rather old to their children, you know." He patted her shoulder. "I expect this second marriage and the little ones will have given her a new lease of life—I'll warrant she'll look ten years younger, and it's you who'll look old to her!"

"Oh, I must go to Chefoo at once, Mr Penfold. But how soon will she know about me?"

"Very soon—a message is already sent by urgent dispatch to the Chefoo Consulate and we'll arrange your passage there as soon as possible. Our Hong Kong Consul, Mr Meadows, wants to see you this afternoon, to hear all about your experiences and your brother's continuing captivity."

"Does Mrs Penfold know this? I must go and tell her myself. You've got your story, haven't you, Mr Callum?"

"Indeed yes, Miss Greenwood, thank you." He sprang to open the door for her, but she hung back. "Is there anything else? You'll certainly capture the headlines tomorrow as it is."

"Oh . . . no, I forgot, about ladies going out first, I mean. It isn't like that in China, you know."

Callum grinned delightedly as she ran out, remarking to Mr Penfold, "It's funny how every other foreigner in Hong Kong thinks he *is* in China—except Miss Greenwood."

"Ah yes, she has much to learn in certain directions—and she'll need some careful handling for a while. But don't put that in your story, young man!"

Careful handling . . . Mr Penfold recalled his own words late that afternoon as he penned his weekly report to the General Secretary of his London headquarters. "Miss Greenwood," he wrote, "impresses me as a young woman of considerable character and, more importantly from our point of view, she has acquired a thorough knowledge of the language and customs of the country which is very rare among foreigners here. I feel"—he paused, bit his quill, watched two butterflies chase each other among the magnolia blossoms outside—"that it might be a mis-direction of her valuable talents if she were to become too deeply influenced by the doctrines of the China Inland Mission into which her mother has now remarried. She is very much her father's daughter and I believe her potential for mission work is great. I'm therefore arranging that she travel to Chefoo in the company of Miss Ida Palmer, one of our most zealous recent arrivals from the Islington mission-college. I shall instruct Miss Palmer confidentially to keep me informed of Miss Greenwood's progress and do all she can to guide her towards eventual enrolment in our theological study-centre in Shanghai." He concluded, "It would be a most wondrous instance of the workings of the Divine Will if Miss Greenwood should turn out to be God's instrument for the Opening Up of Hunan to the Word . . ."

*   *   *

Ida Palmer's thin fingers, encased in pink cotton gloves, gripped tensely round the deck-rail of the China Merchant Company's coastal steamer, *Mandalay*. She was filled with excited anxiety at the thought of leaving Hong Kong for the mysterious China beyond, and it was rather provoking that her travelling companion seemed not to share these feelings. Instead, Alice was gazing with calm detachment at the crowds of well-wishers on the quay.

"You know, Alice," Ida began in the gaspy voice that had been the despair of her college oratory tutor, "I am still so often struck by the thought of just how *many* Chinese there are. One is told in college, of course, but one doesn't quite grasp it—so many millions to be saved, such a gigantic task for one short lifetime, don't you feel?"

"I can't say I've thought of it like that," Alice replied briskly. "But then I'm not a missionary."

"Ah, Alice, not yet—but consider all the valuable work someone like you could do for the Cause..."

"Frankly, Ida, the only causes that interest me are seeing my mother again and getting my brother out of Hunan."

"Yes of course, that is understandable," Ida plucked nervously at her glove, "but these are just passing temporal causes. I'm talking of larger issues altogether—of causes that can take a lifetime."

"Well, I intend to take things little by little, in bite-sizes as they come." Alice was thinking irritably that ever since she had reached Hong Kong a week ago the talk had been of lifetime-size causes: converting the heathen, bringing modern civilisation to the Chinese, conquering new dominions. The English seemed so earnest about everything, but not, how could she put it—not philosophical. That was their trouble.

Ida edged closer, trying to be conciliatory, for she had already decided Alice was a prickly little thing. "What is going to happen about your brother, Alice?"

"I saw Consul Meadows again yesterday and he's sending a detailed report on it all to Sir Hugh Digby in Peking. Probably I'll have to go there and explain everything myself." She felt rather grand about this.

"My, that would be thrilling, wouldn't it! And meeting Sir Hugh for a *tête à tête* too! My room-mate Celia saw him at a tea-party once and says he's ever so distinguished-looking. How old is your brother, Alice? Oh look, there goes the pilot boat...wave...now we're really at sea." Ida gazed back longingly at the solidly reassuring buildings along the Bund. If only Papa and Mama could see her now, how proud and anxious they would be. Poor Father, he had always wanted to see the world; he had gone to Boulogne for three days once and it whetted his appetite, he used to say. But if you were in Father's position with his business and the family, there was not much point in having it whetted, really. Nor would there have been for her, except that, at the age of twenty-three and still unmarried, she had heard the Call. Ida sighed. "And how old is your brother, Alice?"

But there was no response, for Alice had moved across the deck and was deep in conversation with a young native wearing a very odd-looking combination of Western and Chinese dress. Ida sighed again; it was not for nothing that her brothers called her "Ida-the-Sigher". Really, this Miss Greenwood had very little sense of the proprieties, and she must explain to Mr Penfold how difficult it was to keep an eye on her.

"You're going to Tientsin then? How strange..." Alice looked at the young man, feeling a pang of nostalgic grief at the familiar name.

"Yes—a college is just opening there for the study of Western-style military and naval tactics and I hope to enrol."

"Goodness, how things have changed since..."

"Since what?"

"Since I lived in Tientsin years ago."

He looked at her curiously. "Did you? Where do you live now, may I ask? Your Chinese is so unusually fluent for a foreigner, but the accent is unfamiliar to me."

"It's Hunanese, that's why...You see I..." Again she paused, overwhelmed by a sense of bewildered disbelief which she later characterised as "that rabbit-hole feeling". For it suddenly seemed as if, for the past few years, she had been down a rabbit-hole in a land that had seemed real enough while she was there, but, once you left, was impossible to explain. Or contrariwise, she thought, I have *now* fallen down a rabbit-hole—for how could she tell this stranger, standing so confidently in his half-Western outfit on this half-Western steamer, about everything that had happened to her? In any case, with Frank still in rabbit-hole land, it would be foolish to breathe a word of it.

"My parents were missionaries, you see, and I learned most of my Chinese from a Hunanese convert."

"So you're a missionary?" His tone was both challenging and disappointed.

"No, certainly not. My father was; he's dead."

He nodded abruptly. "If you'll excuse my saying, and with no disrespect to the honourable dead, it is not your Christian religion we Chinese need—it is your knowledge of mechanical objects and technical skills. We don't even have a correct word for what makes vessels like this move, for example! And we're still making wooden war-junks equipped with lances and pikes!" He banged the steamer rail hard in emphasis, then smiled warmly at her.

I like him, she thought, he's bold and different from any Chinese I have ever met. Quite handsome too; how would he be in bed, I wonder? She looked up at him searchingly and he stared back, confused and startled; both of them suddenly tongue-tied.

"What is your name?" she asked softly.

"Lin Fu-wei, I am from Canton."

"Ah, a hot-blooded southerner."

He smiled. "You could say so... And your name?"

She told him, hoping he had not read the recent issue of the *China Mail*, and added, "But you can call me by my Chinese name, if you like—Uncut Jade."

"Ha—very good. From Li-chi—'an unserviceable vessel'?"

They drew up deck-chairs and sat down facing the sea. "Are you travelling alone?" he asked.

"No—I have a companion and she is a missionary, I warn you!"

"Like most foreigners I meet. They're not really interested in the new China and the urgent need for change. In my view, we must start by improving the material lives of the peasantry." He spoke as if from a recently-learned lesson, but Alice had no idea of its source.

"But why should the Chinese want to change? They seem well enough as they are."

"The masses are oppressed and ignorant—enslaved by all our ancient customs. No, they must be taught new philosophies by new leaders."

"Like you?" she teased, but he replied in deadly earnest, confidently, full of his own sense of mission.

"That's why I'm going to college—to learn as much as I can and become a leader of the people."

"I see," she picked irritably at the never-opened parasol Ida insisted she carry. "I feel my education has been much neglected—you make me realise how ignorant I am about what is going on."

"Well, most girls are. They don't need to know really."

"Don't they? But I want to learn—so tell me one thing for a start. Would there be more chance for your 'new China' if the Manchus were overthrown?"

He raised a flat hand, warning her off. "That's a very big question, Uncut Jade, and I'm certainly not answering it fully here—to you, a stranger, in a public place."

"But the Manchus are still very much in control?"

"Oh yes, the Empress Dowager has consolidated her power since the death of T'ung-chih. And her nephew—he's only a child—is on the Dragon Throne." He bent closer. "The situation seems hopeless at the moment..."

Really it was too much, Ida thought as she came round the bulkhead, to see Alice and the native whispering secretly and literally *tête à tête*. She straightened her back. "Alice my dear, there you are. I've been looking for you everywhere. It will soon be supper time and you haven't even unpacked. May I meet your new acquaintance?"

"Good afternoon and how do you do? My name is Lin Fu-wei." He rose stiffly, his English was very poor.

"How nice to hear you speaking English...Where did you learn?"

"A teacher, I have..." He was near the limit of his powers and a pause followed.

"Well now, Alice, you must come and dress for supper."

Leaving, Alice flashed back at him in Chinese, "We'll talk more later, won't we?" He grinned agreement.

"Alice," Ida broached the subject when they had retired to their cabin for the night and Alice was able, gratefully, to loosen her stays. "You do realise, I trust, that it is not quite seemly for young ladies to accost strange foreign men on boat-decks, as you did this afternoon?"

Alice leaned her hot forehead against the cool metal bunk. The cabin was airless and she looked with distaste at the appearing details of Ida's pallid, angular body. How much more fun to be sharing a cabin with Mr Lin!

"I didn't accost him. He asked me the time in his very poor English and I replied in my very good Chinese, so we began talking. And we're the foreigners here, not him!"

Ida sighed with extraordinary depth even for her. "Of course your command of the language is a great advantage—a gift of tongues, one might almost say. But like all gifts it must be used circumspectly. And you mustn't let it lead you into too intimate familiarities with...strangers."

"We weren't talking intimately, we were discussing Chinese politics."

"Alice, really—must you contradict everything I say like this?" From her bunk's edge, Ida blinked up in helpless indignation.

"Oh, I didn't mean to—I'm sorry but...well, it's hot in here. I'm just going on deck for a breath of air before turning in."

"But Alice, it's not proper to..."

Ida's wail was lost as Alice shut the door. With trembling fingers she pulled on her nightgown. What could one do with such a perverse creature? Alice did not seem afraid of anything in the way most girls were, she was so unpredictable and her Chinese fluency looked like being a very mixed blessing.

A yellow half-moon hung low over the South China Sea and the only sounds on deck were the rhythmic swish of water and thud of engines as the *Mandalay* steamed northeast towards the Straits of Formosa. Alice leaned against the rail, feeling both elated and troubled as she thought about her short stay in Hong Kong. She had been made much of. The men had questioned her earnestly about the conditions of the interior provinces and the customs of the natives; the women had petted her, presented her with gloves to conceal her work-roughened hands, and bonnets to shade her weather-beaten cheeks—tokens of respectability in the civilisation to which she had returned. One and all had lamented her years of absence from a good moral Christian home and had been too concerned with her spiritual well-being to enquire closely about her material circumstances and how she had managed the journey back. Her lack of social graces had also worried them, and Alice remembered with shamed irritation how, during her first supper with the Penfolds, she had picked up her rice bowl and begun slurping rice into her mouth with a fork till she became aware of their scandalised disapproval. They must have taken me for a little barbarian, she thought wryly, and been most relieved to ship me off to Mama at the first opportunity. For the truth is—no one really knew what to do with me.

Now, as she sailed north, she began to worry about the coming reunion with her mother. Looking up the yellowed file labelled "Tientsin Massacre, 1870", Mr Penfold (who had adamantly refused to let her see its entire contents) read out that Mrs Greenwood had been rescued from the burning

117

Mission at the last minute by the *yamen* guards and had taken a long while to recover from her injuries and the shock of her husband's murder. About six months later, he continued, flipping over several pages, Alice and Frank had been officially listed as dead and Eliza had been on the verge of returning alone to England when, as he put it, "she somehow got mixed up with the C.I.M. people". He did not elaborate, but his tone was clearly disapproving.

Alice had never thought much about her mother's religious beliefs before; now she feared she would be unable to ignore them. Oh, if only Frank were here! He was Mama's favourite and it would have been so much easier with him by her side. She stared at the mellow, low-slung moon, thinking resentfully of the free-and-easy life he was still leading in Changsha—practising javelin-throwing, exercising Han-li's horse... But a javelin—what an absurdity in this modern China that Lin Fu-wei had talked about this afternoon!

She chewed her lip anxiously, for her short experience of Treaty Port life had convinced her that Frank must be brought "home" as soon as possible, for his own good. And that was why she had already resolved to tell no one about the "Carr loot", now carefully sewed into her reticule lining. Funds would undoubtedly be needed for Frank's escape and where else could she get them? But if she had told the story of that strange encounter with Stewart Carr, she would have had to give up the treasure. So: Carr's little Flossie had to wait till her little Frank was safely out of Hunan! In any case, she comforted herself as she returned to the cabin, Flossie had no more right to the loot than she did—by right it should be handed over to the Chinese authorities.

"Oh Alice, I've been so worried, where have you been, wandering about alone at this time of night? It's not safe you know." Ida was dozily reading the latest issue of the *Missionary Gleaner*, having vowed not to sleep till Alice returned.

"Of course it's safe. Whatever could happen to me on a British steamer like this? It's no use, Ida," Alice peeled off her dress, "you can't expect me to worry about things like that, when I've travelled hundreds of miles alone in the interior and come to no harm."

"But then you were disguised as a Chinese—more or less—and now you're dressed properly as a Christian young lady, and that makes a lot of difference."

"My father used to say that the idea of clothes making the man, or woman, wasn't part of a good Christian's belief."

Ida pulled the sheet up to her nose. "I don't know what you're talking about." Then she softened. "It's funny you should say that though. My dear Papa often quotes that phrase, only he says it's the belief that clothes maketh the man which keeps him in business."

"Really? What does he do then?"

"He owns a drapers and outfitters in Bromley, Kent—it's the oldest established firm in the High Street," she added defensively.

Alice yawned. "You must tell me about it tomorrow, Ida. About Kent and all those places in England I've forgotten about."

"Forgotten about *Kent!*" Ida positively jumped up and the *Gleaner* slid to the floor. Alice picked it up as she climbed into her bunk. "My father was born in Norfolk, so I remember about that, but I can't quite place Kent. Good-night, Ida, and sweet dreams."

Alice was asleep in minutes, but Ida lay awake staring wide-eyed into the vessel's thrumming darkness, listening fearfully to the metallic scramblings of the cockroaches, praying that God would show her how Alice could be persuaded to enrol in Shanghai's theological college straightaway. It would seem her only hope of salvation.

However, as the ship sailed leisurely north-east, Ida's vigilance relaxed. The seas were calm, the days balmy and it was pleasant to sit in a deck-chair listening to the waves and the flapping awnings, writing letters eventually destined for the High Street, Bromley. Meanwhile, Alice was profitably occupied in teaching her young Chinese friend more English; an innocent enough pastime, though Ida might have felt differently had she understood everything Mr Lin—"Lin" as Alice soon familiarly called him—told Alice.

"Father says we Chinese must learn your language because we are so ignorant of Western culture and technology. And that makes us weak and vulnerable—he fears we're in danger of being overrun by the powerful European nations within the next twenty years and must strengthen ourselves to preserve the Celestial Empire."

"Your father must be unusual to view things in that way," Alice said cautiously, remembering the Chus' unconcealed, unthinking disdain for all things barbarian.

"Yes, he is. You remember those wars over thirty years ago, when you British came into Canton and insisted on new trading rights—including the import of more opium, which hasn't been good for us? My father was quite young then, and went on a delegation to the foreigners with his father—my revered grandfather—who was one of the Canton commissioners. Anyway, my father met a young Mr Clark who kept boasting about the British Empire overseas and how your small island was just about the richest country in the world. Mr Clark didn't have much time for missionaries—I remember Father telling me that! Anyway, most of the Chinese delegation didn't believe a word he said. But my father listened—that's why he's unusual, and, to cut a long story short, that's why he's sending me away to college now."

"To learn how to defeat the British?"

"To learn how to defend our own country against greedy European traders and power-hungry foreign governments."

Alice looked at him doubtfully, having never heard such sentiments before. He stared back quizzically, then melted into one of his charming smiles. "What strange and pretty eyes you have—hints of green and blue, like jade out of the far western mountains, cut and polished." He touched her arm and she leaned receptively towards him. But he dropped his hand quickly and returned to his earlier theme. "I understand that, in your country, thousands of people work in factories producing goods that sell in world markets—your industrial revolution sounds so full of promise. That is what we need here—it makes my heart ache to see our poor ignorant peasants bending wearily over the paddies, working so hard for so little."

"'To only see the sky when it is reflected in the mud'," she quoted at him.

"Well said. And when I think how much more educated and prosperous your working classes must be... aren't they?"

"I hardly know... I suppose so. I've never seen them." He looked amazed and she added, "You see, I've never been to England. I was born here and I've always lived here—so far."

He liked that about her immensely, it made her less of a barbarian than most. It also explained her lack of that arrogance which seemed bred in most English bones he thought, as, soon after, he watched Ida Palmer piloting Alice towards the tea-room. Every movement of Ida's conveyed a shrinking, if covert disdain for "the natives"—and yet she was but a small-town shopkeeper's daughter, Alice had told him. What effrontery! And he drifted into a pleasant fantasy in which Ida was kneeling bound hand and foot before him, and he, with a chopper in his hand, was telling her quite calmly that he was going to cut off both her breasts unless she immediately recanted her Christian faith, shaved her head and became a Buddhist nun. What would she do in such a situation, he wondered? Would she clasp her hands in prayer and bare her bosom for his blade? He was both excited and repelled by the vision, wondering what *he* would then do? No, she would have to be rescued at the last minute—by Uncut Jade of course. Who would plead for Ida's life, which he would grant in return for—the sweet little Uncut body of course. But for Uncut he would need no other weapon than his own manhood, and there was something in those strange eyes of hers which suggested the encounter would be a delight.

The next day the *Mandalay* stopped at Swatow, then at Foochow and Ningpo, so it was ten days after their departure that Shanghai eventually hove in view one misty morning. As they moved slowly up the Woosung estuary, Alice could just discern the outlines of the international settlement and the tower of Trinity Church. Her heart sank. More missionaries dwelled here, including one Miss Hilda Stubbs of the Church Missionary Society who was going to show her and Ida around during the day's stay in port. "And you'll be able to see the work of the Mission School and visit the theological college and I'm sure you'll find it all most inspiring!" Ida had promised her. Alice had prevaricated, hoping Lin might go ashore with her instead, but he was meeting some naval students and was totally uninterested in her arrangements. The breakfast gong sounded just as the ship docked and Alice went below, pondering the day's unattractive alternatives: to see Shanghai with Ida and Hilda, or not to see it at all.

"Miss Greenwood?" a steward approached as she was finishing her toast. "Please to the Purser's Office, very much important—quick."

"Oh dear, what can be the matter now?" Alice jumped up.

"Shall I come with you?" Ida offered.

"No thanks—perhaps it's another newspaper reporter."

At the door of the Purser's office stood a tall, erect man wearing a smart, light tweed morning-coat, his blue eyes set deep in a bronzed face intently scanning each passing face. He stepped forward hesitantly as she approached.

"It is... isn't it? Alice, it must be you?"

She stared up wonderingly. "It's... it's Uncle Robert! Can it really be?" She clung to him joyously, tears in her eyes. "But however did you... Why are you...? I mean, you used to be in India?"

He squeezed her shoulders. "Oh I'm still stationed there,

but I'm here on leave. And I'd planned to go from here to Chefoo to see your mother. Then yesterday a dispatch arrived from her telling me the wonderful news of your return. The Consulate thought you'd be on this ship. Your mother's overjoyed and so am I, my dear... it's absolutely astonishing, after all these years!" He stepped back to look at her, eyes shining with joy. "And you're so grown-up and so well-looking, thank goodness... But come to the saloon where we can talk quietly."

After hearing the details of Alice's talk with Consul Meadows in Hong Kong, Robert consulted his watch and jumped up. "Well obviously the best thing is for me to come up to Chefoo with you—see your mother and we'll decide what best to do about Frank. I'm sure I can get compassionate leave in the circumstances—after all, Frank is my nephew and I always felt that not enough fuss was made over that dreadful Tientsin business at the time. But that was the missionary angle of course—turn the other cheek and all that. Anyway, I'll go back to the mess, pack my kit, pay my chits and be aboard before teatime. We sail at six o'clock, I believe?"

"But, Uncle, please let me come with you—I've never seen Shanghai and the other passengers are going off for a look round."

"Well—alright then. Get your hat and gloves and we'll be off."

As they climbed into a double rickshaw on the quay, Robert pointed out the workshops and dry dock of the Kiangnan Arsenal where, he explained, the few Chinese endowed with get-up-and-go were learning to make Western-style ships and weaponry.

"I hear they're turning out five thousand rounds of Remington shells a day now—well, good luck to 'em—it's about time they used their gunpowder for something other than firecrackers!"

Leaving the docks, they bowled past the Public Gardens where carefully spaced clumps of wallflowers wilted in the alien soil, the Seamen's Mission, the Oriental Bank, the Circulating Library, the grand portals of the four-storey-high Shanghai Club and the gilded ones of the recently-opened Lyceum Theatre where the farce *You Never Can Tell* was playing to packed houses. At the entrance to the officers' mess, Alice waited while Robert hurried inside, returning shortly with a jolly-looking, paunchy officer.

"Alice, this is a chum of mine, Major Cartwright from Bombay, who's kindly agreed to look after you while I go to the Consulate and set things moving. You'll end up at the Grand for luncheon, then, Basil? And I'll join you as soon as I can."

"Absolutely delighted, my dear fellow. There's a sorry lack of charming feminine company here..." He shook Alice's hand vigorously. "And this young lady is famous too, by jove! I'd just been reading all about her adventures in last week's *China Mail* when lo and behold, up comes Robert and asks me to escort the celebrated person herself around town..." He climbed in beside her. "I only wish there was more of interest to show you... Now if this were Bombay—but these Chinese stations are godforsaken backwaters, real mongrel settlements in my view... Ourselves, the French, Germans, Americans and lord knows who else all hugger-mugger... As for the natives, you'll scarcely believe this, Robert, but I was chatting with old Harry Chambers after breakfast—and well, you know that little stretch of railway our engineers are just laying down near the Woosung docks? Well, the local Chinks don't like it, if you please and they're threatening to tear it up! Nasty noisy iron monsters—that's what they think of steam engines! Can you credit it? As I said to Harry, what hope is there for a race like that?"

Robert tutted sympathetically. "Well you know what they say, Basil—there's nothing like a sharp dose of John Chinaman to make one appreciate the merits of your common or garden Indian wallah... But I must get moving... Take care of my precious little niece, won't you? We can't afford to lose her again!"

And indeed it was with the most elaborate and attentive care, as if she had been a fragile porcelain doll that Major Cartwright proceeded to show Alice what he termed "the sorry little sights of Shanghai". The race-course was the first of them, with its new grandstand and the white-railed enclosure to separate foreigners from natives; then to the cricket pitch where, he explained, the Duffers were to play the Feebles on Saturday and it was a pity she could not be there. Inside the dim cool of Trinity Church Alice read some of the older memorial tablets—to Mrs Agnes Colyer who died of swamp fever in 1848, to Ensign L.F. Smith who was killed aboard ship in pursuit of his duty in 1851. Then, in search of fresh air, they strolled along Bubbling Well Road, past Tundall's the drapers, Boles the saddlers and Fraser & Crawford the grocers who, said Major Cartwright, were guilty of day-light robbery when you compared their prices of Lea & Per-rins Worcestershire sauce and Skippers tinned salmon with the cost of the same commodities in Bombay.

As for Shanghai's Grand Hotel, albeit under the expert management of Monsieur Pierre Gastone formerly of the Champs-Elysées, Paris, it was, the Major said, a mere lodging-house compared to the well-appointed hostelries of Calcutta. But to Alice, who had never before set foot in any comparable establishment, the Grand fully lived up to its name.

Quaking inwardly, she tried to assume a thoroughly grown-up and dignified air as they walked into the dining-room where each table had its white starched cloth, glass cruet, hovering waiter. The only Chinese in view were the waiters, bell-boys and shoe-cleaners squatting behind the potted palms, she realised, thinking how furious Han-fei would be to see all these lordly rich-looking "foreign-devil-barbarians" ordering "the natives" about, and no one even finding it odd.

As they settled at table, Robert arrived and set about ordering the local specialities of boiled shad with cucumbers and roasted spring snipe, together with a celebratory bottle of champagne. "I've sent a dispatch for transmission to Calcutta asking for four months' compassionate to be added to my present leave," he announced. "The Consul here agrees with Meadows in Hong Kong that Frank's case is a matter for the Minister and he's told me the legalities of the situation. Doesn't sound too promising actually, but we'll see . . . Ah," he smiled as the waiter popped the cork. "And I think you should have a little too, Alice. Here's to you my dear. It's a very happy day for me to have my favourite niece returned, almost from the dead, as it were, and such a charming young lady she's become too!" The gentlemen raised their glasses and Alice gulped with delighted surprise.

"Anyway," Robert resumed, "the most extraordinary thing is that the present Consul here is Mr Waters—who was Consul in Tientsin at the time of the massacre!"

"Waters?" Alice looked up. "I remember the name. I don't think Father liked him much?"

"Not much love lost, I gather. But he seems a decent fellow, and told me things I'd not heard before. I was away up on the North-West Frontier when it all happened, you know, Alice. Didn't hear for months, and a great shock it was, I can tell you."

'Were any other foreigners killed that day, Uncle?"

"No my dear, just the Catholics and your poor father. The French kicked up the deuce of a row about their *religieux* but our people didn't do much."

"But why was our Mission singled out for attack?"

"Oh it wasn't that... it was just damned bad luck that you happened to be situated nearest to the cathedral which was the mob's main target. So when they'd polished that off, they headed for you next. After a while the authorities managed to get control—which was why your mother was saved."

Alice shivered and Major Cartwright laid a fleshy hand on hers. "Enough of all that on a day like this! Come, drink up, m'dear. This lovely bubbly will soon buck you up."

He refilled her glass and she drank readily. Robert also drank, watching her. Such a bright, lively young creature she had become—though her complexion and hair were a sorry mess. And full of commonsense it seemed, unlike her father who had been so kind and good, but hopelessly impractical and unrealistic. Consul Waters had told Robert confidentially that the Greenwoods could probably have been saved if they had sought the protection of the Consulate sooner, as the other Protestants had. "But your brother was a stubborn man," Waters concluded. "He always thought he knew best when it came to dealing with the Chinese, and that God would always protect him... You see what happened? And what purpose did it all serve? The only ones to profit were the Tientsin shopkeepers who turned a quick *tael* selling 'massacre fans' with scenes of the slaughter in all its gory detail!" With his last sip of champagne, Robert silently vowed to do everything he could to get young Frank out of Hunan alive; it was the least he could do for that poor, dead, misguided brother of his.

The remainder of the day passed in a happy haze for Alice, who had never before drunk champagne. During her second glassful, the room ballooned into a golden ball of joy and, by the time they left, she decided the hotel was the funniest place she had ever seen—all those solemn obedient Chinese in their neat black Western suits holding doors open and bowing to large barbarian ladies and gentlemen.

"You know what is puzzling me, Uncle?" she shaded her eyes as they emerged into the glare of the Bund. "I can't understand why the Chinese let us do all this in their country... It's absurd. If a few thousand of them got together and decided to push every foreigner and all their belongings into the sea one afternoon, they could—and think no more about it." She giggled. "It would look funny, wouldn't it? All those knives, forks and cruets sinking straight to the bottom and the ladies' feathered hats bobbing about on the waves!"

Robert smiled grimly. "I'm glad it amuses you, my dear, but you've forgotten a few points—such as the power of the British Army and Navy. We've had absolutely legal treaty rights to trade and reside here since 1842, don't forget, and I imagine your 'few thousand Chinese' would soon regret trying any hanky-panky of that sort. So you mustn't worry."

"Oh, it doesn't worry me in the least... I just find it hard to understand."

But then, there's a good deal I don't understand, she thought a while later, as she and Robert stood on the *Mandalay*'s deck waving goodbye to Major Cartwright. A golden sun was setting over the western hills beyond the port and golden circles of lamplight began to flicker from the warehouses and mat-huts along the shoreline as the vessel slid away in the gathering twilight towards the East China Sea. I wonder why it had to be my father who was killed and my brother and me who were kidnapped? Father used to say that things happened according to God's plan, but, according to Uncle Robert, it was just that we happened to be in the wrong place at the wrong moment. And what does Mama think of it all? After seeing Father die like that?

She squeezed Robert's arm. "I'm so glad you're here with me now, Uncle. I was getting a little anxious about seeing Mama again. After all, I was only a child when I left and now I'm practically grown-up. And she's got new babies and a new husband... But now you're here, it'll be alright, I'm sure."

Robert chuckled. "I don't know how much good I'll be. I haven't seen Eliza myself since... '69 was it? When I visited you all in Tientsin the year before..."

"Yes, and you told Frank and me all about the Lucknow campaign you'd been in as a subaltern, do you remember?"

"Can't say I do, but I'm glad an old soldier's yarns made such an impression. Anyway, don't worry about your mother. She's longing to see you, and I don't suppose she'll have changed much, except for a few grey hairs, maybe."

The two of them kept that encouraging thought well in mind when, five days later, they again stood on deck as the *Mandalay* moved towards Chefoo harbour. The remainder of the voyage had been uneventful. Ida Palmer had been most relieved to hand over the chaperonage of Alice to Robert though, as she wrote in confidence to Mr Penfold, she was not sure his influence on her spiritual development was entirely good. For Alice, the only disadvantage of Robert's presence aboard had been its effect on Lin Fu-wei. To be honest, and Alice always tried to be honest in such matters, the young Chinese had simply transferred his attention from her to Robert because the latter had much more useful information to impart.

To what extent did the British government control the policies of its army, he had wanted to know. What was the firing range of the new breech-loading gun he had heard about? Was anyone in England trying to depose Queen Victoria? In such exchanges, Alice was relegated to the role of translator, and when the discussion ranged beyond her powers of immediate comprehension, both men grew impatient, wishing they could dispense with her services altogether. Nor did Lin evince any further interest whatsoever in the colour of her eyes; but when, as sometimes happened, Robert's enthusiasm for international debate waned, he was quick to compliment him on his acute grasp of world affairs and even, on one occasion, on his excellent military posture.

Well, bother him, I don't care. He only wanted to pick my brains because there was no one better available, and I don't suppose we'll ever meet again, Alice was thinking rather despondently as the vessel drew near the land and she began trying to identify the distant figures on the quayside. There was a tap on her shoulder and Lin was smiling down at her.

"Goodbye for now, Uncut Jade," he said softly, "it's been a great pleasure sharing this voyage with you, and we'll meet again some day. This is a Western-style farewell I believe?"

She took his outstretched hand, saying impulsively, "You think we'll meet again? I was just thinking we probably never would."

His eyes shone confidently. "Ah you barbarians have no perception of such matters. We shall meet, and in the meantime, to paraphrase the sage, 'I shall wear a hair-shirt for the world to see and carry a jade next to my heart!'" He bowed, half-mockingly, and she glowed with delight.

Robert jogged her arm. "Could that be your mother—standing with those gentlemen?"

Alice strained forward. "No, not possibly, that lady's too tall, and too fashionably dressed, unless Mama's changed a lot!"

There were only six foreigners among the several natives on the quay and, having studied them all, Robert concluded, "She doesn't seem to be there then. There's no one else possible." Alice sighed and turned for a parting word with Lin, but he had vanished. "Let's make for the gangplank," Robert said briskly. "She'll probably arrive any minute."

As Alice stepped ashore carrying her shabby reticule, a small woman in a Chinese robe of faded blue cotton rushed up. "Alice—my darling darling child! It is you, isn't it? I thought it was, but then you seemed to be escorted by a gentleman and so I...oh, Alice, it's a miracle to see you again, my dear, dear daughter!" They clung to each other, laughing shakily through their tears, though even in her joy Alice was shocked by the grey, weary frailty of her mother's looks.

"The gentleman is Uncle Robert, Mother. He's come up with me."

"Robert here too! Oh I'm so glad he's come, he'll be such a help. And you look so grown-up, my dear. Why, you're as tall as I am!"

Alice squeezed her thin shoulders. "But that's not very tall, is it, Mother?"

Robert hurried up, followed by the baggage coolies. "My dear Eliza, how very good to see you. I'm afraid we just didn't recognise you from the ship in those clothes." He could not entirely conceal the disapproval in his voice.

She greeted him warmly, then looked up with that mixture of timidity and defiance he remembered as being characteristic of her. "But you know it is our practice—that of the China Inland Mission to which I now belong—to wear native dress. Our founder, Mr Hudson Taylor, of whom you must have heard, firmly believes that by so doing we help to break down Chinese distrust... It is no mere affectation, I do assure you."

Alice hugged her. "Dear Mother, I don't know about all that, but I'm quite sure that what you're wearing is far more comfortable than these clothes Mrs Penfold insisted on buying for me in Hong Kong."

Robert controlled his indignation with an effort, though his collar felt hot with it. Really, his sister-in-law looked quite dreadful—like a little old peasant woman in those clothes, her weatherbeaten face, and straw sandals, if you please. He turned sharply to the coolie. "You—wait there, I'll get a couple of rickshaws."

"There's no need really, Robert," Eliza protested. "Rickshaws are in short supply here because of all the hotels, and are very expensive. So I've brought the Mission wheelbarrow." She indicated an old barrow propped against a wall.

He glowered at it. "And I suppose you expect me to push it?"

Alice giggled "I'd like to see you, Uncle!"

"No Robert, of course not. Our mission boy will do it."

So they set off, the boy trundling the luggage-laden barrow; Alice suited her pace to her mother's slower one and Robert, stalking ahead, hoped he would not meet any of his fellow officers—to whom he honestly did not want to introduce his sister-in-law. But he need not have worried, for they soon turned away from the foreign quarter and down increasingly narrow dirty alleys into which no sane man would penetrate except in course of urgent duty. He stopped to wait for the women, who, oblivious of their surroundings, were talking animatedly.

"This is our Mission's recuperation home," Eliza pointed ahead to a building which, Robert was later to tell his sympathetic officers in the mess, looked like a derelict, rat-infested warehouse. "We only rented it a few months ago, so it's still a bit makeshift, but very clean inside." Eliza sensed Robert's disapproval. "There's just Miss Beales, Miss Agnew and me here at present—and the babies of course. Oh Alice, you have heard about them, haven't you? My new chicks— and my new husband. I assumed you knew, but we've been talking so much about Frank."

"Yes Mother, of course I know. Mr Penfold told me in Hong Kong."

"That's a relief and I'll tell you more later . . . but come in. This is our communal room, and we've bedrooms ready for you."

"Oh not for me, thank you, Eliza. I shan't be staying for more than ten minutes."

"Oh but Robert, surely . . ."

"I wouldn't dream of imposing on you here. Besides," he lied, "I've already engaged a room ahead at the officers' hotel and I must go to the Consulate first thing in the morning. So I'll leave you two to get to know each other again and return tomorrow to discuss our future plans."

"Well, if you insist, Robert. I certainly want to talk to Alice for hours and hours." Eliza smiled fondly at ther daughter. "But first you must come and see my precious little ones."

The two babies lay in their mother's bedroom and a smell of milk, vomit and carbolic soap hung about them. At their approach, the punier of the two wailed distressfully. "This is Adam," Eliza picked him up. "Not yet two, and life's been so trying for him, poor mite. He's always ailing—he's a rash of some sort now, you see. And many's the time I've thought I'd lose him."

Alice looked at the damp, spotty creature, feeling nothing. "And this?" The other baby gave her a broad smile of welcome, waving a chubby fist.

"That's Alison."

"Alison—but that's almost my name!" Alice protested indignantly, as the baby curled its fingers round hers.

"My dear, it was meant to be. As you must know, we eventually gave up all hope of ever seeing you and Frank again. So when these two little ones arrived, they seemed some recompense for my dreadful loss. Edward wanted the boy called Adam because, though he has a grown son from his earlier marriage, this baby came after his conversion to the true faith. And I wanted Alison in memory of my dear daughter—not quite the same name, but almost."

Alice picked her up and, as the child snuggled against her, felt a surge of quite unexpected happiness. This little girl, she thought, would need a big sister. Robert peered at her, poked her tummy and the child chuckled.

"Quite a little bundle of sunshine, that one."

"Sunshine." Alice held her high. "That must be her name, Mother. Sunny—the part of her name that's different from mine. It suits her and we can't keep two such similar names in the family."

"Well, I don't know, it's not a proper Christian name. But if you really like it—and certainly she's a sweet-natured, robust child. But oh, my goodness, how could I have forgotten to tell you? William—he's on his way out here at this moment, from England, and bringing his young bride, Isabel, with him. I've not yet met her, of course."

"William—coming here and *married*! But he was still a schoolboy when . . . oh Mother!"

"Well, he's a grown man now and he's joined the Imperial Maritime Customs under Sir Robert Hart. It's not what your dear father would have wished, I fear, but there was no persuading him otherwise . . ."

"A fine career for a young man," Robert broke in crisply. "As I wrote and said when I first heard, Eliza. Secure, chance to travel, to climb higher . . . So where's his first posting?"

"In Foochow, as the chief's assistant. He and Isabel will be landing there any day now and there's a letter waiting with the wonderful news about Alice and Frank. But we can't meet yet, because, when they've settled in Foochow, I'll be hundreds of miles away, back in Mukden, with Edward. It's all so difficult...oh, the times I've wished China was the same size of Scotland!"

Robert chuckled. "And part of the British Empire with decent trains and a telegraph system—that would help a lot!"

"Still it's marvellous news, Mother, and we're all bound to meet again eventually." Alice was happily imagining a reunion party with Mother, William, Frank, Uncle Robert, herself. But there were these worrying newcomers on the scene: the babies, the unknown Isabel and the shadow of a strict stepfather.

"Well dears," Eliza touched their arms, "at least we three have come together, and that's a miracle in itself. But I can hear Miss Agnew playing the evening hymn so it's nearly suppertime. You're sure you won't stay, Robert?"

He grabbed his kitbag firmly. "No thank you, Eliza. I really must get settled before dark. So I'll say goodnight, ladies." He chucked Alice under the chin, whispering, "Hope your supper isn't too awful!" She smiled, thinking how little he knew about her.

"I'm so glad you eat the native food with such relish," Eliza remarked, as Alice scooped up the last shred of cabbage. "It's quite dreadful how many Europeans, even some missionaries, I'm sad to say, feel the need for tinned meat and butter and such luxuries. So expensive and unnecessary."

"But I ate only Chinese food for years, Mother, so I'm certainly used to it. And the Chus are wealthy, so they fed well."

"You really must tell me everything about them, dear, I know so little of what has gone on."

Miss Beales, a round young woman who had eaten hugely and said little during the meal, cleared away the bowls, asking sorrowfully, "I suppose they were quite unredeemed heathens? Has the word of the Lord penetrated to Hunan at all yet?"

"Not to my knowledge, but I was mostly confined to the house, so I don't suppose I'd have heard anyway."

"Now, Mrs Blake," Miss Agnew bustled in, "as this is your very first evening with your daughter, we'll leave you together. Miss Beales will put the babies to bed and I'll bring some tea—and perhaps a cushion instead of that hard stool, Alice?"

"Please, and I'll put on my comfortable Chinese robe—it feels more home-like."

In the gathering twilight, mother and daughter talked quietly, feeling their way, almost as strangers. "But one thing is still not at all clear to me," Eliza said, after Alice had explained briefly how, though not really why, she and Kau had left Changsha. "Why couldn't Frank manage to get away with you? He is well, I hope? You are not concealing anything dreadful?"

"No, Mother, of course not. But for one thing, we seldom saw each other, he worked in the farmyard and..."

Miss Beales came in, looking harassed. "I'm sorry to disturb you, Mrs Blake, but I can't get Adam settled and now he's being sick again. Could you just...?"

Eliza hurried away and Alice moved restlessly about the dim room. She lit the brass paraffin lamp so that a pool of light shone over a bowl of wild marigolds on the table, and sighed as she touched their glowing petals. So often during the long, lonely journey from Hunan she had dreamed of an occasion like this. How she would bury her head in her mother's lap and pour out the whole story: her early misery, the beddings with Lung-kuang, her pregnancy and miscarriage, Frank's refusal to leave, and the meeting with Stewart Carr. Now she realised with a sinking heart that it was impossible to reveal any of these things. She had not bargained for the extent of her mother's naive piety, nor her middle-aged frailty, nor her obsessive concerns with new babies and a new husband. How could Alice burden her with these distressing, unpalatable truths? It would upset her so much and she seemed often close to tears already; moreover the full story would only confirm her worst imaginings about the diabolical practices of the heathen Chinese.

As she reached this reluctant conclusion, Eliza returned, rocking a wailing Adam. "Oh he is such a poor bairn, he ails and ails. There, my wee one, sleep now, don't you cry..."

Watching her bent head, Alice felt both desolate and resentful. Then her mother smiled up timidly at her. "Oh how glad I am to have you with me, dear. You'll be such a help to us all, you were always a willing little girl... Now where were we?"

"I'll do what I can, Mother." Alice curled up on the cushion. "But you've not yet told me anything about yourself, or about my stepfather. Where did you meet him?"

"Well my dear, after the tragedy I was in that little Tientsin hospital for weeks. I really didn't want to live at all—my husband and two children all gone in one dreadful afternoon. But the Lord supported me and reminded me of my duty. When I recovered somewhat, I did all in my power to find out about you both—pestering the Consulate and the C.M.S.

with letters and visits. But it was of no use, you'd both just vanished and eventually I was told you'd been killed in retribution for the execution of the riot leaders. After that I felt I couldn't bear to stay longer in such a dreadful country, so I boarded a steamer for Shanghai, intending to return Home.

"As it happened, the Reverend and Mrs Drew were aboard, friends of ours in the early C.M.S. days. Anyway, at their suggestion I disembarked with them at Nantung to see their mission—I think they hoped to dissuade me from leaving the China field. And it was in Nantung that I met Mr Blake, who was affiliated to the China Inland Mission... Oh, he was so full of hope and enthusiasm, Alice. It was marvellous to listen to him, after all I'd been through."

"Had he been in China long?"

"No, less than two years. Before that he was a schoolmaster. He's a very clever man, Alice, and taught Latin and History in a boy's school near Lewes. But there was an outbreak of scarlet fever in the school and his poor wife, Clara, and his baby daughter both died of it. It was the year before your father's martyrdom. Soon after his wife's death he attended a missionary meeting in Lewes Civic Hall and heard Hudson Taylor crying out for people to sacrifice their all to go out to China and save the heathen. And Edward was called. He'll tell you the full story himself one day. But, do you know, he gave up his schoolmastering, sold his house, put his son Theobald into boarding-school, sent his daughter Laura—who must be about your age—to live with an aunt, and, in course of time, came out here. Nantung was his first station."

She paused, smoothing Adam's brow. "Bring the lamp over here, Alice, he's asleep now and it won't disturb him." As Alice did so, Eliza smiled at her. "How pleasant looking you've become, dear, with those greenish-blue eyes, not really like mine or Thomas's. But you have his hair. And you seem so sensible and grown-up too and I'm very proud of you, my child—how courageously you've withstood all your trials."

Alice felt a lump in her throat at the remembrance of all her mother didn't know, but said lightly, "I wondered how I'd seem to you, Mother... I'm glad you approve. But you haven't yet told me what manner of man Mr Blake is? Is he very schoolmasterish?"

"Well, he's a schoolmaster turned missionary, which makes him a little severe. And when he's sure of a thing nothing will alter his mind. That's how he was about me, you see. I spent only three weeks in Nantung and we talked together about our bereavements and God's purpose in it all. The day I was leaving on the coastal ferry for Shanghai he came to see me off and just before I boarded he drew me aside and... well, proposed to me. He felt utterly certain that it would be for my own good, for his and for the heathen Chinese if I stayed on as his wife to help him with his work. He was most persuasive..." She hesitated, remembering the relentless intensity of his sombre, lantern-jawed face.

"But it seemed such a big step to take alone, without advice, and I felt I scarcely knew him. So I said I'd go to Shanghai anyway, and think it over there. As I went up the gangplank, he grasped my hand and said, 'There'll be a sign very soon, Eliza. I shall pray for it and it will show you that your true duty lies here with me in China.' And do you know, Alice, that very night, soon after we set sail, a typhoon blew up—out of nowhere it seemed. And the little boat plunged about in the storm and I clung to my bunk listening to the terrible roar of the wind and waves, thinking again and again of Edward's last words to me. After several hours, just when I thought the ferry would break in two, the wind abated a little and we managed to crawl back to Nantung.

"The next morning I woke up feeling happy and certain. I simply cancelled my passage and walked back to the C.I.M. It was calm and sunny, I remember, and everything sparkling after the rain. Edward himself answered the door and I said, "Here I am, come back already.' And he replied, 'I knew you would, Eliza, it is even sooner than I expected that God has shown you the way.' And about two months later we were married." She sighed tremulously.

"He sounds very sure and determined, Mother."

"Yes—or rather, sure of God's will in him, as he would say. But you'll meet him when we return to Mukden together. I hope—I mean I think—your father would have approved. And I'm sure you'll grow to like him, Alice." The baby whimpered and Eliza rose, cradling him carefully. "It's more than time for bed, my dear. You must be tired after all today's excitement."

Alice was indeed tired; she slept late and was just helping Miss Beales clear up when Robert appeared on the morning scene, looking pleased with himself.

"Everything is going according to plan," he announced. "I've seen the Consul here who also advised us to go straight to Peking and see the Minister about Frank—only he can authorise any action. So I think we should leave as soon as possible, Alice."

"Surely you needn't take her with you?" Eliza looked alarmed.

"I'm afraid so, Eliza. She really is the only person who can tell the Minister about the exact situation in Hunan. So she must come, for Frank's sake. You won't mind, will you, Alice?"

"But I'm longing to go—of course!"

"I thought you would. So we'll be off tomorrow. I'll go and book a passage to Tientsin and we'll travel on the overland cart service from there."

Eliza sighed. "Well if you say so, Robert. But please take great care of my long-lost daughter... Also," she added, as Alice rushed off to tell Miss Beales the good news, "please remember that Tientsin is full of painful memories for us both. I wept sorely when I had to go through on the way to Mukden last year."

"I had already thought of that, Eliza. I may be a rough and ready soldier, but I'm not without sensitivity, I do assure you. We shall be there only briefly and I shall see to it that Alice isn't unduly distressed."

But when, four days later, they disembarked at Tientsin, Alice insisted they take a walk round the town while waiting for the overland cart. As they strolled along, she was again assailed by that rabbit-hole feeling: it seemed incredible that she and Frank used so often to trot along on either side of dear old Wo-wo to buy fruit and vegetables in this same busy street-market, and there, in the dusty park along the waterfront, she had first bowled a hoop and Frank had pretended to ride Dobbin.

The humble Protestant chapel in Taku Road still stood and inside was the same slab commemorating the birth of "The first Christian child born in the town" in 1861. She had been called Annie Innocent and had died two years later; Alice always remembered the name; it rang with such sweet melancholy. The Catholic cathedral destroyed in the riot was now rebuilt in the same square, looking even grander than before. Leaving Robert gazing at it, Alice started down a side street.

"Alice, where are you going?" He hurried after her.

"To see if the Mission is still there."

"It isn't—it's in a different place now, your mother told me. And you're not to go upsetting yourself."

"I shan't, I promise, Uncle. But I must look at the old street—just once, then I'll never need to come again."

Outmanoeuvred by her determination, he fell in step beside her and they turned a corner. "It was left—along there somewhere—just there, I think?" She paused, watching a man sitting on a stool in the afternoon sunshine peacefully twisting jute cord to make a fishing-net. For a moment, the scene swam before her misted eyes as she remembered her father's voice telling her that missionaries were like fishers of God who cast their nets upon the waters, bringing up, now and then, a soul to be saved—and that was what made all their endeavours worthwhile.

"It *was* there, where that man's sitting. It's a boat chandlers now."

"Yes, I'm sure you're right." Robert put a hand on her shoulder. "Now come on Alice, let's go. No tears, you promised."

As they turned and walked quietly away Alice decided she would never make sense of the world. She looked timidly at her uncle wanting to ask how it all seemed to him. He looked so full of assurance and understanding, but she wondered suddenly if he really was? Did anyone, ever, learn to make sense of the world?

6

It was mid-morning when Alice and Robert first saw in the distance the capital of the Celestial Empire, its bell and drum towers, its circular pavilions, balconied pagodas and gated citadels outlined on the level plain. Strings of mule-carts, laden camels and horses, coolies bent beneath packs were converging on the southern gate and churning the infamous Peking dust into clouds that hung hazily in the warm air.

Robert brushed his spruce jacket, "It's incredible, isn't it? Here we are, approaching what is supposed to be one of the most ancient and glorious cities in the world, and there's not an inch of macadam or a drain in sight—but you can certainly smell it!"

Alice, oblivious to the dirt, the odours, the sad hordes of ragged beggar children and lepers, thrilled with excitement as they came up to the thirty-feet-high walls and joined the queue of travellers passing through the imposing gateway. Robert, bent diligently over his guidebook, read aloud, "The city is divided into three sections, the Tartar, the Chinese and the Imperial. The walls enclosing the whole measure a total length of twenty-one miles and the top of the wall that divides the two main cities is broad enough for pleasant evening perambulations by visitors."

As they approached the centre, Alice saw the tower of the White Ming Pagoda and the yellow-porcelain roofs of the royal palaces sparkling above the red-plastered walls that enclosed the Imperial City itself, wherein dwelt the mysterious and unapproachable Son of Heaven, the Celestial Dragon, the four-year-old Emperor of China.

"Can you see two gates in the walls with peaked towers?" asked Robert, still reading busily. "They're called the Meridian and the Gate of Spiritual Valour. Inside, which we can't see, there's another Gate of Supreme Harmony, apparently, and a Hall of Purity, a Palace of Earthly Tranquillity and a Hall of the Blending of Heaven and Earth. I'd like to see what goes on in there—sounds quite messy!" he chuckled.

About half a mile from the Imperial City they came to the Foreign Legation Quarter with its embassies; in the street beyond, their cart turned suddenly into a secluded courtyard.

"This must be the Mission," Robert jumped up, "though it looks more like a temple, by jove!"

And indeed the building in which Dr and Mrs Sturgeon had established their first Church Missionary Society station in Peking eight years previously had once been a Buddhist temple, with bronze dragons snarling from every roof-corner. The dragons seemed not to mind their dispossession however, for the place had a wholesome, settled Christian air—with its plain white-washed chapel, living-quarters and a large shed that served as a dispensary. Mrs Sturgeon, a plump, rosy-cheeked woman who looked as if she had just emerged from a Sussex farm-kitchen, greeted them warmly, installed them in bedrooms, offered lunch.

While waiting for the meal, Alice wandered into the chapel, and now it all came back to her: the same kind of rough benches, the altar table with its silver cross, dog-eared books and magazines—*Peep o'Day*, *The Messenger*, *Golden Grains of Truth*. She opened the register: Catechists, 5; Dispensary Assistants, 3; unpaid active workers, 14; Backsliders, 38. Oh, it was all going on just the same, and with just as little success and Alice's heart ached to think of the continual defeats and failures of the Sturgeons' lives, of her father's life. Poor, dear Father. She stood before the cross, hands clasped in prayer, but no words came; just the silver very bright in the sunlight, for there was always some elderly female convert of the Wo-wo type to keep the crosses shining, happy in the new-found knowledge that cleanliness was next to godliness.

"But of course the Mission is doing much better these days, isn't it, dear?" Mrs Sturgeon comforted her husband who, during supper that evening, had given his visitors his habitually lugubrious recital of their trials, and now left his wife to provide her customary jolly reminders of their small successes. "We have a core of truly faithful converts, about six regular attenders in Sunday school, and my three Bible women are miracles of faith and perseverence."

Robert, who had informed his elder brother many years before that he considered the business of trying to convert the Chinese to Christianity a thorough waste of effort and money, mumbled an excuse and, leaving Alice to bear the burden of the discourse, went for a surreptitious smoke in the courtyard. It had been a promising beginning, he thought, puffing happily. He had made an appointment with the British Minister for the morrow, and then taken Alice to see some of the foreign sights of the capital, for he felt she had already had more than enough of things Chinese. They had visited the old Portuguese burial ground where some early Jesuits were interred; the Russian cemetery near the Tartar wall containing the graves of twelve Europeans treacherously killed by the Chinese during peace negotiations of 1860; and the Roman Catholic cathedral which housed the famous natural history collection of Abbé David, who had lived there for years and made long journeys north every summer in search of rare specimens...

So far, so good, Robert thought, tapping out his pipe and sucking a lozenge to disguise the tobacco-smell from his hosts. But the most difficult task lay ahead—to enlist the help of the Minister in getting young Frank back to civilisation.

That evening it seemed perfectly reasonable to suppose the Minister would immediately put a small expeditionary force at Robert's disposal for the purpose, but, the next morning, as he and Alice reached the Legation, he was assailed by doubts. "Now, Alice," he instructed, "be quiet and ladylike and leave most of the talking to me—just be sure to tell the Minister what a fine, upstanding lad Frank is and how desperately he wants to be freed."

"Yes, Uncle," she said in a small voice, wishing she hadn't come.

Sir Hugh Digby's study was panelled in wood and smelled of vellum and leather; bookish dust danced in the shaft of light that streamed through the dingy velvet curtains.

"Miss Alice Greenwood, I am indeed pleased..." The Minister rose with a courtly inclination. "My wife was telling me more of your amazing experience only the other day, she'd been talking to some missionary acquaintance, I believe...yes...." he trailed vaguely. "And Major Greenwood," he shook hands, aware of the soldierly grip, the worried, defensive eyes. "Pray sit down, I've asked for coffee..." Sir Hugh entrenched himself behind his desk. "You must indeed be delighted to have your long-lost niece so unexpectedly returned to you, Major? From the dead—almost. Though I must say you look uncommonly well after your dreadful experiences, Miss Greenwood."

"They weren't all dreadful by any means, not after the first few months," Alice corrected humbly. "The Chu family were quite kind to Frank and me according to their lights—though they did think of us as 'little barbarians'." She knew that phrase made Europeans smile.

Sir Hugh smiled. "Quite so—the racial pride of the Sons of Han is beyond belief. Still, it is indeed lucky that you fell into fairly good hands, my dear. But you have no idea why the Chus kept you so long? As I'm sure you know, you were originally captured as hostages for Lung-pao's son, one of the instigators of the massacre. Lung-pao was the uncle of the Deputy-Governor in whose house you were imprisoned—as we've recently discovered. But it is remarkable, to be honest, that the Chus kept you alive after Lung-pao and his son were dead."

"I think they forgot about us," Alice said lamely. "It's a very large household and somehow we were just fitted in and made to work for our keep."

"Well, it says much for the Chus. For I do believe many of our honourable Celestials don't hesitate to, as it were—quietly put down—any barbarian of whatever tribe they consider superfluous, as indeed they do some of their own female babies. And it is equally astonishing, is it not, that you managed to return to Hong Kong unscathed?"

Robert coughed. "As to the matter of return, Sir Hugh, you realise that is what I've come about? It's the boy, my nephew Frank Greenwood, who's still a prisoner there, you know."

"Yes, I do know," Sir Hugh's back straightened just as a servant appeared with coffee. Both Robert's and Alice's hands shook slightly as they took their cups; Sir Hugh's remained steady as he sipped, saying nothing, not helping.

Robert, burning his tongue, asked, "Well, I wonder what you propose to do about it, sir? A young lad, nearly sixteen, a British subject, held there against his will..."

"Against his will? We are sure of that, are we, Miss Green-wood? You see, I've wondered why your brother made no effort to escape with you."

"But he couldn't. He couldn't possibly have disguised him-self as a Chinese because he's big and blond, and he felt it would endanger my chances..." Her voice was not totally convincing, for she was trying to blot out her last picture of Frank refusing to leave.

Sir Hugh turned to Robert. "So your nephew left his sister to do the brave thing and return to her own kind alone?"

"You can't judge so harshly, he's only a lad..." Robert began.

Alice added, "No, it wasn't like that at all. I *had* to leave and... he knew little about my plans. We seldom met, you see—he minded the horses and practised military arts with the other boys and I was in the women's apartments. It's the *custom*," she finished defiantly.

"Quite so, and, Major, please let's not get heated over this. But you say you had to leave, Miss Greenwood? Did something particular happen to make you feel that? After all, you'd lived there reasonably happily, it seems, for several years?"

Alice stared at the rows of gilt-lettered books on the op-posite wall. Tamao would have known how to deal with this, she was good at turning things aside with an apt quotation, something from Confucius perhaps... Robert was watching her anxiously.

"No, nothing sudden," she murmured, "but I was growing up. When I was a child there it was different."

Sir Hugh nodded soothingly. "Different of course. More so for you as a girl than for your brother perhaps?"

"Well he's younger and being a boy was allowed rather more freedom... Yes, different." She bent her head, staring at her tightly-clenched hands, feeling the men's unspoken questions eddying about her. Probably, she realised, they guessed more than they were saying. After all—they all did it, Englishmen just as much as Chinamen. Sir Hugh had a wife, Lady Digby, and he must have been with her many times, as she with Lung-kuang. She looked up at him curi-ously.

"And difficult for the young lady you have become?" he prodded; she only nodded.

A deferential young man entered with some official papers and as Sir Hugh glanced at them, Robert shifted uneasily, feeling the interview was not progressing well. He did not care for Sir Hugh's questioning of Alice, though he too had wondered privately if anything...unpleasant...had happened. The Chinese had no respect for the female sex and liked them young, apparently. As the secretary tiptoed out, Robert said, "We really mustn't intrude too long on your valuable time, Minister, so perhaps we could return to the main point which is—what does the British government and you, as its chief representative in China, propose to do about my nephew? He's been in captivity for nearly six years and now Alice has escaped his position could well be more perilous."

Sir Hugh brushed the back of his hand with his quill. "I'm afraid, Major, the short answer is—not very much, at least not yet. We've already sent a strong protest to the *Tsungli Yamen*—the Chinese department of so-called international affairs, and they, with their usual courteous circumlocutions, deny all knowledge of the case. I've suggested that protests be sent to the Governor of Hunan, but we must tread warily there, and frankly the *Tsungli Yamen* has little power in that quarter. The Hunanese, unfortunately, have long been renowned for their strained relations with the Manchus and their special dislike of matters barbarian, so I don't hold out much hope..."

"But we can't just leave it like that, Minister."

"I fully appreciate your concern, but the fact is that relations between the Chinese government and ourselves are relatively cordial just now, since the Chefoo Convention. So there's simply no question of our upsetting the status quo with any kind of official rescue operation—if that's what you had in mind. It could even lead to an international incident, and that isn't in our present interests."

"So my nephew is to be sacrificed to political expediency, is he?"

"Not exactly sacrificed, Major. After all, we've every reason to suppose that he's alive and well and will remain so. We'll endeavour to do what we can through the usual diplomatic channels and, probably, sooner or later, there'll be a good reason for arranging something—an unfortunate incident, some loss of life, a flare-up, these things inevitably happen from time to time. Then we can say to the Chinese, well now then, we'll overlook this or that you've done—but there's that lad you've got tucked away in Hunan, how about releasing him? You'll see, there'll be a diplomatic solution eventually, but it will take time."

His tone suggested that the matter had been amicably

settled, but Robert jumped up angrily, "Time? How long? Six months? A year? Five? It's young Frank's life we're talking about. And what guarantee have we that he'll survive that long? No, it's not good enough, Sir Hugh, just not good enough."

Alice looked at him admiringly; his stiff unyielding stance reminded her of dear Father when he used to stand before small groups and preach. The memory brought an ache to her throat. "My father laid down his life for the missionary cause, Sir Hugh. He was such a brave, good man—it would grieve him deeply to know that Frank was held in captivity and you, his own countryman, were making no effort to release him."

Sir Hugh smiled tightly, for his sympathy with those whom he privately termed "the pushy Prots" was strictly limited. He sprang from a long-established Anglo-Catholic family and believed that the Catholics had found a more enlightened way of bringing the Christian message to the Chinese. Sometimes, wearied by the burdens of office, he would take an evening perambulation along the Tartar wall towards the northern city, there to ponder the remains of the old astronomical observatory built by the Jesuit Fathers. Finest among them was the globe of heaven, made of solid copper, with figures denoting the stars and constellations still visible on its surface. That was the way it should be done; he was certain.

He said, "I take your point, Miss Greenwood. But you must be aware that the British Government takes a somewhat, shall we say, ambivalent attitude to the whole question of missionary endeavours in China simply because their excessive zeal and indiscriminate proselytising have led to several unpleasant incidents in the past, which could perhaps, with more judgment, have been avoided and which had unfortunate political repercussions." He turned briskly back to Robert, "Anyway, Major, there is surely a good chance that Master Greenwood will escape himself, as his sister did? But as for any overt action on our part, no, I'm sorry, it is impossible." He laid down his quill, signalling the interview's end.

Robert stood his ground. "Then what about sending a few people to Hunan secretly?"

"It would be wiser, certainly, but I'm not prepared to commit us at all, for the reasons I've given. In a year or so, things might change, one can never predict the future when dealing with Orientals." He glanced pointedly at the papers awaiting his attention.

Robert barked, "That's all you care about it, isn't it? Frank's just a pawn, to be forgotten or bartered or made a cause of to suit the requirements of the moment. Well, he's my dead brother's son, and if you won't do a thing to help him, then I'll go and get him out of there myself, secretly, as you say."

Sir Hugh weighed him carefully. "It's not something I would advise, Major, indeed it would be extremely foolhardy. You don't know the country or the language, and the Chinese don't take at all kindly to foreigners wandering about their interior provinces."

"I am something of a geographer and an experienced traveller and it won't be the first time I've gone into unknown native terrain."

"And I shall go with him—because I do know the country and the language," Alice burst in eagerly.

"Come now, Miss Greenwood," Sir Hugh was brusque, "of course you will not—a young lady like you..."

Robert added, "No, Alice it's not a job for you, my dear."

She shut her lips for it was pointless to argue here, but the idea thrilled her. Why not? Just herself and Uncle Robert—what an adventure! And how delighted Frank would be to see them and they would all travel back together. She could immediately imagine the three of them bumping along in an ancient cart and Frank telling her the latest news of the Chu household.

"It's not in my power to actually forbid your going," Sir Hugh was saying. "But I must repeat that the idea is both foolish and dangerous and you should abandon it before it takes hold of your mind. And I warn you, if anything should go wrong, it would be entirely on your own head."

"Naturally I could hardly expect a rescue expedition in the circumstances," Robert smiled dourly. "So I'll wish you good day, Minister. Come, Alice."

As she rose to leave, Sir Hugh said, "Major, before you go, I'd like a brief word—perhaps you'd wait in the anteroom for a few minutes, my dear."

Alice went out, feeling hot and anxious. What an unfeeling man Sir Hugh was, with all his talk of cold-blooded diplomatic bargains. She kicked angrily at the carpet—probably he considered her own father guilty of, what was it?—"excessive zeal and indiscriminate proselytising". Oh, what a dreadful man! And he had tried to pry out her reasons for leaving Changsha too, as if he had guessed she was concealing something. She shivered, wondering what they were discussing in her absence.

Sir Hugh had resumed his seat; Robert stood tense, ready for further battle, but the Minister smiled disarmingly, "No, I'll say no more about your nephew, Major—it's about your niece I wanted to talk." He gestured to a chair. "It's a rather delicate point, and you can tell me to mind my own business, if you like. But when I asked her her reasons for running away, she became most evasive, didn't you think? I didn't like her look. I wonder if you know, in complete confidence, exactly why she left? For one thing, if we are to try and negotiate Frank's release, it is best to know the full story, and I've a suspicion we don't?"

"I know no more than she told you, Sir Hugh. I've wondered myself, to be honest, and I did notice her reactions. I think there may be more to it, but I could only hazard a guess..."

"Exactly, I too can guess. As you must know, the Chinese don't treat their womenfolk as we do. And the system of concubinage is very prevalent among high-ranking families of the kind in which your niece was living. How old is she?"

"Almost eighteen."

"By which time nearly every Chinese girl is betrothed, married or in concubinage of some sort."

"And you think that is why...?"

"I should be very surprised if any young female living in such a house were exempt from the system, barbarian or not. But she's said nothing? Not even to her mother?"

"No, of that I'm quite sure. Eliza would have been so shocked, I'd have heard." He leaned forward, man to man now. "The fact is, my sister-in-law is, well, very missionary, especially since she remarried into the China Inland Mission." He did not conceal his distaste. "One couldn't even hint of such matters to her, and Alice would realise that. She's a canny young lady and she'd keep anything of that nature to herself."

"Which could be very damaging for her in the long run, in the emotional sense, Major. What she could have experienced as a young girl, then have to keep secret."

"Well, I'll see what I can do, sir. I'm very fond of Alice, she's got great spirit. But I can hardly... as a mere man..."

Sir Hugh smiled understandingly. "May I suggest my wife talk to her? She's a woman of the world, and something might come of it. If what we suspect is true, it's a heavy burden for

Alice to bear alone, and she might crave the understanding sympathy of an older woman. But it's entirely up to you, this is not really my business, nor my wife's . . ."

"It's a very kind offer, Sir Hugh. I suppose with all the worry about Frank I've pushed this aspect from my mind. But if your wife would see her, it couldn't do harm and it might do good."

"Quite so," Sir Hugh rose. "A private invitation will be sent to her. You'll be here for a few days yet, I assume?"

Left alone, Sir Hugh wrote on his memo pad, "Talk to Helen about Alice G.". He stared at it for a moment. The young lady in question had indubitably picked up a good deal of Oriental inscrutability during her years *en famille chinoise*—and perhaps the habits of concubinage to boot? She had certainly looked at him with a bold knowingness quite unlike other young missionaries' daughters of his acquaintance. He smiled wryly—he had always thought concubinage had things to recommend it. "Give me a child to the age of seven and he's ours for life," the wily old Jesuits used to say. It had not been quite like that for Miss Greenwood, but she was certainly out of the ordinary run. Interesting—and a meaty tit-bit for Helen, who was thoroughly bored with the narrowness of Peking's diplomatic circles compared to their previous posting in Rome. She would enjoy the chance of a confidential chat with the girl from Changsha.

The envelope with the Legation's seal was handed to Alice the very next morning by a liveried messenger. She and Robert had just returned from a discouraging visit to the *Tsungli Yamen*, where they had tried to find out if anything could be accomplished through those slow-moving "diplomatic channels". But, despite Alice's powers of persuasive interpretation, they had been faced with blank incomprehension bordering on hostility. The official Chinese view was that Frank Greenwood did not exist.

Alice opened the envelope wonderingly: Lady Digby, tea at 3.30 pm. "But it's today," she turned to Robert in dismay.

"Just a ladies' tea, my dear."

"But I don't know any ladies here . . . Need I go? They'll only ask me lots of stupid questions about the Chinese."

"Of course you must go, Alice, why, it's quite an honour to be asked. There are ladies in Calcutta who'd give their eye teeth for an invitation like that!"

"But I'm not good at tea-parties and I don't suppose I'll like Lady Digby any more than her husband."

"Come, don't be childish, Alice," Robert admonished,

knowing she hated the term. "You mustn't judge people before you've met them, and what's more, here's a chance to put in a good word for Frank. So write an acceptance and give it to the messenger straight-away."

Alice did so, but when, at the appointed hour, she rang the bell of the Minister's residence, wearing her best blue muslin dress, her body clammy inside a tight bodice, hands clammy inside tight gloves, she ardently wished she had refused. Ushered into a boudoir furnished with chintz-covered chairs and occasional tables, she looked round puzzled, for there was no sign of the formidable array of ladies and silver teapots she had expected, and she could not decide whether to be more, or less, alarmed by their absence. Arrayed in a corner cupboard were collections of Venetian glass and French porcelain and Alice went to look at them closely— having never seen such beautiful objects of this sort—and her nose was pressed in covetous admiration against the glass when an elegant, soft-blonde lady in a loose tea gown of beige net bustled in.

"My dear Miss Greenwood, I am delighted, I've heard so much about you and wanted to meet you just as soon as possible. Ah, you're looking at my little European treasures, I see. Now pray sit down. I've asked for tea here, so much cosier than the formal drawing-room when one just wants a chat..." She pulled a chair closer to Alice, smiling warmly. "Now, my dear, I know we haven't met before, but I want you to feel as if we had—I don't want you to think of me as the Minister's wife, tiddley-pom, but as someone to whom you can talk quite freely. You must have had such fascinating adventures, but probably only your family has heard of them so far?"

Alice felt rather overwhelmed, then a bubble of laughter rose in her, for she was unaccountably reminded of the Duchess in *Alice in Wonderland* who dug her sharp chin into Alice's shoulder on the croquet ground saying, "And the moral of that is, 'tis love that makes the world go round." And Alice had replied, "Somebody said that it's done by minding your own business..."

"Well now, so how do you like Peking, Alice? I may call you that, mayn't I, as we are to be friendly?"

"Of course—and I love Peking. It's like coming back to China."

"But you've never left surely?"

"No, not really. But when I reached Hong Kong and then went to Shanghai and Chefoo, it seemed different. The Treaty

147

Ports aren't like China somehow, not real, not properly any-where. So coming to Peking is like returning to China proper."

Lady Digby looked at her shrewdly; it must have been quite strange to have seen Hong Kong for the first time in one's life through her eyes. "Yes, I understand, dear, and it must be difficult for you, after all these years away from everybody and everything familiar... Yet now you're expected to behave as if nothing much had happened, isn't that it?"

"Yes, exactly," Alice agreed eagerly. "And the Chu family were quite good to me in some ways, but no one seems to believe that, or be interested in them."

"Well, I'm interested, I assure you, Alice. Quite an important family, I believe? The Deputy-Governor of Hunan?"

The tea arrived and as they drank and ate cake together companionably, Alice found herself talking more freely than she had to anyone else about her experiences.

"Well, Alice," Lady Digby exclaimed eventually, setting down her cup. "I think that's one of the most fascinating stories I've ever heard. And in some ways, you're most fortunate. Very few English people in China today, and probably none of your tender years, have as much first-hand experience of the country and its languages as you—and we must see it's not wasted."

Alice's eyes shone. "Oh, Lady Digby, thank you for that. Ever since I reached Hong Kong people have been feeling sorry for me and asking about my dreadful experiences. They've never wanted to know how much I've learned."

The Minister's wife smiled gently, feeling a genuine concern for this intense little person who was half-woman, half-child, half-English and half... well, something different. "Most of the people have been missionaries, I expect?"

"Yes, that's the trouble. They have such fixed ideas about the 'heathen Chinese'—as if heathenness were the only important thing about them."

"Quite so. Well as you grow up you'll make up your own mind on such matters, I've no doubt. Personally, I'm very glad to hear of the good times... In fact, from what you've said, I'm a little surprised you decided to leave. You took a dreadful risk, just leaping off into the unknown and away from the Chus, where, as you say, much was agreeable?"

Alice felt herself flushing. "Well, I was growing up... and I desperately wanted to see my mother again."

"Natural enough too, my dear. But I do wonder, if you'll

forgive my asking, if something perhaps less than pleasant made you feel suddenly you had to go, at whatever cost?"

Alice realised that a total lie would not, at this juncture, be believed; moreover, even the telling of a half-truth would be a great relief.

"There was something, yes... I haven't told anyone up to now, not even Mama. But one day Eldest Daughter took me aside and told me that Honourable Father, Lung-kuang... was, well..."

"Go on, my dear. I shan't be shocked, I assure you."

"... that he was intending to take me as his wife—or rather as his third wife, for he already had two, his official wife and another. She told me I'd probably have a baby in time, she explained things like that. But I was shocked of course, I felt I was too young and..."

Triumphant, Lady Digby jumped up, squeezing Alice's arm. "My poor dear child, so you risked all and ran away to save your virtue? Indeed your mother should be proud of you. There's no disgrace in that, for you did not succumb to the easier but immoral way. It was a thoroughly brave and right thing for you to do! Really, however cultured the Chinese may be in some respects, their system of concubinage is an abomination... just think what might have happened to you! Come, let me order more tea, it will cheer you up, dear."

While she summoned the servant, Alice realised that her half-truth had been a success as clearly the whole truth would not have been. So it was the "easier but immoral way" she had actually taken? Yet it seemed so natural and right at the time. "And the moral of that is, the Duchess said..." Alice grinned and had another good idea.

"You see, Lady Digby, that's why I'm so dreadfully worried about Frank. He's nearly sixteen, and among the Chinese, boys begin doing things much earlier, well... only men should do... And I'm afraid..."

"Oh dear me, that hadn't entered my mind. Something must indeed be done. He could become thoroughly corrupted for life in no time at all..." She frowned anxiously. "But it isn't an easy matter and there can be nothing in the way of an official expedition, as my husband has told you. Ah, the tea..." She poured fresh cups.

"I think my uncle has accepted that. He's determined to go to Changsha secretly himself though, but there's the expense—carts, guides, provisions. If he could just get a little financial help, unofficially of course, it would make such a difference. And how can we possibly just leave Frank there, in the circumstances?"

"Well, I'll speak to Sir Hugh, Alice. It might be possible... taking into account... your brother's youth... and so on..." She trailed vaguely into the hopeful but noncommittal phrases that had become her diplomatic second nature. People were always asking her to speak to Hugh on their behalf, and usually it was tiresome or boring. But this particular case was extraordinary and she really intended to do her best, as she told Alice on parting, adding, "Now remember my dear, I am your friend, and if you want any help or advice while you're in Peking just let me know."

It was a relief to emerge into the bustle of Legation Street, for Alice could not accustom herself to the silent, empty spaces in English homes where one did not speak loudly for fear of creating disturbance. Indeed her mother had already told her several times to lower her voice. "Shush, Alice, you sound like a market woman calling her wares," she had reproved, and Alice sighed, for in the Chu household there had always been people about shouting, laughing, arguing, scolding and one had to speak up in order to be heard at all.

At the corner she paused, reluctant to return to the solemn late-afternoon dullness of the Sturgeons' mission; instead she strolled aimlessly till she reached the street of the fanmakers near the Imperial City walls. Each open-fronted shop was hung with fans, the cheapest made of translucent paper, the most expensive of exquisitely coloured silks decorated with traditional designs—dragons among clouds, carp among lotus, lions among peonies, phoenixes among cherry-blossom. In the shop recesses, the makers and their families, surrounded by piles of bamboo struts and material, were cutting, folding, stitching. Alice lingered, enjoying the scene and the slight stir she evoked by inquiring about prices in a totally comprehensible fashion. Then she espied the fan she wanted —of creamy Hangchow silk, embroidered with clusters of jade-green buttons enclosed in black circles.

"But that is a gentleman's fan," the shopkeeper protested, "taken from the design intended for Mandarins of the third rank. But for you, how about this?" and he flourished a brilliant silken arc of gold and crimson butterflies.

She shook her head; it was too complicated to explain. "It's for my uncle, he's going on a long hot journey to the south," she extemporised.

"Ah so, very good... A southern journey you say? Where

is he going? Has he everything organised in the way of mules, carts, guides?"

"Not really, he's only just beginning."

The fanmaker grinned. "Your uncle needs David."

"David? A foreigner?"

"Not exactly, but not a Son of Han either. David's a Mongolian, the only one I know with a barbarian nickname. . . . Here, you lazy whelp," he shouted at his second son, "go and find David. Tell him there's a foreigner wanting to travel. Hurry now . . . Sit down and wait a while, he'll come soon."

Alice hesitated; even as she did so a stool was brought and she sat, accepting the course of events. "So, who is David?"

"He's a real character, everyone knows him. When he was a lad, still wet behind the ears, he went with his father—who was a camel driver—on a long journey to some godforsaken place with this barbarian Jesus-man called David."

"Oh I know, Abbé David. I saw his collection in the cathedral yesterday."

"That's him. Well, he taught the lad so much, all about animals, birds, plants and the like, that when he came back he was always boasting 'David told me this or that thing'. So *he* got called David and he's been a great traveller ever since, with his own carts and mules. Foreigners often hire him, they're always travelling about, stupid creatures. What's so green about the grass five hundred miles away? Still it's good for business, and David's the man for your uncle, I'm sure."

And so he was, as Alice knew the moment he appeared. He had twinkling eyes set deep in a pudgy weathered face; he was stocky, his legs bandy from straddling many steeds, but he walked with a springy vigorous stride as if no piece of ground could hold him for long. He had, he told Alice, been in more provinces of the Empire than any other transport-master and no one could equal him in the provision of strong pack-animals, reliable carts and knowledgeable guidance. For had he not made three journeys to the northern extremities of the Empire with that strange, clever, old Jesus-man? And had he not learned more from him than most common sons-of-dogs drivers learned in a lifetime? He sat four-square on a bale of cloth; whenever he grinned he showed rotting yellow teeth and whenever he moved a heavy smell of animal dung wafted from him. But the fanmaker was right—he was the man for the job and Alice promised to tell her uncle so that very evening.

It was nearly dark when she left the fanmakers, feeling inordinately pleased with herself, for, in one afternoon, she had enlisted in the cause of Frank's rescue the sympathies of the Minister's wife and the services of Peking's best transport-master. At the Mission gate, she took out the green and white fan, caressed its smooth silk, stowed it in her bag. It was not for Uncle Robert; one fine day she promised herself, she would present it to Frank, saying, "From one Uncut Jade to another."

Mrs Sturgeon met her at the door, looking anxious yet oddly excited. "Alice, at last—where have you been? Do Lady Digby's teas go on this late?"

"No, but we had a long talk and then I..."

"Well never mind, dear, it's just time for evening prayers and...there's a present waiting for you in the sitting-room. Just go straight in and find out."

Smiling, she opened the door and Alice walked in, wondering if her mother had remembered her approaching birthday. A man stood in the room's dusk. He was in shadow, but there was something about his stance that made her heart lurch in terror for a half-second...He was like...but he...

He stepped forward and she ran to him. "Oh, it's... William...William..."

"Alice my dear, dear little Alice," her elder brother caught her in his arms and held her tightly. They clung together and he kissed her warmly. "But let me look at you properly, dear. I hadn't realised how dark it has become." He went to light the lamp, turning away so she should not see his joyous emotion. The lamp glowed and they looked at each other steadily by its light.

"My, but you've changed, Alice. Mama told me you had— you're a lovely young lady now, though not a very tall one!" He patted her hand teasingly. "Oh Alice, I'm so very happy to see you and we've so much to tell each other, so many years to catch up on! I don't know where to begin, so let's work backwards, as it were. I'll tell you how I got here, it's rather funny."

He led her to a chair and she sat, quite weak with delight. He had grown to be a man very like her father—the same build, the same look of earnest reliability. "Oh William," she wiped her eyes, "how wonderful to see you. I thought you were still at sea. Mother said your ship was only just due."

"It was sheer luck. We had a marvellously calm voyage and reached Hong Kong ten days ahead of schedule. And there we were, all ready to disembark, Isabel and I, our baggage on the deck when..."

"Isabel—you must tell me about her. You are married, William. Isn't that strange to think of?"

"It's very nice, I can tell you." He laughed happily. "You'll like Isabel... but back to Hong Kong. There we stood, when a man from the Consulate came rushing up the gangplank calling my name and I thought something else dreadful had happened. But he said, 'This *is* your sister, isn't it, Mr Greenwood, read that!' and handed me a copy of the *China Mail* with the story of your return from Hunan. You must have seen it?"

"It wasn't quite accurate."

"But it was you. I could scarcely credit it. Anyway, I rushed off to see the Consul who'd been in touch with the Imperial Customs in Foochow and I was granted indefinite compassionate leave to come and see you and sort things out about Frank if possible. So I sailed straight on to Chefoo—leaving Isabel behind, because she's expecting our first child—isn't that splendid, though? But when I saw Mother she told me you and Uncle had just left, so I followed post-haste, and here I am!"

"That's so utterly marvellous! Now you'll come with us to get Frank, won't you?"

"You bet, it sounds most exciting. Uncle's been telling me. I arrived just after you left—for tea at the Legation, I hear? Well Miss Greenwood, you're a young lady of consequence now, everyone wants to know you!"

Alice laughed. "But I can't get used to being a young lady of consequence, having been a very low-ranking female barbarian for so long. I'll tell you all about it in time, but just now it's almost too much, and, in a funny way, your arrival is like a dream coming true."

"What do you mean, dear?"

"Well, when Frank and I first got to the Chus, we were kept inside the kitchen courtyard where we sat for hours looking at the farmgate because we had this silly dream that one day a whole regiment of British soldiers would come marching through to rescue us, led by you and Uncle Robert. We were only children then, remember, with no idea of the difficulties and distances. But now, you and Uncle and I are going to rescue Frank, so it's like a dream beginning to come true."

William frowned. "When I think of the terrible times

you've had... what you actually saw when, as you say, you were still children. No, it doesn't bear thinking about." He stared into the Mission's enclosed courtyard. "And how I wish I'd come to search for you, but we were told so definitely you'd been killed. After a while, Mother wrote to say she was coming home—but then the next thing was, she was marrying a Mr Edward Blake."

They looked at each other, then, by mutual consent, looked away. "I've not met him yet," Alice said neutrally.

"Neither have I. Apparently he can't be spared from his Mukden mission. But the babies are splendid, aren't they? Fancy, a little half-brother and sister, that was a real surprise for you, wasn't it? But talking of brothers, tell me about Frank. What's he like now?"

William listened eagerly as Alice diverted him with tales of Frank's prowess in archery and horsemanship. And, "No, really? Why, we'll have quite a little medieval soldier on our hands..." William was saying when Robert hurried in.

"Medieval soldier? No reference to me, I hope?"

William jumped up. "Certainly not, sir, you're a very modern nineteenth-century warrior. No, Alice was just telling me that Frank is a dab hand at bows and arrows!"

"Extraordinary, isn't it? We must get him away from there... Well, isn't this a grand surprise, Alice? But come— we wanted you to have a short time together, but now supper's ready and the good doctor is waiting for grace."

It was a merry meal. Alice sat next to William and they kept looking at each other in delighted amazement, while Robert only wished he could have raised a glass of wine to their reunion, but that would have offended his hosts. So much was there to say that the table was cleared before Alice remembered to tell them of David.

"And he's coming to see us early in the morning," she concluded. "I'm certain he's just the man we need, Uncle, and he's a really experienced traveller, which is rare, you know."

At precisely the appointed hour next morning David appeared, which was also rare, as Alice pointed out. And, by lunchtime, Robert was so impressed with the Mongolian's expertise in matters of carts, animals and provisions that he began congratulating himself on his ability to "spot a good man when he saw one", as if he, not Alice, had first judged David's worth. But she was too involved in the excitement of their preparations to be annoyed.

Later that day, she and Mrs Sturgeon's cook went to the market and bought sacks of dried pulses, rice and spices, and jars of preserves, beef extract, arrowroot and tins of meats from the German shop in Legation Street. Dr Sturgeon prepared a medical kit with plasters, castor oil, salves and tinctures, and Mrs Sturgeon packed everything in the large "itineration baskets" for carriage in the provision cart.

Then the blow fell. Late in the afternoon, Robert quietly disappeared and, when he returned, drew William aside and they went into the sitting-room. Watching them, Alice's heart sank, for she recognised the tight-drawn line of Robert's mouth as indicative of some obstinate and unpopular resolve. Summoned to the room in her turn, she found Robert at his most upright behind the writing-table, William hunched at the window.

"Ah Alice, there you are!" Robert's geniality was forced. "I thought you'd like to know, I've just returned from the Legation and with good news. First of all, a dispatch granting me four months' compassionate leave has just come, and then I must say you seem to have worked wonders, dear. The Minister has now offered me a sum of money to help defray the costs of the journey and given me a document saying that I'm a harmless traveller engaged in amateur scientific research. All unofficial of course, and if anything should go wrong, our people will deny any knowledge of my real business. But it's certainly a great help, and many thanks to you, for his change of heart seems mainly due to the chat you had with Lady Digby."

"But how splendid, Uncle! When I was shopping today I began worrying about the cost of things, but now we can just 'set off gladly, regardless of short or long'—as some poet wrote..." Her voice trailed uncertainly as Robert drew a deep breath.

"Now that's the other point I want to make—you say 'we' set off. Now listen, my dear, Sir Hugh has told me what you explained to his wife—why you felt and most properly too, that you had to get away from the Chus at all costs. It was an admirable course of action, Alice, and both William and I are very proud of you. *But* that story has most definitely convinced me of one thing—under no circumstances are you going back to Hunan with us. I absolutely forbid it. I owe it to your mother never to expose you again to the risk of falling into Chinese hands. Their ways are not our ways, especially with regard to women, as you yourself discovered. William

155

and I could defend ourselves to the death if necessary, but for you, an innocent and undefiled young lady, there could be even worse perils... So when we leave, I insist..."

Alice broke in with a harsh cry of anguished rage. "But that's not fair, it's not fair! I'm not frightened of the Chinese, I've lived among them for years. I know them, they won't do me any harm, you're talking nonsense... Oh Uncle, please let me go with you. I can speak the language and be your interpreter and..."

"Now hush, Alice, you mustn't shout in that unladylike way. I remember your mother reprimanding you about it..."

"But I don't want to be ladylike—I want to come with you. If I were a boy you'd take me."

"But you're not, Alice," William interposed gently. "That is just why you'd be in special danger, as Uncle has explained. I was horrified when I heard the fate you'd escaped from. Uncle is absolutely right, we cannot possibly allow you to return to a part of the country where concubinage is practised."

"It goes on all over China," Alice snorted furiously. "It's just their way, that's all."

"And a very immoral and deeply wrong way, as you surely understand."

Alice battened down into herself, trying to get a grip on her emotions. She looked at the two men, so kindly, yet so ignorant of what she was really like, of what had really happened. She had a reckless urge to break out entirely and shout at the top of her voice, "But I liked it, liked it! I was Lung-kuang's unofficial concubine for many a moon and I sometimes long more than anything to go back and spread my legs on that red quilt and feel his caress and the thrust of him..." Such a confused storm of intense desire, rage and frustration broke upon her that she shuddered and turned very pale, clenching her fists on the knowledge that she must never, never utter that dreadful truth.

"Come, Alice, don't take it so hard," Robert said briskly. "Enough is enough. And when Will and I leave you'll return to your mother in Chefoo. After all, it won't be much fun travelling across China in a mule-cart in the heat of summer. Surely you've done enough of that sort of thing?" He tried to pat her on the head, but she jumped away, bristling with rage like a cat.

"Well I haven't, so there! And it's just not fair! I know fifty times more than either of you about the country. I found David for you, I talked to Lady Digby and it's through me you're getting this help—and this is what I get for it! It's hateful...it's..."

Robert barked sternly, "Alice, that's quite enough of your shouting, I won't have it. I thought the Chinese taught their children good manners whatever else their failings, but you don't seem to have learned any."

"But I'm not Chinese, and I'm not a child...I'm, I'm...just me. Please, Will, let me go with you. Frank's my brother as well as yours, and he mayn't even leave unless he sees me."

"Oh nonsense, Alice, of course he will. No, Uncle is absolutely right, this isn't a job for a young lady."

"Then I'll have nothing more to do with it, I won't help you anymore, you can manage without me...oh, it's too bad!" And she fled to her bedroom where, burying her head in the pillow, she sobbed and sobbed.

The two men exchanged troubled looks and William sighed, "I feared she'd take it badly."

"Only a childish tantrum, she's very headstrong, as you see—which is another good reason for sending her back to your mother for some sound, home-based discipline." Robert began studying a map of Hopeh province, for he was a man who, when relationships became difficult, preferred the more measurable ups and downs of physical terrains. William sighed, vexed by his sister's behaviour. She had shown such courage, everyone had praised her, he had been so delighted to see her again—but now she must realise she was only a girl and he and Robert should take matters over. Only—there had been a wild and passionate recklessness in her outburst that disturbed him.

"I suppose she feels she doesn't quite belong anywhere, just at present?" he inquired of Robert's bent head. "And that must be upsetting for her?"

"She'll soon get over it and settle down."

But Alice had no intention of quickly getting over it. Refusing supper, she rolled about on her bed in paroxysms of frustration and anger, berating herself for having confided in Lady Digby, telling herself that she would never again trust anyone with even half the truth; cursing, in full-blooded native fashion, the injustice and stupidity of being forbidden to return to the place that only she knew and loved.

Eventually, after nightfall, utterly exhausted by her emotional turmoil, she lit a lamp, dug a few sugar-plums from her bag and, sucking them hungrily instead of supper, began to think. "Remember Confucius," she said aloud, "what did he have to say? There's always something apt..." She paused and chanted, "Confucius heard the cattle-boy singing. 'Is the water of the T'sang river clear? I can wash the tassel of my hat. Is it muddy? I can wash my feet.' Make the best of circumstances, clear or muddy, Alice, and turn them to advantage, so says Confucius."

She pondered a while longer, then took from the lining of her reticule the pearl necklace and put it under her pillow. Still desolate, but consoled by a new resolve, she slept.

"Is Alice still sulking?" Robert asked at breakfast the next morning, noticing her empty chair.

"I'm afraid she must be," Mrs Sturgeon replied. "I knocked on her door as I came down."

"Shall I call her again?" William asked.

"No, leave her a while longer," Robert ordered. "The more attention you pay to young ladies' tantrums, the longer they last, isn't that so, Mrs Sturgeon?"

"I'm sure you're right, Major. Alice has a sunny nature really, she'll shine again before you leave."

"And we must be off to the money-changers' bazaar straight-away," Robert urged his nephew. "They start dealing early, you say, Doctor?"

"Yes—best go now. Get as many silver sycees as possible or the brass cash, they're the only reliable currency outside the capital. They're awfully heavy and the silver must be broken up and sold en route, but there's no choice—don't be palmed off with paper notes, they may be counterfeits or useless in the provinces."

"All sounds the devil of a business... sorry, ma'am," he bobbed apologetically at his hostess, "but let's go to it, Will, my boy."

Though Robert and William reached the money-changers early, Alice had been there before them. She had exchanged the necklace for two bars of silver and a pile of local paper money which she had just thrown on the table in the shed at the animal-dealers' market where David transacted his business. He looked at the pile, then at Alice, weighing the two.

"It's a small amount of money," he conceded casually.

"It's quite a lot of money, count it if you like."

"All in due time, Miss. And what exactly do you want me to do to get this money?"

"You have to let me travel hidden in the provision cart for the first week of the journey to Hunan so that the two gentlemen don't know I'm there."

David's round face seldom registered the amount of surprise it now showed. "In the provision cart! But why?"

"Because they've refused at the last moment to take me with them just because I'm a girl, and they think it's dangerous...so utterly stupid, when I've already travelled hundreds of miles through the country all alone, and much further than either of them!"

David grinned. "You should see the women of Mongolia, they don't go boxed up in chairs or hobbled like the Chinese. They're broad-footed and wear loose trousers and gallop on horseback over the plains like the men."

Alice's eyes widened. "I should like to go and see them sometime...perhaps you'll take me one day, David?"

He grunted non-committally, picked up the bundle of notes and counted them with his dirty, splayed thumb. In spite of his boasts, he knew that the axle of the provision cart was in bad need of repair; there was enough here to buy a new one. He looked at her speculatively, "And what happens after this first week?"

"When we're so far away they can't possibly send me back, I'll come out of hiding." She said it confidently enough, though the very thought of her uncle's anger made her quail. But what was the alternative?

"And what about me? When they realise I've been hiding you away, they could dismiss me at once."

"What—out there in the interior with no other transport-master within hundreds of miles and you the owner of the carts and horses? What's more, my uncle is in a hurry, he has only four months' leave to get to Hunan and back. No, they'll have to accept the position and go on—taking me with them."

David grunted, counting the money again. "There's not enough. I'll have to bribe the drivers to keep quiet."

Experienced in such transactions, Alice took another bundle from her bag.

"There—that's all I have."

He counted again, and nodded. "Done—but where will you sleep?"

"In the cart. I've slept in many carts before now and travelled in many provinces. I'll tell you about it, if you keep our bargain."

"You've been to Hunan already?" She nodded. "Then I'll be interested to hear about it. I'll bring the carts to the Mission late this evening to load because we must leave at

159

dawn, there's always an early queue at the Tartar gate."

"I'll get in the provision cart then, so please leave a little space for me!"

"Alright—you're not very big, for a foreigner."

"And it is customary for the provision cart to travel well behind the passenger one, isn't it?"

"Yes, there should be no difficulty . . . You're a strange one, miss," he added, as they went across the outside enclosure. It was full of horses, camels, pack-asses, bullocks, mules, oxen and men from far-off parts—Tibetans, Manchurians, Koreans, Mongolians like David. The market had become one of the sights of Peking and foreign visitors often came to contemplate its picturesque disorder, stepping carefully between the piles of dung and holding handkerchiefs soaked in eau-de-cologne to their noses. But Alice, David noticed, paid no special regard to the scene, taking it for granted, like a native. Moreover, she knew how to bargain, she had not pressed him hard enough, but she was no novice.

"Why do you want to go back to Hunan then, miss?" he asked curiously.

"Ah, you'll find out in time. You have your money, I have my secret." She put her small fair hand into his broad dark one to seal the bargain and hurried away.

The rest of that day was tiresome for everyone. Returning to the Mission, Alice found it in uproar. A dispensary assistant had accidentally spilled some boiling water over the ulcerated leg of a baby boy. The baby was shrieking wildly, his mother was yelling vituperations at every barbarian swine in sight, and Mrs Sturgeon was trying to placate with salves and tea. Alice was called upon to help and by the time peace was restored, her non-appearance at breakfast was forgotten.

Robert and William were also too busy to pay her much heed. They had been to the money-changers and come away with sycees and several thousand cash—heavy brass coins with square holes in the middle, strung on straw twist and worth, Robert estimated, about a shilling a yard. They had also shopped in Legation Street for two hunting rifles, two pistols, two mosquito nets, Goldflake tobacco, Sporting & Military chocolate, six bottles of claret and twelve of French brandy—the last of which Robert, in deference to his hosts' teetotalism, stowed unobtrusively among the provisions.

Supper was tense and uncomfortable. The Sturgeons feared the morning's mishap had lost them several potential converts; Robert was fretful in case anything vital was forgotten; William was feeling guilty about leaving pregnant

Isabel; Alice was simply quiet. As the meal ended, David's two carts trundled into the yard and the men rushed off to supervise their loading. Showing no interest, Alice stared moodily at her plate. Why did it have to be like this? She hated deception—why could she not be out there, eagerly and openly involved?

"Come, Alice," Mrs Sturgeon said gently, "I know how you're feeling... But once they've left, you'll realise how right your uncle is. It's no easy journey for a woman, you know, and think how you can help your dear mother with her two little ones—that is where you can do most good now."

"But I don't want..."

"Ah, but Alice, what we think we want for ourselves is not always what God has in mind for us. And sometimes, for a Christian, 'I want' must give way to 'I ought'."

"I don't think I'm a very good Christian," Alice mumbled sulkily.

"I'm sure none of us can claim to be that, we can only try... So now, put on a brighter face for the menfolk when they come in."

Alice sighed, but gave an obedient half-smile when William poked his head round the door. "Come on out, Alice—everything is ready to go—and cheer up!" He chucked her under the chin.

Spring moonlight shone on the canopies of the carts in the yard. The larger contained straw pallets and personal luggage for the travellers, the smaller looked absolutely crammed with provisions—but, Alice thought anxiously, there had to be room for her as well. Not daring to inspect closely, she went to Robert, saying in a small voice, "Well goodbye, Uncle. I shan't get up at dawn to see you off. I wish you an easy journey and please bring Frank back safely, won't you?"

"Of course we will, if it's humanly possible. Now, that's better, give me a goodbye kiss, dear. Take good care of yourself and give my love to your mother, she'll have had my letter. Dr Sturgeon says there's a Mrs someone-or-other, American Presbyterian, going to Chefoo at the weekend, and you can travel with her for an escort."

"Yes, Uncle." She clung to William for a moment, longing to confess everything—if only he was not so respectable and strait-laced.

In her bedroom, Alice tiptoed about packing clothes in a calico bag and, in her reticule, her new copy of *Alice in Wonderland*, the poems of Li T'ai, the silk fan and, in its false lining, the Carr loot; when all was ready she threw back the shutters so the cool air might keep her wakeful. Looking out, she could see, outlined against the clear night sky, the distant circular white-marble three-storeyed Pavilion of Heaven, its domed roof, tiled in deep blue, shining silver-azure in the moonlight. Gradually the Celestial City subsided into a brief, dead-of-night silence. It was very beautiful and very mysterious, the hour when all the gods—of the mountains and oceans, of the thunder and wine, of the grass, the rain and the corn-stalks—came into their own and entered the dreams of the two million inhabitants who slumbered within its walls.

At last she heard the distant drum in the tower of the southern palace thudding the end of the night watch. She rose, stretching wearily, pinned on her pillow a letter addressed to the Sturgeons. In it she had written that she could not bear to remain in Peking now the men had left, so she had taken the early mail cart to Tientsin and would go from there to Chefoo. They would worry a little, say she should not have gone alone and then, in the harassed bustle of their days, forget about her.

She took her bags and crept outside. The provision cart creaked noisily as she clambered aboard and the Mission's gatekeeper stirred in his sleep. In the cart's centre, sacks had been stacked and covered with straw to make a cosy nest. She sank into it thankfully, covered herself with her cloak and dozed. Dimly she heard a cock crowing, then the tramp of boots and hooves, the sound of voices; there was a jerk as the shafts were lifted and the mules backed into them, one behind the other.

In her half-sleep Alice slipped back into her childhood, to that first frightening journey with Frank into nowhere. She hugged herself with excitement, feeling happy and secure by comparison, for now the voices outside belonged to Uncle Robert, William and David. There was the general bustle of departure, whips cracked, Dr Sturgeon called goodbye from the Mission doorway, and the carts trundled off in single file towards the Tartar gate and the plains of Hopeh. Before they had left the city, Alice, curled in her straw nest, was deeply asleep.

7

They travelled due south across the plains of Hopeh bright
with flowers of yellow rape and white bean. Larks sang, and
from the fields came the constant creak of water-wheels
turned by buffaloes with pink, fly-encrusted eyes. The main
street of each village was a smelly quagmire of broken flagstones and open drains and the inhabitants who curiously
watched their passing were mostly old crones, spotty children, mangy dogs, for the able-bodied were working in the
paddies. Often they had to fight for space along the narrow
tracks against advancing carts and barrows stacked with produce. On windy days, some of the latter sported cloth sails
that flapped cheerily and aided the coolies' pushing.

Usually Robert and William sat on a box behind David,
feeling increasingly thirsty as each day wore on. And "Why
the deuce didn't we bring beer with us?" Robert asked at
least twice every afternoon. Although David pushed the animals hard their progress was slow and "Why the deuce
doesn't any of this water run north and south?" Robert asked
each time they came to a tributary river carrying vessels
speedily from west to east. And "Why the deuce haven't the
Chinks learned to pep up their food with curry?" he asked
each evening, faced with yet another bowl of insipid boiled
millet or rice, with vegetables.

William replied soothingly to all those purely rhetorical questions, privately deciding that Indian army officers were not half as tough now as they must have been twenty years ago in the good old Mutiny days. Whether it was the absence of beer and curry or an over-sufficiency of millet, Robert could not say, but before long his indigestion was "really giving him jip", as he complained on the afternoon of the sixth day out.

"I'll have to give it a rest this evening, Will—arrowroot in warm water, that's all. Not that I'll be missing any gastronomic delights by the look of things." He looked glumly at the squalid village shack ahead which, David said, was to be their resting-place for the night.

Robert staggered stiffly down from the cart, a griping ache in his belly. The usual knot of villagers gathered at once, peppering him with questions he fortunately could not understand. One youngster plucked curiously at his trousers, then climbed up the cart-wheel to peer under the awning. Robert grabbed him by the scruff of the neck and threw him away so violently that he fell backwards, hitting his head on a stone. He jumped up and tore off, yelling, blood streaming from his head.

"Thieving little brat," Robert snarled in self-defence at David, who frowned.

"William, get me into a room quick, I think I'm feverish, this sun is going right through my skull." By the time William had secured a room off the inn-yard, dislodged a couple of specially audacious pigs and a goat, supplied his ailing uncle with arrowroot, the sun had gone down. He ate his supper inside the cart; every now and then a villager poked his head into the circle of his hurricane lamp, muttered unpleasantly and withdrew. Lord, what a country, William thought dismally. Would he ever take to it? If it had not been for his mother, he might have joined the Indian Service, which was much more civilised, according to Robert. But then he would not have been involved in this expedition. Of course, he would not have missed it, he told himself; though being a natural conservative, part of him yearned to be sitting, at that very moment, round a well-ordered supper table with Isabel in Foochow.

David pushed through the men still sullenly standing about. "Not good place, not like you." He put a hand behind his head in a chopping motion.

"You mean our heads off?" William asked alarmed, but David only mumbled vaguely, for his English was rudimentary. He handed William a note from Robert: "Not feeling good. Please bring brandy—in provision cart I think."

William, remembering the villagers' mood, slipped his pistol into his pocket before walking to the other cart which stood propped against the inn's back wall. As he parted the awning, a dim figure half-rose before him, and he stepped back, yelling, "Hey, David, here quick, there's a thief in the provision cart." He jerked out his pistol in panic, "Come out, you bastard! No messing about, I'm armed." He fired a shot in the air that resounded sharply through the quiet night.

"William—stop! Don't shoot for heaven's sake, it's me..."

He lowered the weapon in disbelief and grabbed the small figure who crouched on the cart floor. "You—Alice—what the devil are you doing here?"

"I've been riding behind all the time. Don't be angry, please, William. I just couldn't bear to be left behind..."

Alerted by the shot, David and some villagers rushed up. "Oh David," Alice ran to him. "I've been found out, but it's alright. I bribed him," she turned to her brother, "it wasn't his fault."

The men were growling angrily at William's pistol. "Tell him to put that away, they don't like it," David said to Alice.

She did so, then, turning to the men, explained in a loud voice. "It's alright. The shot was a mistake. I'm this man's sister—but he mistook me for a thief."

They sniggered. "His wench, I suppose she means," one sneered. "He'll be able to fire his little pistol in another direction tonight then." They shuffled off, disappointed by the anti-climax.

William drew himself up. "We shall have to send you back, Alice."

"But how could I possibly go back alone from here?" she mocked. "Oh, Will, let me come. I've done all this and risked so much. I was going to come out of hiding soon anyway, only I couldn't quite screw up the courage."

"Courage?" William chuckled, for her audacity amazed him. "Alright, Alice, I give in without a struggle, but heaven knows what Uncle will say. He's not feeling well, by the way, which is why I came to get him some brandy. You'd better take it to him—that will either kill or cure!"

Alice walked into Robert's room carrying in her shaking hand a large tumbler of cognac. He was dozing on the straw bed, hands locked across his grumbling stomach, and half-opened a weary eye. "Ah, Alice, you've... Alice? What the devil?" He sat upright.

William, apprehensive in the doorway, prepared for a tough fight, but, on that particular evening, Robert had little fight in him. And, as the brandy sent its cheering message round his empty insides and he heard how Alice had got there, his sternness evaporated and he suddenly burst out laughing, "By jove, Alice, you're a real chip off the Greenwood block I must say. Stubborn as they come, just like your poor father—or me, when I get a mad idea in my head!"

"So I can come with you now, Uncle?" Alice was demure.

"I suppose so. Damn it, what else can we do with her, Will? And certainly you'll be useful when it comes to getting a bit of sense out of this wretched country. Look at this quilt," he shook it in disgust, "crawling with vermin."

She giggled. "And this place is called the Inn of Irreproachable Purity, did you know?"

"What a farce! And these yokels keep peering in and shouting, they're the nastiest bunch we've met so far. I suppose this is the village of Unimaginable Harmony? I don't know what the hell's the matter with them."

"I'll try and find out," Alice said nonchalantly, though she did not much like the look of the group near the door. "I can't understand their dialect very well," she reported back, "but it's something about an injured child that's upset them."

"Oh lord, that..."

The trouble was, as David had tried to explain, that the parents of the boy Robert had struck down had had to buy some healing paste from the doctor. "And they all say you should pay for it, as it was your fault," Alice grinned. "You're a very rich barbarian and the paste cost as much as a fat duck in the market."

"Oh well, if that's all..." Robert counted out the requisite cash and gave it to the child's father who bowed sheepishly and slunk away.

"There—you see how useful I can be!" Alice plonked down triumphantly on a stool, reaching for the glass of brandy.

"Alice—that's mine, and don't start getting above yourself, miss." Robert grabbed it from her, and she hung her head theatrically.

"But, Uncle, it is my eighteenth birthday!"

William kissed her forehead. "Goodness—21st May, so it is. I used always to remember it, when I thought you were dead I mean, and feel so sad. But now you're so nicely alive and here—that surely deserves a little celebration, Robert?"

"Alright, pour another glass—it's certainly helping to settle my stomach."

William raised it. "Happy birthday, Alice, and may your next eighteen years be happier than your first!"

Finishing her ration of brandy, Alice went to collect her reticule from the provision cart. It was a balmy night; plain and village silent and small under the stars. She threw back her head and stared upwards, the starry pinpoints of light doing a little brandy-jig before her eyes, and the thought of the long excitement of life making her tingle with joy. To steady herself, she traced the shape of the Weaving Lady astride her stool who, Tamao used to say, rolled up her sleeves seven times a day as she wove the webs of the years. "I'm eighteen," she said aloud. "Aren't I lucky!"

It was late June before they reached the watery region north of Changsha which Alice and Frank had once assumed to be the end of China. The Tung T'ing lakes were dotted with the high mat-sails of fishing-boats, men on bamboo rafts were fishing with cormorants, and cunningly constructed wicker fish-traps floated among the reeds. Rice sprouted in delicate green, yellow rice-birds pecked at the tender shoots. The journey had been remarkably uneventful, for Robert's money and his official document, allied to David's travelling acumen and Alice's translating skill had seen them safely across every provincial border. But now Hunan was upon them and they grew quiet with apprehension at the temerity of their undertaking.

They decided it safest to reach Changsha just at dusk, and fortune favoured them for, on the evening they arrived, there was not only the usual motley of itinerant cobblers, fortune tellers, barbers, apothecaries, herb-, book- and pipe-sellers crowding into the gate, but merchants with strings of porters carrying wrapped packages containing larvae of the white-wax insect from the valleys of Kweichow bound for the glossy green trees of Kiangsi where they would multiply exceedingly. The watchmen pounded their gongs and shouted to announce the gate's imminent closure, and in the impatient surge forward past the guards, the Greenwoods' cart went through unnoticed.

Reluctantly, Robert and William remained in concealment during the day, for such a novelty as two foreigners in the city, however unobtrusively dressed, would soon be known to the authorities. So they stayed inside the big cart, which came to rest in the stinking yard of an inn called Flowery Happiness, while Alice, accompanied by David and wearing what William called her "peasant outfit", went to reconnoitre.

The first stage was easy, for every street vendor knew the whereabouts of the Chu residence. As they approached the stretch of mud-brick wall topped with blue and red tiles, the familiar sound of the Heavenly Clouds temple-bell quivered in the air and Alice's heart thumped with excited recognition. The main gate was open, the same lame gatekeeper was squatting there and gossiping; as they passed, she saw a servant scraping the flags with a broom, another carrying a bucket. She fought back a strong urge simply to run inside, calling "Younger Daughter—I'm back." Surely it would be alright? They would all understand and she and Frank could leave openly together. But what if they went for the magistrate instead? And what if Lung-kuang wanted her back in his bed? She shivered and David at her side whispered, "Don't be afraid, but don't stare so long."

"I'm not afraid," she replied crossly. "I'm just wondering what to do. I think we'd better sit in the cart till I see someone who doesn't actually belong to the house but can take a message in to Frank."

David positioned the cart where they could see the gate and Alice, having mastered the oriental art of biding time unworriedly, sat on its floor, sucking melon slices and contemplating the scene. The Chu residence was like a shell, she thought, which, when she had been inside, seemed impregnable, but which now seemed very vulnerable to change, to breakage. The people within were living as they had for generations—Lung-kuang and Hidden Glory worshipping regularly in the ancestral hall, Han-li ploughing through the wisdom of the ancient sages, Eldest Son's new wife sitting patiently in the women's courtyard, podded perhaps with the seeds of the future. For they still assumed the future would be like the past. But how could it be when the fringes of their Empire had already been over-run by barbarians who rode in iron-clad ships, sipped wine in grand hotels, pressed up the rivers with their foreign merchandise and Bibles? She thought of Lin Fu-wei on the *Mandalay;* was he too not a destroyer of all this in his fashion? The shell of the Chus would not be safe in his hands.

In the course of the day the gate opened several times as people passed inside, but Alice had already decided whom to approach. The scavenger's cart arrived at sunset as usual, and there was the familiar clattering as the day's detritus was thrown into it. When it left, Alice and David accosted the driver, drew him aside, dangled before his wide eyes a string of cash longer than he had seen for many a day. A message

168

was handed over and they returned to the inn.

For two long, hot, fly-ridden days they waited, leaving the inn only at night, eating food provided by the inn-keeper who had been told that two escaped convicts from another province lay ill inside the cart. A water-carrier brought the reply on the third day: "Dear Alice, it was luvly to here from you. I was serprised. Cum to the outside wall wair it gos threw the litel wood tonite. I will be there if I can. Luv frank." Robert and William were shocked by its illiteracy; if they needed further justification for this mad endeavour, here it was! The lad was nearly sixteen; he wrote like an eight-year-old.

An owl hooted from a nearby tree and Alice twitched nervously. They had been waiting for over three hours, spaced out along the boundary wall as it went through the little wood and they were stiff with tension and fatigue.

"Sssh! Here he comes..." she heard Robert's warning and looking up, saw a figure straddle the wall further down; as they ran towards it, another figure appeared beside him. "Wait, there's someone else!" Robert, fearing a trap, pushed them in the wall's shadow. But, as the two figures lowered a rope ladder to the ground, Alice broke cover.

"Frank—it is you, isn't it?"

"Yes, Uncut, it's me..." He sprang lightly down and she ran into his arms.

"Frank—oh, thank goodness, you're safe and well... Frank, this is Uncle Robert, you do remember him don't you? And William...."

They clapped each other's shoulders awkwardly, William amazed to see how his little brother had grown. "But who...?" Robert peered at the figure behind Frank.

"Why—it's Youngest Son... how lovely to see you," Alice slipped easily into Chinese greeting him with a bow. "But why are you here too?" For she was apprehensively aware that Frank had brought not the smallest bundle of possessions; but he had brought Han-li.

"Can he be trusted to keep quiet?" Robert asked tersely.

"Trusted? Of course—he's my pal, the youngest son. We hunt and ride together now and I'm better than him at archery, but he's cleverer at books than me."

"Well say goodbye then and we'll be off. It's damn risky to hang about. David, our driver, is waiting with a cart at the edge of the wood."

"Goodbye, but you've only just come! And there's so much to ask you..."

"But we're all going, Frank," Alice grabbed his arm tightly. "There'll be lots of time to talk once we're safely out of the city."

He shook her off. "No, I'm not going with you. I guessed you might want me to, which is why I told Han-li about it. I still want to stay here."

"You what?" Robert exclaimed. "Stay here? After we've come hundreds of miles and risked our very necks for you? Don't be mad, boy, of course you're coming with us."

Frank's voice took on that mulish tone that William recognised as an unhappy family trait. "But I'm not, I told Alice when she went away—whenever that was—that I didn't want to leave."

"You told...?" Robert spun on her. "But you never said..."

"Now listen please. I'm sorry, yes, it's true. Frank did refuse to leave with me at that time. But you said you would later, Frank, if I came back for you—you did. And now you've seen us all again and we've come so far for you and we want you back so much. It's for your own good, honestly Frank, I thought you'd have realised that by now!"

"Well it seems he hasn't." Robert contained the anger he knew was useless. "Now listen, Frank, since Alice has returned to Western civilisation she's begun to understand how much she needs to learn, how much she's been missing. Isn't that so, Alice?"

"Yes... yes... in a way. But there's another thing, Frank, Mother is alive and well."

"Mother?" He looked up from his obstinate contemplation of the ground.

"Yes—she's remarried and we have a new little brother and sister, twins called Sunny and Adam. Frank, how could we possibly return to Mother and tell her you didn't want to see her anymore... She's just aching for you."

He stood nonplussed. "I've forgotten what she looks like," he muttered sullenly. "And it's more fun here."

For a mild-tempered man, William then became extraordinarily angry, shaking his brother's shoulders violently. "Fun?—Is that all you think about in life? Well, I'll tell you something, laddie, life's about a lot of other things, like duty to one's family and one's country and learning to grow up a decent man able to earn your own living and hold your head up in the world! And you won't do that riding around on horses and playing bows and arrows."

Frank glared back defiantly. "It's not like that here—you

know nothing about it. And why should I come away now, just to please you? You all forgot about me and Alice for years and years."

"But, Frank, they were told we were dead. It wasn't their fault."

Han-li, uncomprehending, plucked Frank's sleeve. "Whatever's the matter? Don't they like you anymore?"

"They want me to go away with them, and leave you— but I won't."

Alice, understanding, gave a teary sniff. "It'll just about break Mother's heart, Frank, and mine..."

There was a deadlocked pause; into it fell the sound of a watchtower gong reminding them all that dawn was not far off. Frank grabbed Han-li's arm and backed away, muttering, "Perhaps I'll come back myself—later."

"You can't go just like that, you can't," Alice restrained him. "Tell me about the family, how are they? Eldest Daughter, Younger Daughter—did the Honourable ask for me when he returned? Did they miss me?"

"Not for long," Frank said cruelly, again making to leave. Suddenly with one accord, Robert and William fell on him, throwing him to the ground. Frank yelled and fought back, arms flailing. Then there came the sound of someone rushing through the wood.

"By God, someone's heard us—shut up, Frank, you silly sod!" William cuffed him across the mouth.

"Go and raise the alarm, Han-li," Frank called in Chinese, just as David pounded up.

"Whatever's happened?" He stared in bewilderment.

"Help us hold him—he won't come," William panted, as Frank, well versed in arts of self-defence, lunged fiercely upward, knocking Robert off-balance and bringing William to his knees.

"Oh, oh, David—help!" Alice rushed forward, then realised that Han-li had gone. "David—quick, we must stop him!" They raced after him and David grabbed the lowest rung of the ladder just as Han-li was about to pull it up after him. He teetered on the wall's top, it was too high to jump down the other side. "Han-li, come back down please," Alice called desperately. Han-li jerked the ladder; David held on firmly; he came slowly down.

"Youngest Brother," she caught his hands, "we were always friends, weren't we?"

"But you went away."

"I had to, Han-li. I didn't entirely want to, but I had to

return to my own people, my own family. You could never leave your own people forever, could you? I'd always have been an inferior barbarian among you, and it's the same with Frank—only he's so young and stubborn and never thinks beyond the end of his nose, does he? But you do, Han-li. You're much more sensible and deep down you know it would be better if Frank came back with us. We can all meet again later—when he's grown up and sensible."

The sounds of the scuffle receded and Alice saw that Robert and William were dragging Frank away. "See—he's got to go, and please, please, don't betray us. We might be thrown in jail if we're discovered. Pretend you know nothing—and one day you might decide to come and see the world and find us. There's so many modern, different things going on—things you never dream of here. I wish I'd time to tell you. This is such a small pond, Han-li, and Frank and I weren't born in it. You do understand?"

Han-li shuffled his feet; he did understand, though he did not much want to.

"Promise me you'll keep quiet and we'll be forever in your debt, me and Frank too."

"Alright, Uncut Jade, I won't tell. Frank's gone and I suppose his first duty is to his family, as mine is . . ."

David said, "Someone's coming back for us, miss. Let him go now, or there'll be more fuss." He stood away from the ladder and Han-li shinned up.

Alice called, "How is your Honourable Father?"

"Another son is just born. By the new woman he has. He's pleased, more sons are always good."

"Yes . . . I'm glad. And Han-li," she quoted at his departing shape, "'May you ever perpetuate the fragrance of books in your ancestral home'."

Robert panted up. "He got away?"

"We let him go, he's promised not to betray us."

"Huh, a typical Chink promise, I suppose. You believe him?"

"Yes I do. You think all Chinese are thieves and liars just because you've never met the well brought-up honourable ones!"

Robert ignored her outburst, saying hastily, "Well, there's nothing to do now but get out of this infernal city at the double. The east gate opens at dawn and we must be there."

Early sun glinted on the full buckets of the water-carriers and the piles of lake trout bound for the morning market. Alice, in her peasant's garb, sat beside David; in the cart

172

behind them, Robert, William and Frank lay hidden under sacks—it having been made clear to the last that, if he raised the alarm, all their lives might be forfeit. So he was silent, half hoping for discovery, but also excited at the prospect of the unknown world beyond. It might be good fun; he was not going to kick against the pricks.

Above the gate hung cages containing the still-dripping heads of three recently executed bandits; their cart passed below unmolested. Within a few miles the city's clatter fell away and the changeless country sounds took over—honk of wild duck, trundles of wheels, insects humming over the paddie-mud. Alice leaned against the cart frame, sleepy after the night's activity. She smiled at William as he came to sit beside her. "You know I sometimes feel I've passed more of my life so far jolting along in carts than doing any other single thing! Don't look so anxious—I'm positive Han-li won't raise the alarm, and Frank will soon settle down and make the best of things—he always falls on his feet!"

"Stupid young dolt! What gratitude for you—after we've come all this way. He doesn't deserve to fall on his feet!"

"But he will, he's the type, so there's no point in having another row."

"I shan't—but that laddie's got a lot to learn."

And just how much was brought home to them some time later, when they halted for what Robert called a "convenience stop".

"Alice, Frank—get down and stretch your legs!" Robert hustled them out. Alice breathed the fresh air gratefully; Frank leaned against the cart shafts.

"Where are you taking me?" he asked sulkily. Alice looked at him critically. He had grown beefier since she had last seen him and had a certain swagger she had not noticed in him before, though she had seen it often enough in Han-fei and his cronies.

"We're all going to Shanghai," Robert said crisply. "By the quickest route—north-east across the Chiuling Shan mountains and reaching the Yangtze at Chiuchiang."

Frank yawned with elaborate lack of interest, untied the cord holding up his trousers, let them drop and began urinating against the cart-wheel. William pounced.

"Frank—what the blazes d'you think you're doing—right here in front of a lady?"

"Who—Alice? She's seen men do it hundreds of times."

"Oh Frank, Frank," Alice burst into embarrassed laughter. "You mustn't really, not like that, not now."

Frank reached for his trousers. "Don't those garments even have flies?" Robert inquired with distaste.

"No, they don't. So where do you all do it then?"

"We go out of sight—at least I do," and Alice giggled. But Robert did not see the joke for he was busy explaining that, in his view too, Frank, had much to learn.

What Frank came to believe was that he could do nothing right. His social manners were boorish, his posture slovenly and his clothes filthy, Robert informed him; his spelling, William added, was at kindergarten level, his spoken English sloppy, his outlook selfish and frivolous. And all in all, Frank decided on the fourth day out, he would have sneaked away and headed back to Changsha, if it had not been for Alice. But she did not chide him with his shortcomings, for she understood them too well, and he could not resist her pleading when she talked about Mother and the new babies and the exciting things going on in what she called "the new China".

"I've discovered that the Chus are very old-fashioned in some ways," she told him. "And a lot of Chinese in the Treaty Ports don't regard foreigners with the ignorant contempt they do. That's what I told Han-li—to come out in the world and see for himself. I bet he's partly envying you, for Hunan really is a backwater, dear."

She could be very persuasive when she chose and after she had left, he had missed her more than he had cared to admit. He had felt very lonely and forgotten and, in self-defence, had begun to imitate Han-fei's bullying swagger. But if he went too far, he was simply mocked. "Look at the barbarian runt!" Han-fei had shouted one afternoon at the archery butts. "Ordering my servant around as if he were a Son of Han—pick up the arrows yourself, you streak of dog's piss!"

At the time, Frank had tried to ignore such insults, but now, sprawled on a grass verge near the big cart, waiting for William and David to return from the nearby village, he reminded himself that what he had left behind was not entirely sweet. It was pleasant to have Alice's company again, he thought, as he spotted her coming up the bank towards him. She wore her sun-faded tunic, straw hat, open sandals. "You look just like a peasant!" he called in parody of Robert's crispest bark. She grinned, putting a finger to her lips, for, as he then saw, Robert was toiling behind. Apparently he had not heard, for he threw himself on the grass, took off his hat to mop his forehead.

"Phew—it's hot. Oh to reach the Yangtze. We bought some duck eggs back there. The others aren't back yet?"

"No, David's getting that wobbly wheel repaired on the other cart, it might take some time."

Robert looked quizzically at his nephew. "Feeling better about things, young Frank? We are your family you know, not a bunch of kidnappers."

"I suppose so," he muttered evasively. "Come on, Alice—let's see if we can get some peaches, there are orchards full around here."

As they walked off, Robert thought despairingly that they looked exactly like a couple of young peasants, but there was nothing to be done about it just then, so he put his head down on his hat and dozed.

"Frank, there's something I've wanted to say to you, and now we're alone...but it's a bit difficult, so wait and listen to me." He did so, looking down into her tanned face framed by the coolie hat.

"When I was turned out by Eldest Brother, did you ever find out exactly why?"

He coloured. "Not really, but I guessed later. It was because of the Honourable, wasn't it?"

"Yes, but I couldn't explain it to you."

"No, I understand. But after you left I was allowed to go out more, riding in the hills with the other lads, I suppose they knew I wouldn't run away. And after hunting, we'd go to one of those tea-houses in the plum groves, you know?"

She frowned, puzzled, "No—I don't know."

"Well they didn't just serve tea, there were pretty girls there too—for us. So I learned a lot I didn't know before, about what goes on—between girls and men, I mean."

"Did you enjoy it?" she asked anxiously.

He studied his knuckles, "Yes, mostly...It was exciting and fun. But the girls often teased me, about the yellow hair on my body—and...other things. They were quite shameless. So then I put two and two together, about you and the Honourable. It must have been dreadful for you?"

"Oh...yes and no," she shrugged drearily; a conundrum she could not solve. "But the point is, Frank, that I've not told anyone what really happened to me. And you mustn't either. Do you understand? The English look at these things so differently from the Chinese—you'll find out. But promise you'll keep quiet?"

"Of course, Sis, you can count on me."

"And if I were you, I shouldn't mention the tea-houses in

the plum groves either!" They laughed conspiratorially and continued on their way to the peach orchards.

Supper that evening was merry and satisfying, with eggs, rice, peppers and pork ribs cooked over an open fire, and juicy peaches to follow. Afterwards, they sat on the bank in the warm night air; fireflies darted green and gold across the ditch below and night-jars called in the bamboo groves. Seated a little apart, Alice watched the men's faces lit by the embers of the fire. William had been talking about his father-in-law who was a merchant in Singapore, and held very strong views on the subject of the British Empire, and this prompted Robert to describe his experiences of the Perak War in Malaya the previous year.

"But do you think the British might come marching into this country like that?" Alice asked.

"Very different kettle of fish—but it could happen, if the Russians or French started moving in here."

"That's not what you said to Lin, the young man on the *Mandalay*. You assured him the British hadn't the slightest intention of ever interfering in Chinese affairs."

"Not wise to tell these ambitious young Asiatics too much, Alice. There's a similar breed growing up in India, heads stuffed with clever revolutionary ideas from France, and they could be dangerous one day."

"But I thought you liked Lin?"

"He seemed a nice enough fellow, but that's got nothing to do with it."

"To do with telling him the truth?"

William rose, kicking apart the last embers of the fire. "That's enough, Alice, you don't understand anything about these international affairs. And it's time we all turned in. There's young Frank fallen asleep with all this political chat."

They shook him awake, went off to urinate at discreet distances, washed in the communal bucket, then all slept soundly in quilts on the cart floors.

A few days later they reached Chiuchiang from where they were going to Shanghai by river, leaving David to return to Peking with the carts. They had come to rely on his cheery resourcefulness and: "We'll miss you," said Alice, as they stood on the quayside where the muddy Yangtze rolled towards the distant China Sea. And Robert slapped him heartily on the shoulder. "Been a great pleasure, David, and I'll give you a written recommendation for any other barbarian madman wanting to go through the interior in a cart. Translate that for me, Alice."

She did so and a broad grin cracked his face. "He says it's the best way of really seeing the country. And remember," she turned back to him, "some day when I'm rich I'll pay you to take me to your Mongolia where the women wear trousers and ride freely over the plains."

He bowed. "It's a bargain, young lady. I shall be at your service."

They shook hands on that before loading the baggage aboard the *Red Pearl* junk. Frank had never seen so many sorts of boats and people as he did from the junk's high poop during the week's journey to Shanghai. As he watched the traffic of the great river, he dreamed of spending his days sailing it, bargaining for cargo, shouting at the tow-coolies, commanding from the bridge—a respected junk-master whom nobody would dare call a barbarian dog. Near Shanghai, they passed go-downs proudly emblazoned with the names of successful European merchants—Jardine & Matheson, Guthries, Dent & Co—and his dreams enlarged. Why the master of only one junk? Why not own a whole fleet? Greenwood & Co ships would be famed for their speed and size and Alice would help him, and Mother too; only she was married to someone else.

Mother. "Your mother tells me in her letter that she's had to return to Mukden, Frank," Robert said hesitantly. They were in the hall of Shanghai's Church Missionary Society where Frank and Alice were staying, while he and William put up at the Grand. "She sends you this letter with much love."

Frank fumbled it; "I can't read it very well."

"Oh dear, of course, here... She writes: 'My very dearest Frank, The thought that you, my long-lost son whom God has returned to me will read this letter fills me to overflowing with gratitude and happiness. How I wish, my dearest child, that I could be with you at this moment. But as you must know, I have other duties too and my presence is urgently required in Mukden where your stepfather, Mr Blake, labours alone. I've asked Uncle Robert to arrange for Alice to join me in Mukden for her help there is badly needed. I long to see you come with her, but I'm trusting Uncle to decide the best course for you. Once the future is clearer, we will I know have a happy reunion somewhere. Please write, my dearest boy and tell me how you are. I cannot think of you as sixteen, and no longer my curly-haired little treasure whose favourite toy was Dobbin. Do you remember, dear? This comes with much love to you and Alice from your loving Mama.'"

Frank turned away. "Dobbin was the old wooden horse, wasn't he? Fancy her remembering that..."

Robert looked at him sympathetically; having brought his nephew all these hundreds of miles, it was pretty cool of Eliza not to be here. But that was the way with women; new husbands, new loyalties. And it put more of a burden on him, Robert thought later that evening as he enjoyed the last pipe of the day on the balcony of his hotel room. Obviously this Edward Blake fellow had no interest whatsoever in his wife's long-lost children, and William, about to start his own family, had no money to spare for them. It was not so important for Alice, she was just a girl and picked things up quickly anyway. But his nephew—unlettered, uncouth, raw-boned—he needed at least two years' good hard study and discipline if he was to make anything of himself. It was lucky for Frank, Robert told himself, that he had an uncle with a deep sense of family loyalty who had put a few coppers by. A growing sense of virtue suffused him as the half-formulated plan he had been considering for several days became a certainty. There was no alternative—he must write to Elsie and put her off again.

No one knew about Elsie, the daughter of a bookseller in Sheringham, Norfolk. Robert had been sixteen when he first met her—a shy, studious young lady fond of quoting Mr Shelley's poetry. Two years later, when on holiday at Sheringham, he had walked with her along the promenade one summer afternoon and told her he wanted her to be his wife. She had been wearing a brown linen dress with little blue flowers on it, a straw hat, and faded lemon-yellow gloves that did not match the dress very well. He had kissed her cheek in the shelter of the sea-wall and told her he was going into the Army and might be away for years, but one day he would return and marry her. He had promised her faithfully; Elsie had believed him and waited.

He had sent for her to come out to India once, after he had been commissioned, but her father was dying at the time. He continued to visit her in Sheringham on his infrequent leaves. As time went by, her dresses became plainer, her gloves less of a match; she spent years nursing her mother till she died too. But she and Robert continued to correspond and now the date of their union was definitely fixed for two years ahead, when he was to resign from the Army and go Home... Definitely that is, till this business of young Frank blew up.

Looking along the Shanghai Bund—the rickshaws, carts,

sedan chairs with their bobbing lanterns, the stir and bustle of it all—he pondered Elsie and Sheringham. She had always been a quiet woman living in a quiet place and sometimes such peace seemed infinitely desirable; at others it seemed rather—well, dull. After all, as this recent expedition had proved, he was still a man of considerable resource and stamina—qualities that would find little outlet in Sheringham. But if he were to resign in five years instead of two, he could afford to do something for young Frank now and have more behind him when he eventually went Home and married. Dear old Elsie—she would understand of course; she always had. He knocked his pipe on the balcony rail, went inside, drew a sheet of hotel stationery from the writing-desk: "My dear Elsie . . ." he began.

As Robert often said of himself, he was not one to shilly-shally once his mind was made up, and the very next morning he acquainted the family with his plan to send Frank to Bishop Hart's boys' college in Shanghai for two years at his expense. William was delighted and grateful; Frank reluctantly acquiescent; Alice went very quiet, then said, "You're very lucky, Frank. I wish I had your chance."

"Oh you'll be alright, Alice," Robert said quickly. "As you know your stepfather's a former schoolmaster and he's offered to help you catch up with your studies once you've settled in Mukden."

Alice's mouth snapped shut and the pause was broken by Robert's conciliatory, "Well Frank, get yourself smartened up, the Consul wants to see you this afternoon to hear about Hunan. And probably there'll be a reporter from the *Shanghai Mercury* on your doorstep next."

"Won't he want to see me too?" Alice asked petulantly.

"You're a bit too fond of the limelight, aren't you, miss?" William reproved.

"But why shouldn't I be included? After all, I made the journey from Changsha alone, I didn't wait for people to rescue me."

Frank scowled. "You know that isn't fair. I didn't want to leave when you did. I wasn't scared . . ."

Alice was saved from his blunder by Robert's reminder that what mattered was not past mistakes but their present happy reunion. "And I've been thinking," he contined, "it might be a very long time before we're all together again like this, and I think we should mark the occasion with a short holiday before we separate. My ship doesn't sail for two weeks—how about a few days on a houseboat to the lakes

179

beyond the Sung-kiang hills? Treat on me of course. We can hire a boat in a jiffy, I'm told, and the shooting is excellent just now—the wild fowl gathering to fly south for the winter." The idea was carried unanimously, and Robert went off to make arrangements.

Their houseboat was moored along one of the artificial canals that linked the lakes together; the shimmering flatness of the paddies on either side was broken only by the humped backs of the peasant women harvesting rice. Reclining in a deck chair, Alice watched dragonflies and butterflies buzzing about the banks, for, having no love of firearms, she had elected to remain on board while the men went shooting over the nearby marshes. Through half-closed lids she saw the women moving slowly through the mud, pausing only to shift the weight of their baskets or brush flies from their eyes. Then a swish of water announced the approach of another house-boat, more imposing than the Greenwoods' comparatively humble craft. A blonde English girl was leaning over the rail and, as they edged past, called along the deck, "Oh Mother do come and look at these peasant hats—they're the biggest I've seen yet! Can't we stop while I do a sketch?"

"You'll see thousands like that Evelyn, so please don't fuss now." Mother's irritated reply reached Alice as they glided out of earshot.

She smiled wryly—Evelyn looked about her own age, just off a steamer from Southampton probably and China like a quaint picture-book to her. Was it a pity that she herself could never see China like that? She knew only too well about the flies, the mud, the heavy baskets and the sweat that gathered under the picturesque hats. How stupidly the world seemed to be arranged! Until recently, her life too had been a continuous toil as it was for these peasants. But now, as a civilised young lady, no one required more of her than to sit in a deck chair, sip lemonade and sketch, perhaps, like Eve-lyn. She shifted and sighed; the chair creaked as she moved.

"Anyone at home?" a voice called from the gangplank and a young man appeared, dressed in the customary white ducks of the English sportsman. He halted, smiling pleasantly. "Oh, I do beg your pardon. Am I on the wrong boat? I'm looking for a Major Greenwood."

"He's my uncle," Alice sat upright, "but he's off shooting."

"Ah—then I'll explain. I met him on the marshes earlier, with his nephews . . ."

"They're my brothers."

"Well that younger brother of yours is a superb marks-man—what an eye! I just had tell him so and we began chatting. Then they invited me back for a drink before supper as I'm travelling alone—just upriver from you."

"In that case, please sit down. They're due back any time."

"You're sure? I'm obviously too early..." He hesitated, then held out his hand, "I'm Charles Grant."

"I'm Alice Greenwood. Do have some lemonade and take a seat."

He did so. "Phew—it was hot on those marshes—and the mosquitoes. You know, I was thinking as I came along—are you *the* Greenwoods?"

She smiled. "I like to think so. But what do you mean exactly?"

"The brother and sister who spent years in captivity in the interior and have just returned. I read the story in the *Mercury* yesterday."

"Yes—that's Frank and me."

"But how exciting, I thought the names were familiar. Now please tell me all about it. No one I've met in the Treaty Ports so far seems to know much about the real country—or even to care."

"You've not been here long then?"

"A few weeks only, and this is my little holiday before returning to India. I came to look at new trading opportunities in Shanghai and perhaps upriver...it's bound to open up more soon. So anyone who's been in the interior interests me—especially when it's an adventurous young lady like yourself."

"Well..." Alice paused teasingly, liking his winning enthu-siasm, "it's a big subject, Mr Grant. Where shall I start?"

"You're right, I should get my thoughts in order first, as my father used to say."

Boots tramped up the gangplank and Frank appeared, triumphantly waving a brace of plump teal. "Look at these—and the boys are loaded with ducks."

"Not to mention every pin-tailed snipe that didn't take off for India yesterday!" Robert said behind him. "We'll all grow feathers eating this lot—ah, there you are, Mr Grant. You found us then?"

"Yes, I fear I'm a duffer in the field compared to you two, so I gave up—and met your charming niece instead."

Robert clapped his hands. "Boy, bring more lemonade, beer, glasses."

They settled down with drinks; flocks of still-unscathed

wild fowl wheeled against the sunset over the marshes. While Frank explained why Chinese archery practice had made him such a good marksman and Robert warned that the only real hazard of shooting in China was the stupid propensity of the natives to jump out of ditches without warning and get in the way of the occasional bullet, Alice considered their guest. She liked his crinkly smile, the timbre of his voice; she wondered why he was travelling alone.

"Come along with us tomorrow if you like, Mr Grant," Robert was saying, "and pick up a few tips from young Frank to stun the locals when you get back. You're an India man like me, didn't you say?"

"Not entirely—but I've Anglo-Indian relatives going back three generations. The country's become a family tradition you might say, which is perhaps why I'd like to break away to somewhere else. So I'm looking for trading prospects up the Yangtze, as I was telling Miss Greenwood."

"Risky business, trading with these yellow men," Robert shook his head, "never know where you stand with them."

"Inscrutable, hey, Uncle?" William teased.

"Devious and dishonest—think of the trouble we had with bribes on the journey."

"Oh come, Major, you sound like my father—he talks as if every Indian were a paragon of integrity by comparison. All Eastern peoples have different standards from ours in money matters."

"Maybe," Robert was stubborn, "but you still know the Indian, even when he's robbing you blind . . . So your father's not keen on your starting up here then?"

"No, I can't say he is. He and George, my brother-in-law, have been in the I.C.S. for years, and my wife's family too. So they all expect me to follow in the jolly old footsteps, but I'm not really a desk man."

"And your wife, Mr. Grant? What does she think? Isn't she here with you?"

"Not yet. Maria's pregnant again and as this is just an exploratory trip, she decided to stay in Madras. I'm not sure she wants to move, but I believe China offers so many more opportunities—it's challenging in a way that India isn't anymore."

"But it's all very uncertain here," William warned him. "I'm about to start in the Maritime Customs Service and the whole question of duties and tariffs isn't yet fixed. What's more, the currency is in a dreadful mess—Hankow taels with different values to Shanghai ones, and that sort of thing is hardly conducive to business. It'll be years before we get things properly organised and controlled. What's more, the Chinese themselves are getting a grip on the upriver trade, I'm told—chartering their own steamers and even going into marine insurance!"

Grant laughed. "You could say they're entitled to! But anyway, who wants certainty all the time, Mr Greenwood?"

Alice clapped her hands delightedly. "Mr Grant, I so agree with you—Uncle, supper is ready. I'm sure there's ample for Mr Grant, if he'd like to stay?"

He accepted readily, and as the meal began, Robert continued, "Now yours is a typical young man's reaction, if I may say so, Mr Grant. But there's much to be said for certainty—for institutions like law courts, public works departments and so on that we've set up in India. For example, I shudder to think what might have happened to us if we'd been discovered in Hunan. Hauled up before some benighted oriental magistrate, chop, chop, heads off, say no more about it, maybe. Things like that can't happen in India . . . And take the roads here, scandalous! Your main route south from Peking is worse than a Himalayan hill-track in places. How can you move goods over such terrain?"

"I bet that would be a way to make a fortune, wouldn't it, Uncle?" Frank burst in excitedly. "Build some decent roads and railways, like in India?"

"It might be, boy, depends how you go about it."

"Well whatever you others say about risks and difficulties, I entirely agree with Mr Grant," Alice announced, "China is much more exciting than stuffy old India."

Robert turned on her, "Please, Alice, you know nothing about it, and don't forget that 'stuffy old India' is the mainstay of the British Empire, and where would we all be without that?"

"You're right there, Major," their visitor smiled, "but that still leaves me plenty of room to experiment elsewhere."

Robert signalled the boy to remove the plates. "Well, Mr Grant, if your own father can't dissuade you from China, I don't suppose I shall. And you may make a go of it—Will here is about to try and I imagine Frank will too, once he's got some education behind him."

"I'd like to build railways," Frank declared. "I'm going to be a railway millionaire with a stable of racehorses in Shanghai and a fleet of trading ships as well!"

Alice wandered to the boat-rail, all this having little to do with her. If only, she thought bitterly, her relatives would evince one scrap of interest in what *her* future held. But they did not; nor did this handsome, married, stranger who was planning his own future in a way she could not possibly do. The boy had lit the lanterns, the men were smoking and sipping a brandy nightcap; there was no point in sulking, she told herself grimly, and rejoined them with a smile. "I think I'll go to my cabin, I'm rather sleepy. So goodnight everyone—and, Mr Grant, don't let my uncle change your mind about China!"

Charles sprang up. "Indeed he won't. And thank you for making me so welcome. It's rather wearisome travelling alone and talking pidgin the whole time."

"Then you must join us again tomorrow. We can promise you some more truly British conversation, I'm sure."

Charles Grant frequently returned to the Greenwood boat during the remainder of the holiday—days that Alice long remembered as among the least troubled of her life. For the boat was a private, serene world, and, as they moved along the water, she forgot the difficulties of both past and future. Further west, the countryside became more beautiful, with ranges of low hills covered with teabushes, larches and flowering tallow trees; in the valleys nestled thatched huts and Buddhist monasteries. She woke each morning to hear the boys sluicing the decks, and the voice of a tow-coolie nicknamed Beancurd chanting wild songs from his native province of Szechuan. After much shouting and banging about, the vessel got underway before breakfast, while the cook fried eggs over the kerosene stove. In mid-morning they tied up in a backwater and while the men went off with satchels of sandwiches and guns, Alice and the cook strolled to nearby villages for provisions. At sunset, they forgathered with Charles Grant as they had on the first evening, and talked about the day's bag, the strange ways of the East, the vagaries of British politics.

But on the last evening Charles did not come to supper for he was packing up his own boat, and the Greenwoods ate quietly, cast down by the shadow of imminent partings.

"Come on now, you boys, jimp to it!" Robert tried to dispel the gloom as the meal ended. "We've got to oil all the guns and pack the fishing gear—can't trust the coolies with that."

"Can I help?" Alice asked.

"No, I don't think so—tell you what, can you get it across to the cook that we must leave at dawn for Shanghai, dawn mind you, so they ought to start packing up now."

She nodded listlessly, knowing that the cook would be

smoking his nightly opium, that tomorrow he would dismantle his entire *batterie de cuisine* in ten minutes, that nothing would persuade him to do it sooner. Instead, she went on deck. A low mist hung over the paddies, not dense enough to conceal the beauty of the starlit night beyond. She pulled her cloak round her and, on impulse, donned one of the coolie hats hanging near the gangplank. She walked down and along the tow-path, and soon the only sounds were lapping water and frogs croaking in the ditches. A coolie with an ox-halter slung across his back padded past. "Misty night," he said. "Yes, quite thick." She smiled gleefully to herself; she was still of the country. Then she heard heavier feet and a large shape loomed out of the mist. She bent her back as he approached and pushed rudely past her on the narrow track. She turned: "Good evening, Charles." He stopped, peered back, holding up his lantern.

"Good heavens, it's not you, Alice? Whatever are you doing out here?"

"Just taking an evening stroll."

"But all alone and dressed up like that!"

She smiled. "I'm not dressed up, I just borrowed a coolie hat because of the damp—I always think they rather suit me!"

So do I, he thought, looking into her upturned face, framed by the simple straw.

"I'm not sure your uncle would approve."

"He doesn't know. They're packing up the gear and not to be disturbed—very important job, like moving a regiment!"

He chuckled. "I was coming along to say goodbye, but you think I wouldn't be welcome?"

"Wait a little—the packing won't take long, but Uncle enjoys making a great fuss about it. I was just going to that little temple we passed earlier, why not come too?"

He fell into step beside her, offering his arm attentively at every patch of rough ground. How strange, she thought, five minutes ago he pushed me roughly aside, thinking I was a Chinese peasant; now I seem to need help over every pebble. If I had the lightest bag, he would offer to carry it, but if a peasant women bent double under a heavy sack passed, he would not lift a finger . . . So this gallantry in men does not have much to do with their physical strength after all. What then does it have to do with?

She was still puzzling this as they reached the temple steps, up which Charles helped her as if she were lame. As he pushed open its creaking door, a string of flapping bats flew out and they both recoiled. Inside, a peeling gilt Buddha squatted in a niche hung about with cobwebs; there was a fusty smell of incense and bat-droppings.

"Not much used by the look of it..." Charles swung his lantern round. Alice made a quick obeisance which she hoped he would not notice; but he did.

"What does that mean, Alice? You're not a clandestine Buddhist surely?"

"No—but I remember my father's story about a convert who went to all the Buddhist and Taoist festivals as well as attending his mission, because, he told Father, he was hedging his bets. Father had to laugh, though he didn't approve of course."

"So you hedge your bets too?" Charles was amused by her as usual. What a splendid wife she would make for some lucky fellow out here, with her knowledge of the country, her lively attractiveness. He though of Maria; his marriage, unlike his choice of career, had been considered eminently suitable by his family.

"My wife wouldn't agree with hedging of that sort either, but she's more devout than I am."

A silence fell between them, he moved to the door and looked out over the misted landscape. She joined him. "It's a beautiful night in its way, isn't it?"

"My wife doesn't want to come to China at all," he blurted out. "She's praying that I'll return from this trip agreeing with my father and all the others who say 'Stick to India'."

"And shall you?"

"No. For the reasons I've mentioned. So she'll have to put up with it. Shanghai at least will suit her well enough once we're settled."

"But why doesn't she want to come here?"

"Her relatives are in Madras, you see. And she's not lucky with child-bearing. We've been married four years and Peter, our first-born, is fine. But she's lost a child since and this pregnancy isn't proving easy..." He sighed, with a sudden memory of her lying leadenly in their marital bed, nightgown raised, eyes beseeching him to leave her alone. But what was a fellow with normal male appetites to do? He shifted uneasily. For Alice his words had conjured very different thoughts and she shivered, so that he put a protective arm on her shoulder. "Are you cold? Let's go back, there's an autumnal nip in the air."

"I'm quite alright, thank you." She looked up at him smiling gravely and suddenly he had his arms tightly round her, pressing her to him, kissing her gently and then, feeling her warmth, with increased purpose. She fastened her arms round his neck and clung closer, nibbling his lips. Stimulated by her knowingness, he thrust his tongue deep into her willing mouth. Then he pulled back sharply, untwining their arms. "Alice, we must stop this at once, it's quite wrong. Here am I, a married man, years older than you..."

"Only about eight."

"So you've worked that out? Never mind, you're an innocent young lady and if your uncle saw us now he'd call me a complete rotter, and rightly so."

Determinedly be broke from her and started down the steps, stamping down his ardour as he went. He stopped at the bottom. "Come on, Alice, let's go back."

He extended his arm and she pulled herself in tightly. "Alright, Mr Grant."

"Now please—we've been on Christian name terms for days, don't be so formal. You're not angry, are you?"

"Of course not," she replied distantly.

He chucked her under the chin. "We can be friends, I hope?"

"Well we could be, but I don't suppose we'll ever meet again."

"I hope we will—but that's certainly reason enough for not doing anything we might regret."

"Yes, and it's nice you wanted to kiss me."

"Of course I did. I have several times in the last few days, as a matter of fact. But you'll keep it secret, please? Promise?"

She promised; they squeezed hands and returned along the tow-path in a companionable but rather depressed silence. Approaching the boat, they saw its lights ablaze, heard the Major's voice barking into the darkness. "Alice, where are you? Alice, are you out there?"

She giggled nervously, "Oh dear, we..."

"It's alright, Major Greenwood, she's with me," Charles squared his shoulders as they met him at the gangplank.

"Alice, wherever have you been? I was about to organise a search-party—and in that outfit. I've never known such a girl for slipping away—and turning up in unexpected places!"

"I only went for a walk, Uncle."

"Alone and at this time—why on earth didn't you ask one of us to escort you?"

"But you were all busy, and then I met Charles and he escorted me."

Robert regarded them suspiciously. "I was just coming to make my farewells and share this with you perhaps, when I met Alice..." Charles produced a bottle of brandy from his jacket pocket and Robert looked somewhat mollified, for it happened that the Greenwood spirit supply was exhausted.

"A good thought on your part, Charles. Well, as there's no harm...we'll say no more. Come and join Will and me in the main cabin. As for you, miss, to bed at once. I've just sent young Frank off, he nearly blew his head off cleaning a gun—the pair of you are enough to turn a fellow's hair white, eh Charles?"

Charles followed him obediently, but at the cabin door turned to look at Alice where she still stood, under the hurricane lamp on deck.

"Goodbye, Alice, and good luck, whatever you do."

"Goodbye Charles, and good luck to you too. And I hope you'll return to China."

"Nothing will stop me. You can count on that..."

As the door closed on the men's voices, Alice went to her cabin, sat on her bunk and sighed. Charles Grant was the first Englishman she had ever enjoyed kissing; but he was married and going away. There came a quiet knock and her heart leaped hopefully, but, "Uncut Jade," a voice whispered, "may I come in?" Frank slipped inside grinning. "Uncle and Will were getting in a paddy about you—I kept telling them you'd be alright."

"Of course. I always am."

"Yes I know. I felt I had to see you alone before we're packed off—you to Mukden and me to this wretched college. You know I was thinking, Sis, once that's over, I really do want to go into business like Charles Grant with a company of my own—and I'll let you in it too—Greenwood & Greenwood, doesn't that sound grand?"

"It's a fine idea—we'll buy a junk and go trading upriver..."

"We'll only need a little capital to start..."

"Perhaps I can find some," she said lightly, thinking of the Carr loot. "Oh Frank—that reminds me, I've a little present for you. I bought it in Peking and vowed to give it you one day." From her reticule she took the jade-button fan.

"A memento of our past, dear—from one Uncut Jade to another."

"It's beautiful, Alice, thank you very much..." He stroked it, swallowing hard. "We'll stick together won't we, Sis? We really understand each other because of what happened to us, don't we?...That sounds like Charles leaving...I must go."

They kissed lightly and he slipped away. Alice stowed the reticule under her bunk. Earlier she had vowed that, once Frank was safely out of Hunan, she would return the rest of the loot to Flossie Carr. But now she was increasingly reluctant to do so. How could she ever explain her long silence over the matter? And how could she possibly trace her? Perhaps Flossie was dead by now or married to a rich man with no need of the treasure anyway...at least, not as much as she, Alice, had. For what if life in Mukden proved unbearable? How could she ever leave unless she had some money of her own? It was her only source of independence.

"You're an unprincipled, wicked young lady," she told herself as she snuggled into her bunk. But her dreams were not guilt-ridden for all that; rather they wove themselves round the handsome figure of Mr Charles Grant...

Part Two

8

"To trust God when our warehouses and bags are full and the table spread is no hard thing; but to trust Him when our purses are empty, but a handful of meal and a cruse of oil left, and all the ways of relief are stopped, herein lies the wisdom of Christian grace. For, whatever your wants are, want not faith and you cannot then want supplies."

Edward Blake's sonorous voice stopped; he snapped shut the book from which he had been reading and announced, "That passage, from the wise old divine, Mr Charnock, concludes our little prayer offering. Let us now offer up also our silent meditations to Him."

In the ensuing pause, he surveyed the small gathering on the schoolroom benches before him. Doorkeeper Peng, christened Gabriel upon his conversion, was gazing at him with unctuous incomprehension; equally unreachable was his neighbour, the cheerful widow christened Ruth, their only Bible woman, who also helped in the house. The only native who had understood some of his words was the interpreter Be-dien, a scrawny man in faded silk gown and dingy skull cap who at the age of forty was still trying to gain a literary degree. In the course of an undivulged past, Be-dien had travelled in the Treaty Ports and picked up a smattering of pidgin. It was an excruciating mongrel tongue and, having once heard himself described as "Number One Topside

Heaven Man", Edward often wondered what versions of God's peerless message were transmitted to the natives through his imperfect instrument. Now Be-dien sat impassive, eyes closed, just sufficiently awake to keep his jaw clamped shut.

Next to him Eliza wore a meditative expression, but Edward guessed that on this particular day she was much too excited to be concentrating correctly. Beside her sat Alice, whose clear greenish eyes were looking glassily past him to the summer sunlight streaming through the open door. Edward had encountered many recalcitrant spirits during his fifty years of life—in his own family home, in the school where he had once taught Latin to unruly boys, and certainly during his six years in China; but never one more so than his stepdaughter's. She was like a prickly new broom that you could take and bend but which always snapped back to its original shape the moment you let go. He had never found a key to her, and so they bargained, he and she. The bargains, begun soon after her arrival those months before had, as time went on, become more complex, more hardly driven on both sides. Most of the words he uttered at these Sunday prayer-offerings were directed at her—it was she who wanted that faith, that wisdom of Christian grace to which old Charnock referred; but she had not been truly listening, he knew.

Beside Alice, Adam suddenly jumped up, saying, "Please, Father, 'scuse me," and waddled quickly out. Sunny watched him disdainfully, then smiled smugly at big sister Alice; she never had to leave in such an undignified rush in case she wet her knickers as Adam sometimes did.

"Thank you, Edward. Come Alice, Sunny..." Eliza moved towards the door. "We have so much to do..."

But Alice was at her school-desk, taking out her text books.

"Oh Alice—not today surely? Must you study? There's the fruit to peel and chop for the cake and..."

"I'll help you later, Mother. It's my Latin lesson day and you wouldn't want me to miss that, would you, Stepfather?"

She looked at him boldly; it was one of the bargains that had to be kept or she would leave—as she had nearly done soon after the confines of Edward Blake's China Inland Mission in Mukden first closed around her. It had been winter then, northern, long, lightless and harsher than any she had known. The harshness was inside as well as out. It permeated the bare interiors of the former grain-chandlery where the Mission had been founded three years before; it emanated principally from stepfather Blake himself, whose stern voice was raised day after weary day on the themes of the unregeneracy of the Chinese soul, the proximity of Satan's dominions, the relentlessness of God's righteous wrath.

It was only when driven by all this to the point of reckless departure that Alice realised she held a trump card that could make life a little more tolerable: she could speak and write Mandarin, and that was a skill of inestimable value to a missionary who had no fluency in Chinese but was yet determined to convert several thousand Mukden residents to his uncompromising brand of Christianity. And so the bargaining had begun, tacit and indirect because of the innocent optimism of Eliza who could not accept that Edward was not won over by her attractive, high-spirited elder daughter, or that Alice felt no spark of regard for her worthy, diligent, educated second husband.

The first bargain was that for two hours of every weekday Alice should help Be-dien improve Edward's grasp of the native tongue; the second, that for one hour daily he should teach her—or at least make available books for her from which to acquire—the basics of history, geography and Latin. The last had been Alice's over-ambitious mistake, for at Latin she proved stupid. Edward was excellent at it of course, but extremely poor at Chinese, so, but for the mistake, her linguistic ascendancy would have been absolute. As it was, she usually concealed her satisfaction at his ineptitude and merely pointed out some of the more obvious absurdities of a literal translation of the Bible into Chinese. Edward found this hard to accept, for, he was fond of saying, Wycliffe had pressed Bibles into the hands of England's rude ploughboys, and they had got the message—so why could not the Chinese?

He said now, as Alice reached for her books, "No, Eliza, Alice mustn't miss her lesson, even today, for she needs the mental discipline that study induces..." And Eliza nodded, for she seldom contradicted Edward.

Left alone, Alice studied her grammar unenthusiastically, then fell to thinking about another of their bargains which was that on her "free" Sunday afternoons she usually went to visit Dr and Mrs Campbell at the hospital of the United Presbyterian Church of Scotland Mission. But today it would be difficult to go on account of the cake-making and preparations for the morrow. Still, her heart warmed pleasurably at the thought, for tomorrow Frank was arriving from Shanghai to spend his first summer holidays with them. She wandered out, staring at the bright, dry sky of the North China summer and leaned against the warm mud-brick wall of the former grain store, wondering how it would be when Frank came. It would not be easy, of that she was sure, for how could Frank warm to this dour, stern, religiously-obsessed stepfather any more than she could?

"Old Tombstone Face" the Chinese called him behind his back and so did she, for it aptly described the straight graven furrows of his brow and mouth. The Chinese thought he had been forced to leave his homeland because of some crime he had committed, for why else would a man choose to live in a foreign land? They thought Alice was his concubine, brought in to console him for the insufficiencies of his grey, often ailing official wife. They felt this arrangement a preferable way of satisfying his wayward desires than plying his female converts with aphrodisiac pills so that they threw themselves lustfully upon him—for did not many teachers of the Christ-religion behave so? And was it not rumoured that Jesus himself had been the son of a prostitute and licentious with both his male and female disciples?

All this Alice had soon discovered because of her thorough understanding of the language which was not fully realised by the local gossips. She had not passed on any of these horrendous titbits, which would have only confirmed her parents' opinion of the natives as little better than half-savage degenerates. Also she feared to imagine the effect it might have on Edward, from whose cold eyes a glint of tantalised lust occasionally peered at her. Experienced as she was, she sometimes played on it, mockingly, out of a bored contempt that she then turned upon herself.

For she was bored. After the upheavals and challenges of her earlier years, Mukden was an emotional desert. Its other foreign residents—the Campbells and a few European merchants with whom the missionaries seldom fraternised— were, in her youthful opinion, commonplace souls. But like them, her Chinese acquaintances were now limited to servants, shopkeepers and the converts—the "Eaters of foreign rice", the "secondary devils" who sought out the Mission for their own dubious purposes. At least, she thought restlessly, as she left the sun-warmed wall and went to help Mother in the kitchen, Frank's coming would enliven the scene.

"What does bruvver Frank look like?" asked Sunny digging a spoon into the cake mix Alice was stirring.

"He's got blond hair, like Mama used to have, dearie, and he's quite tall."

"Taller than Papa?"

"No, not that tall."

"And please try to remember," Eliza said gently, "that your Papa is not Frank's and Alice's Papa—because he died many years ago."

The child didn't like being in a minority. "But my Papa is Adam's Papa, isn't he?"

Adam, playing with toy bricks in the corner, said, "Stupidy Sunny, of course. The Lord brought us into the world at the same time and it was a gweat twial."

Eliza laughed, leaving her baking to hug him. "Fancy your remembering that silly phrase of mine—but the 'twial' was worth every minute..."

"What does that mean?" Sunny asked.

"Oh you'll find out one day when you're a grown woman, and so will Alice, I daresay."

Alice lowered her eyes. Often she was tempted to throw into the complacent pool of the Mission's narrow world some unspeakable truth about her past. The intense dramas that would follow such dire revelations enlivened her daydreams, but she always resisted the temptation for her mother's sake. As she did now; briskly finishing the cake and the preparation of glazed sugar plums that were her special offering to Frank. She wiped her hands: "I'm going to the Campbells' now, Mother."

Eliza looked resentful as she usually did when they were mentioned. The Campbells were decent and true Highland Scots which was greatly in their favour, but Eliza felt their whole approach to missionary work was deeply misguided. They were far too concerned with healing of the flesh, not sufficiently with the deeper ills of the native spirit. The only Way, as she and Edward knew, was a straightforward going forth with the sincere Milk of the Word. It was an abiding grief to Eliza that, in spite of years of effort, her own ability to offer the Word in the native tongue was still sorely limited; it affronted and saddened her that Alice, whose linguistic capacity was of God-given proficiency, should absolutely refuse to preach directly, yet was willing to translate patients' symptoms for Dr Campbell's benefit.

"But surely they won't expect you today, Alice?"

"Why not? The doctor relies on me to tell him about the new admissions." Eliza sighed; Adam comically imitated her; Sunny seized the chance to steal a sugar plum and turning away to hide her bulging cheeks, mumbled, "Bye Alish..."

Alice guessed, smiled, and left.

The difference between the Scottish Presbyterian and China Inland Missions in Mukden reflected the considerable disagreements over method that divided the Protestant movement in China. Alice had now heard a great deal about those differences—from her stepfather and Dr Campbell separately and on the infrequent occasions when they met, in default of other more congenial Christian company, to celebrate the commonly-binding festivals of Christmas and Easter. She was thoroughly tired of hearing about them. She sympathised with the C.I.M.'s insistence on unadorned, native-style living (which had the bonus of allowing her to wear native dress) and she shared her stepfather's scorn for those numerous missionaries who confined their labours to the comfortable security of the Treaty Ports. But there was a naive and wasteful silliness about so many of her parents' efforts, an ignorant refusal really to understand the country that often irritated and depressed her. In the Campbells' Mission, by contrast, an air of purposeful endeavour centred on the hospital and Alice had sometimes seen patients' eyes shine with hopeful faith because the foreign medicine had relieved their sufferings.

"He says he feels as if he's got nests of white ants growing in his belly," Alice reported to the doctor as they stood looking down at a young muleteer on a hospital pallet. He looked most woebegone and unbuttoned, for, as Dr Campbell often said, the Chinese made the most of their illnesses.

"Where exactly does he feel this?" He prodded the pallid flesh. "And what's he been taking for it?"

"A special medicine made from crabs' livers and crushed dragons' teeth from his doctor—it hasn't helped."

The doctor jotted in his notebook: "Admission No. 3—white ants; 'dragon teeth'" as they moved through the jumble of rice-kettles, teapots and food bundles that the patients always brought in with them.

"We've seen her before," Alice said of the next patient.

"Have we? It's dreadful how they all look alike..."

The wizened little woman on the bed held up a withered arm pitted with festering sores. "The local quack's been burning those moxus of amaranthus on her by the look of it," Campbell snorted. "Nothing I can do except heal the burns."

"You remember—she's the widow with two daughters who says her fingers are too stiff to make firecrackers anymore and they're nearly starving—she threatens to commit suicide by swallowing lucifers."

"Well, her daughters must do it, I suppose. I'm not gifted with miraculous powders, I can't cure withered arms."

"Do you wish you could, Doctor—like Jesus?"

"Come, young lady, don't be flippant. I believe, if you seriously want to know, that some people have a certain gift of healing, but it's a great responsibility... Now, let's go and sample May's delicious scones... And I expect it's another of my novels you'll be wanting the loan of?" he continued in his pleasant Highland burr as they crossed the courtyard. "I see you've returned *Rob Roy*."

An unspoken bargain Alice had struck with the Campbells was that, in return for her translating help, she had the run of their considerable library. And last winter, by lantern-light and surreptitiously because her stepfather disapproved of such trivial literature, she had read *Pride and Prejudice*, *Adam Bede*, *Waverley*, *Lorna Doone*, *Pickwick Papers*, *Lavengro*, *Henry Esmond*, *The Mill on the Floss*, *Northanger Abbey*, *Vanity Fair*, and, at the doctor's insistence, every air, prayer, poem and song penned by the great Robbie Burns. She now had a richer if still rather quaint picture of that small, distant homeland she had never seen.

"And how did you enjoy the harum-scarum adventures of Rob Roy, gentleman, Alice?"

"Oh well enough, thank you. But George Eliot's Maggie Tulliver is still my favourite."

"Och well, your tastes will not be fully developed yet— you grow into things, I do myself. Take Emerson for example, Ralph, Waldo, an American—never thought anything of him, but I just received a volume of his essays, 'Society and Solitude' published recently. Now listen to what he says on the subject of books..." He took out the volume, adjusted his spectacles. "And he's not only writing about the sacred books of Christendom, but of Epictetus, the Buddhist texts, the Upanishads, and your favourite Confucius to boot—they're all, he claims, 'the Bibles of the world... majestic expressions of the universal conscience.' He goes on, '... These are scriptures which the missionary might well carry over prairie, desert and ocean, to Siberia, Japan and Timbuctoo. Yet he will find that the spirit which is in them journeys faster than he and greets him on his arrival—was there already long before him. The missionary must be carried by it and find it there, or he goes in vain.' Now that's a strange thought, Alice, and I'm not sure how I take it, for to tell you the truth, the 'universal conscience' of the Chinese eludes me. But you know, lassie, I read in Blackwood's magazine recently that Emerson's philosophical approach is very similar to the Chinese. He doesn't ever reach for one complete and logical system of ideas, but deals in momentary truths, temporary opinions if you like, refusing absolute definitions, as the Chinese do. Now what do you say to that, Alice?"

Rather out of her depth, she said hesitantly, "Certainly the Chinese sages seem to contradict each other, even themselves sometimes, but it doesn't seem to bother them as it would us. And they get carried away by flights of fancy, not minding about logic..."

"Aye well, that's a bit Emerson's way too, but he's an eloquent man for a' that."

"Can I read it, Doctor?"

"When I've finished mulling it over myself you can."

Indoors, they met May Campbell with the tea-tray. "Hello, Alice dear. Phew, it's hot baking scones at the stove today—look at my face!" Alice grinned, for May's cheeks were even more deeply flushed than usual. Both the Campbells had retained the ruddy Highland complexion of their youth and were called "the two purple plums" by the sallower natives. This Alice knew, but, as with many things, felt unable to reveal.

"And I doubt if the tea will be up to scratch—I hung the mare's milk in the well to keep cool, but it's almost sour, it's that hot."

Alice did not much care for this hard, dry-as-dust inland heat that pounded down on the flat town, cracked its mud tracks and walls, yet left chill shadows. There would be no rain for another month, but the surrounding fields were already parched and the wells too low for the efficacious cooling of milk.

"We've been baking a special cake for Frank—Mother's been saving fruit and sugar for weeks."

"Och aye, she'll be excited today?"

"Oh yes—Frank was always her favourite."

Dr Campbell smiled quizzically. "Sons often are—with mothers."

"Yes, Mother always said I was Father's."

"Never mind, dearie," May patted her hand. "Have another scone? And it will be grand to see your brother again, won't it? Is he a bit of a bookworm like yourself?"

"Oh no, Frank's the outdoor type. According to his letters he's best at sports, and he's longing to leave school and go into business."

Dr Campbell's scone-crumbs blew in his mirth. "Oh dear, dear. That won't sit well with your stepfather, I'll warrant. Your brother'll have to mind his Ps and Qs."

But Frank had never worried unduly about the Ps and Qs

of life and did not do so in the company of his family as they all sat round the tea-table the following afternoon. He had arrived off the overland cart from Newchwang that morning—a strapping youth with a loud, easy laugh and hammy hands, his broad physique well set in its manly mould. Only his blue eyes still sometimes held the look of a furtive, bewildered, uncertain boy who knew life could produce some nasty surprises for the unwary—and that wariness was not his strong point.

"More cake, dear?" Eliza leaned to touch him, as she kept doing, in happy wonderment that this really was her long-lost son.

"No thanks, Mama, but I'll have another sugar plum—quite like old times, eh Alice?"

She nodded. "But have more cake as well—it's a special treat."

He looked at it dismissively. "You can get scrummy ones at the new confectioners on the Shanghai Bund—with whipped cream, cherries and thick thick chocolate on top like so." He held up two fingers.

Sunny's eyes rounded. "An' cream, an' cherries an' chocolate all on one cake?"

"Yes—and nuts. I forgot the nuts."

"I wouldn't like them," Adam chimed in. "They make me choke."

"Stupidy Adam, you could scrape them off and give them to me."

"You wouldn't be there, you're only a girl. But I'd be there eating lots of cakes with just Frank, wouldn't I?" For Adam had already taken an enormous shine to his stepbrother.

Frank laughed. "Oh come, Adam, that's not very gallant. When you're bigger you'll all come to Shanghai, Alice and Sunny too. And I'll buy you all cakes, with nuts or without, and icecream, strawberry or vanilla."

Sunny sighed deeply. "I've never had icecream."

"Yes dear, you had some in Chefoo once, but you were too young to remember," Eliza corrected.

Edward Blake coughed, folding his napkin like a prayer-sheet. "Well I think it's time I returned to my labours. I'm greatly hoping that the carpenter from Sparrow Lane who called at the street chapel yesterday will return, Eliza. He seemed a very genuine inquirer. And I trust we'll soon hear something of your actual studies, Frank? The news so far has been all of cricket matches, rowing contests and the consumption of cake."

Frank said curtly, "I study of course, Stepfather, but I'm not clever with languages and stuff like Alice."

"Well, you are competent in something other than hitting a ball I trust?"

"I'm not bad at geography, maps and things. Uncle Robert's pleased about that and suggests I might go in the Army. And I'm fair at arithmetic and that's good for business—which I really want to go into."

"Business, dear?" Eliza clattered the plates nervously. "Whatever kind of business?"

"Shipping of course, that's where the money is. Sending foreign goods upcountry to remote places like Changsha. That was Charles Grant's idea too—you remember him, Alice?"

"I do indeed. Did you ever hear from him again?"

"Not a word—I suppose he stayed in India after all."

Edward coughed again. "Am I to take it then, Frank, that your ultimate ambition in life is to become an upriver trader, making profits out of selling to the Chinese such items as kerosene lamps, cotton goods, glass baubles, and various mechanical contrivances which they've lived quite happily without for centuries?"

"Oh please, Edward, let's not discuss these matters on Frank's first day here." Eliza put a timorous hand on his shoulder which he immediately removed.

"My dear, I had no intention of so doing. But when my stepson talks of money-making as his *summum bonum* and this is all his education is presumably fitting him for, then I cannot but express some dismay—which you'll surely share, Eliza?"

"Of course, Edward, I'm disappointed that up to now neither he, nor Alice for that matter, seems to have found the true Path. But they're still young..."

"But I shall be..." and "Nineteen's not..." they protested simultaneously.

"Yes, dears, that is still young," Eliza said firmly. "After all, Edward dear, it was many years before you saw the Way clear to your life's work..."

He bowed humble assent. "And wasted years they were too in some ways. I only hope your children won't waste so much of God's precious time. But at least..." he rose, "I was never wedded to the notion of making money in trade."

Frank's lips went into a familiar pout. "There's nothing wrong in making a little money, Stepfather. It takes a man much further than one without any..."

It was perhaps fortunate that, while everyone's attention was elsewhere, Sunny had been devouring as many sugar plums as possible and now got a stone stuck in her throat and choked violently. In the ensuing diversion, Alice whispered, "Don't go on any more like this please, Frank—for Mother's sake."

Edward, thinking similarly, gave a frosty nod and departed to the street-chapel where he spent two hours kneeling on the earthen floor, praying in vain for the return of the Sparrow Lane carpenter.

"I don't know how you bear it, Alice," Frank said the next morning as they set off on a tour of the limited Mukden sights. "Stepfather's even worse than our French master and he's the worst in school. And you have to live in the same house."

"But I shan't always, I keep telling myself. Only Mother does need help with the little ones just now, she's not strong."

"No—she looks so much older and greyer than I remember, I was quite shocked."

"I suppose it isn't surprising, after all she's been through..."

"And now married to that man..."

Alice gave a twisted, sad smile. "She saw it as God's will for her—and who are we to gainsay that?"

"Oh all this praying and Bible-thumping, it's not good for you, Alice. You should come to Shanghai where there are so many dashing young bachelors in the shipping offices and consulates—and even 'in trade'," he imitated Edward's tone of heavy disapproval. "And not enough pretty young ladies to go round. Why, you could take your pick and have such a jolly time!"

She tossed her head. "Oh, I don't fancy that sort of gent somehow. I've seen a few—so pleased with themselves with their smart moustaches and smart jokes and smart jackets— they seem so young and silly to me."

"I always guessed you'd be hard to please, Sis, not like the rest of the English lassies."

"Well, how could I, after what's happened to us?"

"Did Stepfather and Mother ever find out how we really lived in the Chu house?"

"No, they didn't want to hear about anything pleasant and they still think we were kept in some sort of prison, because that's how 'the heathen' would behave, in their view. And there's so much I just couldn't explain—Mother would faint clean away!"

Frank chuckled. "It's the same at school. I once told a chum that I'd been a groom in the service of a Deputy-Governor's son. He just jeered, but when I swore it was true, he advised me never to mention it because it was letting the side down."

"So we just have to keep it to ourselves... But I often wonder how they are, don't you?" Her tone was wistful.

"Oh I expect they're alright. Anyway, in a couple of years we'll set up that company, Greenwood & Greenwood, remember? So blow stepfather! And we'll get rich in no time and buy a splendid junk painted red and gilt and go sailing back to Changsha together!"

Laughing in that golden dream, they turned a corner and were nearly trampled by a string of horses trotting to market. "Gosh, look at those!" Frank's eyes widened. That's what I want, old girl. They're true-bred Mongolians, I've seen them at the Shanghai races—yes, I often go, you see some real swells there, but don't tell Mama! Fierce little brutes they are, they bite and arch their backs like cats when they're angry, but they go like the wind and never give up. We call 'em 'griffins'—the same name they use for green youngsters just out from Home. Now if I could only afford one of those— let's find out what they cost anyway—I've still got some of Uncle Robert's allowance!"

They followed the animals to the market where dealers from the north were bartering mules, sheep, goats and pigs and the pelts of foxes, ermine, sable, squirrel, dog and racoon as well as the sprightly Mongolian horses. Their price, Frank discovered, was less than half the going rate in Shanghai. "Our first trading venture—we shouldn't miss a bargain like this!" he pleaded with Alice.

She hesitated thinking of her tiny hoard of coins, then smiled. "Bags I the front half then!" So they returned to the Mission that afternoon with a springy steed called Griffin; he had a bristly tail and mane, wickedly glinting eyes, and had cost their every penny.

But he was worth every brass cash, Alice soon decided, for it was only the fun, first of training Griffin, who had very much a mind of his own, and then of teaching her to ride him well, that kept Frank contented for most of his holiday. Even then, boredom set in during the evenings when, instead of a stroll along the Bund, a cricket or rowing practice, came the Mission routine of prayers, a sparse supper, book-reading, early to bed.

"Let's play draughts again, Alice," Frank suggested with

a yawn as the sun sank in a fiery glow behind the tiled Mission roof. They got out the board; Eliza took up her sewing, happy just to have them with her and hoping guiltily that Edward, who had gone to see a convert, would return late. So her heart sank a little when, within the hour, she heard his heavy tread in the passage. He stood in the door surveying the scene, until Alice, feeling the waves of his rising anger washing over them, raised her very cool eyes to his tired, red-rimmed ones.

"Won't you sit down, Stepfather? Would you like some tea?"

"Tea—what I want is more than tea, miss."

Eliza looked agitated. "But Edward, what... ?"

"Help, madam, that's what I need and what no one in this unfeeling household will offer me. Do any of you know or indeed care what I've been doing this evening? I've been trying to bolster the sorely-tried faith of our poor ploughman, Lo-shi. He's being persecuted by his neighbours and his farm tools have been stolen—yet he clings to his new-found conviction in the Word. And while I struggle thus, you sit here—playing draughts, if you please!"

"But Edward, they..." Eliza was now at his side.

"And you, Eliza, many's the time I've heard you say, 'Folded arms will never save sinking souls'—yet here you sit with your arms folded while I labour alone without support."

"But Stepfather, we do help in many ways," Alice began mildly, seeing Frank's face darken with rage.

"But not in the way that is most valuable—you should be my interpreter, the instrument through which the most marvellous message in the world could be transmitted to the unbelievers. And Frank too, he can speak the tongue with the utmost fluency—yet he sits here eating the bread of the house every day, yes and the cake too, but won't raise a finger to..."

"Well if that's how you feel, Stepfather, I'll leave tomorrow!" Frank blazed. "I've very little money, but I don't want your charity thrown at me."

"Please Edward...children, stop..." Eliza's wail was lost.

"No money?" Edward sneered. "Just enough to buy horses, hey? And enough time to go riding over the plains all day like a gypsy without a care in the world."

Frank leaped up, spilling draughts on the floor. "If it wasn't for Mother, why I'd..." He doubled his fists, pushed violently past Edward and out of the room. Eliza hurried after him, flinging back at her husband, "If these were your children—your Theobald and Laura—you'd never speak to them so, Edward. How dare you send my darling boy away like this?"

"I'm not sending him away, I'm only asking..." he shouted as she ran out.

Alice began picking up the draughts with shaking fingers. There was a silence.

"And you, miss?" he towered over her. "What can be done to break that stubborn and wilful spirit of yours—which has been tainted, yes I use the word advisedly—tainted through too much close contact with heathendom during your formative years. I pray on my bended knees for you every night, Alice, that God may reveal His purposes to you, that you will realise the hopeless spiritual coma in which you live."

She straightened. "Tainted you call it—by something you know nothing whatsoever about. You tell me the people are sinful idolators, don't you? Well, I won't believe it. I've lived among them as you say and I don't think they're any worse, or any better come to that, than we are. And what you call idolatry is people going to pray and give thanks at the graves of their ancestors. What's so wrong in that?"

"Are you trying to tell me that I don't recognise sin? That I don't know what wrong is—when I see it on all sides, in this town, in this house, in your very eyes at this moment, Miss Alice, I see the powers of darkness lurking, goading me..." He raised his arm dramatically, pushing a greater distance between them. He was deathly pale and trembling with a passion that first repelled her, then stirred her to pity. She stepped towards him and he backed violently, "Get out," he said in a low voice, "begone from my sight this instant, woman."

She flew out, brushing the draught-board as she went so that it too clattered on the floor. Left alone, Edward fell on his knees beside the scattered game, grasped his large bony head in his large bony hands and tried to pray.

In response to his mother's and sister's entreaties, Frank did not leave immediately; but, he told Alice angrily, he would only stay on condition he paid for his keep. Stepfather could consign his soul to perdition for all he cared, but he was not going to label him a sponger, so, as Frank's entire allowance was tied up in Griffin, the horse would have to be sold. Alice pleaded, but her brother could also be stubborn, and the result was that Alice slipped off to the money-changers the next day with a perfume bottle from the loot-box.

"Now his hind quarters are mine too," she laughed, pressing money in Frank's hand. Wisely he did not ask where it came from; he simply took it and paid his protesting mother a "mess bill" for the remainder of his stay. It was short and rather uncomfortable for them all. Edward usually maintained a haughty, wounded silence, interrupted by the occasional querulous bark at Adam, who had taken to following Frank about like a timorous, adoring lap-dog. Eliza lived in a continual twitter of anxiety, fearing more rows, while Alice simply withdrew, glad of a respite from the front-line of battle, but uneasily aware that, when Frank left, tensions would probably increase. Only Sunny bounced gladly through the days as usual, happy that Frank's presence meant more tea-time treats, happiest of all when, clinging to the front of Griffin's saddle, she and Alice trotted to market.

Two days before Frank's departure the twins went down with chicken-pox, so only Alice saw him off on the Newchwang cart, kissing him lightly and joking about the rigours of his journey to conceal her misery and envy at the thought of his immediate prospects compared to hers. "It won't be for long, Sis," he promised. "One more year of school grind, then I'm going to make a fortune for us both and you can leave Stepfather to stew in his own miserable juices! I hope *I* never see him again!"

As the cart trundled away, Alice turned Griffin's head and rode north-eastward out of town. Bright morning light flooded the plains and the stony ground was dotted with clumps of wild marigolds, daisies and yellow daphne, about which flitted pale violet butterflies. At the sound of hooves, ground-squirrels skittered into their tunnels and rock-partridges rose cackling into the air. Higher in the sky soared kestrels, buzzards and flocks of magpies bound for the reddish-brown millet fields that were higher than Griffin's head. Heaps of already-harvested grain were piled against the mud-walls of farmsteads and from their yards came the beat of threshers' flails and the tramp of oxen pulling stone rollers. Near the settlements, strip-fields were still planted with late summer beans, barley and tobacco; foul-smelling hemp was steeped in shallow pools; flocks of ragged sheep and goats nibbled at dried turf. As the sun rose higher, she reined Griffin to a halt.

"We have to go back," she told him, and he turned a wild, disbelieving eye on her, his quivering nostrils exulting in the fresh smells from the distant hills. She sat there numbly. "You're wondering why?... And so am I!"

On the way back, Alice made a detour to the tombs dedicated to T'ai Tsung, a seventeenth-century leader of the Manchus. The tombs, containing T'ai Tsung, his official wife and favourite concubine, were out of sight behind high walls, but the surrounding park was open—a veritable oasis of trees, flowering shrubs and grassy hillocks. Alice rode slowly down the wide flagged path leading to the tomb-enclosure, and flanked by stone statues of camels, horses, lions and elephants. Grey, ruffled doves were cooing in the dark pines, green lizards basking on the camels' humps and suddenly, a yellowish snake slid over the stones ahead and vanished behind an elephant. Griffin snorted warningly and she halted him. The hot silence enveloped them both.

The place, which she often visited, always spoke to her of death, especially of her father's. Whenever she remembered that dreadful summer day in Tientsin, her heart lurched in sad panic. To her mother, Thomas Greenwood was the very exemplar of the Christian hero who had gone so bravely to his martyrdom in the defence of his faith, but, as she grew older, Alice found this version increasingly hard to accept. There had been such a wasteful silly chancefulness about the whole episode—as if God's attention had been elsewhere that afternoon. The first time such an idea came to her, she had felt horrified and guilty; now she accepted its implications. And every time she came to this secluded spot—impregnated as it was with the short-livedness and short-sightedness of all human endeavour—she felt more certain that her reckless, stubborn, dearly beloved father had died in vain, though her heart ached none the less for that.

But then, as she sat on, the sun pouring on her head and Griffin's sweating flanks, and she looked at the garden animals, the trees and sky, she was overcome by an awareness of the beautiful unimportance of her own life and the reassuring inevitability of its passing. She murmured,

> "Green, green the cypress on the mound,
> Firm, firm the boulder in the stream.
> Man's life within this world
> Is like the sojourning of a hurried traveller..."

That made her feel better, put into perspective the small trials that awaited her back at the Mission—the twins' illness, her mother's depression over Frank's departure, her own loss of his company. What did it all matter? She was a young and buoyant traveller with a long road still to explore. A lark burst into a sparkling chain of song high in the blue; she leaned forward and tweaked Griffin's ear, "Come my lovely, my very own lovely—it's alright to go back now."

Although there had been no hint of it in the clear sky of that morning at the tombs, the torrential late-summer rains began a few days later and the evenings began to draw in early and chill. Alice slipped away to the furriers' market and with the money left from the sale of the perfume bottle, bought a fine cloth jacket, luxuriously lined with sable. Because of its cost and beauty, she dared show it to no one, but sometimes, in the privacy of her bedroom, she wrapped herself in its elegance, dreaming of a time when she would be draped in furs—in the lobbies of grand hotels, on the way to glittering balls. She hungered for the challenge and excitement of young people's company, longed to find out how she would fare in what her mother termed the "worldly" world that had so far been denied her.

She had no one in whom to confide her longings for they would have shocked her parents, but the Campbells at least realised Alice's lack of congenial and eligible companionship. So they produced Josiah Simmons for her as if he were a Christmas present. He arrived on 22nd December, and the Campbells decided he and Alice should be properly introduced, for the meeting might be momentous—and what better time than the goodwill season when doctrinal and personal differences were put aside? So it was on Christmas Day, when the Blakes and Alice arrived at the Campbells' for dinner that May beckoned forward a chubby-cheeked, bespectacled young man with curly hair and a shy smile. "And *this* is Mr Josiah Simmons, Alice."

They shook hands; she had heard of his impending arrival of course. He was the new Mission assistant and May had told her all she knew of him. He was twenty-two, unmarried, the son of a factory-owner in Birmingham; he had spent two years at the Society's Mission at Hankow on the Yangtze and its head had written to Dr Campbell that Josiah was energetic, willing, devout and a good musician. May had great hopes of Josiah, for she felt, as she told her husband, that poor Alice was rather a lost soul, though with great promise. What she needed was the guidance, support and love of a decent, God-fearing young man. So May beamed as she ushered them into the sitting-room, where her little Jenny and Sunny passed round home-made biscuits, young Andrew Campbell played with Adam behind the sofa, and Eliza sat pink-cheeked by the stove roasting chestnuts. Dr Campbell produced some ginger wine which Edward sipped as if it were cough linctus and Josiah, as was fitting, talked to Alice.

He spoke enthusiastically of the advance of mission-work in Hankow compared to Mukden. "Why, there are American Presbyterians, Episcopalians, London Missionary Society, Methodists, Canadian Baptists—as well as pioneers such as the C.M.S. and ourselves there," he explained. "Quite a community, and the bolder spirits among us—of which I was one, I may say—formed a 'Sowers Band' to work jointly with the young natives. We'd have a sing-song every Saturday evening in one of the Mission parlours with an harmonium, fiddles and several of us singing. Do you play or sing, Miss Greenwood?"

"I'm afraid nothing like that goes on here, Mr Simmons, and I have no musical accomplishments."

"Ah well—we must remedy that. We're so few here to 'make a joyful noise together' that it's a case of all hands on deck surely? Perhaps Mrs Campbell could be persuaded to teach you the harmonium accompaniment anyway—singing is really my forte."

And later, as twilight fell and they all sat replete from the generous Christmas feast, he showed that it was. As his rich baritone filled the room, Eliza hummed softly in the background, tears just behind her eyes, for she was remembering earlier Christmases when the children had been young and she and Thomas had put oranges, toy whistles and sweets in their stockings. Staring at the orange glow of the wintry sunset, Edward's thoughts drifted in his own similar directions, to a particular Christmas of years ago: fair Clara lighting the candles in the window of their Sussex home; Theobald poking his chubby fingers in a trifle and little Laura shrieking with laughter on finding a silver horseshoe in her pudding. Whatever would Clara think of him now? Of his drab and humble Chinese robe, this harsh, alien city on the Manchurian plains, and he with no comforts, no truly congenial company, hardly any money? He shivered, for he could almost hear the little tinkling laugh of scorn she used to reserve for the less sophisticated members of the school staff. Ah, but Clara had been fair, very fair—but alas very worldly.

To Alice the songs meant little, so she considered the singer. He reminded her of a picture of the young Schubert on May's music sheet, with the same bumbling over-eagerness she felt the composer might have had. One of her stepfather's favourite sentiments was that the Gospels contained "Shallows where the lamb may ford and depths where the elephant must swim": Edward certainly considered himself in the elephantine class; Alice suspected that Josiah was among the lambs.

Whatever Alice's private reservations, May Campbell decided that the first meeting between the two young people had been promising and encouraged Alice to take up the harmonium. From the first, Josiah found time to help her—singing encouragement and explaining the difficult passages. When the weather improved and Alice resumed her riding over the plains in the early mornings, she often heard the thud of hooves behind—and there was Josiah, on the doctor's plump steed, his spectacles steamed up with exertion. To entertain her, he reeled off the names of every plant and bird; he brought lumps of iron-ore or soapstone for her inspection; when the first jonquils of spring appeared, he gathered a huge bunch and presented them to her, smiling shyly. She found his company pleasant enough, and it was a relief to hear little of Christian dogma, for, as Josiah readily admitted, men like her stepfather could soon tie him in theological knots.

"It's enough for me to be here doing what little I can as a practical Christian," he explained earnestly. "I think God intends to use me in this way."

"But Josiah, how can you be so sure of God's intentions?" she asked. "I never am. What makes you so certain He wanted you to become a missionary? My stepfather now, he vows he received a direct message from God in Lewes Civic Hall where he heard Hudson Taylor preaching. It was only a few months after his first wife, Clara, died, and I've often wondered if he'd have heard that message if Clara had lived, or if he hadn't gone to that meeting."

"But it's very difficult to explain about Calls, Alice, especially to those who've not yet received them. People are more open to them at certain times of their lives—perhaps your stepfather was made receptive by his bereavement. In my case, I must confess I first wanted to be a singer, but Father disapproved, saying it was no life for a Christian gentleman. So I was feeling very discontented and disheartened when I started attending missionary meetings."

Sometimes, secretly, Josiah himself wondered why and how it had all come about, though he did not regret his life's choice. He was however beginning to repent somewhat of the excessive zeal that had urged him to leave companionable Hankow for this Mukden outpost, where there was such a dearth of charming feminine company—except of course for

Alice. And Josiah was a susceptible young man whose emotions tended to bubble over easily like his voice and, on the desert of the Mukden scene, the sight of Alice's trim figure riding over the plains, her merry laughter and teasing, the withdrawn, sometimes harried look in her green eyes, held him in thrall.

There was a certain mystery about her that tantalised him, a strange boldness that slightly awed him. He did not fully approve of her Chinese clothes, of the novels she read, of her merciless derision of her stepfather, or even of her over-easy familiarity with the natives. But he never dared to hint his disapproval, for he had once seen her eyes flash with anger and guessed that, in any battle of words, he would surely be vanquished. So he played admiringly to her tune—which was, had he known, the last strategy to win her affection. And when, after several months, this seemed of no avail, he steeled himself for a more direct approach.

He chose his time carefully, wishing there were some moonlit ruins or picturesque glen as fitting backdrop for his essay. But Mukden was singularly lacking in romantic spots and he had to make do with the strip of formal garden laid out by the foreign residents for promenading. It was located unfortunately close to the animal-dealers' market and, though screened from it by trees, the garden's air was so feculent that promenaders were few. On the evening that Josiah determinedly steered Alice there after an harmonium practice, it was quite deserted. The smell, he realised with dismay, was strongly animal, but there was at least a moon; a few tattered streamers hung on the rose-bushes, and firecracker-cases littered the paths.

Josiah kicked one. "Looks as if the natives have been celebrating again."

"Of course, the Ching-ming is just over, when they visit the family graves and pay homage to their ancestors, didn't you know *that*?"

He reddened at her asperity. "Yes, silly of me—they have so many festivals, I get confused."

"You wouldn't if you'd actually been along to the tombs with a family—as I did when in the service of the Chus."

He put a tentative hand on her shoulder. "Poor little Alice, how absolutely rotten it must have been for you."

"They didn't treat me so badly and it was more interesting than life here, in some ways."

"But you were so alone and young—then to escape like that, was so brave, Alice—indeed I think you're quite wonderful altogether." He stopped, pulled her against him and, in a sudden rush, covered her cheeks and mouth with moist kisses.

She drew back in surprise. "Why... Josiah... no, please stop. You really must..."

His body trembled violently like an eager puppy's and, for a moment, he simply held her tighter in his shaking arms. "Oh Alice..." he released her with a gasp, "dear, dear Alice, I've wanted to kiss you so often—please don't be angry with me. I know you must be innocent of a man's feelings, how he has to struggle with himself sometimes... I haven't offended you, have I, dear? Please say not..."

"No, Josiah—I'm just so surprised. You see, I'm not... well, you mustn't think of me in this way."

"But how else can I think of you, Alice? You're so pretty and sweet."

"Josiah, I'm not sweet." She laughed lightly. "Why, you've often told me, and quite rightly, that I'm critical and impatient—and not nearly as devout as you."

"Ah but, Alice, I'm sure you are in your own way and would become more so, if you were to... I mean, I don't want to hurry things, but if you could begin to think kindly of me, in this new way... I mean I could come and see your stepfather soon... if you'd like, now I've kissed you like this and..." His voice trailed away, and he looked down at her hand he was still forlornly rubbing.

"Oh no, Josiah, why whatever has made you think that? We can be friends of course, but I couldn't possibly consider..."

"But dear," he pleaded desperately, still squeezing her limp fingers, "it's hard for a man not to want something more than friendship, when he's with a lovely young lady like you so often. I want everything to be proper of course. I'm sure the Campbells would be very pleased—they've even hinted as much. My prospects are quite good you know, and the Doctor thinks well of me."

"I'm sure he does, Josiah, and so do I. But I'm not at all a suitable person ... I mean, I've no idea what *my* prospects are..."

"Oh I know you must think carefully about such matters, Alice, and perhaps I've been a little hasty, considering your inexperience..." He drew back again, polishing his spectacles; Alice turned away, biting her lip, for his words, allied to a specially pungent odour from the market, filled her with a huge desire to laugh.

"Come, Josiah," she gasped instead, "we must go back or Mother will fret. And please let's not say another word on the subject, it's quite out of the question."

"But, Alice," he blinked at her, "I really don't understand why you should say that. What's the matter with me? I mean, your present situation isn't very appealing surely? So why couldn't you just consider growing slowly fonder of me, as fond as I am of you?"

She faced him firmly. "You don't understand, you know so little about me, really, Josiah, and that's how it should be. I shall never be a missionary, nor the wife of one, and that's that. Everyone's been trying to persuade me in that direction ever since I returned from Changsha—the Penfolds and Ida Palmer, my mother, my stepfather, the Campbells. And it's quite largely because I speak Chinese fluently and they see me as a sort of instrument for conveying their messages. Well, I've told them all to forget the idea and I'm now telling you the same. Please let's go—this garden really has the most abominable smell, haven't you noticed?"

He fell sulkily into step beside her as they returned to the Mission. In their mutual silence Josiah was wishing ever more fervently that he had never left Hankow, while Alice marvelled that the Campbells and perhaps her mother too could imagine she might want to wed Josiah. The thought depressed and angered her, for it meant they did not take her own declarations at all seriously—they had simply assumed that if the "right young man" came along she would gladly become a missionary's wife after all. Did they not realise how extraordinary she was—or at least felt herself to be? Probably, she decided with a flash of uncomfortable insight, only her stepfather had a perception of that.

What her stepfather did perceive in Alice was an independence of spirit unleavened by Christian humility. He, for one, was not surprised to learn—for the news soon reached him—that Alice had refused Josiah's advances. "I expect," he remarked tartly to his wife, "she doesn't consider him good enough for her. I sometimes fear your daughter doesn't believe that Christ Himself in all His Glory is good enough for her. And I must confess, Eliza, that considering her age and sex, I find her degree of self-pride quite overweening."

The desire to humble that pride, to force Alice to accept her manifest destiny as one of God's instruments for converting the heathen, goaded him constantly. As he had said, he prayed for her soul every night. How could she remain totally unmoved by that power which had urged, nay, almost forced him to forsake his all to come and labour in this alien soil? Again and again his mind furrowed along these tracks, but in spite of all his prayers throughout that next summer, Alice showed no sign of "growing in grace".

For her too it was a barren time. She saw much less of Josiah, who had been quite shocked by her adamant rejection, not only of him, but of any connection with mission work. Prudently he started writing warm letters to Mildred Thistlethwaite, one of the single young ladies in Hankow and an accomplished harmonium player. From the outside world came tantalising news: William and Isabel, now the parents of Charlotte and little Joel, had been posted from Foochow to Port Arthur on the Liaotung Peninsula where Frank now spent his summers. Alice could not help feeling jealous, for again it seemed Frank had all the exciting opportunities, whereas she had nothing but obligations in Manchuria to fulfil.

The seasons passed. Spring brought jonquils, but also premonitions of heat; during the late summer rains, swarms of mosquitoes hummed above the town's flooded drains and Alice noted with a depression of the spirits the familiar portents of the long, cold northern winter. The tracks where she rode were churned into a yellowish, flowerless mire by the carts of sturdy Mongolian traders already swaddled in their padded sheepskins; overhead came the rhythmical wing beats of wild fowl flying south; the grazing herds of antelope and gazelle vanished from the foothills.

It was in a mood of nostalgic melancholy induced by the season that Alice sat in the school-room one autumn afternoon practising calligraphy to show Be-dien. She had chosen to copy the poem "Jade Flower Palace" by the admirable Tu-fu, and, as she wrote, the scene in the Chu courtyard when Lung-kuang first really looked at her returned vividly. "The colours of autumn are fresh in the wind and rain... though the virgins have all gone their way to the yellow graves... in dark rooms ghost-green fires are shining..." She shivered at the line, sensing, as she sometimes did, that the Mission itself, the former grain-chandlery, did not like their barbarian presences. The building was reputedly set in an ill-omened *fen-shui*, meaning it had an unlucky relationship to the elements of wind and rain and certainly it was true that, from whatever quarter they came, they blew with exceeding ferocity through every crack.

As Alice rose to secure a blowing shutter, Josiah came

riding through the gate and called to her, "Oh Alice, come out—there's such a pother. Mrs Campbell fears she's beginning premature labour and the doctor has just gone off on a two-day itineration. She wants me to go and fetch him back at once and wonders if your mother will come and stay with her till we return..."

Eliza hurried off with Josiah at once, leaving Alice in charge of the children.

"Why is Mrs Campbell having another baby, Father?" Sunny asked as they all sat round the tea-table. "Doesn't she have enough?"

"Ah but it is God's will that she should bring forth more fruit."

Sunny looked puzzled. "But Father, I said a baby, not fruit."

He lowered at her. "It's a manner of speaking, children, fruit of the womb, fruit of the loins... But these matters are quite beyond your understanding."

"Perhaps we could say that Mrs Campbell's baby is the fruit of the gooseberry bush—babies are sometimes found under them I believe?" Alice suggested maliciously.

"It may be the simplest explanation for now, yes, Sunny."

"But Mrs Campbell doesn't have any gooseberry bushes in her garden."

And Adam said, "There aren't any gooseberry bushes in the whole of Mukden. What do they look like? Do gooses eat them?"

Edward rose hastily. "I have a return of the colic, Alice, and I don't wish for more tea. I shall go to study some characters in readiness for the morrow's lesson. Ruth will help you with the children."

Edward had been a martyr to the colic for the past year, due, he decided, to an excess of boiled millet and not enough good red meat. To counteract this, Dr Campbell had prescribed a brownish tonic and a small glass of port every evening. These Edward now dutifully swallowed before his nightly wrestle with the Mandarin. After a while however, his concentration was disturbed by noises from the nursery. "It's time they were asleep," he muttered crossly, going to investigate. Alice's voice reached him through the door.

"'You are old said the Youth, as I mentioned before, And have grown most uncommonly fat; Yet you turned a back-somersault in at the door, Pray what is the reason for that?'"

Edward walked in: the twins tucked in bed were giggling loudly at Alice's lively rendering of "Old Father William".

"What balderdash are you reading them? You know that is not what they should be hearing! This is their bedtime book, surely?" He indicated the copy of *Noble Tales for Little Boys and Girls* with which Eliza usually sent them to sleep.

"That's not nearly so nice and funny," remarked Sunny.

"I like hearing about the White Rabbit much better—'oh my fur and whiskers...I'm late, I'm late...'" squeaked Adam, giggling up at his father, holding his hands like paws.

"You see how you've over-excited them?" Edward grabbed the offending book. "*Alice in Wonderland*—ah, that Mr Carroll, I've heard of it, and he's a don I believe? What nonsense! He should know better..." He glanced through it disdainfully. "And how unfortunately typical, if I may say so, Alice, that you'd choose a tale with a heroine bearing your own name—further increasing thereby your sadly overblown sense of your own importance, I suspect."

"That's nothing whatever to do with it! I adore Wonderland Alice because she's a real heroine. I'm not nearly so brave...why, if I were I'd..."

"And what exactly would you do?" he challenged, throwing down the book in disgust.

"I'd get out of this miserable house for a start, that's what I'd do. It's like a prison, filled with your narrow ideas, so grim and depressing. What's wrong with telling the children a light-hearted fairy story for a change? They don't have much fun, poor little doves..."

Sunny began to cry noisily and shaking Adam buried himself under the bedclothes, for he hated rows. "Now look at the state you've got them in! And no mother here to comfort them—be quiet, Sunny. Go to sleep like good children, and tomorrow night I'll read you a suitable story myself as Alice's taste is obviously not to be trusted."

She scooped up her book. "I wonder sometimes if you've ever really laughed at anything, Stepfather—or if you were ever a child, it's hard to imagine!"

And with that she bolted, leaving him to deal with the children. When they were eventually settled, Edward returned to his books, but now his stomach positively stabbed with choleric bile. Those pictures of a pretty little girl with her silly animals—self-aggrandisement, that's all it was; how dare she fill his children's head with such trivial stuff? The colic griped him; he groaned and, going to the cupboard, tossed back more tonic and port. But still he could not concentrate, tortured by her gibe about the lack of laughter and light in his house. How could he be light-hearted, surrounded

215

as he was by these heathen masses in dire need of redemption? How could he joke and smile, when he was plagued by so many backsliders, by lukewarm adherents even under his own roof? Now if only he could count on the wholehearted support of his stepdaughter—again his belly stabbed; again he downed the hopeful remedies, then, giving up all pretence of study, sat in a leaden gloom listening to the wail of the rising wind from the northern hills.

The evening deepened into chill night and the town's Drum Tower bell tolled the watches. Edward's belly stabbed relentlessly as he reviewed the unsatisfactory circumstances of his present life, and was only temporarily calmed by further recourse to the port bottle. When at last he rose, his head reeled unaccountably and he stepped into the yard to clear it. He looked at the sky, seeking for some sign, however remotely construable, of God's supporting presence.

All that caught his eye was a light still shining from Alice's bedroom. What could she be doing awake at this late hour? What new unsavoury mischief might she be brewing—that hard, unredeemed, young female spirit? He stumbled back inside, along the passage and burst into her bedroom; his face, though he did not know it, was glowing and he was breathing heavily. She was sitting up in bed, reading by lantern-light, the sable-lined jacket thrown round her shoulders.

"What's this now?" he pounced at her, tearing away the book. "*Wuthering Heights? Wuthering Heights?* So it's not enough to fill my children's heads with romantic nonsense but you fill your own, hey, miss? And this—this finery? How did you come by it? I've never seen this—it's a very expensive garment, I can tell that much. How could you—what devilry's been going on here?" He was bellowing with rage and his words slurred slightly as he slung the novel away, tore back the bedclothes and jerked the coat off her.

"Stop it, stop it!" She clung to it. "It's mine, mine. How dare you come bursting into my room like this?"

"How dare I?—How dare you sit here in my house reading trash, adorning your person with garments you could never have come by honestly? Oh Alice, I've had my suspicions about you before—there is not enough innocence about you, not enough Christian humility. It is time for you to be forcibly shown the way to repentance, Alice, for your own good I shall..." With shaking fingers he untied the thick waist cord of his robe. "This headstrong spirit of yours must be tamed, child. There is something of evil in you, I fear..." He breathed harshly over her, the cord in his hand, and she screamed, pushing him away, trying to duck under his raised arm.

"Stop it, Stepfather, stop it! You've gone mad... how dare you...?"

"Dare, me dare... why I dare to..." He lunged, caught her round the waist, lifted her bodily and, sitting back on the bed, slung her face down across his lap, holding her neck towards the floor with a steely arm. She cried out again, kicking her legs violently till he pinioned them down with one of his stronger ones.

"Don't resist me, Alice," he panted. "This chastisement is for your own good—it had to come. I won't tolerate this worldly light-mindedness under my own roof any longer. Humble yourself, Alice, subjugate yourself to my will. You have been contaminated by heathendom and it is my bounden duty to..." As he spoke he pulled up her night-gown and began to whip her bare thighs and buttocks with the cord. She struggled helplessly, clamped down over him, shaking more with rage than pain.

"Stop it—you beast—I hate you—"

"You are still defying me, Alice. Your spirit must be humbled—there and there again. Oh, submit yourself willingly to this punishment, Alice, accept this small pain I'm inflicting on you for your greater good..." He was almost whispering now. "Ah Alice, let me chastise this rebellious flesh, this sweet but tainted fruit... Let me feel your closed spirit opening to my will, let me just..."

As he clamped her even more tightly across his lap, she became aware of a growing bulging thrust against her stomach and, knowing she could not be mistaken, gave a sudden violent upward push of revulsion, tearing at the front of his loose robe and rending it open.

"Look at you!" she screamed. "Look at you—you filthy old man! Look, that's what you really want! Oh, it's hideous, hideous..."

For a second they both stared in mute horror at the penis which was quite unmistakably in a state of large erection beneath his merino-wool combinations. He leaped up in a frenzy, hastily gathering his torn robe over the obstreperous organ with a whimpering snarl.

"Oh dear God... what have I...? How could it...?"

"Get out," she gulped, suddenly very close to tears as the full enormity of the situation struck her and her flesh began to sting. "Get out—you're quite odious and disgusting and

I hate you . . ." He made as if to move towards her in a gesture of conciliation, but she shrank back, covered her eyes and screamed very loudly, "Get out, get out I say . . ."

He rushed away, leaving the cord on the floor. She stared at it numbly for a minute, then, putting a chair against the door, examined the weals on her skin. They were pink and sore but the flesh hadn't been broken; she lay face down on the bed and cried softly for a long while. Neither of them slept for the remainder of the night. At the first glow of dawn Edward emerged into the yard, saddled the mule and rode slowly away without a backward glance. After watching him go, Alice too rose, packed her clothes, books, the map of China and the loot-box in her calico bag.

Downstairs in the kitchen where the air smelled of charcoal, soy, pickled turnips and stale animal grease, Alice stared at the scrubbed-wood table where the family had shared so many meals, so few of them pleasurable. She visualised Edward at its head, bony hands clasped in prayer for yet another frugal repast. Never would she be part of that group again, the very thought of him there made her feel sick. She wrote a note to her mother explaining that she and Edward had quarrelled so badly she had determined to leave at once for Port Arthur, where she would stay with William. No one, she added, need worry about her in the least. Then, in a panicky haste lest Edward should return, she gulped down a bowl of purplish sorghum porridge, saddled Griffin and rode away, wrapped in her sable jacket.

All that day she travelled south, forcing herself to keep her sore buttocks on the saddle in case she was pursued. But no one followed and, by the second night, she felt securely enveloped again within the ample lap of the uncaring country. But, as her physical wounds healed, she felt more deeply hurt and outraged by what had happened. The inescapable conclusion was that her stepfather had been aroused by whipping her and this filled her with a nauseous dread, for it suggested a brutality that she had never sensed in Lung-kuang. So which was the more "civilised" way—Lung-kuang's unashamed sensual enjoyment or her stepfather's desire to subjugate and hurt her, all mixed up with his horrible secret lust? Surely Edward did not feel the same when he made love to his own wife, her mother?

Questions like these throbbed in her head like an aching tooth and every time she probed them she experienced a burning disgust so strong it was like a bad taste in the mouth. Again and again, though she tried desperately not to, she saw that large unsightly bulge beneath Edward's underwear; the way his hands had clawed to cover it; hands she had so often seen clasped in prayer. Stirred and weakened by these thoughts, she longed to lie beside Lung-kuang's trim body, to feel again his gentle knowingness. One morning, waking in a dirty village inn, she got out the map of China with the wild idea of simply riding south-west for hundreds of miles till she reached the gates of the Chu.

But this, she knew, was impossible, for the winds, blasting straight from the Mongolian wastes, were daily more bitter, the tracks between the villages iced-over mires, and her freedom was but a temporary respite, for the family would be in anxious contact about her, and she had no other home. So she spurred Griffin down the broad mountainous spur of the Liaotung Peninsula until, on the tenth day out, she reached that point where it narrowed to little more than a bridge separating the Bay of Korea from the Gulf of Chihli. Then the land widened to small-island size, and there ahead, on the very last tip, huddled at the base of stony hills called The White Wolf, The Dragon Ridge and The Eagle's Nest, was Port Arthur.

9

Both Alice and Isabel long remembered their first meeting and learned to laugh about it; but its actual occurrence, on a wintry evening in the year 1880 at William's house next to Port Arthur's Imperial Maritime Customs office, was uncomfortable. Making herself known to the servant, Alice was shown into the drawing-room and she was tentatively running her fingers over the luxurious wine-velvet of the armchairs, when Isabel came in. No one had told Alice that her sister-in-law was beautiful—or at least striking, for her nose and mouth were too full for classic beauty. But what Alice first saw was her statuesque figure, splendidly arrayed in an evening gown of emerald brocade with a sweeping satin train, silken gloves covered most of her arms, her creamy shoulders half-bared, and a diamanté necklace glittering at her throat; above all shone a mass of natural auburn curls, coiled back from her face in a glowing chignon. In the eyes of foreigners this was her crowning glory, though the Chinese had a special aversion to such a hue and her nickname among them, Alice later learned, was "Number One Red-Devil".

Painfully aware of her travel-stained jacket, baggy trousers, the stench of roadside inn that clung to her, Alice simply stood and gaped. Isabel too paused involuntarily, then stepped valiantly forward, silk-encased arms outstretched in welcome. "You must be Alice?" It was almost an incredulous question, and Alice replied, "Yes, but I don't always look like this, only I've ridden a long way on a horse."

Isabel's face lost its majesty as she replied with a broad smile, "Never mind, I don't always look like this either, only William and I are dining with the French Consul tonight."

Then William hurried in, gathering her into his arms, smell and all, saying how delighted he was that she had arrived safe and sound. And then, when the pair went off for dinner, Alice had a bath, a good supper and slept in a bedroom that seemed a veritable bower of luxury and elegance compared to her room at the Mission. Isabel soon made her feel at home, for she was a kindly, sensible woman devoted to her husband and two children, four-year-old Charlotte and baby Joel and quite prepared to include within their tranquil circle her husband's sister, whom, she felt, had so far spent a rather wretched life. It was little wonder, she told William, that Alice had determined to leave Mukden, for what sort of life was there for a spirited girl in a remote mission station unless she were a missionary? Alice, she declared, had been put upon enough, and what she needed now was a little social polishing, a bit of wholesome fun and a radical reappraisal of her wardrobe.

William seldom gainsaid his wife in such matters and Alice was so grateful to be offered a home without the asking of awkward questions that she fell in eagerly with Isabel's plans. So the two spent many earnest hours closeted with Madame Claire, the town's French dressmaker, where Alice was fitted for a tight cuirass bodice moulded to her waist and hips, for a day-dress of astrakhan cloth, for a lemon-yellow tea-gown with ruffled lace sleeves, and a velveteen tie-back walking dress that she wore with an ermine muff and saucy fur hat. And in due course, when it was the Greenwoods' turn to invite the French Consul to dine, Alice appeared in a blue silk polonaise gown, looped at the sides and draped at the back, trimmed with white and rose ribbons; moonstones glowed at her neck and brown curls framed a face that looked almost too demure, were it not for the mischievous greenish eyes that were always knowing, alert and clear.

Monsieur Félix Fauré, the Assistant French Consul also present, was much taken with the Customs Inspector's sister, as Isabel guessed he would be, for Félix was intelligent, if a little affected for her taste. His dark moustache was long and droopy, he wore velvet waistcoats and the silk facings of his dress-coats were rather flamboyant, his manner and accented English most dashingly Gallic; but, a Parisian by birth, he undoubtedly possessed savoir-faire and was just the man to teach Alice the social ropes.

Félix too wanted to cultivate their acquaintance, for not only was Alice the most fascinating English sliver of Chinese jade he had ever met, but she was thoroughly conversant with Mandarin, the mastering of which was his only serious ambition. Soon after the dinner-party therefore, it was arranged that Alice should go to the French Consulate every Friday afternoon to help Félix with his Chinese, for which she received generous payment and a lavish pastry tea. As the days shortened, the tea-hour lengthened into suppertime, after which Félix escorted her home. At least that was generally the practice, till the evening Félix suggested they call for a night-cap at Epimoff's.

At that time Port Arthur was little more than a fishing port except for the newly opened Chinese naval college on the outskirts and the cluster of Western-style buildings near the harbour. Here stood the consulates of various European nations, of the Americans and Japanese, and the Customs office where William presided. Here too was Epimoff's, the only hotel and known to everyone, though Alice had not been inside before because William did not think it quite respectable. This view would have infuriated its owner who claimed to run the only thoroughly reputable hostelry between Shanghai and Vladivostock.

A Russian Jewess of ample proportions and experience, Madame Epimoff had opened her establishment three years before and its dining-room, with huge oak sideboard, glass chandeliers, tinkly piano and a corner bar, was famed for its bortsch soup and brown sourbread. Olga, her daughter, wore tight satin gowns and played French chansons near closing-time and was an added attraction to the regular clientele. Most were of French, Russian or American extraction and of the male sex, for Madame considered the British, Germans and most women to be unutterably boring and the Chinese totally inexplicable. Alice, though lacking the requisite qualifications, was allowed in on sufferance at Félix's request, for he was a favourite of hers.

Madame had also been persuaded to offer table-space to some of the Chinese naval students who in tight-buttoned jackets, serge trousers, and peaked caps provided a touch of comic relief that was irresistible. Earnest, argumentative, puzzled young men, they tried in vain to seem at ease in this alien setting, spooning soup self-consciously, sipping hesitantly at the famous Epimoff cocktail made with vodka, melon juice and angostura bitters, losing their shyness in violent political debate as the evenings progressed, and fleeing instantly when Olga began to play, for they found the noise unendurable.

Soon the Friday visit to Epimoff's became a high point of Alice's week: she developed a taste for bortsch and vodka and liked the cosy familiarity of the scene on long winter nights when only habitués gathered there and Madame's aged father-in-law, sole witness to the existence of some long-departed spouse, sat in the warm stove-corner playing chess with the Russian doctor.

As the season warmed the port livened up again. Local fishing boats ventured out into the Gulf of Pechili and trading junks loaded cargoes of soy, bean-cakes and sesame seed oil from the warehouses. Larger vessels came nosing into harbour from afar and Félix and Alice, arriving at the hotel on the first balmy evening of late April, were surprised by the crowd of new faces.

Two Korean sea-captains and three Russian tea-merchants were eating bortsch, and propping up the bar was a portly grey-whiskered man called Harry Snow, owner of a schooner called the *Snowdrop* in which he hunted sea-otters along the Korean and Japanese coasts; draped at his side was a blonde woman in a low-cut sequinned dress. The Chinese students also seemed more animated than usual, Félix thought as he elbowed a way to the bar, cosily nudging the blonde en route.

"Alice *ma chérie*," he handed a cocktail, "there is something in the wind with the students—they are all drawing ships on bits of paper. Find out what it is, my little Jade, and come and tell your old French uncle." He rolled his eyes at her. Félix was in fact only a few years Alice's senior, but it was a game he had instigated to avoid any hint of seriousness in their relationship. Through the visits to Epimoff's, she had however proved a useful source of information about what was going on among the naval students, some of whom were hot-headed political reformists. It was for this reason that the French Consul was always ready, if required, to vouch for the games of cribbage with which Félix and Alice were supposed innocently to while away Friday evenings. The Consul's reward was the satisfaction of being generally better informed than his rival British counterpart, who had never considered Alice's diplomatic value.

Alice, innocent of such stratagems, simply enjoyed the

223

students' company and their ambitious plans for the future of China excited her. So when she returned to Félix, her eyes were sparkling.

"Yes, there is news. Li Hung-chang has finally persuaded the Empress Dowager to go ahead with the building of that shipyard here."

"Really? It is official, not just another rumour?"

"Official yes. That lecturer, the one they all call 'The Leader' who never comes here, has just returned from Peking where he had a meeting with the great man himself and got the direct word. They are to begin building at once and some students have just arrived from Foochow Arsenal to take navigation courses. It will really put Port Arthur on the map at last, they say."

The blonde leaned over Félix's shoulder, "Well it's sure time something put this godforsaken hole on the map. And your French friend tells me you live here year round, Miss Greenwood? That's tough."

Alice smiled. "Oh I don't mind, I've lived in worse places, Miss...?"

"O'Hara, Mrs Bella O'Hara. Well, at least there's a good selection of real full-blooded gentlemen round here—which must be a compensation." She looked roguish, but Alice flushed and stammered, "Oh I don't... I mean, I only come here on Fridays with Félix, you see my brother doesn't know and..."

Félix grinned. "Poor Miss Greenwood had the dire misfortune of being born into a missionary family, Mrs O'Hara. She's on the road to recovery, I'm pleased to say, under the tutelage of her *bon oncle*, but still has much to learn..."

"Is that so?" Bella, losing any spark of interest in Alice, turned to him, "Well my gallant Parisian, perhaps you can tutor me a little... Who is this Chinaman, this Li someone-or-other who orders shipyards to appear? Is he the President?"

"*Hélas, non,* the Chinese, dear *madame,* do not espouse the enlightened republican ideas of you Yankees and we French. *Non,* they have their Emperors still, or rather now they have mainly an Empress, the old Buddha, the arch-she-dragon of all times, the avowed enemy of all change and progress who lavishes her country's money on the building of yet another grand edifice in the grounds of her glorious Summer Palace near Peking where there are already Halls of Sparkling Brightnesses, Pavilions of Southern Fragrances and what not. Naturally she has no interest whatsoever in such ugly monstrosities as shipyards, but this Li Hung-chang, the Governor of Chihli, is powerful and persuasive. He sees further in front of his flat little nose than most of his compatriots and realises that 'when a series of changes has run all its course another change ensues'—as he quotes some worthy sage or other. And he sees that if, in ten years' time, there is still nothing more terrible to behold in China than fragrant pavilions and men brandishing muskets, the place will be in a hopeless mess. Someone will over-run it. Already the nations of the West are watching 'like birds of prey and grey wolves with watering mouths and eyes'—as they graphically put it. Nevertheless Li believes, and he may be right, that the first invaders of the Celestial Empire will be the little yellow Japs from the East who are learning, oh so fast, to build ships that go under their own steam and fire breech-loaders. So—the astute Governor wants his country to be the proud possessor of arsenals and shipyards and vessels made of iron instead of wood, with trained technicians to make them work, and he must have gained the Empress Dowager's ear recently. And *that* is why our young Chinese friends over there are happily designing grand and quite improbable warships and dreaming of the days when they'll all be admirals of the fleet, conquerors of all Asia, and Heaven knows what else!"

Bella, laughing in appreciation of this discourse, proceeded to ask Félix about the scandalous court revels in which the Empress, her intimates and eunuchs were rumoured to indulge, while Alice twirled her glass disconsolately and eavesdropped. People were talking of fishing, buying tea and selling timber, of otters, stormy seas and places she had never seen. Only she had nothing to say, for her life had become lacklustre and static, she thought resentfully. Who would want to hear about Lottie's new tooth, Isabel's new evening-gown, the jam tarts she had made for tomorrow's picnic? Finishing a second cocktail, she lapsed into a discontented sulk, feeling ever smaller and of less account as more people crowded into the bar chatting animatedly and ignoring her. But suddenly she gasped, staring incredulously at a latecomer who had just joined the nearby student table.

"Félix—that student over there... it's... it must be..." Excitedly she pushed through the crowd and tugged his sleeve. He turned.

"Han-li, Younger Brother—it is you!"

Seeing his familiar face, so little changed under its absurd peaked cap, she felt as if a rabbit-hole had opened at her feet. The years fell away from them both and they clasped each other with shining eyes. For a minute everyone quietened at the extraordinary sight till Han-li drew back in embarrassment.

"Uncut Jade—you. Is it possible?"

"And you, Han-li, in that Western uniform. I am astounded!"

"But let's go and talk quietly over there, everyone is watching us."

After a word of excited explanation to Félix, she joined him, bubbling with curiosity. "You—a student here? But however did you manage it? What are you studying? Your Honourable Father has actually permitted this? And how is he—the respected Dragon Brightness? And Tamao and Mei?"

He butted in eagerly. "And your brother, my barbarian horse-groom, where is he now?"

"Working as a clerk in a Shanghai hong—quite a young man about town now, and still mad on horses. But you...?"

"It all started with Younger Sister really. She was betrothed to a Changsha man of good family, you remember? But just before the wedding he died and she was broken-hearted."

"Mei was fond of him?"

"She scarcely knew him, but she desperately wanted a husband and sons. So she pestered and pestered till Father let her marry another man—a young fellow and restless by nature. He took her off to Canton and went into business. Father didn't much like it, but it meant I was able to visit her." He looked at Alice shyly. "You remember when we last met you said there were so many things in the modern world I'd never dreamed of? Well when I went to Canton I began to understand, and I begged Father to let me stay there to study after I did well in my Eight-Legged Essay examination—and eventually he agreed."

"But how is it you are here, in Port Arthur?"

"I studied maths and Western naval science at Canton, then at Foochow, because I'm good at these strange things. Now I'm here for a short while because of the new shipyard. But you, Uncut? Is that your husband over there?"

"No, Han-li, I'm not yet married. I live here with my brother, the older one you never really met—except in the little wood near the boundary wall!"

"But you're quite old now, Uncut, surely you should be married and having children?"

226

His question wasn't intentionally rude, but she replied curtly, "We Western women don't marry so young, you know."

He smiled. "I'm sorry, I didn't mean..."

Félix pushed through the crowd. "Alice, I hate to interrupt this happy reunion, but there'll be a grand confrontation with your brother if you're late." He held up his watch. "Fifteen minutes to ten."

"Oh botheration, and we've only just met. But I'm afraid you're right. I'll tell Will about Han-li... but oh dear, I'm not supposed to be here at all. Félix, why is it I always seem to be deceiving people though I never want to?"

"Because you are something of an original, *ma chérie*, you don't easily fit the mould. But you're not quite original enough to break it altogether, if you see what I mean?"

"Only too well." She laughed wryly and he patted her arm.

"There are worse fates, I am similar in a way. But come, I really must see you home."

"Oh dear! Younger Brother, I know—you must come to our family tea on Sunday and meet everyone—my brother, his wife, the children."

The arrangement was made, though Han-li looked rather anxious about it and Félix, drawing her into the shadow of a verandah on the way home, warned gently, "This meeting between the Chu lad and your relatives may not be easy, Alice—a great exercise in international diplomacy for you, *hein*? You'll have to be careful."

"I was just thinking that. It will be so odd to see them together, I'm not sure I'll like it."

He chuckled, tilting her face to his. "But it will undoubtedly be interesting, and think, if I'd not taken you to Epimoff's, it might never have happened. So do I not deserve my usual reward, Little Jade?" He began kissing and cuddling her gently, which he regarded as an hors d'oeuvre for his customary Friday visit to the little piece of Chinese porcelain who was waiting for him in nearby Green Peacock Street. Finally he kissed her nose. "There—does Mr Jeffrey Winthrop make love to you so nicely?"

Félix was slightly jealous of Jeffrey Winthrop, his counterpart at the British Consulate who'd been courting Alice recently with what Félix considered typical British phlegm. In Jeff's shoes, Félix would have soon made sure of Alice, but he had a fiancée of his own Catholic faith waiting in Tours, not to mention the lady of Green Peacock Street.

Alice tossed her head. "That's my business is it not,

Monsieur Fauré? But he's coming for a picnic on the hills with us tomorrow, so you'd better watch out!"

"Ah, *le pauvre Winnée*, he's somewhat slow, is he not? He'd bore the pretty little socks off you in no time, such a big sack of rugged northern grit!"

Alice giggled; and did again the next morning when they all set off for the hills and she considered the shape of Jeffrey Winthrop riding ahead with William—his solid bottom planted squarely on his horse, his hair, she suddenly thought, very similar in hue to the gritty slope up which they were climbing. Sun sparkled on the wavelets of the distant sea below; the wiry undergrowth was greening and butterflies flickered over it. She sniffed the balmy air and smiled, for spring was her favourite season. On the hill's crest, Will and Jeff waited for the rest of the party: Alice on Griffin, the cook-boy driving a laden donkey, and two covered litters, one for Isabel and Joel, the other for Charlotte and the amah.

"Look down there—quite large trees and even a tinkling brook," Will pointed. "What better spot for a picnic?"

On that they all agreed and slithered down into the valley where the cook-boy, resigned to these barbarian follies, unloaded the donkey and the bearers bathed their arms in the water. "A proper coppice," Jeff marched about triumphantly. "Birches in new leaf, alders, gorse, even a bit of grass." He dug his heels in the tough tufts. "Reminds me a little of the Dales, know that part of the world, Will?"

"No—but it reminds me of those spinneys near the North Norfolk coast where I used to go on holiday with Aunt Sarah."

Jeff jeered. "It's a coppice, not a spinney and it's all Dales!"

Isabel clambered from the litter, brushing dust from her skirt, "What nonsense you men talk—it's a grove, made for green thoughts in a green shade, ten a penny in the Cotswolds, and the streams smell better there!"

Alice, leading Griffin to water, said tartly, "Why can't it just be a Chinese wood—as we're in China?"

Isabel smiled gently. "Oh Alice, I keep forgetting you've not seen the beautiful English countryside yet—meadows of lush grass and wild flowers, the variety of trees. Once you have, you'll understand why we talk so, pretending to be Home for a while."

Jeff frowned into the budding birches. "Yes it's seeing something like this, just familiar enough to make one homesick suddenly. It's more than time you saw the old country, Alice, we'll have to do something about it, don't you think?"

He smiled towards her encouragingly but she was busy

with Griffin, for conversations about Home always made her apprehensive and resentful. "You must come back with us on our next leave," Isabel had already promised, "that is, if some handsome young man hasn't already taken you as his blushing bride!" Was that what Jeff had in mind now, Alice wondered, intercepting a meaningful glance between her brother and Isabel.

"Well, we'll not get all melancholy about Dales or Cotswolds," Will said briskly. "As Alice says, it's a Chinese wood and we're about to have a proper Chinese picnic—and you wouldn't get bean-sprout salad at Home, so we should count our blessings!"

They all laughed, then Isabel settled in the shade to feed the baby and William gave Cook-boy a lesson in the art of chicken-carving, while Jeff and Alice mounted again to ride up and look at the hill-top view. As Isabel spooned mush into Joel's mouth, she said, "Jeff hasn't spoken to you, has he, Will? I wondered when he mentioned Home just now."

"About Alice? No—I daresay she could nobble him if she tried harder, but I suspect she prefers Félix."

"Who's oozing with Gallic charm, unlike our solid Jeff from t'Dales. Anyway, it's hard to guess what Alice really thinks. You know, we were out walking with Charlotte recently and some of those naval college students greeted her most familiarly, and I wondered then how they knew her. Then last night she tells us she just met this younger Chu son by chance, but I doubt it somehow. She's rather secretive, you know, and I'm not being over-critical I hope, because I love her dearly."

Will came to kiss her, holding the carving knife playfully at Joel's forehead.

"Papa, don't, he might jump into the knife!" Charlotte squealed.

"I'd like to see him—go and help the boy, Lottie," and she trotted off, enjoying taking knives, forks and dishes from their padded hamper nests and spreading them around the white cloth.

"Yes, she is secretive, Uncle Robert used to say so—never quite know where you are with her. And I'm not sure it's at all a good thing, this young Chu turning up out of the blue. The real trouble is, she's twenty-three and it's time she was properly settled. Now if Jeff were to propose I'd be all in favour."

"Well, I doubt if she'd accept. She doesn't look at him in the right way."

229

"Oh, you ladies and your looking!"

"But there isn't enough choice for her here, she'd be better off in Shanghai which is bursting with lovelorn young bachelors, I believe."

William sighed, arranging chicken slices carefully on the plates while the boy watched, apparently lost in admiration. "But I can't send her to Shanghai without chaperonage and Frank's leading much too wild a life with that horse-racing fraternity to be relied upon... Lottie, don't tip the salt on the ground, there's a good girl... No, we must wait for something to work itself out." He looked up the valley where the two had just reappeared, riding leisurely in single file. "Perhaps something has?"

Isabel, following his gaze, smiled fondly. "Don't be silly, Will, if any momentous subject had been broached, they wouldn't be returning in that ordinary sort of way."

Commonsensical Isabel was right of course; Jeff had not proposed, though he had said how he enjoyed riding with Alice and how dull life had been before her arrival. And Alice had been a trifle flirtatious in return, reining close to him at the hill's top where they looked eastward across the glittering sea.

"And beyond the horizon lies the Hermit Kingdom—the last bastion of oriental exclusiveness soon to be broken down because the old king's just been deposed," Jeff said sententiously. "The Americans are opening a consulate in Seoul soon and my boss wants to be the first British rep on the scene. He says everyone will have diplomatic relations established within a year."

"Really? The Koreans I've met don't think so..."

"Oh? Where have you met any, Alice? I can't tell them from Mongols."

"Their language is awful and they smell of that dreadful pickled cabbage they eat so much... As to where I've met them, wouldn't you like to know, Mr Winthrop?"

She teased so winningly that he wanted to crush her in his arms and get the truth from her, which, he suspected involved that foreign frog Fauré. But his northern caution saved him. "It's none of my business of course, Alice... Let's go, your brother will have carved the chicken to perfection by now."

So they had ridden back in their ordinary sort of way to eat the chickens, the salads, Alice's jam tarts, all washed down with claret, and then lounged in the shade of the English-seeming birches while the amah crooned lullabies for the children. As the sun set they had ridden home, and later, as the moon rose, Alice gazed at it from her bedroom window, relieved she had not been pressed towards any decision that day. Jeff Winthrop was pleasant enough, the stuff from which worthy Vice-Consuls are cut, as Will had said in an unguarded moment. But she did not want to be the wife of a life-long Vice-Consul whose grit-coloured hair was already receding to reveal a life-long freckly skull.

So what did she want? Her encounter with Han-li had unleashed the haunting secret memories of lustful beddings with his father. Undressing, she looked sorrowfully at her firm, young, unused body and, shivering with untimely desire, traced faintly on the chilled windowpane the characters Lung-kuang, Dragon Brightness—the only man who had yet penetrated her. Tomorrow, she thought as she climbed into bed, she must discreetly learn more of him from Han-li and oh, how pleased she was to have met him again!

But when he was ushered into the drawing-room the next afternoon her pleasure shrivelled into apprehension as she seemed to see two simultaneous but conflicting scenes. For Han-li, there was large William drawing himself up importantly and smiling with no warmth; Isabel, cool, unknowable, with that dreadfully unnatural coloured hair, and the children wide-eyed at the idea of a Chinaman come to Sunday tea. And for William there was an undersized student, looking much younger than his twenty-one years, in his absurd ill-fitting naval academy suit, twisting his cap in his hands and darting inscrutable glances at them.

Alice made the best of the introductions; Han-li sat on the very edge of a straight chair, and Isabel asked kindly, "You are studying here at the college, Mr Chu?"

"Yes," he mumbled carefully.

"And have you ever been in a real English home before?" William inquired, looking round his heavily-furnished room and thinking it must be quite an eye-opener for the lad.

"Yes. In Foochow."

"Ah . . . We lived there for a while. Quite a fine little dock-yard you Chinese have there now, what?"

Han-li turned to Alice, pleading in his own tongue. "Uncut Jade, you'll have to help. I've learned a lot of English from books and I can understand, but I can't reply quickly enough, please translate for me . . ."

After that conversation flowed rather more easily until

Isabel took the children to wash before tea and Alice said, "Will, I must ask Han-li about the family and that's easier for me in Chinese."

"The family—what an odd expression for you to use. But go ahead, don't mind me." William began to read a copy of the *Illustrated London News* with ostentatious attention which was distracted nevertheless by the irritating clack of an alien tongue in his Sunday drawing-room.

"Tell me about Tamao and Weng first." Alice drew her chair closer to his. "Are they well—and little Custard Apple?"

"Ah yes, they live in tranquillity and lighten the home for everyone. There is another son now—a real scamp. We call him Pepperseed because he shows signs of the Hunanese quick temper already."

"And Han-fei, Eldest Brother?"

Han-li shrugged. "He still doesn't please Father—he's so touchy and irresponsible. His new wife is prettier than silly old Dull Thorn, but she too only bears daughters." He sniggered. "So he has three now—including the poor little runt who should have died when her mother did."

"Han-li, what a cruel thing to say!"

He glanced at her. "But it would have been better. Oh I know you Westerners look at it differently—all babies are sacred so your missionaries say. But your soldiers think nothing of killing hundreds of babies—and their parents—when they go grabbing other nations' territories."

Alice bit her lip. "I suppose I never thought of it quite like that. You're learning the ways of the world fast, Han-li."

"This is no time for slowness, that's what Father found hard to understand. When I eventually persuaded him to let me study foreign matters he said, 'Can you not wait? It will mean losing you forever, my son.' And in a sense he was right. I can never go home again, not really."

He looked at her gloomily and she patted his hand. "I know just what you mean, Younger Brother, because, when I think of them all—even Vegetable Aunt with her fits and Spots with his ducks—it seems almost like home to me too. A lost home."

Irritably William threw down his magazine and stalked out saying, "Tea is served, Alice."

"I don't think your brother likes me, Uncut?" Han-li whispered.

"Oh it's not you personally—I suppose it's because he's not used to having Chinese to tea."

Han-li grinned wryly and rose as Alice put a hand on his shoulder. "And your Honourable Father? Is he healthy? Is he happy? I often think of him kindly..."

"Ah yes...he has now two sons with his unofficial wife and that gladdens him. But he grows a little weary and it worries him, I think, that Eldest Brother will one day be in charge of the household. How he and Brother-in-law would quarrel!"

"But the Dragon Brightness is not that elderly surely?"

"Not yet—but he shows his few grey hairs with pride and says he wishes he had time to cultivate chrysanthemums as his Honourable Father did before him. The years pass..."

"Yes indeed and you are a man now, like Frank."

"Frank, now tell me..."

They went into tea chatting gaily and Alice, ignoring the frost that emanated from her brother, reported defiantly, "Han-li's been asking about Frank. He's going to call on him in Shanghai when he leaves here. Won't that be a wonderful reunion for them?"

William mumbled noncommittally, thinking it was pretty cool of this Chinese whippersnapper to be claiming friendship on an equal footing with his brother and sister. But they would not see it that way of course...Damn and blast that dreadful Tientsin business; there never seemed to be an end to it. Finishing his second tea-cake, he asked, "So you're learning something about modern science, are you, young man? It must be a great puzzle? Can you read a compass properly yet?"

Han-li scowled. "We Chinese have used compasses since the days of the Han dynasty, sir. It's only recently that we've fallen a little behind in these technical matters, but we're catching up fast."

"Ah yes, I forgot...Still, you've quite a lot of catching up to do at the moment. It seems to me that the vast majority of your countrymen have no desire to learn anything new whatever—poor ignorant wretches. And you few young idealists will find it difficult to drag them into the modern world. Progressive, enlightened civilisations like ours in Britain to-day are built on solid foundations, you know."

"And you don't think China has a solid foundation of civilisation?"

Han-li's eyes glinted and Isabel broke in: "Now, Will, have more cake and stop this political talk, it only causes friction. Cake, Han-li? Now tell me about your father and mother.

Are they not curious to visit you and see Treaty Port life for themselves? All the modern changes, the grand buildings and foreign ships?"

Han-li smiled wistfully. "My father is a very busy man in Hunan, he couldn't be spared, madam. And he wouldn't quite know what to make of it all, would he, Uncut?"

"But your mother, she has more time surely?" Isabel insisted politely.

The very thought of Hidden Glory in Hong Kong made Alice laugh aloud. "Oh Isabel, no—Han-li's mother only leaves her house two or three times a year. She knows of nothing—nothing beyond Changsha, and precious little of that."

"But how dreadful, you never told me that, Alice. Really, the way Chinese women are treated..."

"It's different, Isabel. The seclusion seemed cruel to me sometimes and I could never live happily within it, but..."

Han-li, partly understanding, added stiffly, "Please explain to your relative, Uncut, that my mother is quite tranquil in her home. She would be most unhappy in the common bustle of the world that seems so desirable to you Western women."

Isabel, bridling at his tone, rose abruptly. "Come children, it's bedtime. Say good-bye to Mr Chu. He used to play bows and arrows with your Uncle Frank when he was a little boy— isn't that odd to think of?"

Indeed it was and Charlotte and Joel stared in renewed astonishment at Han-li as Isabel and Alice led them away.

William, folding his napkin, wondered how he could make it clear to this young Chinaman that, whatever had happened in the past, he could not expect to be "one of the family" in this house. "I hope you enjoyed your first real English tea, Han-li? You must visit us again sometime, though I'm sure you understand that, in my position here, I have to be careful about local contacts?"

Han-li bowed, saying merely, "The tea was very nice, thank you."

When Alice returned they moved towards the drawing-room and William decided to reinforce his message. "I don't suppose you've much time for anything but your studies here, Han-li? And you must stick at them. China's going to need promising young men of vision like you who've realised the errors of the past and broken free from the backward old ways of their families..."

A flush mottled Han-li's sallow cheeks, and the fierce pride of the Sons of Han gave him the ability to say directly in

English what had been smouldering in his mind for the past hour. "You call my country uncivilised and my people ignorant. Our ways are very different—our ways are deep in the past, centuries and centuries. You know nothing about us. My father is an important man, he has power and dignity but you call him backward, and my mother also. You do not want to know me, his son. But when your brother and sister were in our household they were the ignorant, uncivilised barbarians and at that time your brother was grateful to be my horse-groom and your sister my father's woman."

"What—what did you say?" William grabbed him by the collar while Alice wailed in dismay. "Oh Younger Brother—what have you said? He didn't know that—oh dear heaven..."

Han-li, red and trembling, looked at them both, realising where his fury had led him. He blurted, "I'm sorry, Uncut, I assumed he knew—and I lost my temper. I cannot stand his attitudes. I must go now, please..."

William shook him. "Alice, my little sister, and your father. How dare you suggest such a filthy thing?"

"It's true, William. I never told you because you'd have been so shocked. Well now you are. And stop shaking Younger Brother. It wasn't his fault, he was only a boy at the time."

"And you only a girl, only..."

"Fifteen, yes." Sadly she handed Han-li his cap. "He'd better go. I suppose it was a mistake his coming here, but I so wanted you all to like each other."

"Like each other—when his father..."

Han-li glowered at William, unrepentant. "My father is an honourable man, civilised, not backward. He was very kind to the Uncut Jades called Greenwood. Goodbye to you."

Hearing the front door slam, Isabel rushed down. "Has he gone? But what's happened?"

Alice's voice trembled with sympathetic rage. "Han-li couldn't stand anymore of your patronising airs and graces about his country and people. And when Will started on his family he lost his temper and I don't blame him. It's never once occurred to you, has it, brother William, that this whole house and everything in it would fit easily into the Chus' courtyard? Oh you just have no notion how proud and fine it all was!"

Her voice broke and she began to sob noisily. Isabel reached for a handkerchief.

"There, there, never mind, Alice. I was afraid this mightn't work out well."

"But she's not told you the whole—the parting shot from our dear Younger Brother. Not only was Frank his horse-groom apparently, but Alice was his 'father's woman', as he bluntly put it."

"He said that? Alice—oh dear God—that can't be true surely?"

"Yes Isabel, that's why I ran away from the house."

"But my dear, how very very dreadful. You just a child and he... he forced you to...?"

"Yes, but I soon escaped."

"Oh dear, oh dear. Will, you had your suspicions years ago." She put an arm on Alice's shaking shoulders. "But you can't blame her—a mere child and forced to it."

"No I can't blame her for that, it's just too horrible to think of. But I certainly do blame her for inviting that insolent lad here, to our house as a friend, after the crime his father committed on her."

"It was the custom. He didn't see it as a crime at all. No one there did." She sniffed. "In their eyes it was far superior to being a skivvy—the other kitchen maids quite envied me."

Isabel shuddered. "Oh Alice, how can you think of it in that way? Using innocent girls, keeping them in concubinage, a sort of harem—men like that are not civilised."

Alice's face flamed. "Well, what's so civilised about many men of our race? They have their women just the same—I've seen them along the waterfront—miserable creatures often without any homes. At least a proper concubine has a roof over her head. But you're all so hypocritical—pretending such things don't go on among us, that we are whiter than the driven snow compared to the 'immoral Chinese'... Oh, how I hate that expression, Stepfather used to say it and he... ugh!" She shuddered, her tears drying in remembered outrage.

"The men you speak of are foreign sailors and such—the riff raff of the docks," William snapped. "But the subject is closed, Alice. What happened to you was most shocking and you were an innocent victim. It's a thousand pities you weren't completely honest years ago, then this needn't have happened now. Naturally I don't want you ever to see that young Chinaman again—and I say again, you must put the whole unsavoury episode of your captivity right out of your mind, that is the only healthy solution."

She snorted bitterly. "Episode—we're talking about years of my life, and Frank's."

William raised his head at a distant wail. "I hear Lottie

crying. Why don't you go and soothe her, Alice? She listens to you..."

"The only one here who does," Alice muttered as she stormed out and Isabel, shrugging at her husband, followed.

William poured a sherry to steady himself. What a stubborn, argumentative little minx his sister was. No wonder Mother had not tried to get her back to Mukden! So—she was not virginal, somehow he had always suspected it; there was a look in her eyes sometimes. He began to speculate on what had actually occurred in the house of the Chu. Dragon Brightness—ugh! Had Alice really been one of several women in his harem, draped in soft silks, smoothing him wherever he wished, satisfying his every whim? His skin tingled. How much did his sister know about the pleasures of the flesh? Perhaps more than he did. The thought disturbed him profoundly and, for the first time since her arrival, he devoutly wished his sister would go away.

In spite of William's prohibition Alice looked for Han-li at Epimoff's the next Friday and, when he did not appear, sent a note via his friend begging him to come the following week. In the interim, she rehearsed how she could soothe his wounded pride, convince him that she shared none of her relatives' stupid prejudices. And, when Friday came again, Han-li was indeed there, but bursting with eager importance and saying, before she could open her mouth, "Uncut Jade, I'm to take you to the Leader at once. He's asked me to..."

"The Leader? But why ever should he...?"

"I don't know. I happened to mention my meeting you again. I didn't tell him everything, don't worry. And he simply instructed me to bring you this evening. One doesn't ask a man like him questions."

Alice turned in puzzlement to Félix. "I should go, Alice. There can be no harm, he's a respected college lecturer, and you may learn some interesting political tittle-tattle. But back before ten..."

Han-li and Alice bowled along in rickshaws to the old quay where fishing junks were moored near some seedy, two-storey dwellings with overhanging verandahs. He led her up a narrow stair, knocking carefully on a door. "One and two, three-four-five—the special knock for the Leader's friends," Han-li whispered as the door opened and the man stood looking at her. First her scalp then her whole skin prickled with excitement as if she had known all along who it would be, but dared not think who, inevitably, it was.

"Uncut Jade," he said softly. "So we meet again, as I knew we would."

"Lin Fu-wei, the man on the *Mandalay*," she gasped.

"You haven't forgotten me surely?" He sounded quite shocked.

"No—but I'm surprised to see you here."

"And I you—till Han-li told me of his reunion with a certain English girl called Uncut Jade who once lived in captivity in his household... But why didn't you tell me that when we first met?" He drew her courteously inside, saying, "Thank you, student-boy, it is indeed she. You may go now, but return at the right time to escort her back." Han-li bowed reverently and fled.

Lin had filled out in stature and bearing since their earlier meeting; his face showed signs of authority, though his eyes were still as bold and quick, his mouth as full and mobile. His room was simply furnished with every chair piled high with books; a writing-desk stood in the verandah window. As he cleared a seat for her, she noticed his hands were trembling and guessed why, for she too was tongue-tied, remembering his exciting nearness as they had talked on the *Mandalay* deck, and his words at their parting. He was considering her carefully.

"You are a grown woman now, Uncut Jade, but you are still Miss Greenwood and unmarried?"

"Yes—it is not a disgrace to be single among us you know, we aren't like the Chinese."

He grinned. "I am aware of that, Miss Greenwood, or Uncut Jade as I hope I may still call you? I'm sure one so charming would easily find a husband if she chose."

There was an embarrassed pause till Alice said, "And you have grown into a position of importance now, Lin? The students call you Leader, do they not? When they spoke of you at Epimoff's I wondered why they used that title—in English?"

"But don't you remember at our very first encounter, I told you I wanted to be a leader of the nation? I could tell you didn't take me seriously, but I kept the name in English to remind myself of the ambition I first expressed to you."

She flushed with pleasure. "I'm glad I helped in my small way. But now, five years later, how does leadership feel, Lin?"

"Ah that is the trouble—I'm not a leader of the people at all, only a college lecturer with bright new ideas that I can't knock into my addle-pated students! It is all so much more complicated than I thought then . . ." He cleared another chair and sat down. "There is so much stubborn, deep-rooted conservatism in this country, so many die-hards in powerful positions. I've recently returned from Peking where I met an American, Mr Martin, who runs a school for the acquiring of Western knowledge, the *T'ung-wen Kuan*."

"I've heard of him, wasn't he once a missionary? My stepfather says he's been seduced from the true Way by the false dawn of modern science."

"Huh, the stuffy, old-fashioned missionary view . . . No, Mr Martin's a good man, but getting so dispirited by us reactionary Chinese. I'll give you an example—recently he wanted to teach his students how to operate a telegraph system and had one sent over especially from America. When he demonstrated it to some officials in Peking they thought it was just a great big joke! They were blind to its potential, his students won't soil their hands with it—so now it's mouldering in a school cupboard . . . He showed it to me there and I felt sad and ashamed."

"I'm sorry, yes I can see how difficult it must be—you with original ideas among so many without. At least I hear you have the ear of the great Li Hung-chang?"

"I met him certainly—an able, powerful politician. To many he seems a great reformer—for doesn't he want to set up schools of navigation and science, build steamships, dockyards, arsenals? Yet even he doesn't think far beyond that. Give us technical and industrial power comparable to the West and all will be well, that's his view. But that won't be enough for China, Uncut Jade. It isn't merely a matter of material progress, I understand that now. I've a friend, Yenfu, in Tientsin with all the qualities of a true leader—vision, energy, and deep understanding of our country's problems. But I fear he'll never gain power, his ideas are too radical, too selfless, too far-sighted even for men like Li Hung-chang, and as for the masses, they are stuck up to their Manchu pigtails in the ancient slime of the ages and there is no moving them."

She listened spellbound by that vehement conviction which had first attracted her.

"And your Tientsin friend, what is it he sees that others don't?" she encouraged him.

"That one cannot separate the process of change and industrialisation from the fundamental culture of a country. That you in the West believe in this abstraction called 'modern progress' which grows naturally from your civilisation.

Now we Sons of Han have a totally different civilisation and we don't basically understand or believe in this progress of yours. It is an alien ideal, perhaps we don't even need it in the same way... The government sent me to England and there I..."

"You—Lin, you've been to *England*?"

"Yes, I studied in your famous naval college near London, at Greenwich... But I'm still a bad linguist." He smiled ruefully.

"But... oh, that's dreadful... oh..." She jumped up in agitation. That she, a true-born English girl had never been Home, yet the government sent him. It gave him a tremendous advantage and a different dimension altogether; it was, she obscurely felt, terribly unfair. Bad enough listening to her relatives discoursing on the different sorts of English wood, but that Lin also had seen them was too much!

He was watching her in puzzlement. "I thought you'd be pleased that I've been there but you look downright angry?"

"I'm—just envious I suppose. Everyone pities me for not having been yet, you see."

"But you'll go soon, with your relatives or your husband when you deign to marry?"

"Oh that's the trouble with being a woman!" she scowled fiercely. "You always have to wait for a man—relatives or husbands—to make things happen. Why can't I just go Home alone if I want? Or why won't the government send me?" She was teasing now, trying to dissolve her vexation. "I could be so useful—there aren't many foreigners as fluent with Chinese as I am."

"Ah that's true enough," he put a calming hand on her shoulder. "You're a white jade of rare value, Miss Greenwood. And putting aside the claims of the government which has its own translators, think how you could help me and my students... You see these books? They're full of new, fascinating ideas that we Chinese need to fully comprehend. I struggle with them, but I'm ashamed how poor my English is..." Endearingly helpless, he held out a copy of J.S. Mill's treatise on Liberty. "The sagacious Yen-fu is intending to translate this for example. But he's hampered and overworked as I am... Now if only you..." She flipped through the heavy tome.

"I don't know, I mean I've never read this, it looks difficult even in English."

"But you are unusually intelligent for a woman, Miss Greenwood, I always remembered how interested you were in my ideas. Surely books written in your own tongue wouldn't daunt you? And you could learn from them too, as I try to..."

She opened a page he had marked, and translated, "'The despotism of custom is everywhere a standing hindrance to human advancement.'"

"Ah yes, and he talks of the Chinese in that context and what exactly does he say?"

"That their sages and philosophers 'impress the best wisdom they possess upon every mind in the community, but they've been stationary for thousands of years, government for them is a staying still... If they are ever to be improved it must be by foreigners.'"

"There—just as I was saying. Now when your thinkers make arrogant statements of this nature we need to understand exactly why they do—what to accept, what to reject. And you will help me in this, won't you?"

Her eyes shone. "Oh Lin, it would be grand, but how am I to?"

"We'll think of a way," he said, and in fact already had, for it was soon arranged that she should meet his college principal who would formally hire her to teach the advanced students and help Lin with translations. "And we'll work together at the texts, here or at the college," he added.

"But I'm so afraid my brother won't approve, especially since..." she trailed off vexedly.

"He's in the Maritime Customs is he not? I made it my business to find out when I learned your identity."

"And if you'd come to Epimoffs we'd have met sooner."

"Well, the place sounded rather a waste of time—people just drinking and vaguely theorising, I believe? Of course, if I'd known you were sometimes there..."

"You'd have come?"

"Yes," he said deliberately, consulting his French pocket watch. "But student-boy will soon return for you. As for your brother, don't worry, we'll find a way to him. There's bound to be a little unofficial help we can give, you understand...?"

She nodded, but did not really understand until one evening the next week when William announced that he had been called in unexpectedly that day for a confidential chat with the naval college principal about plans for the shipyard and the coastal defences.

"Did he say anything else?" Alice interrupted eagerly.

"About what?"

"About me."

"He—mentioned you, yes. I suppose he'd heard of you through the Chu lad."

"What did he say?"

William looked uneasy. "Never mind what he said, Alice."

"But I do mind. It's not nice to be talked of behind one's back, you say so yourself."

"He simply referred to your excellent knowledge of Chinese. I suppose Han-li had told him."

"And?"

"Oh you're so abominably persistent, Alice, it's not at all ladylike. He asked if you might be interested in doing some translating and teaching there, if you must know."

"And what did you say?"

"I said you would not. It all sounded extremely dull anyway."

"But how dare you—just like that, as if you had a right to speak for me. You're my brother, not my keeper you know, and I've got a tongue of my own."

"That I never doubted for a moment."

They had been sitting waiting for the supper bell when William had made his announcement and, at the first hint of trouble, Isabel had slipped out to avoid acting the mediator between the two yet again. Alice drew herself up, strong with a sense of utterly justified indignation. "It's just the chance I wanted. Here I am—one of the few English in the entire Empire with an absolutely thorough grasp of the Mandarin and the colloquial, written and spoken—and doing nothing whatever with it. At last I can be of some use and earn a little money of my own beside—and I'm going to."

"You are not because I forbid it."

"And what right have you to...?"

"You are living in my house and under my protection and I have every right."

"Then I shall leave your house and your protection, as you call it, this instant!"

He groaned. "Alice, calm down please."

"Calm down yourself." She was busily collecting together her embroidery tapestry and silks as if about to carry out her threat.

"You know my reasons very well. I simply won't let you mix any more than is necessary with the natives. After what has happened to you in the past it's simply not—fitting. I don't thoroughly trust you in that regard, to be honest."

"And what do you mean by that?"

He quailed slightly at the intensity of her passion. "What

I say. I think you could easily be led astray—in several directions. You are young, vulnerable and rather too sympathetic towards the Chinese generally."

"And that's a sin, is it? To be sympathetic towards the people I've lived among all my life?" She had her work-bag over her arm now, ready for immediate departure and her voice was controlled. "William, I've thrown myself utterly on the mercy of this land and its people three times before, and I'm quite ready to do it again now. Either you'll allow me to make some good use at last of the only real skill I have—or I shall go to the college tomorrow, take both the work offered and a room in their teachers' hostel, and move in there—much as I should hate to hurt Isabel and leave the children. I shall do it, Will. Short of putting me under lock and key, you couldn't stop me."

He knew defeat at her hands as he had before and, as before, reluctant admiration mingled with his chagrin. "Yes I fear you would—if only to spite us."

"I don't want to spite you, Will, only to have a say in the conduct of my own life."

He grunted, preferring not to rise to that. "I'll find out from the principal exactly what he has in mind and then, perhaps—strictly on a short-term, part-time basis, mind...At least it will enable me to maintain contact with the college and that could prove useful."

Two weeks later Alice was appointed as a temporary tutor to the senior students and translation adviser to Mr Lin Fu-wei, lecturer in Western science and philosophy. She enjoyed the teaching, and the students treated her with rare deference, but better yet was the translating work with Lin. Excited both by the ideas in the European texts they studied and by his warm physical proximity at the writing-desk they shared in his lodgings, time passed all too quickly, and she was always reluctant to leave at the stipulated hour.

"So, to summarise..." Lin, drawing another session to a close, glanced through their rough draft, "it seems Mill believes that unless liberty is permitted—even 'conceded in spite of prohibition'—to the moral nature of man, baneful consequences will result? But this 'in spite of prohibition' is totally irreconcilable with the teachings of Confucius, is it not? For does not the sage say that the moral man always conforms himself to his life circumstances, carrying out his duties calmly and behaving strictly in accordance with the demands of society?"

"But couldn't there be a path of compromise?" Alice

frowned thoughtfully. "After all, Mill also says it's morally wrong to affect others adversely through the pursuit of purely selfish ends."

He went to open the verandah lattice, staring down at the sun-drenched sea. "Huh—it's too hot to think properly anymore... Yet the dilemma is simple—most of my moral and intellectual desires are at some variance with what society expects of me, but if I suppress them baneful consequences will follow, so says Mr Mill. If I express my own nature at the expense of others—and there is no other way of doing so—I am but a vulgar and ignoble brute, so says Mr Confucius!"

Alice joined him. "It's the same with me. Often I have to dissemble, to deny my real nature because I'm allowed no space to develop it truly and freely."

He turned in surprise, unaccustomed to the moral problems of womankind. "Really? But what is it you want that is not in accord with the moral laws of your society, Uncut?"

"I want—oh so much. Freedom to travel and work at what I like, to meet different sorts of people in my own way, I want to be bolder and more ambitious, like a man, I suppose."

He put a hand on her neck. "Come, Miss Greenwood, you've been reading too much philosophy. You wouldn't want to be a man surely? You're much too pretty as you are!"

"No, not be anyone else really, but have more liberty to be myself, as Mill says."

"Ah sweet liberty, and how would you use it at the moment, little Uncut? Perhaps as I would—in a fashion that isn't entirely in harmony with the moral laws of either East or West..."

As he drew her into his arms, her voice quivered, "Yes... I think, I'm afraid that..."

"Don't be afraid, my green jewel, for haven't our bodies made up our minds for us in this one direction at least? Perhaps Mr Mill would approve, I don't know, nor at the moment do I care..." He closed the lattice and half-carried her to his narrow bed; his lips moved over her face and neck as he fumbled with the unfamiliar fastenings of her dress and bodice. She smiled, helping him until he could gather her bare breasts in his hands. "Ah they are full and lovely as I often thought of them—like plump white gourds topped with luscious cherries." He licked her nipples.

"But are they too big?" She was a trifle disconcerted by his comparison.

"Bigger than any I've known, but then I've never before fondled the breasts of a Western woman."

The very idea fired him, with trembling hands he pulled off the rest of her clothes and, slipping easily from his loose robe, spread her thighs and thrust urgently into her before she was ready. Then he withdrew, struggling for control. "Ah—I am much too excited by the unfamiliarity of your Jade Gate, I must pause." He caressed her again and she clung to him tightly. "My dear little Uncut, you are the only barbarian I've ever wanted."

"Did you then—when we first met?"

"Yes, but my desire was unformed and seemed almost unnatural, I was a little ashamed, to be truthful. And you?"

"I'd but recently come from the bed of Lung-kuang in the house of Chu, so it seemed natural enough to me then. It was only later I learned the shame. But this, between us now is not at all like that, is it, Lin?" She moved under him happily.

"Of course not, we shall be lovers in the modern way and there is no shame in it, my sweet Jade. And now you are with me, are you not? Your red flowers have begun to open and burn?"

"Yes, oh yes my darling." He poised over her erect, raised her legs high round his waist and went deep inside her till she cried out, kissing and biting his shoulder joyously.

After their union when they had sponged away the dampness of heat and sex, they stood in the verandah watching the sun set. "Oh Lin," she grasped his hand, "we must be so careful, no one must ever suspect this, must they? I daren't imagine what my relatives would think—or the people at the college. It's all very well for Mill to talk about 'intelligent deviations from custom', but not so easy in practice, is it?"

He kissed her forehead. "Exactly so—you see what I guessed in the abstract is already proving true in the personal and particular. We've just enjoyed the liberty of our own impulses—in spite of prohibition, but it would be most foolish to take a public stand in the cause of the future betterment of mankind... At least I won't!"

"Nor would I" she shuddered at the thought, turning into his arms. "Yet I still want you and don't feel ashamed either, just a little worried."

"There's no need, so long as we behave as if nothing untoward had happened. And so you must go as usual now."

"And come next week as usual?"

"Indeed yes—at the same time, but not, alas before and I hope not later."

As she walked along the quayside all her senses were quiveringly alive. The junks were setting out for a night's fishing; globules of lantern light illuminated the ships' masts and the figures of the men below who were banging about with baskets. There was the smell of fish offal, seaweed, kerosene, the swish of ropes casting off as boats nosed into the dark waves like antediluvian monsters. Primitive craft, Lin said of them dismissively, doomed as the dinosaur in the new world of steamships. But there, "Things never are the same for ever, nor even for as long as we think they will be", this also he had said and it was unquestionably true. Her world had changed often already and now it had taken a new direction that she both desired and feared. Her flesh still tingled with the joy of it, but her thoughts sheered away from the new deceptions it would involve. And how could this intimacy possibly turn out well? Even then, right at the beginning, she dreaded the end, feared pain, loss, disgrace, tried hopelessly to imagine how they could be avoided. The only way would be to withdraw now, before the sweet tangle of their lust and love enmeshed her. As she left the sound of the night sea and headed for the Customs House she almost persuaded herself into this prudent resolve, and yet, at a deeper level, she knew she would not and could not keep it.

And nor did she, for once back in Lin's room with his warm eyes and light hands upon her, her only resolve was to enjoy him and be enjoyed, to love and be loved for the first time in her life. The pace of their studies slackened considerably during the long hot afternoons of that summer as the intensity of their love-making increased. Entwined on the narrow bed, touching each other towards further excitement, Lin would murmur snatches of popular love poetry:

> "Her robe is a cloud, her face a flower,
> Her balcony glimmering with bright spring dew
> Is either the tip of earth's Jade mountain
> Or a moon-edged roof of Paradise..."

And she, unable to respond in kind, would rub her face against his chest, delighted by such Oriental extravagances.

Lin, proud of his lover's prowess, encouraged her to compare his lovemaking with that of Lung-kuang. "But I cannot," she giggled, "I was so young then too."

"But was his organ bigger than mine? Of the same mush-room-shape?"

"I don't remember, dear, does it matter?"

He squeezed her nipples. "Not really I suppose. Do you know, there was an Empress Wu long ago who had a lover whose stem was so big and strong she called it the 'Wonderful Thing' and said the whole Empire was less valuable by com-parison. But then she took another lover whose organ was small and she called it her 'Little Monk'—but he was as active and subtle as a snake in his thrusting and it was he she made her Imperial Adviser."

Alice moved her loins against him, "I don't compare you with a snake or a dragon-brightness, my darling, just be my wonderful thing—that's all I ask!"

As they lay quiescent after their vigorous and tender unions he would talk to her about his family—of his proud, sad, aristocratic father who was disillusioned by the present state of China and harked back to the glorious ancient days, of his spendthrift younger brother who had gone into trade, and of his much-loved mother who kept the old-style family life going. He spoke too of his brief stay in England where he had seen so much to amaze him: cows moving in those lush meadows, railway stations and horse-buses, carriages in Hyde Park; the busy docks on the Thames, and people splash-ing about in the sea at Brighton just for the fun of it.

He asked little of her in return for he was not used to women's confidences and she was disinclined to speak, for her life seemed thin and pointless in comparison. So she simply cuddled close, listening, aware that all too soon the sunlight through the lattice would fade and she would have to leave—carrying her books in an innocent bag, all signs of their heated dishevelments expunged.

It was with this customary demeanour she returned home in the dusk of a late summer evening and came upon Isabel sewing in the drawing-room. Her auburn curls glowed under the lamp and she looked, as always, orderly and calm. She smiled, asked Alice if the translating was going well, said supper would soon be ready and then, rummaging in her workbox, added, "Oh Alice, I've a bit of news for you—I think you should be the second to know, after William that is."

"What is it, what's wrong?" Alice guiltily assumed news must be bad.

"Nothing wrong—I'm going to have another child, that's all."

"Isabel—how lovely, for you and for Will!" She kissed her warmly, feeling, as always, a secret tug of ambivalence on the subject of birth—what she had lost, what she was even now risking. She asked lightly, "So which do you want? A sister for Charlotte or a brother for Joel?"

"I don't much mind, but a girl would be called Polly after my favourite aunt, and a boy Thomas after your father—Will and I were just discussing it, and he wants your father to have a namesake."

"I'm so glad he thought of it—and Mother would be pleased too."

"Oh yes, talking of your mother, this news has made us decide to make the effort to go to Mukden at last before I find travelling difficult. As Will says, it's too bad that she's not clapped eyes on me or the children yet and we've not met your stepfather."

Alice groaned at the word. "Come, dear, I know you don't care for him and he sounds dreadfully straitlaced and missionary, but he must have some redeeming features, so we'll go and find out—all of us."

Alice backed in alarm. "But not me—you'd have to drag me every inch of the way!"

"Yes, Alice, of course you too. I know you had deep disagreements with them, but that's all over and done with now, and it's silly for families to harbour bad feelings."

"No, I just can't see him—or that place again. You don't fully understand, Isabel, and I can't fully explain. but I won't go."

"But, Alice, just think how disappointed your mother and the twins will be if you don't come with us!"

"There's another thing, the college term begins next week and I can't possibly be away then."

"But, Alice, that's only a little job and . . ."

"Oh yes, all my jobs are little, aren't they? Well, I won't let my students down and I won't go, so there."

The supper bell rang and Isabel folded her sewing with a sigh. "I can't think what your brother will say—we'll only be there a fortnight because the journey takes so long, so for that short time you could surely bury the hatchet?"

"No, I wish you joy of the place and him, and I'm sorry not to see Mother; but I won't go, whatever you or Will say."

And though William said quite a lot on the subject it was of no avail and on a bright September morning two weeks later Alice rose early to see them all off in the Customs House mule carts. As the sound of the wheels faded she looked round the walled courtyard where pots of chysanthemums and daisies bloomed and stretched her arms above her head with a glow of delight. Dearly as she loved her relatives, it was so pleasurable to be alone for a change, to be the sole mistress of a house. What would it be like to actually live alone, she wondered? How free one could be—going out at odd times, entertaining whomever you liked. And why should she not entertain now? The cook and boy were still here, with little to do. She plucked three chysanthemums—bronze, ruby, white—imagined them gracing the centre of the dining table with she at its head in her polonaise dress and her guests around her—Félix and Jeff, Olga Epimoff, dear Han-li, Harry and Bella of whom she had grown quite fond, and at her right hand, Lin of course. Oh, it would be so much more fun than the usually stuffy collection of consular and customs officials. Why could she not do things like that sometimes? Because she lived as a dependant in her brother's house; because respectable unmarried young ladies did not have their own establishments. But one day, when she and Frank were rich and living in Shanghai, they would have magnificent dinner-parties with people of various nationalities and Lin, her acknowledged lover, would bring the leading Chinese intellectuals of the day to her table. She tripped indoors, arranging the flowers in a vase and imagining how the conversation would flow at her ideal dinner-party.

When she left the college that morning, Lin fell into step beside her, "Lets go to a fish restaurant I know near the docks," he suggested. "You don't have to hurry back, do you, for your relatives have gone to Mukden."

She gasped, "You always seem to know what goes on in our house before we do ourselves."

"It's part of our Oriental mysteriousness—we get messages through the air much quicker than those through the telegraph wires you Westerners have just put up between Tientsin and Shanghai!"

"Oh fiddle-de-dee—you just have your spies everywhere!" And that was nearer the truth for it happened that Lin's houseboy was a relative of the Greenwoods' cook and both were eminently bribable.

"Moreover," he continued, "I hear your Customs House food is excellent but for the next month you've no one to share it with. Will you not invite me to supper tomorrow, Uncut Jade? You've seen my humble abode many times, but I've never seen yours."

At first it seemed an outrageous idea, but then, remembering her day-dream of that morning, she laughed recklessly. "Yes why not? Why shouldn't you come? You're a very respectable college lecturer after all! Tomorrow—at seven."

At first the difference that the unfamiliar setting made took them both unawares. She was carefully dressed for the occasion in a peacock-blue gown with a low neckline and drooping pagoda sleeves, and he too looked different in a dark stiff Western suit usually reserved for college functions. They sipped sherry awkwardly like strangers and Lin prowled about examining the ornaments and family portraits on the drawing-room tables, then stared at her with a heavy intensity that was both tantalising and vexing. "I've never seen you look like that before."

"In this evening gown you mean? But you've been in England and know what women wear there."

"Yes, and it's foreign. I never supposed you could look like that."

"Oh I'm too short to look really well in evening dress. You should see my sister-in-law, she's larger and formal gowns suit her—I wish I was like that."

His face lightened and he teased, "But remember the words of Chuang-tse, 'The duck's legs, though short, cannot be lengthened without dismay to the duck and the crane's legs, though long, cannot be shortened without misery to the crane. That which is long in nature mustn't be cut off and that which is short mustn't be lengthened. Thus will all sorrow be avoided.'"

"Oh that's lovely—I'll remember next time I see Isabel looking magnificent!"

He came over and squeezed her encased waist. "I sometimes wondered in England how hard women's waists were, but never found out." He began kissing her fiercely, murmuring, "Oh you foreign bitches show off your shapes—your bulges and curves. Tying yourselves so tightly..." He prodded her stays and bodice in a mood of sudden hostility laced with heady desire. "A fashion meant to tantalise poor men, I suppose?"

She moved away. "I don't know about tantalise, but men of my acquaintance don't behave like this before supper."

"Only after—when they've gazed their fill at every part on display I suppose?" Again he grabbed her and again she broke away. "Oh stop it, please. Don't you like this dress and this room then? You wanted to come, remember!"

He slumped in a chair and began examining the contents

of Isabel's workbox. "I forgot how flaunting foreign women can look, that's all."

"It's not flaunting, it's just the fashion—but you don't like it?"

He shrugged. "I am Chinese. Our women don't show off for men in this way."

"But they bind up their feet to make themselves desirable and that's worse."

"And you bind your waists so tightly for the same reason. What's the difference?"

"Look I'll go and change if you want, or you can leave, this isn't a bordello, if that's what you're thinking..."

"No, no, Uncut, keep the dress on, it's very attractive, as I've told you in my fashion. And it will serve as a reminder of the strange temptations of the West. How foreign it is—and you are, to me. Give me another sherry and I'll behave like a proper English gentleman, I promise. But eventually you'll let me unlace that tight little middle, won't you?" he added in a whisper and she had to smile with the pleasure of him, as they allowed the tension to cool.

At the supper table, arrayed with the best silver and a bowl of chysanthemums, Lin tried half-apologetically to explain himself. "You see, Little Jade, I deal mostly with the abstractions of your Western civilisation and find much to admire, as you know, particularly the methods you've devised to make the wishes of the masses known to their rulers. But then, when I encounter certain Western-style realities, I'm slightly shocked, almost threatened and my pride in our Celestial Empire reasserts itself. Do you understand?"

"Partly—but threatened, here in your own country?"

Meditatively he traced with his finger the pattern on the silver flower-bowl, "I think it is this casual prosperity, these small but certain statements of your imperial power. Much of it dependent on quite ordinary materials like coal, iron and oil which won't last forever of course. But for the present your people enjoy much economic security compared to ours. And the struggle for existence is being generally replaced by the struggle for more enjoyment, more possessions, is it not? I look around—amazed to see how much is considered necessary for your family's comfort, yet your brother is quite an ordinary, run-of-the-mill Customs Officer."

"But surely you don't think it nobler to spend one's life just struggling to exist as many Chinese do?"

"No, but what happens to people when they get more money? My family is quite wealthy but our tastes are discreet as have befitted our class for generations. But in the Treaty Ports you find the Chinese nouveau-riche—isn't that what the French say? They are despised by our scholar-gentry for their lavish habits, they have no political influence or standing and are given few opportunities to improve themselves. Yet we need more young men of confidence and ability from all classes of society—Wang T'ao, an early reformer, wrote that twenty years ago, and it's still true... These things depress me, Uncut, as I sit at your table," he smiled at her wryly.

"So you are rude and pounce on me as if I were to blame? But what about the Japanese, Lin? Jeff Winthrop was talking about them recently. They seem to be adapting very quickly to Western ways and the Meiji Government is full of men of ability, so Will said."

"Oh pooh to the Japanese—pushy, conceited, shallow-minded dwarf-pirates! And I hear they've taken to your silly games and fashions—billiards, lawn-tennis and their women wearing those ridiculous bulges over their bottoms."

"Oh bustles—yes, I suppose they are rather absurd. But you're certainly hard to please in the matter of ladies' dress, honourable sir."

He leaned across to stroke her cheek. "It's what lies beneath the garment that really interests me, jewel."

She glanced round anxiously. "Hush, Lin... the servants."

But the servants had discreetly vanished from the scene, almost as if they knew, which indeed they did, exactly what was going on. Lin led her quietly up the stairs, pausing at the top, "Show me your brother's room, Uncut."

She opened the door, her lamplight falling on the heavy flowered quilt of the double bed. "Ah—truly spacious, designed for the couplings of large barbarians, is it not?" He bounced down on it, holding out his arms. "The very place to unleash the generous breasts of the lovely green-eyed foreign devil!"

"Oh Lin no, not here—we must go to my room..."

He pulled her to him, smothering her protests with kisses until the novelty, the recklessness of it fired them both as they tumbled in a state of disarray and soon of nudity on the flowery quilt and at length slept—entwined in a sticky heap under the fine linen sheets.

The next month passed in a happy dream for them both, each utterly absorbed in the other, filled with an urgent, insatiable need for each other's presence, feel, taste, smell, look, a passion that seemed to grow remorselessly with every meeting. And they met constantly in a way they had never done before; walking and working together, eating and sleeping together, and several times stealing away to the little wood in the hills where they nestled together under the birch trees. Often the spacious delights of the barbarian bed drew Lin to the house late in the evening and he came to the side gate, conveniently left open by the cook, and crept upstairs where Alice waited in a fever of excitement and guilt. Their passion, always strong, was the more intense because they knew this period of completely abandoned union was brief and dangerous and must end when Will and Isabel returned to reclaim their bed and regularise Alice's life.

And so the night came, when after their lovemaking, Alice whispered that he must not come again. "I must go to Epimoff's as usual tomorrow evening, and then they're due back." She stroked his head sadly.

He turned in her arms, mumbling, "Such a shame, we are so well together here. But that is the way with human joy, as Li-po says, 'ten thousand things run away forever like water towards the east'. I wish I could offer you a double bed in my humble place—but you'll come next week as usual?"

"Of course, my precious." They held each other close and he crept away before dawn as was his custom.

But, on returning from Epimoff's the next evening, she was surprised: Lin stepped from the shadow of the door. "Uncut—let me come with you, just one more night here." He pressed inside the hall. "It's a waste of that good bed to remain empty."

"But Lin it's risky, they are due tomorrow..."

"Ah tomorrow is tomorrow, tonight, tonight—where's your philosophy, dear?" Her small resistance melted as he ran his hands down her body and they stole upstairs like guilty children.

It was about three in the morning when the Customs cart came into the courtyard and William congratulated the driver on the speed of their progress. He roused his wife, "Now wasn't I right? Much better to carry on even at this hour than spend another night in a foul inn."

She yawned. "Yes dear, I suppose, certainly we've made good time. Now you and the nurse carry the children in and straight to bed they're so sleepy, poor mites." They went quietly inside and lit a lamp in the drawing room. "I'll just take my cloak upstairs, then make a nice cup of tea for us..."

Alice sprang awake in instant panic at the sound of steps on the stairs. "Lin, I think there's someone..."

The door opened and Isabel came in with a lamp. "Why

Alice—you, in here and..." Her voice rose to a little shriek as she saw the black head rising from the other white pillow. "William—William—come here at once, it's Alice and... she's, oh my God, I can't believe it, William..."

He pounded upstairs, terrified that his sister had been murdered, and there the two of them were, holding the bedclothes round their nakedness, Lin's normally sallow face a deep red, Alice, pale and crying out, "Isabel, oh, I'm so sorry... that you should see... oh, what have I done? Oh please, please go away for a minute and let us put something on..."

"But Alice—who is this, this native—you here with a man, a *native*, in our house, our very bed?" William passed a hand over his eyes to wipe out the sight. Then he roared, "Who the hell are you—you fornicator? Get out of here—"

"Yes, can, but clothes..." Lin's English broke completely under the strain as he reached for his nether garments.

Isabel took William's arm, "Come away for heaven's sake, it's too dreadful to look at... so upsetting... Let them dress."

"You—fellow—I'll see you downstairs in five minutes." Will slammed out.

"Oh dear God, oh help me, oh Lin what have we done?" Alice quivered under the sheet like a terrified animal as he fumbled with his clothes.

"It's my fault I fear, Uncut. If only I hadn't returned tonight, it was greedy of me, and I'm terribly terribly sorry... I'll tell your brother I led you astray for you are younger. And I'll tell him who I am—at least he should be glad to know I'm not just a bounder off the streets!"

"But, Lin, what if he throws me out?"

"Oh he mustn't, can't do that. He's a kind man, you always said so. But I must go and face him, it is only right. I'll take what blame I can, I promise..." He did not touch her but rushed out with a set face now turned unnaturally pale.

Alice cowered in the bed, feeling sick and weak, listening to the bawling of the thoroughly awakened children; the front door slammed and Will came up the stairs. She met him at the door in her nightgown and they stared at each other in silence for a moment. "I'm very sorry, Will, it was terribly wrong of me to let this happen here—in your house. I know it was... But you mustn't think it's just a casual sordid thing between Lin and me. He's a very intelligent, charming person and... I love him, Will, truly I love him..." Her voice broke.

"You what, Alice? Love—a young native like that? It's quite loathsome to think of—this shameful, horrible infatuation between you, and that it should have gone this far, and in my house...I'm utterly shocked, utterly disgusted. I'm ashamed of you as I've never been in my life before. You were terribly corrupted in your youth, my girl, and now it's all coming out—like a festering sore! No, it's no use your saying another word. Go to your room at once. We're wretchedly tired after the journey and as for my poor dear wife, to have returned to a scene like this! She's crying her heart out—she, who's always treated you like a sister, and you repay her, us—with this flagrant immorality, it's..."

"Oh please stop, William, please, I can't bear it..." She reached for him wildly, but he brushed her furiously aside.

"Get to your room, I tell you. But I'll just say this, there'll be no more talk of love, it's lust, disgusting animal lust you've succumbed to. And, as I told Mr what's-his-name Lin, you are never never to see him again. I had grave doubts about your college activities all along and how right I was. If you don't obey me absolutely in this, Alice, I'll throw you straight out into the streets, where I'm beginning to think you belong!"

He clattered downstairs, leaving her looking into the shadows of the hall and shuddering. And there rang in her head not only her brother's harsh words, but her own sad ones— "I love him", she had told William; now she was forbidden ever to see him again.

Breakfast next morning was late and sombre. The children were fretful after their late night, the two women pale and red-eyed. William studied with elaborate attention the mail that had accumulated in his absence, only looking up to snap, "Quiet, Joel" at his son, who had just discovered that beating a spoon on a bowl made a nice noise.

Not until he was about to leave for his office did Alice venture, "Well at least you might tell me about Mother and the twins? I still care for them, you know."

He grunted. "Oh—er yes. How did we find them, Isabel? Healthy I suppose you'd say, though Mother looks worn out."

"And the children so peaky and whey-faced," Isabel added. "They need building up and some good sea-air. Your stepfather keeps Adam grinding away at his studies for hours and the whole place is so shabby and comfortless and grim—you know of course."

"And what did you think of Stepfather?"

Will shuffled his papers in silence till Isabel upbraided him: "Come Will, don't pretend you've changed your opinion on that score just because... We didn't, couldn't like him, could we? He's overbearing and harsh and his views are extremely bigoted in every respect."

"He's the worst kind of missionary, I must agree," Will snorted. "All that prayer and effort to try and save the soul of some poor leprous beggar he's got there, while he makes life a misery for his own family—ugh! We left as soon as we decently could." He glowered at his sister, remembering the result of that. "I must go, there's a lot to catch up on..."

As Isabel wiped Joel's fingers, Alice began timidly, "Please, I'm terribly sorry, truly. You've always been so good and kind to me, and I'm more ashamed about upsetting you than anything else. Please forgive me if you can! I must tell you, as I told Will last night, that I truly love Lin. Doesn't that excuse it a little in your eyes?"

Isabel frowned, picking up her son to hug. "I'm not really narrowminded, Alice—not in the missionary way as you know. But what you've done is quite shameful and it must never, never happen again. And as for love—I don't think you know the real meaning of the word or you wouldn't have behaved so. Anyway, you must put this romantic nonsense from you immediately. I occasionally heard of inter-racial marriages when I lived in Singapore, they never work out well and as for the Eurasian children that result—well, the less said the better."

Feeling fresh tears rising, Alice simply hurried away. Such a term as inter-racial marriage had never occurred to her before; it sounded quite unseemly and not in the least descriptive of their passionate togetherness. But that apparently was how it looked from the outside, even to Isabel... But what right had she or anyone else to decide categorically that it was wrong? She and Lin were different; every fibre of her being said so.

Impulsively she donned her cloak and, telling the maid she was going to the market, walked to Lin's lodgings. He was out, the boy said, and brought her tea while she waited, staring at the by-now familiar scene of the boats along the quay. A grey drizzle was falling, heightening the sense of a cold raining in her heart; coolies slipped about on wet decks, swinging netfuls of glistening fish ashore. She watched numbly, losing all track of time, so that the catches had all been unloaded and the men gone before she heard Lin's step on the stair.

"Uncut Jade, you?" He looked weary. "Your brother hasn't thrown you out surely? He promised he wouldn't..."

She came and put her arms round him. "No, but I had to come, though he's forbidden me to see you again, ever."

"Yes—he said he would." He shook his cloak. "It's a beastly day—pour me some tea, Uncut...I don't know what to say, except that I'm so very sorry, if I hadn't come last night, all would have been well."

"All? I'm not sure about that now, something was bound to go wrong eventually. We'd have been discovered, or you'd move to another job—and what then?"

"I don't know." He stared moodily out, till she turned him to face her.

"Lin...Lin...I love you, truly, I told my brother so, and I want to be with you when you accomplish great things and become a real leader...I want...Oh Lin..." She buried her head in his chest. "I want to be with you, in bed and out of it...I..."

He grasped her wrists tightly. "And I want my sweet little Uncut, in bed and out of it, just the same. Then you must come and live here with me, never mind what people say. And when I move on, you'll come too, wherever I go!" He began kissing her passionately and they clung together like frightened children.

"Oh Lin," her face was alight with joy, "I know my relatives will hate it at first—inter-racial marriages never work, my sister-in-law said this morning. But she's wrong, Lin, we'll prove her wrong, ours will..."

He pushed her away, looking bewildered. "Oh no, Uncut, that is quite impossible, I cannot marry you. I've been betrothed for years, the girl is from a well-known Cantonese family, waiting to be my first wife. In fact, Father wrote recently saying he could allow no further postponement, for he wants the blessings of my sons in his declining years..."

She could scarcely take in his words, they sounded so unlike him. "But Lin, Lin—you never told me—you don't love this Cantonese girl surely?"

"Of course not, I scarcely know her. But my bounden duty to my honourable parents is to marry her."

She was still incredulous. "But this—this is ridiculous. It's so old-fashioned from you, Lin! You who believe in the liberty of the individual, the breaking down of traditional barriers between men and women...and yet now you say..."

"Ah yes, but my revered father is far too old for advanced ideas of that sort. It would be a terrible disgrace to the ancient lineage of our family if I were to...wed a barbarian." He used the word gently, but the cruelty was still there and she stared at him in dry-eyed horror.

"So it's alright for me, is it? I offer to give up everything, knowing how my family would loathe an inter-racial marriage, but you, you won't sacrifice anything for me!"

"But little Jade, dearest, I'm offering you much—to come and share my life and work, in spite of what people will say."

"Together with your official wife and your official children, I suppose? What you're offering is concubinage, Lin, a very ancient institution in spite of the modern trimmings you suggest—oh yes, I made a good concubine, as you know..." She turned away, her voice trembling.

"Come now, Uncut, there is such a thing as free love and companionship."

"At the expense of everything else in my life? My family might eventually and very reluctantly agree to our marriage, but if I were to come and live with you 'in sin' they would, I know, totally disown me..."

He bit his knuckles, looking at her sadly. "You're right, it cannot be—for either of us. We are talking across a great divide suddenly, are we not? You with all the family ties and conventions of your culture, I with the traditions and conventions of mine. You don't fully realise what you ask of me— even were I to disregard the feelings of my parents, marriage to a barbarian would ruin my future. Already I'm labelled a Western sympathiser, an outspoken critic of our ancient ways, a slightly suspect person, and I must tread carefully. No, it is quite impossible."

He turned back to the window, saying huskily, "I'll leave this town at the first opportunity and you must return to your brother's home, your proper life. We must forget this—this dream of romance, secretly we always knew it was doomed, did we not? 'The time has come to pour the wine in the dust.'" he ended formally.

She could not reply because of the aching lump in her throat, but simply buttoned up her cloak with shaking fingers. In the late afternoon grey they looked at each other without touching anymore, neither of them able to break this last, sad silence. At length he walked to the door and opened it, murmuring, "Goodbye for a long while, Uncut Jade—but we shall meet again."

"You said that once before." Tears welled in her eyes.

"And we did..."

"But this time no, it is all over..." She blundered down the stairs.

Outside a rising wind whipped the ropes of the boats, and gulls were squabbling over fish-offal on the quay. The drear, harsh sounds seemed to cut right through her and though it was but chill, her every pore was icy cold.

After a small pretence of eating supper she went early upstairs, and it was only when she lit the lamp by her bed and stared into the rain-flecked night that the full extent of her loss came upon her with such intensity that she gasped. She paced restlessly up and down, hating Lin for causing her this misery and for the burning shame mixed with her pain. For the unvarnished truth was that she had offered all she had, a lifetime's commitment to him, a native—a little yellow Chinaman, the English would label him—and he had refused her. Oh, if only there was someone to whom she could talk, someone who would consider everything on a broader, more charitable light than her relatives ever could. She could think of no one, but the misery of the empty room was too great to bear and the only temporary alleviation she could imagine was a double Epimoff cocktail. She stole very quietly downstairs and out, but in the drawing-room they heard the front door click.

"If she's gone off to join that native again I'll..." Will started from his chair.

"Now calm down, dear, I don't suppose she has. But she's undoubtedly very infatuated and very distraught. She's not a child, you know, and we can't control her every movement, even after this."

"You take it pretty coolly, I must say. I'd have thought you could hardly bear the sight of my sister after that scene last night."

"It was a dreadful shock of course, and if she'd been normally brought up—but I've been thinking it over all day, and Alice just hasn't had a normal life so far. To lose her virginity so young and at the hands of a middle-aged Chinaman—we cannot know how deeply that has affected her. Then, how did she really live with those primitive hill-folk, I wonder? Then, after all that, to be sent to Mukden. We said on the way back how dreadful it must have been for her there and we were feeling sorry for her, remember?"

"Oh yes, sorry indeed, till we got back to find..."

"Yes, yes. But don't you see that Alice's behaviour now has so much to do with her past, for which she wasn't to blame? I can't quite fathom the root of it, perhaps better not to, but we mustn't be too harsh. If we make life unbearable for her here, wherever would the poor creature go?"

He picked up a skein of her pink knitting wool. "You've decided it's to be a Polly, not a Tom, then?"

"I shall knit one pink jacket and one blue."

"Ah, marriage to the right person is such a blessing, is it not, my love? That's what Alice needs, now more than ever— the right man to come along. We'll invite young Jeff to supper. He's due for a posting and I must try and pin him down. I hope to heaven he's not heard rumours about this damnable native and Alice."

Alice, hurrying through the rain, thinking about the damnable native, was acutely aware that she had only to turn in the opposite direction to be with him again in a few minutes. But she stuck to her road. It was slack between-seasons at Epimoff's and in the saloon were only the chess-players and Bella O'Hara flipping through an American magazine called the *Good Housewife*.

"Why Alice—you here, and on a Saturday night. Is Félix coming?"

"No—I'm alone."

"Well come and sit with me then because I'm alone too and bored stiff. Harry's gone off for the last hunt of the season along the Korean gulf. He wanted me to go too, but the weather is lousy—here, have a stool—and I'm sick of watching those poor silly otters being butchered to tell the truth. They come right near the boat you know, all friendly and cuddly-looking with their funny little heads and paws out of the water—and then bang, bang, bang, all that blood and muck."

"It must be quite horrible."

"It is. Of course Harry says I'm just a hypocrite because I love an otter-fur as much as the next lady and help him spend the profits. But there's a limit and I've reached it. So, when he comes back we're off for the gay lights of San Francisco, thank heaven... Would you like a cocktail?"

"Yes please, a double if you don't mind."

Bella looked at her closely. "Is anything wrong? Why, Alice, you're nearly crying..."

"Bella, can I talk to you—somewhere private? I feel I must..."

"Why sure, honey, come up to my room."

Alice had not seen an Epimoff bedroom before, furnished as it was with a worn velvet armchair, tasselled lampshades,

a stained pink rug and bedcover of a similar hue. The taw-
driness, the hint of illicit, unloving sex broke the last shred
of her control and she flung herself on the bed sobbing as if
her heart would break. Bella lit a cigarette in a long holder,
looked at her, went to the cupboard and poured a drink.
"Here—brandy's always good for a crisis."

Alice gulped it gratefully. "I'm sorry, Bella..."

"No need to apologise, honey, just tell me your trouble,
then you'll feel better."

So Alice told her everything, from the time of her first
meeting with Lin on the *Mandalay* deck to their grey, agonised parting that afternoon.

When she had finished Bella lit a second cigarette, poured
a second drink, asked, "And are you pregnant?"

"No—I've no reason to think so."

"Well, that's a plus anyway. And how old are you?"

"Twenty-three."

"Well that makes me just ten years older than you, Alice,
and now I'll tell you a little story. When I was twenty-three
I was living in San Francisco with dear old Pa and Ma, who
ran a dressmaking shop for the bar-girls—and did I ever sew
on a million sequins in my salad days! Anyway, when I was
twenty-three a guy called Cowboy Joe walked into my life,
swept me off my feet and into his bed in no time. He was
tall, handsome, had a ranch out Arizona way, so he said.
Well, time came for him to ride away home and he asked me
to go with him, not as his wife, mind—none of that fancy
religious stuff for Cowboy Joe. But I'd be his woman, his doll,
his favourite lady... Oh I loved that man, Alice, such a fine
figure he had and other pleasing masculine attributes, but
I thought of leaving Ma and Pa and everything familiar for
no security and I refused to go.

"So Joe rode off into the sunset and I cried and cried—
just as you're crying now, and thinking my heart had broken
in a thousand pieces..."

Alice smiled a little through her tears. "And had it?"

"Nope—at least not for ever. There were other gentlemen
after that, and in due course I met nice Mr O'Hara, a ship's
engineer, and we married—you should have seen the wedding dress Pa made for me! Then I had a child and it died
of croup and I cried again, and then Mr O'Hara was blown
to bits in the boiler room of the *Hawaiian Queen* somewhere
in the Pacific and I cried more than ever in my life before.
But why I'm telling you all this, Alice, is that when I was
howling my eyes out at your tender age, I thought the world

had come to an end, but it hadn't, had it? And now there's no more than a tiny ache in my heart where Mr O'Hara used to be, and as for Cowboy Joe, I'm sure glad I didn't ride off into the sunset with him, for he'd have found another favourite lady pretty soon and I might have found another cowboy. But ten years later it wouldn't have been so good.

"And if you went off with your Chinaman there'd be an end to it, honey, because there always is with these arrangements. Maybe you'd find another Chinaman, but in ten years' time, when you'll be as old as I am now and with a lot of life left to live, we hope, where would you be? Because no respectable white man between Hong Kong and Port Arthur would look at you then and you'd be pretty tired of being unofficial barbarian wife number two, three or four..."

Alice picked at the satin coverlet. "So you think I've made the right decision, Bella?"

"I'm darn positive you have, honey. And I'm just looking at it from your point of view, nothing to do with your family or even your lover. He'll take care of himself—men always do. And my advice is—marry a nice well-heeled young English gent as soon as possible. For one respectable marriage always stands a woman in good stead whatever happens later. So stick it out, Alice, even if you have to sit and suffer for a while... And right now, come on down and I'll buy you a double cocktail—won't hurt you, they make 'em mainly of melon juice for the ladies anyhow, the crooks."

Alice went over to the cracked mirror above the washstand. "I look such a mess though..."

"Here—bathe your eyes, then put this stuff on." Bella handed her a box of peach-coloured make-up and stood behind her whilst she applied it. As the two women shared their reflections in the mirror, Alice secretly hoped that she would not look quite as old as Bella at thirty-three. She gave a watery smile.

"Is that better? And you promise me that in ten years Lin will be no more than a tiny ache in my heart?"

"Sure I promise, Alice, and I speak with the voice of experience. And you'll have a lot of happiness in your life well before that, I can tell. There's something about you that won't be kept down and under for very long."

Bella squeezed her shoulders affectionately and the two women went out of the bedroom together arm in arm.

10

The memory of that shocking scene of Alice bedded with Lin caused William such surges of rage and revulsion that he could take no more pleasure in her company. Sometimes he felt she had been let off too lightly; but at other times he decided she looked unhappy enough already and if he said more, she might simply run away—and then what would he do? So instead eventually, and at his wife's urging, he again asked Jeff Winthrop to dine, with a view to making discreet enquiries as to his matrimonial intentions, if any.

The evening did not sparkle; Isabel's pregnancy was trying and she was heavy and listless, as too was Alice, who responded politely but without enthusiasm to Jeff's laborious jokes. It was clear she cared little for him, but this no longer mattered, Will thought irritably; if he could just marry her off to him it would be more than she deserved in the circumstances and she would have to make the best of it. So, when the ladies retired after dinner, Will pushed the port across the table saying, "So you'll soon be off to Canton, Jeff? We'll be sorry to lose you. When do you go exactly?"

"About a month, the governor says, but these things are always uncertain."

"You're looking forward to it, I'm sure? Canton's several

notches up on this dead-and-alive hole. Wish we'd something else in view. But you know what they say about the I.-G., Sir Robert Hart, he has a chart on his office wall with the names of us hapless officers on it and when he's in the mood he takes a couple of pins, sticks 'em in at random—'Now move him here and him there'—and that's it. A fellow can be in some godforsaken backwater for years, or up to head office in no time!"

Jeff clucked sympathetically. "I've heard that was the way. Well, at least if I behave myself I've every hope of being made a Vice soon."

It was the perfect opening, but William hesitated, moodily reflecting on his right to persuade this perfectly decent chap to marry his sister; he himself certainly would not, knowing what he did. She was not to be trusted, that was the devil of it, time and again she had been slippery as an eel and she would twist round this Jeff chap in no time. But she was his sister, very lovable in some ways, and he no longer wanted the responsibility of her. "A Vice, hey? That's pretty good going, Jeff. And you'll be setting up your own establishment in Canton, I expect?"

Jeff smiled, guessing the way of the wind. "I hope to, yes."

"Anyone particular in mind to... well ... share it with you?"

"You mean a wife?"

"I suppose I do."

"You mean Alice?"

"Well nothing pressing of course, my dear fellow... but you've been seeing a deal of her in the past eighteen months, and I just wondered, as her elder brother?"

"Alice wouldn't have me even if I asked her, Will, as I was once tempted to. But I'm over that now. There's something else worrying her, but it's none of my business. She's got a mind of her own, has Alice, and there's no room for me in it, and that's all about it."

He settled his broad behind more comfortably and drained his glass. William sighed. "Some women are like that—it makes for the deuce of a problem. Alice has never been easy and I fear never will be. One more top-up, Jeff, then we'll join the ladies—bless 'em and forget 'em. What'll be your new duties, same as here? More people on the staff of course?"

"Oh yes, several officers and three student interpreters. Canton's a focus for the self-strengthening movement you know, we had a memo round recently—the F.O. wants to know more... Is it gaining widespread support? How dangerous is it to our interests? What sort of people join it?"

"The self-strengtheners haven't got a bat in hell's chance as long as the Old Buddha and her posse of eunuchs hold the reins. In twenty years' time, China will be the same moth-eaten old gunny-sack of ancient tradition, disorder and ineptitude as it is today, I warrant."

"I'm not so sure, some of these progressives are quite persuasive and very determined. The principal of the naval college here for one, and Lin Fu-wei, the man they call the 'Leader', he's quite impressive."

Will looked into his glass. The deuce was he could not decide whether Jeff was deliberately going along this track—perhaps the whole town knew of Alice and Lin? Curse the girl. "Really? I've not met him."

"He's suddenly resigned his post and returned to Canton, his home town, I gather. It could be an indication that things are hotting up down there."

"Well, I wish 'em all luck I suppose," Will rose, "but there'd certainly be a bloodbath if they come into the open and try to start a revolution. Shall we go to the drawing-room?"

It was quiet there except for the crackling of logs, the click of Isabel's knitting needles, the occasional rustle of Alice's books. Jeff warmed himself at the fire, regarding her covertly. She was attractive to him still, in spite of his show of non-chalance. "That's a heavy-looking tome you're reading, Alice. I didn't know your interests extended to the philosophical?" The whiff of a scandalous rumour about her had reached him and he wanted to scent it out.

"I think it's time I stretched my mind a little—it's already over-stuffed with trivial chaff, so my stepfather used to say."

"And you're translating these works at the college, I believe—so you need to understand them thoroughly?"

Her colour had risen. "I *was* working there, as you must know, but not any longer."

Isabel broke in, "More coffee, Jeff? I always think it must be wonderful to have Alice's grasp of the Mandarin."

"Indeed yes—I certainly wish I had, especially now. I was just telling Will the F.O. want us to find out what we can about the self-strengthening movement and several of its members are Cantonese you know, including that man they call the Leader. I think you helped him with some translating, Alice?"

"Yes, but he's gone away now."

Jeff's strategy had not been specially subtle, but it took

little perception to realise from the Greenwoods' reactions that what he had heard held at least some grains of truth. With this assurance Jeff left the Customs House that night with a lighter heart, comfortable in the knowledge that he was well rid of Miss Alice.

"He must have heard something!" William snarled at his sister as the door shut on Jeff. "Harping on about your ex-paramour like that!"

"Not necessarily, Will, but we were so on edge when his name was mentioned," Isabel contradicted.

"Well if he has heard, it would explain why he made it clear to me that he's no serious intentions in your direction, Alice."

"And I've no intentions whatsoever with regard to him. You've known that for months, Will."

"But the point is, no respectable young man here ever will if your scandalous behaviour is public knowledge. I really don't know what to do about you!"

She slammed her book shut and jumped up. "You don't need to do a thing about me—I'll go at once and live in Shanghai near Frank if I'm such a burden to you!"

"You'll do no such thing, Shanghai's no place for an un-chaperoned young lady."

"But you don't really think I'm a respectable young lady anymore, do you? So why not let me go to the dogs—or the horses with Frank—in my own way?"

"Will—you two, stop it!" Isabel also rose. "Alice is not a burden to us. She's behaved badly as we know, but this is her home and here she stays. Indeed, I badly need her now, you know that, don't you Alice?" She caught her hand. "You're going to help me and the little ones through this winter, aren't you?"

Alice laughed shakily, putting an arm round Isabel's neck. "You're a very sweet sister-in-law, Isabel. I sometimes wonder if Will deserves you. If you want me, then I'll stay—unless my brother actually casts me out!"

"Of course I shan't, you women always stick together," Will growled, stalking out.

Isabel wound up her knitting. "I like that! We women have to stick together, considering the way men behave! Now calm down, dear, and have a good night's rest."

In her frigid bedroom Alice undressed quickly, reminding herself of the much more intense cold she had earlier survived in Mukden; yet, in some ways, those drear winters had been preferable to this one. For then life had still seemed full of promise and hope, whereas now she felt sure, with the uncompromising passion of her age, that all the best was behind and she might just as well die, for no possible good lay ahead. But she went through the days doggedly, if resentfully, nevertheless, keeping up a cheerful front before Isabel and helping with the children.

Between times, she worked on the translation of J.S. Mill's treatise which Lin had sent soon after their last meeting, with a formal note telling her of his imminent departure for Canton on both political and family business—and she had bitterly guessed the nature of the latter. He had begged her to continue alone with the work, "for the sake of the China of the future". At first, she had angrily put it aside, but had then taken it up again, first as a continuing link between them and also because it held new meaning for her. For was she not a member of "a subject class", given little chance to use her talents and kept in a state of economic dependence, at everyone's beck and call? "If there is anything vitally important to human beings it is that they should relish their habitual pursuit," Mill had written. But what chance had she to discover a truly relishable pursuit anyway?

Made resentful and restless by the realisation of her powerless position, she sometimes sneaked off to Epimoff's in search of congenial company, but even that had lost its charm. Bella and Harry had gone and Félix was in France, marrying his betrothed; some naval students still frequented it, but Han-li was no longer among them, for he had returned to Foochow to teach the rudiments of intensely-crammed navigational science to others even less knowledgeable. In January, Jeff Winthrop left for Canton, and the following month, to everyone's relief, Isabel was safely delivered of her baby.

"It's a Polly," she whispered to Will as he crept into the bedroom where Alice, who had just witnessed her first birth, was rearranging the bedclothes.

"Polly—little Polly Eliza—we agreed on that, Isabel?"

Alice came to him. "Let me hold her, Will please . . . She's lovely, isn't she lovely? Let me be her godmother, please Isabel, please Will!" she begged in a sudden burst of joy.

He hesitated and Isabel said from the bed, "If you wish it, then certainly, my dear. You've been a great help to us all this winter."

William mumbled, "Yes of course . . . And now I must give the doctor a brandy before he leaves."

Alice touched the button-nose of the wrinkled creature in her arms. "Such a wondrous thing, isn't it? I feel so drawn to her—exactly as I was to Sunny."

"You seem to prefer the girls of the family, Alice?"

"Oh I love the boys too, but the girls may really need me one day, as the boys probably never will."

The miracle of Polly's birth buoyed Alice temporarily, but then she was assailed by a dire lowering of the spirits. What could she look forward to? Was her future role to be no more than dependent aunt in her brother's house? A steadily ageing spinster devoting herself to various good causes as the years went by? Was it for this that she had risked her very life to return to her own people? And now she sometimes wondered to what extent they were her own people—these conventional consuls, customs officials, traders who lived so complacently and myopically on the fringes of one of the world's greatest countries. Could she ever settle contentedly among them? Only, she felt, at the expense of a diminished spirit, a denial of half her being. The Chinese world from which she had fled had been restrictive and harsh in many ways, yet it had been real and rich, lusty and colourful. There was a genteel pallor, a straight-lined dullness about her present life which oppressed her fearfully, making her yearn for another escape.

Alice's restlessness was inadvertently brought to a head by William who, peering at the sky one morning around the "Time of Clear Brightness" announced cheerfully that it would soon be the picnic season again. But the very idea filled Alice with melancholy. The birch-wood—where she and Lin had lain together when there seemed no end to their delight. How could she bear again those long, somnolent family picnics? Mentally she heard Will's meticulous sharpening of the carving knife preparatory to cutting chicken; it set her teeth on edge.

Closeted in her bedroom, Alice contemplated her secret store—the rest of the Carr loot and her savings from teaching. Then she wrote to Frank. Clearly, she began tartly, he was having too good a time to bother about Greenwood & Greenwood Ltd; but she was bored to tears with wretched Port Arthur. She had saved some money, and that, allied to his trading experience, was sufficient for a start. She intended coming to Shanghai that summer. She concluded, "I'm sorry, dear, if I sound like a bossy old spinster schoolmistress, but I'm beginning to feel like one. I'm saying nothing of this plan to Will till I have your answer. He's bound to raise objections, and it's best to present him with a *fait accompli*. Please reply soon—I'm counting on you now."

But Frank was never a brisk correspondent and when, a while later, the weather was sufficiently clement for the first picnic, he had sent no word. The birches were in green leaf and Joel toddled about under them while William carved the chickens and Charlotte laid the cloth. When they were all comfortably settled, William went to his horse and returned with a bundle. "The Home mail," he announced triumphantly, "came this morning, so I thought I'd bring it. One for you from Frank, Alice."

She scanned it, then raised her head with a jerk, but the others were too engrossed to notice. She paused, savouring the drama to come before saying with studied calm, "Frank's about to get married."

They both looked up. "Married—young Frank?" Will frowned. "Well, he's twenty-one of course. But why the deuce haven't we heard about her before? Who is the lucky girl?"

"Her name is Tao Yuan-wang and he calls her Peachy because 'Tao' is the Chinese for that delectable fruit."

There was a stunned silence. "You mean she's..." Isabel moaned faintly.

"Chinese, yes. Her father is a respectable, quite wealthy merchant apparently, who owns several race-horses as well as the most beautiful girl in the world—according to Frank."

"My God, whatever next?" William jumped up agitatedly. "Is this—this arrangement definite? Can I do anything to prevent it?"

"No, it's a *fait accompli*, Frank says. The wedding is fixed for the third of June, which isn't far off. He's sending us all an official invitation by the next mail but wanted me to break the news. He hopes you'll be as delighted about it as he is."

Will knocked his head against a convenient treetrunk. "Is that meant to be a joke? Delighted at his—marrying a native!"

"Oh dear, these inter-racial marriages never work," Isabel wailed. "Yes I know I told you that, Alice, and it's so true. Oddly enough, the girl's family is probably just as upset as we are."

"Oh yes, Frank says they've tried to dissuade her for months, which is why he hasn't told us before. But it's Frank or no one for Miss Peachy apparently, and they've finally given in."

William flopped down and reached for some claret. "Well I'll be damned—and to think of all the pretty young English lassies in Shanghai. It's not as if he's stuck in a backwater like this with nothing but Chinese girls to look at."

"What those Chinese did to you two," Isabel whispered sadly. "How they altered your lives—for that's the root of it, isn't it?"

"First Alice and now this, I honestly don't know which is worse," Will groaned.

"Well you can't stop this and I'm glad—yes, glad that Frank at least has got what he really wants." Alice glared at her brother, suddenly recalling Frank's tale of his youthful excursions to the plum groves near Changsha. "Yes, that's the root of it, Isabel. But it's not as if Frank were marrying a tea-girl, Peachy sounds very sweet and respectable. And you'll come to the wedding, won't you? Because Frank will need all our support—I suppose there'll be dozens of her relatives, if they deign to come...Oh goodness, I wonder what Mother...?"

"God—Mother, it'll kill her," Will gulped his claret. "I suppose little Peachy-weachy isn't a convert by any happy chance?"

Alice consulted the letter. "No—because he says there'll be two wedding ceremonies, one Buddhist and one Christian."

"Oh poor dear Eliza—not only a native but a heathen native! I can just hear Stepfather Blake on the subject, can't you?" Isabel shuddered. "He'll never allow her to attend the wedding. You see what troubles alliances of this kind cause, Alice? But we'll have to put a good face on it—for Frank's sake, as you say. And it'll be fun to go to Shanghai, won't it, Will? We'll do some shopping and see a lot of new faces..."

"And spend a lot of money," he snapped.

"That's right! We'll go to Madame Claire's tomorrow, Alice, and get some new clothes made—everyone's frightfully smart in Shanghai these days. Come on now, let's have lunch, then we'll all feel better about it."

Defiantly Alice raised her glass. "And here's to them anyway—Frank and Peachy!"

They all drank, but then a glum silence fell as they considered the full implications of the news. Alice's feelings were very mixed. She was happy for Frank and jealous of his happiness at the same time; she was both amused and saddened by her relatives' consternation and hated to think how deeply it would distress her mother. Most of all she feared it meant the end of the dream of Greenwood & Greenwood—indeed

Frank had hinted as much, but adding that she should move to Shanghai anyway. "We're going to live in a villa belonging to Peachy's father, with stables and a paddock," he had boasted, "and there'll be lots of room for you, Sis."

So once again Frank was the lucky fish of the family; everything seemed to come his way without any effort, whereas she made so many efforts to no avail. Yet, in spite of its unfortunate aspects, the news of Frank's marriage lifted her spirits. At least it heralded change of some sort, and when, a few weeks later, Alice packed her trunks for the journey to Shanghai most of her belongings went inside, for, secretly, she intended to stay there.

Shanghai of the 1880s was just the place for anyone in search of a bright new future, China-coast hands always affirmed. Stand on the Bund, they proudly bade the newcomer, and look at the view. Westward, the whole of the Old World before you, the largest land mass on the globe; eastward, its greatest ocean, nothing but sea between you and California; in the foreground, plenty of solid, reassuring evidence of the Occident's presence in the Orient: banks and consulates, churches, courts of justice, customs offices, the spacious residences owned by those foreigners who had already manifestly made good.

Frank met them off the Port Arthur steamer, very smart in a suit of white marseilles drill, check waistcoat, leather button-boots. He ordered the coolies to put the baggage in his buggy; "We'll ride in grander style": he nonchalantly indicated a gleaming two-horse carriage with a liveried coachman on the box.

"This your turn-out, Frank?" William asked cautiously as they climbed aboard.

"Not exactly—belongs to my future father-in-law, he's got two landaus and he lent me this to ferry you about in." William raised his eyebrows. "I've a little luncheon in the hong mess for you," Frank continued. "I thought we'd go straight there, and then to the Dawsons at the Customs House—which is where you're staying, I suppose?"

"But Frank, Polly's feed is due and there's the children and amah..." Isabel protested. It was settled by Alice and William going to the hong, while Isabel coped with the family.

"So this is where you've been holing up, looks very fine, I must say," Will remarked as the carriage turned into an extensive walled compound along the Peking Road which was the hong of Guthrie & Robinson Ltd. Facing them was a solid, rectangular, two-storeyed house flanked by warehouses and outbuildings.

"Yes—it's quite large. There's the silk godown, that's the tea and the smaller ones for piece-goods. Then there's counting offices, general stores, rooms for the compradores and the shroffs who check the cash. The taipan's got some grand stables at the back too. My bedroom's up on the left there—it's quite a chummerie and now I'm about to move, I know I'll miss it." He led them into a huge dining-room where luncheon was in progress—an enormous meal, as Shanghai meals invariably were, accompanied by various beverages and considerable conviviality. (This, perhaps, was why the young men of the settlement spent much time in violent exercise "shaking up their livers", while the women, deprived of similar outlets, looked bloated and depressed during the hot summers and suffered much from colic.) It was nearly three in the afternoon before the dessert dishes were cleared, the other hong members left, and the Greenwoods were alone.

An awkward pause fell which William broke with, "So it's settled then, Frank? You're going to marry a Chinese girl?"

"Certainly—and an extraordinarily lucky fellow I am! You wait till you see her, she's expecting us to call later and..."

"Well, I shall have to delay that pleasure, I must go and help Isabel, we've left her to manage everything," Will cut in firmly. "But there's something I did want to ask, though not in front of your chums—you do know how much you've upset Mother, I suppose?"

Frank shrugged irritably. "Of course I know, I had an awful letter from her. She won't come to a wedding between her son and a heathen and what's going to happen to the souls of our children—and all that."

Alice sighed. "But it's very real for her, Frank, the basis of her life—though I've every sympathy for you."

"Well I haven't," William snapped. "I just hope you realise what you're taking on—a woman of a different race, different religion as your mother says—different outlook on life entirely. It doesn't work, you know."

Frank stuck out his lower lip. "Of course it does. I won't be the first white man in China to marry a Chinese, nor the last. And my Peachy is a little beauty, you'll see. Anyway, I love her, more than I've ever loved anyone in my whole life, so there!" He glared defiantly at his brother. "And she

272

loves me too," he added for good measure. "She refused lots of rich young men to marry me."

"Then there's no more to be said, but I can't help wondering what Father would have thought."

It was an unkind thrust as Frank's face showed, and Alice broke in briskly with, "But that's a silly idea, Will. If Father had lived, things wouldn't have happened like this—no Hunan, no Frank alone in Shanghai, nothing the same. So we might as well forget it."

Frank smiled in relief, adding, "But talking of Father—guess who is coming to the wedding? Uncle Robert arrives tomorrow."

"Oh that's splendid news, I do like Uncle Robert, he's so reassuring somehow."

"And what did he have to say about it?" Will asked slyly.

"Oh, he wasn't exactly overjoyed—but it's decent of him to come, don't you think?"

"Very, in the circumstances." William rose stiffly. "Thank you for an excellent luncheon, Frank. Now I must go back to the family. Alice, you go and meet Peachy, it'll be easier without me anyway, you can all chat together so fluently."

"That's typical," Frank sniffed at his departing back. "In fact, Peachy's been practising her best English greeting for him."

"Well, you haven't told us much about her yet, dear."

"Oh, I'm no good at letters... that's all my writing's good for," he signed the meal-chit with a flourish. "But Peachy's counting on you, she's sure you'll take a broader view than the rest of 'em..." He looked at her shyly as they came out into the driveway. "I mean, you do understand, don't you Sis? Why all this rot Will talks about different races and religions cuts no ice with me?"

"Yes Frank, I do understand perfectly..." She stopped to smell a yellow rose by the entrance. "You see, I myself ..." But no, Englishmen did not want to hear such things about their women, least of all their sisters. Besides, it was Frank's wedding, Frank's adventure. "But what Will says it's not altogether rot—it won't be easy."

"Oh I know," he agreed carelessly. "I didn't tell old Will, but several of Peachy's relatives have refused to attend the wedding, and there's been a great to-do about the two religious services and the breakfast has to be in a dreary guildhall because it's neutral territory—but what does all that matter? When you really love someone, that's the only important thing."

His words stabbed her; she wondered, as she had so often, whether she too should have sacrificed all for love. But there was a difference, she thought bitterly, it was at least marriage, not concubinage, Frank was going into—and one with considerable financial advantages, it seemed.

"You say Mr Wang has three carriages like this? He must be pretty well off?" she asked as they drove off.

"Oh this is his least grand turn-out. His old man was in the opium trade I believe, though they keep that pretty dark now. Anyway, Wang switched over to tea during the heyday of the clippers. He's a wily bird and made a small fortune. Tea's quietened down now, but what he's lost there he's made up on horse-racing, I reckon. He's got a grand stable and I have the run of it—his pals call me the Golden Horseboy... It's my hair that does it!"

"And Mrs Wang—is she a lady of consequence in the household or another Hidden Glory?"

He grinned in recognition of their shared past. "There's nothing hidden about Madam Wang—she's a Manchu for a start, and they're very determined characters. Like the Old Buddha, whom she rather resembles."

"Manchu—and married to a Chinese?"

"Unusual yes—indeed that was considered a dreadful inter-racial liaison till I came along!"

"So who made the decision about Peachy's feet?"

"Her mother fortunately. The two elder daughters were bound and when it came to Number Three, mother put her foot down—ha!"

"So she's not bound, I'm so glad. I wondered how you could ever... I mean I've seen bound feet and..."

"Yes, it always rather put me off, I must say, never looked at them." He stared out of the window in embarrassment. "But Peachy is natural from top to toe—all the best qualities of Chinese and Manchu rolled into one!"

And certainly that was an apt physical description of the young woman who greeted them in the reception room of the Wang villa. Peachy's slender form was shaped in a high-necked jacket of iridescent turquoise brocade, patterned with white irises; her wide trousers were of deeper green silk; she carried a painted ivory fan, her jet hair swept up and away from her pale, oval face by jewelled combs. Her features, of a slightly Manchu cast, were well moulded and her smile eager.

"You are Uncut Jade, Frank's sister," she spoke in halting

English. "I ver' please meet you."

"And I you! Why, you are everything Frank told me!"

She looked at him in puzzled adoration. "That good?"

"Excellent, I assure you."

As a servant brought tea she reverted gratefully to Chinese and Alice looked around. There was a great deal of mother-of-pearl about, intricately carved lattice-work screens, huge, colourful Ningpo vases. She remembered Lin's disdainful reference to the nouveau-riche of the Treaty Ports; undoubtedly this was the house of one. But, she checked herself, what right had she to assume his snobbish, aristocratic standards—and what right had he to judge others by them? Oh, he could talk so grandly about the need of equality between classes, sexes, races—yet the traditional divisions still moulded his attitudes. How she would love to tell him that one day!

She smiled warmly at Peachy. "You know, I've not yet heard how you met each other?"

"It was last spring, my father let me go to the races because his horse with my name was running. And he introduced me to Frank—the only barbarian who knew anything about horses, he said! And after that Frank kept calling on me and I kept stealing away to see him..." She giggled, put a hand to her mouth, "I speak English now, for the walls have ears— my father want me marry Chinese man, but I say no, no, no. I have letter from my sister, is in America with husband. She tell me in that country women not have marry men not likee. So I likes Frank, is best man. Many times I say—marry him. My father say no, yellow barbarian, foreign devil, them sillee thing. At las' they say, alrigh', you like old ox..."

"Ox?" Alice raised an eyebrow.

"Stubborn as a mule," Frank explained.

Peachy looked anxious. "You teachee me goo' English, not pidgin, please?"

"Yes, I'll help you to learn good English..."

But Peachy had drawn back, reverting to her own tongue. "Here's my mother coming, she's been playing mah-jong as usual and has returned early to meet you."

Frank and Peachy stiffened as Mrs Yuan-wang swept in. With her oiled hair folded on either side of her square face, her square shape encased in a richly embroidered robe, she was indeed reminiscent of official portraits of the Empress Dowager and the same veiled disdain for foreigners lurked in her hooded eyes, She held out a long-red-nailed hand, her deeply rouged cheeks cracking in a polite smile, but conversation was suddenly very hard to make and it was a relief when she was soon called away on what Alice guessed to be a pre-arranged pretext.

Riding back along the Bubbling Well Road, Alice first reflected that she did not care for the atmosphere in the Wang house, then subsided into a wistful daydream wherein she was married to Lin after all, and was warmly welcomed into his aristocratic and cultured family in spite of her unfortunate barbarism. But, "What nonsense, Alice," she said aloud, as they reached the Bund and she distracted herself instead with the passing scene.

It was early evening and the Bund was at its sprightliest: the gardens along Soochow Creek were gay with roses, lilies, geraniums, heliotrope; from the bandstand came the strains of a popular Strauss polka, and children were darting about the gravel paths watched over by amahs in white coats and wide black satin trousers. Along the main thoroughfare smart landaus with footmen as well as drivers conveyed foreign ladies and gentlemen to their various evening entertainments; buggies pulled by tough Mongolian ponies like Griffin; and little basket-carriages much used by brokers and commercial agents for the conduct of their peripatetic businesses. Visitors and humbler folk of many nations were riding in rickshaws with their hoods down, for the air was balmy, and the humblest natives trundled slowly by in wheelbarrows with platforms on either side of the wheel for people, packages and animals.

Alice stared at it all longingly, wondering how she could manage to stay here without again incurring her brother's displeasure. As she drove up to the Customs House where Mr and Mrs Dawson lived, she yawned mightily, suddenly realising how weary she was from all the activities of her first day ashore.

But there was little time to rest, for Isabel, having inspected the elegance of the Shanghai crowds, was convinced that the garments cobbled together by poor Madame Claire in Port Arthur were quite inadequate for the coming nuptials.

"We shall look like poor relations from the hills," she told Alice at supper, "and quite let Frank down. So we're off to Mrs Dawson's own couturière in the morning and she promises she'll have something decent ready for us in a day."

So the next morning was a whirlwind tour of dressmakers, tailors, milliners, haberdashers; followed by a courtesy call at the Wang villa. Then William rushed to meet Uncle Robert while the ladies went to the hairdressers. Late in the afternoon a weary but satisfied Isabel sank into a chair at the Viennese patisserie where she was to meet Robert and William. She patted her newly-styled hair, ordered tea, began a critical survey of the ladies' bonnets in view.

"Ah, Isabel, hello, my dear!" Robert appeared at her side. After their greetings, he drew up a chair, and reported, "Will's got another touch of fashion-fever and has gone to buy some smart shoes. He may join us later. But it's lovely to see you—and as blooming as ever."

"Thank you, Robert, and I'm glad to see you safe and well. We've been most anxious about you—out there in Kabul fighting those bloodthirsty Afghans. We read about that battle where over a thousand men were lost."

"Yes, a nasty business. I wasn't there fortunately, but I did march with General Roberts' forces to the relief of Kandahar which was quite hard going." He took a chair. "So I feel entitled to a rest—and one certainly gets it on the P. & O. these days, Excellent accommodation and service, better than the old days of sail when I first came East."

Isabel poured tea and they prodded chocolate gateaux while she described the charms of her new-born. "I'm looking forward to making Miss Polly's acquaintance," Robert said, adding cautiously, "I wish I could say the same about Frank's future progeny."

She looked at him; the two had seldom met, but they understood each other.

"It's a great shame and we could do nothing about it, Robert, a *fait accompli* before we even heard."

"Same here, and I was beastly disappointed after all I've done for Frank. But one has to put a good face on it."

"Exactly. And I'm sure it has to do with their past—his and Alice's—what happened in Hunan, and, when they returned, no proper parental guidance. We've all done our best but it's not the same, and Eliza's so taken over by this mission. Will and I visited Mukden last autumn you know, and met Stepfather Blake."

"From what Will wrote, it couldn't have been pleasant for Alice there. I'm so glad she's now with you—and well I trust?"

Isabel was silent, weighing him.

"What's the matter with Alice? Why isn't she here now?"

His obvious concern decided her. "Oh she's perfectly fit, thank goodness, having tea with Frank. But I'm worried about her, Robert. You see in Port Arthur last year she . . . well, fell for a Chinese—just like Frank, that's what's so worrying."

"Good Lord, who? Is it over?"

"Yes. He was a naval college lecturer—quite a young radical."

"Oh I know the type, have 'em in Calcutta these days—want to throw out the white man, start a revolution, put the world to rights...and with a dangerous appeal for clever young ladies! But what happened? Could you break it?"

"Well...we...found them together..." she was blushing.

"Together? What do you mean exactly?"

"In our bed if you must know. We got back from Mukden earlier than expected, and there they were..."

He stared in glassy horror. "Isabel! I can't believe it—little Alice—a thing like that, good God!"

"Now, Robert, there's no use getting upset. Will was furious enough and it was all most unpleasant."

"But how utterly disgusting—in your bed and with a...a Chink!"

"Well, it's over now. The man left town soon after and has now married his betrothed, thank goodness. But the point is, Robert, I have reason to believe Alice's attraction to the natives is deeply rooted—as it is, you see, in Frank. She's been quite miserable since and we've kept a close eye. But I'm so afraid she'll meet another man of a similar type and before we know it there'll be a second wedding as unfortunate as tomorrow's."

"Good heavens, this really is appalling, but I'm glad you've told me. The danger's there alright...But what's to be done?"

"As Will and I have often said, Alice needs a good steady English husband. But the choice in Port Arthur is very limited. Now if she were here in Shanghai, mixing socially with eligible young men...But the difficulty is, who'd keep a check? Frank's offered her a home, but it will be full of Chinese of course and after what's happened...If there were someone older around, if only for a while, just to..."

"I have it, Isabel—I'll stay here myself for the summer! I'm at a bit of a loose end with this long leave until January."

"Robert, what a perfectly splendid idea, it never occurred to me..." said round-eyed Isabel who had been thinking of nothing else for the past half-hour. "And I'm sure you'll thoroughly enjoy Shanghai too."

"Well, I was thinking as I came here, it's perked up a lot since I was last here. And dash it, I've invested enough in Frank, not to much avail, I fear, so it's time I did something for my niece. We can't have her going off the rails like that again. Then I'll have done my best all round, hey?" He beamed. "And let's have two of those delectable-looking nut sundaes to celebrate. It'll give Will a little longer, he must be buying up the shoe-shop."

So they spooned their sundaes and discussed the details of their plan and then, in a relaxed pause, Isabel asked guilelessly, "Robert, I hope you won't think I'm inquisitive, but when we last met I thought you intended leaving the Army and going Home this year? You've changed your mind?"

"Had it changed for me really, Isabel," he gloomed into his sundae glass. "Fact is, I was jilted."

"You jilted—my dear, you're far too handsome and nice for such a fate!"

"Thank you for saying so, but—I'll tell you, as we seem to be exchanging confidences this afternoon. I had a lady friend in Sheringham, Elsie Massingham—known her for ages, since I was a boy. Always thought we'd marry one day and so did she. But things always kept cropping up to prevent it somehow... Anyway, to cut a long story, when I decided to finance Frank at the college here I wrote and told her I was staying in the Army for three more years after all, then I'd go home to her. Well, that was the last straw I suppose. Her letters cooled a bit, but I didn't pay much attention, not enough apparently. Then bless me if she didn't write to say she'd married the Vicar of Blakeney, a widower, quite elderly. Said she'd waited long enough and I'd taken her good nature too much for granted. Quite a horrid letter it was, though with grains of truth, I must confess. So there I was— no Elsie, no villa in Sheringham, no point in going Home really. So I've signed up for two more years, then we'll see."

"Robert you old dark horse! You never told a soul about Elsie, did you? What a shame—and all through your generosity to Frank too. Ah well, you'll have to see what Shanghai can produce for you as well as for Alice. Come, let's give Will up and go—else the wedding feast will be upon us before we've digested this delicious tea."

The day of the wedding was a sparkle of sunshine. As Alice tried on the dress of apple-green silk trimmed with white ribbons that the dressmaker's boy had delivered at dawn, she felt almost as happy as if the ceremony ahead were her own. The previous evening, Isabel had told her the plan she and Robert had "cooked up in the patisserie" and she had been overjoyed. As she pirouetted in front of the glass and tried on her new ostrich feather hat, she felt as if Shanghai was already at her feet and all the worries about Frank's marriage were groundless. Why should he and Peachy not be perfectly happy when they loved each other so much? That, as Frank said, was the only important thing, and surely enough for a lifetime?

She kept that thought uppermost when, a few hours later, she watched the bridal pair climb from Mr Wang's best landau and go into the guildhall for the wedding breakfast. Peachy wore no white, the Chinese colour of mourning, but looked ravishing in pale pink, a veil partially covering her rouged face, and carrying a bouquet of red roses. There were roses everywhere—in the church, the hall, stuck in the men's buttonholes and the ladies' hair, and ever afterwards Alice associated their fragrance with that day, such a sweet, beguiling scent, yet with an elusive hint of melancholy and swift decay.

Earlier the Greenwoods had attended the Buddhist ceremony in the Wangs' ancestral hall, and Robert and William had been fearfully oppressed by the strangeness of it all—the gongs, incense and chanting of the priests. But Alice had been beset with memories of that other wedding long ago in Hunan. She remembered Eldest Son's flushed face, the cowed features of poor Dull Thorn; Lung-kuang doing all the honours with the proper degrees of courtesy. Gross in some ways, that ceremony still had a magnificent sense of occasion which both this and the subsequent Christian service lacked. For there were too many discordant elements, and which was worse, the sight of Frank's blond head bent before the ancestral tablets, or the senior Wang's pigtailed pate making similar polite obeisance before the altar of Trinity Church?

As they filed into the guildhall, Alice hoped that the secular activity of feasting would create a pretence of fusion—and no expense had been spared to that end, for tables were piled with native and foreign food. While toasts were proposed, Mr Wang, looking, Isabel decided, exactly like the hundreds of other natives from whom she had bought fish and vegetables, talked about the fostering of links between England and China, a theme embroidered by other speakers in both English and Chinese. Afterwards, Peachy's brothers and their racing friends gathering in a corner drinking hard and laughing loudly, and the older men grunted together in business pidgin, but the ladies were reduced to smiling politely and pointing at the roses, to show their shared appre-

ciation of their beauty. Seeing Mrs Wang and Isabel so
stranded side by side, Alice was about to go to the rescue
when Charlotte tugged her sleeve. "Aunt Alice, there's a man
at the door asking for you."

"For me—specially?"

"Yes, Miss Alice Greenwood he said."

Her heart leaped; it must be—who else. "But he can come
in—there are lots of Chinese here."

"But he's not Chinese, he's English."

"Oh . . . oh well, I'll come."

It took but an instant to place the face at the door in its
six-year-past slot.

"Charles Grant! Mr Grant—why, how lovely to see you."

"And little Alice—Greenwood is it?" he cast a surreptitious
glance at her left hand.

"But come in and let me get you a drink to the bridal pair.
But however did . . . ?"

He smiled. "I seem destined to read about your doings
in the Shanghai press. I slipped into the Club for a snack
today, picked up a *Mercury*—and lo and behold, the wedding
announcement of Mr Frank Greenwood and Miss Tao Yuan-
wang. I wasn't sure it was the same of course, but it seemed
worth finding out."

"What a shame you didn't come sooner, we've been rather
short on the English team, as Uncle Robert calls it, and now
it's nearly over . . . Here, Will, look who's just arrived!"

William joined them. "Why it's—of course, Charles
Grant, the man on the houseboat, how splendid to see you.
You must come and meet Frank before he whisks the bride
away. Set up in business here now, have you? As you
planned?"

"Only just started really—there have been, delays . . ."

"And your family is here now too, I suppose?"

He avoided their eyes. "No, I fear my wife and the new
baby died, about a year after I was here."

"Oh Mr Grant, I am sorry, how dreadful for you. But what
happened?" Alice broke in.

"We'll talk later, shall we? This is a wedding feast, after
all . . ."

William nodded. "Yes of course—now let me introduce
you to my wife . . ."

As he pushed through the throng that was gathering at the
door, a sudden burst of cheering went up, firecrackers
snapped and Frank and Peachy came running down the

281

length of the hall hand in hand, pelted as they came with rose petals, rice and paper streamers. As they neared the door, Peachy's brothers and friends waylaid Frank, tripping his feet and butting him in parody of the traditional teasing of the bridegroom outside the bridal chamber. Peachy, giggling, fled outside and as Frank tried to follow, a guest caught him from behind, pulling him down backwards. Others fell on him, stuffing rice down his shirt, throwing wine in his face, while one of Mr Wang's dapper jockeys pranced round thrusting out his loins rhythmically and muttering suggestions about the capabilities of a barbarian cock. Frank bellowed with frustration and laughter and, trying to rise, kneed one of his tormenters in the groin; he doubled up, groaning theatrically. As Frank struggled harder, Peachy's brother punched him in the belly while a friend pinioned his head to the floor and rammed a champagne bottle against his mouth. Frank's mouth began to bleed and a cry of real pain broke from him.

The mask of the day had slipped; the flushed faces surrounding Frank were unsmiling now; the man they held to the ground was a yellow-haired barbarian who was going to put his cock inside one of their own kind; the mouth of Peachy's brother was drawn back in a snarl. As Alice looked desperately for discreet help, Mrs Wang suddenly surged up in her brilliant robe of vermilion and emerald, the jewels of her headdress shaking in her wrath. She hissed at the youths in a low whisper and they fell back instantly. Frank stood up and his attackers brushed him down, smiling sheepishly. Mrs Wang dabbed coldly at his cut mouth and he gave her a shaky smile of gratitude as he rushed off to join Peachy in the waiting carriage.

"They're off on honeymoon to the Snowy Valley Lakes," Alice said to Charles brightly.

He brushed her neutrality aside. "That wasn't very nice, was it?"

"No—but then the whole affair isn't very nice in some ways, only we all have to make the best of it."

"Of course, I understand. Look, Alice—if so I may still call you—I'd love to see you again, but I feel I'm gatecrashing on a family affair. Perhaps we could meet tomorrow? How about the Hotel des Colonies in the French concession at noon?"

The date was made and he hurried away. Alice leaned against the door for a moment to regain her composure. The scene she had just witnessed had shaken her and as a result of it, she thought remorsefully, she had been led into her first betrayal of Frank and Peachy. Her words to Charles had been an exact echo of what her relatives had said all along about the marriage. Yet, at the moment of speaking, she had felt them true, and now, at the end of the day, she no longer knew what to think. Indeed, she suspected that its only certain good had been the totally unexpected reappearance of Charles Grant.

Their meeting at the hotel the next day rather confirmed her view, for he was as good-looking and affable as she remembered. "The chef here is Swiss," he explained as they went into the dining-room, "and far superior to the man at the Grand." The prices, he did not add, were also more moderate.

She smiled. "You know I've done nothing but eat and drink since I came to Shanghai."

"But that's exactly what most people here do most of the time . . . so when in Rome, eh?"

She studied the menu closely, remembering her past attraction to him, aware of his close scrutiny.

"It's been six years, hasn't it, Alice? In which time you've grown into a charming and attractive young lady, if I may say so."

"Oh—thank you," she raised her eyes. "And you—seem little changed, which is meant as a compliment."

"But a lot has happened in the interim, I can tell you, if you care to hear. Only it seemed rather an Ancient Mariner's tale for yesterday's wedding feast . . . But you shall hear. I recommend the duck *à l'orange*—and a small Graves," he added to the waiter.

"You returned to India after we parted, did you not?"

"Yes and Maria's baby, a girl, was born soon after. Only, they never flourished, either of them—they just ailed and ailed . . ." He traced circles with his fork on the cloth. "An arduous journey to China was out of the question. I sent them up to Ooty, but it didn't help. Then came an epidemic that summer, fever which often hits the South—they both got it and died quite quickly; the baby was only eighteen months, poor mite."

"Oh Charles, how dreadful for you, I am so sorry."

He smiled twistedly. "Not such a rare occurrence in India, but the sort of thing you always assume happens to others, like avalanches or earthquakes. I went down with the fever myself then, but pulled through eventually. Peter, thank heavens, escaped it."

"And he is well now?"

"Yes and a great comfort. I took him Home to school for a while after it happened and got a job for myself in London... But Lord it was dull, just the sort of thing I'd always tried to avoid. Ah, here's the duck, and here's to you, Alice!" They drank and he continued, "We stayed with my sister Dottie in Hampshire for the next Christmas and I remember we stood looking out of a window at one of those typically colourless English-winter days and Peter said, 'Father, I hate it here, let's go back to the East.' He'd put into words exactly what I felt, and it seemed a sort of sign. When you're a bit lost, you pay attention to signs don't you?"

She nodded with understanding.

"So in due course, we went back to Madras and at least that made Peter happy, he's in school there now. But India still wasn't my cup of tea and Harriet, my elder sister, had really stuck the black sheep label on me by this time!" He smiled charmingly at her.

"But surely it's better to cast around for a while than settle for too little?"

"I'm glad you feel that too," he poured more wine, "so I started casting back in the direction of China again, threw up my Madras job eventually and landed here a few weeks ago. I've taken a recce up the Yangtze and I'm now trying to raise more capital, then I'm opening a trade agency in Hankow. Yesterday, I was in the Club, picked up the *Mercury*... and now you're absolutely up to date!"

Her eyes held his, warm with compassion. "Yes, that is a sad story and you were so full of hopes when we met before. It seems cruel you've been so... battered."

"Well I still have my health and am beginning to hope again, whereas poor Maria..."

He looked away at the potted ferns behind her. "She was lovely in many ways. One always feels guilty afterwards somehow."

"But you did what you could, I'm sure?"

"Oh yes, at the time." His face closed. "But now it's your turn, what have you been doing since we met?"

As she gave him a carefully edited version of her recent past, he listened carefully for clues to the one question he really wanted to ask: why was she not yet married? She had seemed such a lovable, lively creature at eighteen and to this she had added the graces of young womanhood. Was there some odd quirk in her nature that was not immediately apparent, or was it simply that she had been stuck in out-of-the-way places where few matrimonial chances existed?

"And now Uncle Robert's decided it will be good for me to stay here for a few months and he'll keep an eye on me," she imitated his sombre tones. "I'm to stay at the Customs House annexe and we are to have some fun, he assures me."

"Quite right too," he grinned. "And let's kick off right now with a *crème brûlée* and cream—specially good here."

As he ordered she asked casually, "And will you be in Shanghai long?"

"Only a few days, then to Hankow to learn the ropes of the tea-trade on the spot. Later I hope to get upriver beyond the Treaty Ports—Ichang, Chungking...who knows?" he waved an airy hand.

"It sounds exciting, I've never been up the Upper Yangtze region—the River of Golden Sands."

"Sounds damnably dangerous whatever its pretty name. Dozens of boats get smashed to smithereens in the rapids every year apparently. Nearly put me off altogether I admit—not only the risk to life and limb, but many a merchant has lost his entire capital outlay through the breaking of a tow-rope at the wrong moment."

Her eyes sparkled. "I'd love to see how they get those junks up the rapids. And you'll go ahead, won't you, in spite of the risks?"

"No choice—I've really burned my Indian boats this time. It's partly a question of how much to gamble in what. The risks are so great that insurance is enormously costly."

She frowned. "It must be difficult. Frank and I used to dream that we'd form a company and go trading up the Yangtze one day. But now he's married to Peachy and is joining his father-in-law, which sounds safe and easy, but excludes me."

"Really? I never imagined you'd be interested in the sordid business of buying and selling, most ladies aren't."

"But I don't seem to be like most ladies and I'd love the adventure of it, and trying to beat your rivals—though the best time for that is past, isn't it? When the great tea-clippers used to race from the Yangtze to London with the first of the season's crop."

"So I've been told and now it's prosaic steam through the Suez. Trouble is, I always seem to be too late for the real thrills—like my parents' tales of the stirring Mutiny days when I was just a little nipper. Yet being a pre-Mutiny baby is quite a sign of age now, when all the bright young lads coming out were born after it!"

"And I was born just as it ended—so where do I stand? In the old days it was before or after Waterloo that dated you. I suppose it was ever thus? And always will be?"

He reached for the bill. "I wonder what the next great watershed will be, the sort of event historians begin and end chapters with?"

She grinned, "1882 of course—the year Mr Charles Grant went a-merchanting up the Yangtze and opened the Middle Kingdom to the greatest influx of Manchester cotton goods and Birmingham hardware that the Celestials had ever seen..."

"...changing the economy of the entire East and the balance of world trade and becoming a multi-millionaire in the process!" His eyes twinkled. "And with that cheering thought I must go, Alice. I've an appointment with a junior chahsee at Crawfords—not a very brilliant beginning, I fear."

"Well, the Chinese say that to build a mountain you have to start with one bucket of earth. And I'm sure even the humble life of a Yangtze trader will have its excitements."

He glanced at her keenly. "And you'll be enjoying yourself here, I'm sure."

She shrugged. "We shall see—but don't let me detain you. Oh and Charles—Isabel has asked you to join us for supper tomorrow evening—if you can manage it?"

He did manage it and, in spite of business commitments, joined the Greenwoods on several occasions before he returned to Hankow, and Isabel and William to Port Arthur. The tone of his subsequent encounters with Alice was lightly flirtatious, both of them avoiding the deeper currents of their first luncheon together. Alice felt they might have gone too far too soon, and in any case he no longer had the same dazzle for her as when she had met him at eighteen. She still liked his breezy promise of a recklessness that had not yet been really tested; but perhaps his sister was right—he was something of a black sheep, a rolling stone mossed only with vague dreams of wealth. When he left, he kissed her gently, carefully withholding any hint of the passion that had once sparked between them. It was as if, after the first elation of their re-encounter, they were both a little disappointed—but did not know quite why.

11

There was general agreement among the resident foreign
ladies of Shanghai that June was altogether delightful. The
weather was warm and dry enough for the lightest muslin
frocks, but not oppressively hot, and gardens, both public
and private, glowed with flowers; cross-country racing was
forbidden on account of the farmers' rice seedlings, and the
spring snipe had flown north, so that the menfolk did not
spend all their waking hours galloping about the countryside
or peppering it with gunshot; the first race-meetings and
regattas of the year were in full swing and the first contingents
of globetrotters and visiting artistes from Europe and America
brought new zest to the social scene.

Immediately after the departure of William and his family,
Robert Greenwood made it his business to find out forth-
coming events in the community's social calendar. As an officer and gentleman he obtained temporary membership of
the Shanghai Club and from the vantage of its famous Long
Bar easily made the acquaintance of various respectable and
popular citizens. Very shortly, it seemed to the impressed

Alice, he knew everyone worth knowing in the several-hundred-strong British community and there was no shortage of invitations to suppers, picnics and balls for them both.

"I really don't know how you do it, Uncle," she exclaimed admiringly, as he raised his hat to acknowledge the greeting of yet another passing lady as they strolled through the Bund gardens one afternoon.

He beamed complacently. "Shanghai's an easy-come-easy-go sort of place, m'dear. But wherever you are, go at it like a military exercise—do a recce, find out who's who, get the right lines of communication going, invest in the right equipment—well-tailored clothes and wallets of calling-cards for example—get up a few treats for the right people, and Bob's your Uncle... ha! Needs a bit of *savoir-faire*, but this Uncle Bob's been through many a Simla season and that's a social minefield compared to this. Ladies are often better at it than gentlemen. You should watch Mrs Dawson of the Customs House or Mrs Fortescue in action, for example. They only need to keep in trim now for the field is theirs, you might say, but they've certainly employed similar tactics in the past."

She was amused. "I don't believe I'd have the confidence."

"Well you're still young—you need a husband in the background, then you'll be alright."

It had not been a deliberate barb, but he saw her mouth tighten and wondered whether to soften it. But no—Alice had to understand that, though bachelors might proceed in this way, a woman needed the financial and social support of a husband. Alice, well aware of his attempts to furnish her with one, had conscientiously studied the season's form, as Frank put it, but so far without enthusiasm. There were eligible young men a-plenty: juniors in the consulates, the hongs and banks, the subalterns in the barracks, and several of all types happy to escort her on pleasurable excursions. Like Jeff Winthrop, she discovered, they talked earnestly of their families at Home, their future prospects, their recent successes in various sporting endeavours. The bolder spirits held her hand, pressed kisses upon her, told her how charming she was. But they all seemed mere boys compared to Lin Fu-wei, or even to Charles Grant, who had gone away without another word.

The only exception might have been Clifford White, a student-interpreter at the Consulate, until the evening when she had heard him read a paper to the Asiatic Society on

"The Influence of Confucianism in the Chinese Home". A stranger and one of few ladies present, she had not dared question him, but afterwards she had informed him at length that his conclusions were both superficial and inaccurate and that she could have done much better. He had stalked off crimson-faced, saying he wondered why ladies were allowed to come and listen to members' papers if all they could do was criticise. And she had gone miserably to bed, wishing she could learn to hold her tongue.

As they neared the Customs House, Robert said, "Oh, I meant to tell you—Mrs Fortescue has asked us to be of her luncheon party for the Victoria Cup race-meet, quite an affair apparently. She says—do bring a friend, if you'd like."

"Next Saturday, isn't it? I might ask Bertie Tarrent, I suppose."

"I thought Clifford White was the hero of the hour?"

"No—he's abominably self-opinioned and puffed-up."

He looked amused. "Please yourself, miss, you usually do... Now I must go and change for the concert tonight. Mrs Fortescue assures me this orchestral group from Hanover is superb."

"I never knew you cared a fig for music, Uncle?"

"Well I've developed a taste—a love for cultural activities—it comes later in life to some than to others." His tone was deliberately noncommittal and, as he hurried away, she did not quite know what to make of it.

The day of the Victoria Cup meeting, last of the spring season, dawned as fair as many before and with a refreshing sea-breeze which, Alice was assured, would die away within a week leaving them to the mercy of the mid-summer heats with positively no air to breathe at all. Foreign ladies on the arms of gentlemen strolled near the grandstand wearing day frocks of lemon yellow, rose pink, or peppermint green, and crowds of predominantly blue-clad Chinese spectators crowded round the track corners where betting was furious. The drum and fife band from the gunboat *Euryalus* played a selection of lively airs; boys ran in and out of the striped marquees with trays of drinks and the members of the racing fraternity were clustered round the ponies in the paddock.

Frank was among them, giving advice to his father-in-law's jockey while Peachy nearby watched her husband adoringly. Alice, on the arm of Bertie Tarrent, a senior clerk in the Hong Kong & Shanghai Bank who had a good head for figures and a waspish sense of humour, spotted her from a distance.

"Oh—there's my sister-in-law, near the paddock, we must go over!"

Bertie raised his field-glasses. "Where—I can't see..."

"There, near the mounted pony, in pink and orange..."

"Oh... er yes, Chinese of course I forgot... silly of me. And a bit rum for you?"

"Not at all. Peachy's very sweet—let's go and see her."

"If you like, but I think the saddle-bell is about to ring."

Defiantly she started off, but just then the bell did ring and Mrs Fortescue claimed them, leading them to her table in the shade with a good view of the last length. Mary Fortescue had quickly become rather important in Robert and Alice's life. A friend of Mrs Dawson's, she had been delegated by that busy lady to take the newcomers under her wing and was admirably fitted for the task. She was a rather ample, garrulous middle-aged lady with changeless ash-blonde hair and blue eyes of the roguish variety. Early the previous year her husband, Claud, a director of the Hong Kong & Shanghai Bank, had dropped dead of a heart attack one morning; instead of going quietly Home, as most women did in such circumstances, Mary Fortescue stayed on. It was the most unconventional step of her life and she still felt obliged to justify it sometimes—though less often recently as people grew accustomed to her singularity. Events like race-meetings brought out the best in her, for she was a Shanghai-hand of twelve years' standing; she knew everyone, liked the majority and was liked in return for her generous hospitality and an irrepressible liveliness that had survived her widowhood undimmed.

"... Now Alice, Bertie, whom do you know? Major, a chair for Alice please... Why practically everyone, I believe... Mr and Mrs Wetherby and the Misses Wetherby, Clifford White of course—and Mr Hinkson, our dear Hink, you know? And Bubbles Parker, well everyone knows him... Then we'll settle down and think about making our fortunes. Hush now everyone," and she called for silence as, after two false starts, the next race began.

"Lady Luck in the lead yes... it is... yes, I knew it! No, Petronella—come on Petronella... no, it's Lady Luck!" The Misses Wetherby clapped their gloved hands and cried out in excitement as the favourite scampered past the winning post and made them ten dollars richer.

Alice had early realised that she was not to be the most sought-after belle of that Shanghai summer, the position being jointly occupied by Violet and Iris Wetherby, charm-

ing, elegant daughters of a newly appointed shipping director. They had recently come from Home bringing the latest
fashions and social chat and had already impressed upon the
assembled company that today's races were mere comedy
compared to last year's Epsom. Still they had sportingly decided to make the best of it and giggled mightily at the funny
little Mongolian ponies bouncing round the uneven course.

"Now who's going to win next, Vi?" Iris ran a finger down
the card. "How about Taiping? What does that mean? Something Chinese I suppose, Mr Hinkson?"

Mr Hinkson, librarian from the Consulate secretariat,
could scarcely ever have been asked a sillier question, Alice
thought, but he answered good-humouredly. "I wouldn't back
a pony of that name, Miss Wetherby—the Taipings didn't
exactly emerge victorious from the field."

"Oh—people, were they?"

"Rebels against the Manchus who wanted to set up a Heavenly Kingdom on Chinese soil. They were causing havoc
when I first came out here more than twenty-five years ago—
plundering and slaughtering wherever they went."

"Really, how horrible." Iris shuddered. "Then I shan't
back him, I'll have more of that delicious salmon mousse
instead."

"Did you actually see the Taipings in action, Mr Hinkson?"
Alice asked. "My parents did in Ningpo."

"So did I—unfortunately—at Soochow, not fifty miles
from this racecourse. I was a young interpreter with the Ever
Victorious Army commanded by Major Charles Gordon,
'Chinese Gordon' they later dubbed him. The Taipings held
Soochow for a month and I was there when Gordon's troops
recaptured it. A grisly affair altogether, difficult to know who
behaved worst, the rebels or the Imperial Forces storming
through the city like animals, firing buildings and cutting up
innocent people—the ditches overflowed with blood. Hard
to believe now that such things went on not far away, not so
long ago... But here, some salmon mousse?"

"Thank you... And hard to imagine the sort of life that
still goes on among people living not so very far away who'd
be absolutely astounded by a scene like this. The drums and
gongs of the magistrates' procession reminded me..."

He smiled understandingly, his reply lost in the crowd's
roar as the race finished and Iris turned on him reproachfully.
"Oh, it's Taiping I do believe! An outsider too and you told
me not to back him, Mr Hinkson!"

Alice was unsympathetic. "Never judge the jam..."

Iris, looking annoyed, went to join Clifford White and Bubbles Parker, thinking that Miss Greenwood was simply a country-born little person of no possible consequence. "I gather Miss Greenwood has never been Home?" she whispered to Clifford as he poured lemonade.

"I think not—which is why she feels entitled to have so many decided opinions on things Chinese." He smiled at her.

"And I gather her brother is actually married to a native?"

"Yes—he's over there, that blond chap with the dandy Chinaman. Here, take a look..." Bubbles Parker handed Iris his glasses. He was a ruddy-faced man with ruddy whiskers and was reputed to foam at the mouth with rage at the misdeeds of his houseboys, hence his nickname.

Clifford shrugged. "Well, old Frank's married into quite a bit of money, if you like that sort of thing."

Bubbles snorted. "Not my cup of little green tea, thank you... How could one possibly, when there are so many utterly alluring English ladies about?" He bowed at Iris as they moved away from the emptying tables.

Alice felt her cheeks burn, for, though she had not quite heard the conversation, she had guessed Frank and she were its subject. She had just decided to go and talk to Peachy, when Mrs Fortescue drew her aside. "My dear Alice—your uncle's been telling me of your little difficulty about accommodation and I wonder if I could help?"

"Oh that—it *is* rather a nuisance."

The previous day the Dawsons had heard that the Inspector-General of Customs, Sir Robert Hart, had left Peking on an inspection tour. Sir Robert's tours were renowned for thoroughness, unpredictability and size of entourage; clearly the whole Customs House had to be held in readiness.

"I've suggested to your uncle that you come and stay with me and he's quite agreeable, if you'd like to? My daughter Lilian and I just rattle round in my place these days. And Lilian is no sort of company anyway—so I should be delighted and it would give the servants a bit more to do."

Alice's heart leaped with pleasure, for on her one visit she had thought Mrs Fortescue's house, Fairlawns, quite the nicest in Shanghai.

So it was arranged and Mrs Fortescue was to send her carriage round the very next day, for, she explained, very soon no one, except the indefatigable I.-G., would move an inch in any direction on account of the heat. Only when packing her trunk that evening did Alice realise that, in the excitement of the races and the subsequent whirling away to the Wetherbys' house for tea, she had not even spoken to Peachy. She felt vexed; how easy it was for such situations to occur, how difficult to have introduced Peachy to them all. But she knew that her sister-in-law would be feeling slighted, and there was nothing she could do about it.

Fairlawns, into which Alice moved the next day, was spacious and peaceful, its rooms adorned with scroll-paintings, porcelains, lacquerwork, its lawns surrounded by oleanders, magnolias, palms and tulip trees. On Alice's first evening, Mrs Fortescue arranged to be in, for, she said as they settled on the verandah at sunset, "As you are to be staying here, my dear, we should get to know each other better. And," she continued in her usual rush, "I expect you wonder why I've chosen to stay on here? My married daughter in England begs me to join her and so does my son, Edgar, in Singapore, but it's Lilian my youngest who's the bother."

"I don't believe I've met her yet? Isn't she studying for something?"

Mrs Fortescue's eyes rolled skywards in despair. "Indeed yes—and of all ridiculous things, she's fixed on becoming a medical missionary. A sort of lady doctor if you please, dealing with all those utterly repulsive Chinese diseases—leprosy, scrofula, elephantiasis, the Lord knows what. It quite turns my stomach to hear of them. Lilian, I say to her, you are a well-born, well-brought-up young lady, it is simply not fitting for someone like you to..."

Alice decided to interrupt. "But what gave her the idea? Does missioning run in your family as it does in mine?"

"Oh dear no, and I'm sure they do most worthy work, but Claud, my late husband, would send her to the mission school here. She was always his favourite pet lamb," there was no mistaking the venom in the mother's voice, "and he couldn't bear her to go Home to school as the others had. That's how the missionaries got hold of her, body and soul—oh Claud, if you'd but lived to see the mischief you've wrought, I say to myself. She was already inclined to it before he died, but since then there's been no stopping her. She studies nothing but dreadful medical books and some of their illustrations are positively indecent in my view. She refuses to do anything else and if I leave her here, she'll move into the mission hostel and there'll be no hope for her!"

"But there's another side of it, surely, Mrs Fortescue? Lilian is obviously doing what she wants, she has found a mission in life you might say. And I sometimes wish I could. Are not people with a sense of true purpose the happiest, whereas the rest of us—I speak for myself anyway—tend to drift along rather aimlessly?"

"No, my dear," Mrs Fortescue was quite firm, "there are things a woman can fix upon if she's a mind to and I'm sure you will. If Lilian wants to do good—there's the Benevolent Society, those funds for orphans and sailors' widows and whatnot. But missionaries are hopelessly one-track, they don't give a fig for their own kind. And they often make the most unsuitable marriages. Why, a young lady came here with the C.M.S. recently, daughter of a wealthy Sussex land-owner I understand, but full of the word of the Lord, as they say. Well, would you believe it, within the year she'd married a young blacksmith from Aberdeen—now they're going hammer and tongs at the souls of the heathen somewhere in Szechuan! Nearly killed her poor Mama... And that's what worries me most about Lilian—bad enough being a lady doctor, but she could end up marrying a carpenter to boot!"

"Well Jesus Christ was a carpenter." Alice bit her lip, realising she had angered her hostess.

"Come now Alice, that's being frivolous. There are carpenters and carpenters. Your uncle warned me you have strong opinions, but I didn't gather you fully supported the ideas of the missionary fraternity."

"Indeed I don't, it was just a silly joke, Mrs Fortescue. My stepfather considers me quite a lost soul, I assure you."

"Then let us drop the subject and have supper. And after I'll show you the other reason why I stay in Shanghai—of which Lilian doesn't at all approve, but you might..."

And when Mrs Fortescue showed her the long gallery behind the house filled with her collection of Japanese works of art, Alice's approval was wholehearted. "I began buying when Claud and I were in Yokohama in the early '60s," Mrs Fortescue explained. "And the most beautiful things were going for a song then—it was before the Meiji Restoration and Japanese currency was in a sorry mess. It wasn't till we came here in '70 that I realised how clever I'd been, and should have bought more! But it was a start and since I've traded the lesser stuff for works of real quality. See, here's a print of Harunobu's, 'Two Girls by a Stream'—look at those delicate colours, the flowing lines... and here's Shinenaga's 'Descending Geese at Katata'... isn't it droll? But they're only woodblocks, *ukiyo-e*, 'pictures of the passing world'... Come, see over here: this exquisite screen, irises, reeds..."

"Did you like the Japanese as people?" This was a new idea to Alice, for the Chinese spoke of them so disparagingly.

"A wonderful race, my dear, so clean and go-ahead, so admirably effective in every way, compared to slow-poke Chinamen. One day they'll beat the pants off the rest of Asia, as your uncle bluntly puts it. And good luck to 'em... I always wish we'd stayed there, but now I have to be content with occasional buying sprees to Nagasaki and Yokohama. And between you and me, everything I buy sells extremely well to globetrotting amateur collectors with more money than sense! And my favourites, which you see here, give me the added gratification of increasing in value every year... That's why Lilian doesn't approve—quite unprincipled according to her and I should make due penance by donating all profits to the new Mission hospital! So you see my dear, my daughter and I seldom see eye to eye. But would you agree with Lilian in this?"

"Certainly not—it's a marvellous collection and I think you should cherish it, build on it and let others admire it with you." Mrs Fortescue patted her shoulder.

"Well Alice, I'm sure you wouldn't say that just to please me. So please feel at liberty to look round here whenever you like... Some of the works grow on you—you'll see."

Indeed the gallery did open a new dimension of seeing for Alice, who, while quietly absorbing the beauty of the art, gradually realised that its creators could not be as contemptible as she had been led to believe. The relative coolness of the gallery also attracted her during the long summer days when the social pace slackened as the temperature rose, when, along the Bund, the whitish afternoon sun shone with a metallic glare on the stone facades of offices, the zinc-plated godowns, the motionless sea beyond.

After sunset, people began to move again in a limp way and Uncle Robert, who seemed remarkably content with Shanghai life, would come to take Mrs Fortescue and Alice out—to a concert, a supper-party, a drive to the playing fields where the sportsmen were practising. At weekends, parties were made up for excursions into the hills or houseboat trips along the Wampoa with the usual contingent of bachelors, the elegant Misses Wetherby and globetrotters with the right introductions.

Late in the evening, returned from various jollifications, Alice used often to stand on her bedroom verandah enjoying the fragrance of blossom, the croak of frogs from the lily pond, and think—for, as everyone said, it was too hot to do so at any other time. Invariably, a light still shone from the room of the industrious Lilian, a quiet young woman pale of skin and eye, who disapproved of Alice as of everything in her mother's household. To Lilian, Alice was just another husband-seeking, light-minded young lady flitting on the social scene, and it was in vain that Alice told her how she admired her determination to acquire a profession against all odds.

"You could do the same if you really wanted," Lilian had snapped back. "There's a crying need for qualified medical people in mission outposts throughout the world."

"But you see..." Alice began, then stopped, wondering then, as she did when she stood on the evening verandah, why it was that she could not commit herself as Lilian could—wishing desperately to be in some way taken over. For having fun, she thought dismally, was not enough. But why did she feel the odd one out? The other young people seemed never to be afflicted with the sense of dissatisfaction that so often beset her. It was, she supposed, her missionary inheritance that rendered her incapable of prolonged frivolity and had given her a sense of purpose that she could not quite ignore, though it was undirected by any conviction.

I could spend a lifteime on the sidelines, waiting to be convinced by something—or someone—she thought in despair, leaning against the verandah pillar, watching Lilian turn off her lamp at last and kneel in prayer before sinking into untroubled, virginal slumber. But Alice's nights were sometimes haunted by erotic fantasies wherein her body moved knowingly into one of her favourite positions and she became "like a silkworm spinning a cocoon" with her hands clasped about the neck, her feet across the back of her urgent lover, whose face was now Lung-kuang's, now Lin's, now an indeterminate amalgam of Oriental manhood. After such dreams Alice would lie awake damp and troubled in the bright dawn wondering whatever was to become of her.

The first sign of a new becoming occurred on a late August evening when she was dressing for the Mih Ho Loong ball. From outside there came the sound of a thousand beating wings and she went on the verandah, looking into the clear dark sky.

"Hear that?" Mary called from the garden where she was standing with Robert. "It's the snipe returning from the north—they'll be all over the marshes tomorrow and the men will be oiling their guns tonight. It's the beginning of the end of summer."

Alice listened to the lovely rhythms and then went inside, brushing her hair absentmindedly. The end of summer—and then what? She had made no plans beyond that and still lacked the urge to do so. Downstairs, Mrs Fortescue and Uncle Robert were waiting for her in the drawing-room, he in his officer's mess kit, she in a ball-gown of pearl grey silk trimmed with harebell blue; they stood stiffly side by side, posed, like a *tableau vivant* or a studio portrait.

"Is anything wrong? You look so solemn..."

The pose broke and Robert handed her a glass of champagne they were drinking. "Not at all—quite the contrary. We were drinking a little toast and hope you'll share it."

"Of course, I love champagne." She lifted her glass. "To what do I drink?"

Robert glanced at his companion. "To us—if you will. Mary and I have just become engaged."

Alice set down the glass and stared at them, tears springing to her eyes. "You—why—you two? You pair of dark horses... but I never dreamed..." She laughed shakily.

Mary came to kiss her. "You are pleased, I hope, Alice?"

"I'm delighted of course—delighted. But so surprised, I must have been blind."

And indeed she had been, for, with the self-centred arrogance of her years, it had not once occurred to her that their summer friendship was more than a mild flirtation. She gulped down the inexplicable emotions in her throat. "Mrs Fortescue, how lovely for you! I assure you my uncle is a dear man."

"And Mrs Fortescue is a very dear lady, I assure you, Alice," Robert smiled. "But we needn't be so formal anymore. Wouldn't Aunt Mary sound better?"

Mary laughed coquettishly. "Oh Robert, please not! Alice is too grown up to suddenly acquire another aunt—and how ancient that makes me feel! I think just 'Mary' in the circumstances..."

"To Mary and Robert, with all my very, very best wishes for their future happiness..." Alice raised her glass. "And when is the wedding to be?"

"Ah, that was the slight difficulty we've just negotiated successfully. You see Alice, I felt it couldn't be this year—when poor dear Claud only died last. Widowed one year, remarried the next—sounds a bit fast." She giggled into her champagne. "But Robert has to be back in Calcutta by late January. So we've settled on 2nd January. We don't want to seem impatient, but that will give us a little time together before Robert leaves."

"You won't go with him?"

"Oh dear no—that's fully agreed. I'll join him in Simla for a late honeymoon next year, but we both want to stay in China."

"And once I'm out of the Army I'll settle here with Mary for a few years anyway."

"So you'll always have a home now with us." Mary patted her arm reassuringly, aware of how mixed Alice's feelings must be. After all, the original purpose of the Greenwoods' staying in Shanghai was to find a husband for the niece, not a wife for the uncle.

"But come—let's go to the ball and dance the night away!" She tripped to get her shawl, and Alice noted with a pang how Robert put it round her shoulders in a newly proprietorial manner.

The Mih Ho Loong ball given by the Hook and Ladder Company volunteer fire brigade was one of the most select held at the Club. Members of the brigade wore the same scarlet shirts, tight black trousers and leather helmets in which they sallied doughtily forth to fight the frequent blazes that occurred in the foreign concessions. Their dashing outfits gave an extra brio to the evening and encouraged everyone to look their best. Dancing was in full swing when they arrived and Alice was claimed by coolly-waiting Bertie Tarrent for a cotillion; a couple of Highland reels followed—practice apparently for the equally grand St Andrew's Day ball later. Then the band struck up the popular Shanghai waltz and, over her partner's shoulder, Alice saw Robert and Mary float past, happily oblivious of anyone else.

"Well, well, good for Mrs Fortescue," Bertie exclaimed when she told him of their engagement in the supper interval. "I'd have thought her a bit long in the tooth for your handsome uncle—must be over fifty if she's a day."

"But he's . . . let's see, in his late forties. Not much difference."

"And she's very comfortably provided for, is she not?"

"I hope you're not suggesting that my uncle . . ."

Bertie smiled sardonically. "Tut, tut, of course not, my dear." But, remembering the recent liaison of young Frank, he had just coined the term "gold-digging Greenwoods" to amuse his chums.

He looked at Alice keenly. "And you'll have the run of Fairlawns now, I imagine? Cunning of the old girl to have you stay there so that Uncle could keep making highly respectable calls, what?"

"Oh Bertie, I don't suppose she deliberately planned it so."

"Of course she did. A good strategist, Mrs Fortescue. And your uncle didn't have to fall. She simply recognised he was ripe for the plucking."

Bubbles Parker, next on Alice's card, lunged up for his polka just then, leaving Bertie to consider Alice's new position, for the name of Fortescue was still one to conjure with in local banking circles where he was making his way. When the time came to claim her for the last waltz, he whispered in her ear, "The floor's abominably crowded, let's go outside instead."

It was a balmy, star-filled night, the Club gardens awash with late-summer blossom. Bertie drew her into the shadows murmuring softly, "You are a lovely creature, you know, Alice Greenwood, a lovely lovely creature..."

His slim fingers stroked her cheeks and neck, pressed gently into her breasts, and she, still in a happy haze of music and champagne, responded gladly. How odd the world was, she thought, unbuttoning his jacket and putting her hot cheek against his cool stiff shirtfront; men and women catching and clinging to each other—on dance floors, in bedrooms—and she giggled at the marvellously ironic joke of sombre Uncle Robert catching, being caught by, the roguish widow Fortescue.

"Why are you laughing, sweetheart?" Bertie murmured into her hair. "Does what I'm doing only amuse you?"

"Oh no, it's very pleasurable, Bertie...." She wriggled closer, trying to accommodate her small soft body to his tight narrow one.

He kissed her ardently and whispered, "Isn't it romantic—this beautiful starry sky, music in the background and we two alone here together?"

She stared up at him, wondering if he had reverted to his usual badinage, but his expression was humourlessly intent, though no stir of sensuality came from him. Was he really bowled over by passion at last—the cool, flippant Bertie for whom all women were like bank accounts with credits and debits to be carefully balanced? Then she understood and flung her head away from his nestling arms.

"Why of course—Bertie, you great fraud!" She was almost amused. "It's not me you're trying to seduce, is it? It's my new prospects, my sudden credit rating, as you'd call it—a sort of step-niece to Mary Fortescue, owner of Fairlawns, widow of your bank's director?"

He drew back affronted, whipped by guilt into an immediate flash of anger.

"Don't be so insulting, Alice—how dare you accuse me of such baseness? It's because I'm so fond of you—or was, but not if you think things like that of me." He rebuttoned his jacket primly. "I suggest you apologise at once, Miss Greenwood. As if I cared..."

"But you do, Bertie, you do." She wiped the moisture of his kisses off her mouth. The very traces of them angered her. "Oh you hypocrite, Bertie. At least the Chinese are honest in such matters—their unions are unashamedly based on credits and debits with none of this foolery about starry skies and sweethearts. But oh—oh you have to pretend you're madly in love with me all of a sudden. But you're not a man who knows how to truly want a woman, Bertie Tarrent, I can tell that."

"Well, well and I wonder where you acquired so much expertise in the field, Miss Greenwood?" His sneer was icy. "And where you find your truly wanting men? The streets of the native town are full of them, I'm sure. Why not try there—if you've not yet done so?"

She raised her evening bag and hit him square and hard across the face with it. The bag was beaded and he yelped; she did not wait to see if she had drawn blood as she hoped before rushing away across the lawn and down the driveway. The ball had ended and couples were streaming out into the night, some still prancing and singing a little as they came with a swish of gowns, crunch of boots, jewels glinting on warmed flesh, glamorous smells of powder and perfume. Globular lanterns bobbing in the hands of servants, on the poles of the carriage-drivers gave the scene a certain enchantment. It was like a stage set, she thought, leaning against a tree to regain her composure. And were they not all actors, these merry revellers, laughing and flirting in groups, then driving off home together two by two? Would the magic of this evening sweeten those marital beds where resentment, boredom and revulsion so often reigned? She sighed heavily. Why did she know that? See so clearly through Bertie's little stratagems? Why was it that other people—these dancers,

Uncle Robert and Mary Fortescue—found it so easy to fall in love and get themselves properly married off? Disconsolately she walked to the gates, looking for the Fortescue carriage. A Chinese in Western clothes passed, then paused to look through the Club railings. Was there not something achingly familiar about the turn of his head? The miracle—how she needed it at that moment!

She rushed to him. "Lin... Lin can it be you?"

An unsmiling, unknown face stared round at her. "I'm sorry," she fell back. "I thought you were someone else."

He looked at her up and down insolently. "You were at this foreign festival?"

"Yes—a dance."

"You barbarian men and women hold each other close to dance, I believe?"

"Yes, it's quite fun."

"It must be—for the man with you. Will you show me how?"

He came closer holding out his arms and she stepped impulsively into them. "You move slowly and together like this." She pushed him gently into a waltzing motion, closing her eyes the better to imagine Lin's embrace.

The stranger's arm tightened round her waist and he chuckled. "This is worth learning—come to my lodgings and teach me more, foreign woman."

Why not, oh why not, she thought. Her body ached with tension, rebellion, half-roused desire. Bertie, even her brother William had already suggested she was a woman of the streets in thought if not in deed. Why not live up to their expectations? At least with this young stranger there would be no hypocrisy, no play-acting—just direct sensual sex. She could feel it in his sinews. She looked at him, her eyes glittering.

"Come," he tugged at her and she melted towards him. Then she heard pounding footsteps and Robert's voice shouting.

"Alice—it *is* you! What the devil are you doing?" As he ran up the stranger bolted. "Who was that man? Do you know him?"

"No, I was just showing him how foreigners dance."

"Dancing—in the arms of an unknown native in the streets! Really you are an utterly shameless hussy sometimes. It's degrading...disgraceful. Here's the carriage, get in there..." He propelled her so roughly inside that she fell across the seat and lay there inert, trembling, dazed.

"This is becoming quite appalling. We must get that young woman respectably married off quick," Robert muttered to Mary between his teeth as they drove home.

"I'll see what I can do, Robert. Leave it to me."

"Come here a minute, dear," Mary called as Alice returned from giving Peachy her English lesson one afternoon shortly after the ball. She was sitting surrounded by fashion plates cut from European magazines. "I'm trying to decide which of these would be suitable for my going-away. Hong Kong is so smart. But guess who I met in Saxby's this afternoon—he gave me this." Teasingly she held up a namecard, blank side showing. Alice reached for it. "No, guess who you'd most like it to be, and that's who it is."

"But I don't know that..."

"In your heart of hearts you do, Alice, I'm sure. See..."

"Grant and Co.... Why, Charles, back again?"

"Yes, arrived yesterday and asking very particularly after you. So I've invited him to supper with us all tomorrow... Such a charming, handsome man, I've only met him briefly, but... anyway, I should wear your lime-green and gold dress, dear, it's most becoming."

She wore the dress and was glad, for the look of admiration in Charles' eyes when he saw her was the start of a very pleasant evening. He was in high spirits and more than ever convinced that Yangtze trade was full of promise.

"You should see the houses of the tea-men along the Treaty Port bunds—very grand. They've obviously made some tidy piles in very few years. One needs some experience to get in the right swim though and I've been advised to dabble a little in Eastern exotica for the European markets as well."

"What a good idea!" Mary bubbled. "I've always been sure that those jolly little painted fans you see everywhere would sell like hotcakes to English ladies wanting to feel a trifle *outré* in Bromley. And how about pictures? Not good ones of course—you must see my Japanese gallery, Mr Grant—but the hideous scrolls of demons and gods they sell at temples. Yes, I think it will soon be fashionable to have a scrap of the mysterious Orient in every seaside villa hall."

"Why, you inspire me, Mrs Fortescue," Charles bowed. "And what about a few tons of those handbells to summon the maid to dust the scrolls?"

And Robert added, "While we're about it, why not a few thousand of the brass gongs from the monasteries of various heavenly clouds to summon the guests to dine?"

"Seriously, Mr Grant," Mary continued, "I'm sure you're on the right track. Several traders I first met in Yokohama in the '60s have done excellently exporting Japanese trash to America."

"You were in Japan that early—before the Meiji?"

"Indeed yes and what a time it was! Fewer than two hundred of us foreigners cooped up in the Yokohama settlement in rickety clapboard bungalows with just a couple of stores, a few godowns and bars of ill-repute. But it was all so *pioneering*—we ladies felt as if we'd won a gold cup if we secured a bottle of Lea & Perrins sauce or a tin of salmon from Baker & Co when the overseas cargoes came in. And people kept making fortunes and losing them just as fast... oh, but it was such fun!"

Charles grinned. "There you are, Alice—too late for the real thrills again! In India, Japan and now here, I imagine the best of the action is over?"

"Oh that's *your* grumble, isn't it, Robert?" Mary got in first again as usual. "To hear him talk sometimes you'd think he'd be glad to have another Mutiny on our hands."

"Tush, that's putting it too strongly, Mary. But certainly now that Pax Britannica has descended over all and even Afghanistan seems quiet, there's precious little excitement in the military life. I might as well go trading trinkets like you, Charles."

"But you make it sound so trivial, Uncle," Alice protested. "I think it sounds most exciting—merchant-adventuring up the Yangtze."

"Oh for the visionary glow of youth!" Mary sighed, ringing the bell. "Now, do show Mr Grant round the gallery, Alice, and then join us for coffee on the verandah.

"... You know, Robert," she continued, as he lit his after-dinner cigar, "I think that's the man."

"What—for Alice? He's rather old, isn't he? Widower, bit of a rolling stone..."

"But more likely to appeal to her than these Shanghai sprigs. She's old for her years in some ways and is obviously attracted by his sense of adventure."

Robert grinned. "So now you've fixed me up, it's my niece's turn, is it?"

She kissed him on the forehead. "Exactly so. And I shall be good for you, just as Charles would be for Alice. You'll see..."

As they strolled through the gallery Alice was thinking

along similar lines and remarked with a feminine pout worthy of Iris Wetherby, "I haven't heard a word from you since you left, Charles, and I did hope to."

"Did you? I thought you'd be much too taken up with all your young beaux and I didn't feel I should interfere."

"Silly—it hasn't been like that at all."

"But you've had beaux surely?"

"Oh yes, several."

"Anyone—important, if I may ask?"

"No." They stared at the paintings in silence.

"That one would fetch a pretty penny," he remarked at last.

"You do want money, don't you, Charles?"

"Only because I've much less than the rest of my family and they tend to judge me accordingly."

They moved to the end of the gallery, tense with awareness of each other's presence, and, instead of looking at the last painting, he put his arms round her.

"You remember that night—the old temple on the hill when I first kissed you?"

"I've never forgotten it."

"Haven't you? I had to pull myself up then because I was married, but that's no longer the case. So perhaps it's time I kissed you again?" For answer she moved into his arms, feeling her senses stirring as his hands moved round the back of her neck. When they returned to the verandah Mary privately decided then and there that a few prods in the right direction would undoubtedly produce the required result.

These Mary discreetly administered during the next two weeks while Charles lingered in Shanghai, acting as Alice's constant escort and finding it unaccountably difficult to conclude his business affairs. But eventually he had neither reason nor excuse to stay longer. "I have to return to Hankow on the Friday steamer," he told Alice as they bowled along in a double rickshaw one evening after a Fine Arts Society meeting.

Her heart sank. "I shall miss you." She didn't look at him.

"Will you really?"

They listened in silence to the laboured breathing of the rickshaw coolies who, driven near exhaustion at the end of the day, were craving rest.

"Let's pay them off and walk back via the Bund gardens shall we?" Charles suggested. "It's not very late."

The gardens were practically deserted; moonlight shone

on white chrysanthemums in the flowerbeds and Alice commented selfconsciously on their beauty. Under the shadow of a magnolia tree Charles pulled her to face him. "I think I'd better say quite simply what I have in mind, Alice—what has been occupying rather too much of my thoughts for sometime, actually. I am in love with you, dear, and want you to marry me. Will you be my wife?"

She drew in a sharp, thrilled breath, thinking incongruously that she seemed doomed to receive proposals in public gardens. "Oh Charles ... well, I really ..."

"Of course you've every reason to refuse me. I'm a widower, considerably older than you and with the responsibility of a growing son. I have little capital, no fixed profession or even abode and my future prospects are by no means certain. So I shall quite understand if you ..."

She felt so happy that it was easy to tease a little. "So you are advising me to refuse the offer you've just made, I take it, Mr Grant?"

He paused, nonplussed by her banter. "I think I ... No, I'm not. You see I love you very much. I think a little bit of me has loved you ever since we first met six years ago. And that is the most important thing, is it not?"

He took her shoulders, forcing her to meet his eyes seriously.

"Yes Charles, I do love you. I know I do, very much. And I shall be very happy, very pleased to become your wife." It was a formal moment; then embarrassed and pleased they fell into each other's arms, kissing and touching tenderly, while Alice assured him that her family would certainly approve.

After a while they pulled apart, Alice straightened her hair and they walked away together arm in arm. "And you realise, Mr Grant, how useful I shall be to you?" she asked lightly. "There are few Englishwomen in China today with my knowledge of the language and people. And you will let me help you, won't you, dear? I can translate documents for you and manage the compradore and I'm excellent at bargaining."

"You'll really enjoy doing things like that, Alice? It would be a tremendous help of course, for I know so little ... but I wouldn't expect ..."

"Yes of course, we shall be in business together and—oh Charles, I was getting so bored with all these frivolities here—they become pointless after a while. And now this— I told you I'd long dreamed of trading up the Yangtze and

I'd much rather do it with you than Frank. But there's one condition if I'm to help you wholeheartedly." She tugged him to a halt.

"What is it, sweetheart?"

"The firm Frank and I dreamed of would have been Greenwood & Greenwood. I want our firm to be Grant & Greenwood."

He frowned. "But I don't see why... I mean your name will be Grant too." It had not occurred to her and she felt a pang; Greenwood was her name; Uncut Jade stemmed from it. "Well I shall keep my maiden name too then, Greenwood-Grant, some women do."

"But, Alice, I've just had all the cards and letterheads printed—you saw them—and it's not usual for wives to..."

"But, Charles, I'm not quite a usual sort of wife and several very unusual things have happened to me, as you know. You said the other day you like my having a mind of my own, so I want my own name on the firm, our firm."

He sighed, feeling it was a bad omen to wrangle so soon after plighting their troth. "All right, but it will be expensive to get everything reprinted."

"I'll pay for it, I have some money." She tucked an arm into his. "And you must admit that Grant & Greenwood has a grander ring to it?"

He grunted noncommittally, comforting himself with the reflection that, once the firm got on its feet and she had children and domestic duties to see to, the "Greenwood" could be quietly dropped.

As Alice guessed, Robert gladly gave his formal blessing to the proposal and Mary capped it with an inspired idea: why not make it a double wedding on 2nd January? Half the expense and fuss, double the pleasure and purpose, they all agreed, so the new engagement was announced forthwith. Bertie Tarrent, his nose much out of joint, opined that Charles Grant must be a wealthy man because Greenwoods only married into well-feathered nests; Clifford White said it was a blessing Grant knew little about China and was thus a willing empty vessel to receive his fiancée's many fixed views on the subject; the Wetherby sisters thought that Alice must have been rather desperate to marry a widower senior in years and a trader to boot. But the other Greenwoods were delighted; Isabel wrote to congratulate Robert on his cleverness; Frank harboured vague dreams of Greenwood, Grant

& Wang Ltd that would one day monopolise the Yangtze trade; and there was a touching letter from Eliza expressing her gratitude that Charles was apparently a Christian gentleman and offering to come to the wedding with the twins.

Charles' people were less pleased, especially his sister Harriet in Madras who feared that the new bride would immediately lay claim to Peter, of whom she was extremely fond, and fill him with all sorts of Chinese nonsense. To his parents, recently retired to Hampshire, Charles sent a photograph of Alice sitting on a basket chair in the Fairlawns verandah. She looked, decided his mother, quite a presentable creature, but her jaw was too set and her eyes were not looking directly into the camera, giving a somewhat shifty impression. One must not, of course, expect too much of a missionary's daughter of totally unknown background, but, all in all, it was a thousand pities Charles had not stayed in Madras and married dear Belinda Dodds who had discreetly doted on him for years.

When Alice studied her photograph she had the disquieting sense that only part of her was there—like a painting of a half-moon by one who had never seen it at the full. She looked demure and lady-like enough, in a pretty muslin dress, ankles carefully crossed; but she too noticed that her eyes were averted from the camera, detracting from the happy smile on her lips. For she had felt thoroughly happy at the time; as relieved as everyone that the problems of her future were suddenly solved. She did not have to fight against the barriers of race or religion after all, did not have to worry about where to live, what to do next, who to love. She was not going to be an old maid, or a supernumerary aunt or the mistress of a struggling revolutionary; she was going to be a respectable lady with an English husband, just as everyone had hoped. And in a few years, Charles had promised her, when the firm would be thriving, he would take her to Europe at last and they would see all the sights. Such had been the stuff of her conscious thoughts when she posed on the verandah, yet she could not meet the camera's eye in case it saw through to things she most deliberately was not thinking about, of which her fond fiancé had no suspicion.

These things seemed to have accumulated over the years and were a burden to her as never before, because she believed Charles to be an honest man and yearned to be equally honest in return. Often, that autumn, when he had returned to Hankow and she and Mary were engrossed in preparations for the double wedding, she imagined that, when he returned, she would tell him all: the delights of her early concubinage; the distress of her eviction and miscarriage; the wild scenes she had witnessed among the Miao; the meeting with Stewart Carr and her continued guilty possession of his loot; the feel of her stepfather's "jade stalk" rising as he whipped her buttocks; the delicious joys and searing pains of her love affair with Lin. "Only those who are their absolute true selves in the world can fulfil their own natures," she sternly quoted Confucius to herself. But there were so many factors in her life which the sage could not possibly have reckoned with, and she feared to see the love-light die from Charles' eyes, feared to be left alone again with all the problems his reassuring presence solved.

So, when he did return to Shanghai a week before Christmas, her resolve faltered, though, in one respect she found it hard to keep her secrets intact. His passion for her was noticeably increased by their separation, while vigilance of the securely-affianced pair was noticeably relaxed. Thus they were often alone together, and once he pressed and caressed her, murmuring his desire for her, and she, roused in spite of herself, retreated into a coy, girlish teasing that bewildered him. The next day she crept to Lilian's bedroom, consulted her textbooks on the subject of female virginity and decided that something must be done.

"Charles," her approach that evening sounded more tentative than she had intended.

"Hmm?" He was engrossed in the *Mercury*'s list of silk prices.

"Charles dear, will you listen a minute please, there's something I must say."

He looked up reluctantly. "It's quite important, dear, and you mightn't like it."

"Don't tell me you're going to marry a millionaire instead!" He was jocularly confident.

"No indeed, but when you hear, you might wish...well, I'd better say it quickly, only it's embarrassing." She felt her cheeks burning. "You see, Charles, the fact is, I'm not virginal...not a virgin. I, I've...there was a man earlier, only I couldn't help it, I was powerless..."

"No! But, Alice...who? When? You must tell me everything—at once."

She averted her eyes. "It happened when I was in captivity

in Hunan. I was only fifteen and the master of the house took me as one of his concubines... I was forced, I couldn't help it, please, Charles, I really couldn't and then I ran away just as soon as I could." She raised pleading eyes. "You will forgive me?"

"Oh Alice, how simply dreadful—how awful..." He jumped up and patted her head. "There, there don't get upset, little one—what anguish it must have been for you, at that tender age... The brute, the uncivilised savage—and you, an innocent, undefiled little girl—ugh!" He shuddered with disgusted rage.

"You can't blame me, can you, Charles? There was no one to help or protect me."

"No, no Alice I can't blame you—rape, rape, the savage yellow beast!" He spat it between his teeth.

"I've never told anyone before, Charles, but it has been a secret burden to me and now we are to marry, I felt I owe it to you..."

"Yes quite right, dear. It's something of a shock of course. A man naturally expects his wife, when she's single as you are, to be unsullied. But the circumstances are quite exceptional and it would be most unfair of me to hold it against you. I'm sure you escaped from the dreadful situation just as soon as possible?"

She came and twined her arms round his neck. "Of course I did—and it was horrible in every way." He kissed her and she tightened her grip on him. "Well now that's over—and I feel much better for telling you—we can talk of more cheerful matters."

Retreating from their mutual embarrassment, he retrieved his newspaper. "And I'm glad you were honest with me, Alice. Now we shall proceed as if I didn't know and it didn't happen. I can't be fairer than that, can I?"

"No, dear, and thank you. It was many years ago and now I'll try to forget it too. Let me show you Mary's latest additions to the guest list—she really is quite impossible, saying it's to be a quiet wedding while inviting most of Shanghai to come!"

Going to get the list, Alice felt relieved that her way into matrimony was now a bit easier, but, she thought wistfully, even if Charles magnanimously chose to forget, the memory of those early joyous sexual unions must be with her for life and remain with her untold. For she simply couldn't risk a change of course now, caught up as she was in the momentum of the approaching festivities, paddling, as it often seemed, in the wake of the indefatigable Mary. And Mary was in her element; not for many years had every bedroom in Fairlawns been aired ready for use, the finest porcelains brought from her glass cupboards, all the silver polished, provisions of every delectable kind filling the pantries for the glut of jollities ahead.

Isabel, William and the children arrived first, wrapped in furs against the colder Port Arthur winter, bearing gifts of Russian caviare, French cigars and painted wooden toys from Korea. Then came Mary's son Edgar from Singapore with his wife Sylvia and their children, Lawrence and Grace. Edgar had followed his father's footsteps into banking, a lean, saturnine man whose wife did most of the talking, as his mother had before her. They brought charm bracelets of Malayan silver, tortoiseshell knick-knacks, and a thick tiger-skin rug for Alice, which was her favourite present in that present-filled time.

And at dusk on Christmas Eve, just as Mary and Isabel were lighting the candles on the pine tree, Eliza arrived with Sunny and Adam. They brought hand-painted Biblical texts, hand-carved models of Mongolian camels for the children, and for Alice Eliza had worked a tapestry with the words "God is Love" framed in a border of pansies, lilies, roses. But Alice's heart ached to see them—her mother's bent frailty, her hands so work-roughened in a company where those of the other ladies were soft and white, and worse were the skinny, pallid children who laughed far too seldom. Sunny retained shreds of her natural vivacity, but Adam seemed totally cowed, his skin clammy with perpetual fear—of his father most of all, of a vengeful Christian God, of all the devils and heathens in China, and now of the imminent prospect of sailing alone to England where he was to go to school.

On Christmas morning they all went to Shanghai Cathedral where Frank, Peachy and Charles joined them, coming back to the liveliest and largest Christmas dinner Alice had ever known. Such a gathering it was, with Mary and Robert at the head of a table laden with stuffed birds of every variety, sides of roast ham and pork, pâtés, pies, puddings, jellies, tarts and fruits—and both of them aglow with a joy that was infectious. For Mary it was a return to the days of her first prime when her own children were young, and for bachelor Robert it was a belated celebration of the family life he had earlier missed. They joined in the children's games with gusto—charades, consequences, hunting the slipper and thimble, passing the packet and, in the Boxing Day *tableau vivant*, Mary was Queen of the Fairies, Robert her Oberon.

By comparison, Alice and Charles seemed a lacklustre pair. "You'll have to exert yourself if you want to outshine the other bride-to-be!" Isabel had laughingly warned Alice soon after her arrival. But Alice had no desire to do so, for she lacked both the older woman's aplomb and her confident adoration of her intended. Clearly Mary and Robert harboured no doubts about their union, but, as the days of festivity reeled by, Alice and Charles felt increasingly strange together. Almost they avoided each other, on the unspoken understanding that their relationship was too fragile to be tested further in case, like property deals, it might collapse before completion of contract.

Charles sought refuge in what Robert jokingly called "the business team" that also included William, Edgar Fortescue and Frank, who gathered solemnly in smoke-filled corners and exchanged views on the inequalities of export taxes and customs dues, while Alice, seeing her fiancé so involved, glumly realised that this would be the pattern of their future social gatherings. Most of the ladies were in the "mothers' team", headed by Mary, with Isabel, Sylvia and on occasion Peachy. She was heavily pregnant, but her condition was ignored by all except for Alice who recited smiling,

> "Buxom is the peach-tree
> How its fruit swells!"

For Eliza that Christmas was the worst of everything that she disapproved of—the silly games, the copious quantities of food and wine, the other women's frivolous conversations about fashions and recipes. Eliza did, however, find one unexpected ally in Lilian Fortescue for whom her mother's precipitous liaison with a dashing army major was an unmitigated disaster. Lilian shrank appalled from the spectacle of Mary's flighty joyous flirtatiousness and vowed deep inside her thin, tense frame that she alone would keep loyal for life the sacred memory of her beloved father who had so recently died. The heady seeds of martyrdom were sown in quiet Lilian that Christmastide.

On the last day of the old year, Alice and her mother took Adam to the P. & O. wharf and consigned him to the care of a missionary family bound for Home. As he went up the gangplank his peaky, elfin face was whey-coloured with distress while on the quay Sunny shrieked hysterically. "Hush dear," Alice patted her head. "Adam is being braver than you and he's the one leaving."

"But I want to go too, I don't want to stay at the Mission without him—whatever shall I do?"

Having no good answer, Alice's heart ached for her, and for the memory of her own childhood when William had gone Home and she had been left crying on the quay. Eliza turned away from the painful sight of Adam's tiny figure, her mouth working. "Partings like this are always so dreadful! I always wonder when...if...you know."

"Yes, Mother, but I'm sure all will be well. Everything is much safer these days."

"Yes dear, and in about two years we're due for home-leave at last—so you'll soon see Adam again, Sunny...And I'm sorry you won't be coming with us, Alice. But it will rest with your husband now. Perhaps he'll take you Home soon?"

"He says he will, before too long. And I'd love to go—though his relatives sound so stuffy and proper."

Eliza took her arm, they waved to Adam for the last time, and moved off. "Well I'm glad he's a nice gentlemanly sort of man, dear and I'm happy for you...even though he's not in the field of work I'd hoped. But I shan't need to worry about you anymore, as I do all the time about Frank."

"Because of his marriage?"

"That yes, and his general attitude to life. Ah Alice, I can hardly bear to look at Peachy now—to think of that baby's future, the grandparents it will have, an owner of racehorses and a heathen Manchu woman who plays mah-jong every day. Frank told me about them himself, he seems to take a cruel delight in shocking me since I've been here, have you noticed?"

Alice had indeed, and replied carefully, "I don't think he's quite forgiven you for not coming to his wedding, Mother. He was very hurt underneath."

"Oh dear me, I felt it deeply too, but Edward so adamantly forbade it, it nearly caused an open breach between us. And then there was the expense. I had to scrimp and save every penny secretly to come here now...If only Peachy were a convert...that was the bitterest blow of all..."

Alice, thinking with renewed hatred of her stepfather, could utter no word of comfort to her mother and, in silence, they walked past the foreign shops along the Nanking Road. Red and white lanterns glowed above the doors and the lintels were emblazoned with English translations of cheery New Year messages, a good-natured Chinese salutation for the foreigners' festival. "For your New Year—guaranteed Prosperity Dumplings and Lucky Grasses" read one; "May the bounty of the Five Happinesses be yours throughout the Year"; "Cast out the devils of the past, welcome the blessed gods of the Dragon Year". Alice read them carefully, as if they were intended for her alone. And did she not require some special blessing, when, with the year's turning, she would become a different person—a Mrs Charles Grant?"

"It is better to be married isn't it, Mother?" she asked in an agonised whisper as they turned into Fairlawns' drive. Her mother blinked in surprise.

"Of course it is, my dear child . . . Well, there are things that men . . . that husbands sometimes desire to do with their wives that are not always entirely agreeable to us women . . . I trust you know a little about matters of sex, Alice? I haven't said anything to you, but . . ."

"Yes, Mother, I know. I meant that just being married is better for a woman than being single, is it not?"

"Certainly it is, Alice. Very definitely." Timidly Eliza patted her daughter's hand. "You will have a good Christian man to protect you and you will see how pleasant and comforting that can be. And I hope every one of the Five Happinesses will attend you, my dear, for all the days of your married life."

12

Mr and Mrs Charles Grant stood on the deck of a Chinese Merchant Company's vessel waving goodbye to Mr and Mrs Frank Greenwood who had come to see them off. The rest of the family had dispersed immediately after the wedding: to Port Arthur, Mukden, Singapore, and the other newly-weds to Hong Kong. Charles and Alice had spent a short honeymoon on a borrowed houseboat moored in a creek near the Snowy Lakes and were now bound for Hankow. Alice watched the receding figures on the quay: "So many comings and goings... it will be a relief to just settle down quietly for a while, don't you think, Charles?"

He grunted warningly, "But you might find life pretty humdrum after all these excitements."

"Oh I'm glad they're over, I assure you."

She huddled in the shelter of a cabinway, hands clenched in her fur muff. It was drear and chill, raindrops spattering on the muddy waters rolling below. Yes, she was glad it was over and that everything had gone according to plan. Fortunately, 2nd January 1883 had been crisp and clear, pale sunlight on the weathered stone of Trinity Church, the inside decorated with ferns, glossy evergreens and winter jasmine. Mary Fortescue had looked splendid in pearl grey silks, with handsome uniformed Robert at her side; Charles had looked equally well-groomed and assured, while she, presumably, had lived up to expectations—the fledgling by comparison, tentative in a gown of creamy satin, clutching a bouquet of camellias, Sunny and Charlotte treading solemnly behind her in rosy tulle. William had given her away; Edgar had given his mother away; no one had cried except Polly who was teething. When Charles smiled warmly at her as they left the vestry she could have wept for joy. All the Wangs came to the wedding breakfast at Fairlawns and behaved impeccably, and, in Mary's gallery, Mrs Wang had tapped the pictures with her long red fingernails, grunting with envy.

That night, on the houseboat, after she and Charles had stood on deck entwined together and congratulating themselves on the rightness of spending their first night of marriage in a vessel similar to that on which they had first met, Charles had led her to bed. There he had made love to her with slow, gentle consideration as if she were the virgin he had fondly imagined. And she had cried out obligingly at his thrusts so that he could murmur endearments, assuring her it would not hurt for long. His love-making had not hurt at all, nor had it much pleased her and afterwards she propped herself, wideawake, on an elbow, staring at his still boyish face as he slept, wondering how it would be between their sheets in future.

But already the wedding and honeymoon seemed slightly unreal to her, as such occasions often do to their protagonists, though living undimmed in the memories of relatives and friends. For to Alice all the excitement lay ahead—six hundred miles upriver at Hankow. Several wedding guests had commiserated on her exile to such a place where, they said, the racecourse was shocking and society entirely limited to missionaries and merchants. And she remembered their words with amusement when, three days later, the city hove in sight: miles of low wooden habitations crowded across the grey alluvial plains on either side of the yellowish mile-wide tide that divided Hankow from Wuchang, the capital of Hupeh, and Hanyang.

From a distance the three cities looked equally featureless, but Hankow—the Collecting Place of Nine Provinces—had been a Treaty Port for the past twenty-two years and was distinguished, on closer approach, by its waterfront bund bordering the hundred and ten acres of the foreign concession. Loyal residents claimed it was the finest in China, with a broad promenade chained off for the sole use of foreigners, a high stone wall pierced by steps, rows of willow trees and an extent of half a mile, giving everyone the chance of a daily constitutional.

No one was taking that chance on the afternoon Alice and Charles landed, for the weather was at its wintriest, the sluggish waters at their lowest, flanked by filthy mud-banks, the willows wind-stripped bare and most of the finest porticoed houses to the west of the Bund, locally known as "Nobs' End", shuttered, for their residents had briefly fled to cheerier climes. The only people in sight were boatmen, customs officials, coolies and a crowd of particularly diseased and ragged beggars crouching on the steps, holding up skinny, pleading hands.

Charles had been subdued that morning and, as they disembarked, said uneasily, "The house is no mansion, Alice. I did warn you, and it may look worse after being shut up."

She was cheerful. "Oh you told me you weren't at the smart end of the Bund! I'm not expecting anything grand."

And certainly the rickety dwelling at the concession's very edge to which Charles led her was not that. Sounds of scuttling rodents, smells of mildew and bad sewage greeted them as he pushed open the ill-fitting door. "Where's the boy? He should have got things warmed up for us!" Charles roared in embarrassment. He led her down a dark passage with a rotted floor. "The work's done on that side—and we're here." He watched apprehensively as she looked round the main room. It was furnished with two shabby armchairs, strips of shredded matting, two battered bamboo tables that Charles had bought from a departing consul. He had also acquired an old brass bed, washstand, some chipped chinaware and cooking pots stacked in the small, dirty kitchen, and a tin hip-bath now full of dead centipedes. It was propped against the wall of the privy, which stank horribly.

But the place had its bonus—a sizeable verandah which, owing to the risks of summer floods, stood raised on piles, accessible from the living-room by a flight of covered steps. It was, Alice decided, like a top deck, a secret eyrie higher than the rest of the house and with a view of the nearby Yangtze. The view was bounded by the dilapidated Grant & Greenwood godown and the more substantial wall of the Russian factory from which brick-tea was exported to Manchuria and Siberia. The smells and sounds of tea-dust being sieved, pressed and dried arose from it continually and to the end of her days, Alice had only to sniff the inside of a teapot to be reminded of her early married life.

"It looks even worse than I feared, dear," Charles apologised as he came on to the verandah. "The boy's obviously done a bunk and he's stolen the bed quilts to boot, the scoundrel—Heaven knows what we're going to do for food and warmth tonight!"

"Oh we'll be alright, I've had lots of training in native household management, you know!"

And so she proved. Within a few hours she had swept the floors, been to the market, got the stove going and that night they dined on vegetable soup, broiled eels and rice, and then enjoyed a most successful lovemaking warmed by the tiger-skin rug and the glowing charcoal embers. As he sank into satisfied slumber Charles congratulated himself heartily on his choice of a resourceful wife and she, equally content, thought how pleasant it was to have a home of one's own, however humble, and be able to decide for herself the colours of the bed-quilts she intended buying on the morrow.

For the next few weeks Alice busied herself happily with the creation of a comfortable nest. The quilts, chosen on account of cheapness rather than colour, were of padded indigo-blue cotton from Chungking, and for the floors she bought strips of scarlet felt and local grass-cloth. The walls she hung with wood panels painted with writing and bordered with flowers and trees; one read "The sun moves, bamboo shadows steal over the grasses. The wind blows, fir-cones fall on the robe of a guest." Carpenters came to make tables and shelves on which she set bowls of bright pebbles from the Rainflower Hills, writing brushes and perfumed ink-tablets. In the verandah Alice arranged pots of ferns, small orange trees and two long lounging chairs for when the weather improved.

She hired a fat cook-boy who coiled his pigtail twice round his head and spoke with a thick Hunanese accent. His parents were boat-people who hailed from that province and he was called Snow Duck for the literal Chinese reason that the first thing his mother had seen after his birth was a duck with snow on its back floating past a porthole. Snow Duck adored Alice from the moment he heard her speak his very own tongue, he cheated her less than he had ever cheated an employer and, on her behalf, mercilessly bullied the coolie called Number Eight Son who swept the yard and privy.

As the winter retreated, the shutters of the Nobs' End houses were taken down for their owners' return and Alice, the newcomer, was obliged to call on the community's leading ladies. First on Mrs Wilcock, wife of the Commissioner of

Customs, then on Mrs Amelia Telford, wife of "Tommy the teaman" as he was jovially known. It was rumoured that Tommy had made a cool £10,000 profit in the vintage year of 1873 by putting all his teas aboard the clipper *Ariel* which won the race to reach the London market. Amelis Telford however, who wore an habitually pained expression, never discussed matters of trade either in good times or bad. She found the whole subject of tea quite lowering, drank only imported coffee and spent many waking hours in a secret dream wherein she was married to a handsome diplomat instead of Tommy, lived in Vienna by the Danube instead of the Yangtze, and visited the opera regularly instead of playing operatic airs on her tinny piano.

For to be in Hankow at all was bad enough, as she remarked to Mrs Wilcock, but it must be unutterably dreary for poor little Mrs Grant in that pokey hole next to the tea-brick factory. So the resident ladies did what they could, presenting Alice with cast-off cushion covers and saucepans, inviting her to tea and assuring her that the first year in Hankow was always the worst.

Goaded by their well-meaning patronage, Alice soon decided to take more active interest in the other side of the house, where the infant firm of Grant & Greenwood was struggling to grow. The tea-season did not begin till May and the godown thus contained a strange assortment of stranded items: sacks of broken aniseed, lily roots and dogs' skins; bundles of rattans, straw hats and iron rods; barrels of glue made from boiled seaweed, a liquid indigo and Szechuan oil; bales of material labelled "grey shirtings", "bunting" and "turkey red cloth". The pervasive smell was a heady mixture of the fragrant, the fusty and the simply horrible, and the pervasive impression was of immobility—unused rods rusting, frayed hats, and several rat-chewed sacks, their contents spilled on the earth floor.

"But where is it all going and why is it so long here?" Alice demanded of her husband, who sat at an old roll-top desk adding figures. He frowned.

"It's waiting shipment to the interior or Shanghai. But it's a bad time for transit, the waters are still low, junks can't get alongside to load or through the gorges."

"And the material labelled in English, imported from Lancashire? Do the Chinese actually buy shirtings and turkey red cloth?"

He shrugged. "Some of them seem to."

Persistently she leaned over his shoulder and giggled,

"Iron: nail ditto, hoop, ditto, pig; bones: cow, broken, ditto, tigers... That's rather funny."

"Yes, I remember I thought so at first."

"But not anymore?"

"Well, it isn't a joke that bears much repetition."

She twisted a piece of copper wire round her finger. "Don't you think we might do something definite instead of waiting for the river to rise and the tea-season to begin? Why can't we explore a little upriver ourselves and find out what the merchants want? You said you wanted to pioneer beyond the Treaty Ports."

He put down his pen. "It had occurred to me, but..."

"But what? Where's your sense of adventure? Not gone already, has it?"

He flushed angrily. "But it's the money angle. I'm in debt already, Alice, new firms invariably are, but I've money to find for my son's education and it's cost a bit to set the house up nicely... I'm not grumbling, but..."

"Charles, I do wish you wouldn't talk as if it were just your firm—it's ours, you agreed. So why can't I be included in these decisions? Please, Charles..." she rubbed against him, hiding her irritation under a show of coaxing. "Let's go upriver and see for ourselves. Nothing venture nothing win, you know."

He drew her on his lap, stroking her hair. "You are a determined little madam, aren't you? The firm's called Grant & Greenwood remember, not t'other way round. But I admit things are slack and I'm tired of listening to rats chewing up our tiny profits—so perhaps this once we'll let the junior partner have her way. But only as far as Ichang, mind. There's an English couple living there I'd like to meet—A Mr and Mrs Archibald Small. Old Wilcock told me about them. Apparently they've managed to get a sound business going even though Ichang isn't yet a Treaty Port. Rum couple, Wilcock said, dyed-in-the-wool China hands, and both very large which is rather a joke. Anyway, I'll send a message with one of the junk-captains that we're coming. They're bound to welcome a bit of company at this dead time of year."

On a windswept morning a week later they boarded the sternwheel riverboat *Chang-wo;* the below-decks were packed with Chinese and the Grants shared the small saloon with two Belgian nuns also bound for Ichang. The river was still low and the vessel crept along, lurching from one just-concealed gravel shoal to the next. At every grounding, the melancholy note of the leadsmen rose to a wailing crescendo and

319

at every re-floating the nuns raised their eyes to Heaven in gratitude. But the only real excitement in Alice's view was their passing of High Peak Islet that marked the entrance to the Tung T'ing Lake, the great stretch of water that flowed towards Hunan. Hunan. She had never been so close since she left and she stood in the cabinway as they passed and murmured,

> "He is going to the Tung T'ing Lake
> My friend whom I have loved for so many years.
> Spring wind startles the willows.
> And they break into pale leaf.
> I go with my friend as far as the river-bank.
> And my mind is full and overflowing
> With the things I did not say..."

Later, in her cabin, she wrote a long letter to Tamao which she doubted would ever arrive, and that night tossed in her bunk in half-frightened, half-sensual dreams.

As they sailed west along the Great River the plains gave way to terraced slopes and wooded hills; cliffs and promontories reared where gulls and cormorants nested; some of the rocks were enlivened with poetical exclamations in large whitewashed characters: "The river and the sky are one colour" announced one. At dawn on the fifth day they passed through the Tiger Teeth Gorge just below Ichang where ochre-coloured waters poured through a two-mile-long channel. The entrance to the town was spectacular: flanked on the left by a high peak and opposite by a craggy range topped with a Buddhist monastery, its roof gleaming in a shaft of early sun. "All change at Ichang" was always the cry, for only the sturdy, high-sterned junks could negotiate the treacherous "Thousand Rapids" beyond in which dozens of craft came to grief each year.

When the *Chang-wo* anchored in mid-stream, its passengers were poled ashore in hooded sampans, where just one foreign woman stood among the native throng. Her large frame was clad in a sage-green gown that struck Alice as pleasantly exotic, though of no recognisable style. She extended her hand, "You must be Mrs Grant? And I am Mrs Daisy Small... You might as well laugh at that name once and for all!"

Alice smiled. "Indeed I shan't. In any case I'd already heard you were... not small."

"So my fame goes before me. When we first came I made

a point of translating our absurd name to the Chinese and they were tickled pink. Now I do believe we're known as the size-of-two-elephants-foreign-devils in every port between Ichang and Shanghai. But I've often wished to meet you, Mrs Grant."

"Oh—why me?"

"Ah, here comes the baggage coolie with Mr Grant—it must be? How do you do? I was about to tell your wife, Mr Grant, that I heard of her sometime ago in Shanghai. We were dining with Mr Dawson, the Customs Commissioner, and he said, 'Well Mrs Small, there's only one English lady I've ever met with as much grasp of the Chinese, both Mandarin and vernacular, as yourself—and that's Miss Alice Greenwood.' And he told me a little of your early captivity in Hunan—I long to hear more about it."

Charles smiled dismissively. "Oh that's ages past, Mrs Small, time Alice forgot all about it. Is that your cart the baggage-coolie's making for?"

"Yes—could you see to it, Mr Grant? Our humble temple-abode is up the hill there. You'll stay with us of course? There's nowhere better here, I assure you. And we ladies will walk behind and begin to know each other, for I'm sure we've much in common. Are we not both China-born for a start?"

As they walked, Mrs Small explained that she too came from a missionary background.

"But my poor mother died giving birth to me—fifth and last of her oversized brood. Father was more of a linguist than a proselytiser and so I grew up in Hong Kong spoiled and cosseted by amahs and disciplined by the moral laws of the Chinese classics—just like a little Son of Han! But your early experiences sound much more exciting?"

She beamed and thus unusually encouraged Alice was still talking when they reached the former temple on the Hill of Four Prosperities where the Smalls lived. It was a wooden dwelling, with a crumble-tiled roof and an air of aged serenity, set in a grove of pine and bamboo. After luncheon, when Charles went off to meet Mr Small at his office, Daisy took Alice to see the locally-famed view from the hill's top. Its dominant feature, she pointed out, was the Pyramid Peak which had long had an adverse effect on the fortunes of Ichang and to counteract its sinister influences, a monastery had been built, at great expense, on this peak where they stood.

"But you will be familiar with such superstitions?" Daisy eyed her inquiringly.

"Oh yes, there were some rounded green hills near Chang-sha supposed to be of a most benevolent disposition, and I never doubted it, at the time."

"Indeed why should you? Children don't doubt such things, which is one reason, I suspect, foreigners often consider the Chinese childish. But now you're grown-up, how do you feel? Such an extraordinary experience must have influenced you profoundly and I'm sure you've made much of it since?"

Alice faltered; she liked Daisy's directness, but was unaccustomed to it.

"Oh—I've done very poorly with it I fear. I seem to be different in all the wrong ways as a result. I find I'm much too critical for one thing—of many foreigners' narrow outlooks for example. It's quite uncomfortable really."

"But I make similar judgments, so does Archie, and we don't consider it a fault. I've never subscribed to the dictum of judging not that you be not judged—one's simply got to stand up and be counted sometimes, don't you think?"

"Well I always admire those who do, certainly. When I lived in Port Arthur before my marriage I came in contact with some of the young self-strengtheners—I sometimes wish I'd had the courage to be counted with them."

"Ah—such confused, ambitious, arrogant, clever young men! My heart bleeds for them—doomed to all the frustrations and tribulations of reformers the world over, but with the fearful likelihood, in their case, of ultimate failure and disgrace, if not the execution ground at the end. . . ."

Alice looked alarmed. "Do you really think so? I didn't realise it was so dangerous."

"It could well become so, though up to now the Government is too firmly in control to worry much about such hotheads. Do you know any of them well?"

"Not really—not now. I helped one of the lecturers at the naval college with some translating. J.S. Mill's treatise on Liberty mainly . . . then he . . . went away. I've nearly finished it off alone, but I don't quite know what to do with it next."

"But my dear, that's perfectly splendid—Mill's 'Liberty', what more stimulating and dangerously incomprehensible book to offer inquiring young Orientals! We must talk to Archie, he can put you in the way of getting it published, I'm sure. There'll be a tremendous demand—no," she chuckled in self-correction, "not enormous, that's my enthusiasm again, Archie's always telling me off about it—discriminating demand which could be more influential. And oh Alice, I've a marvelous idea for your next translation—you won't mind my speaking so familiarly so soon, will you? Mill again—on the Subjection of Women, you know it of course? The perfect background text for my league for the Abolition of Foot-Binding...But I've not yet told you about it, have I? There I am running away with myself again."

She paused, staring at the younger woman with shining eyes. Alice was leaning against a rock, behind her the budding yellow tassels of a glossy-leaved tallow tree swung in the breeze, far below a bend of the sunlit Yangtze glittered. Her outline was very sharp to Daisy suddenly, the tilt of her head very determined, her greenish eyes very bright and clear. In the silence they both heard the simple tolling of a distant bell and the monotonous chant of the Zen monks who lived in the nearby monastery. Daisy drew in her breath sharply.

"Oh Alice—I've just had such a feeling about you—one of my inexplicable intuitions, that's what Archie calls them, and they're nearly always right. You're going to be an important person in my life, you're going to see and do some of the things that have eluded me—my heiress, just apparent. And not only mine, you will go beyond that—forgive me, but I've just seen it clear!"

Alice coloured uneasily, for her instinct was always to withdraw from such impulsive enveloping. "I...I wish I had your gift of vision, Mrs Small—but I feel no such sense of certainty, in any direction.... But please tell me about Mr Mill's book on women and the league you mention—it's all new to me."

"Come then, it's time we went back for tea," Daisy hooked her arm as they walked back down the hill. "Mill's book you must study for yourself—he puts the case for our emancipation so much more forcibly than I ever could. What a magnificent man he was! As for the league, it began because I just couldn't understand how we foreign women can bear being in this country, constantly closing our eyes to the fact that all around us thousands of our own sex are being crippled for life...Those diseased, deformed hooves of the old tottering grannies, and, even worse, the haunting pallor, the morose suffering on the faces of the little girls as they hobble past, their cries of woe in the night. Have you never heard them? Have they never touched you?"

"Yes," Alice muttered. "In the Chu household, the youngest, Little Piece—I used often to hear her, but the elder daughters seemed quite resigned. It was just the custom, they used to say."

"Ah, several influential Chinese I've spoken to on the subject have said the same and I've reminded them, as I do you, that one of the three universally recognised moral qualities according to Confucius is compassion. And how can any person of compassion look upon such youthful pain without wanting to alleviate it?"

"So you've formed a league? But isn't this more a matter for the missionaries?"

"That is just where you and all well-intentioned foreigners are wrong!" Daisy stopped in her tracks and rounded on Alice. "Missionaries do not have a monopoly of the milk of human kindness and their efforts are often so misguided anyway. We had a pair of fire-and-brimstone Scots here recently, handing out wads of free tracts to all and sundry—which, I heard, made excellent thick soles for the coolies' sandals! Not the sort of soles they intended to save! No, it is just because the people associate the abolition of footbinding with Christianity that they don't take to it. Now my league is based simply on our common humanity—transcending every religious creed, and I'm collecting much supporting medical evidence from enlightened Chinese doctors. You will help me in this, won't you, Alice? Your knowledge of the language would be invaluable—and just remember the cries of the little Hunanese girl in the night. How can you fail to respond to that memory now its relevance has been made clear to you?"

"But what can I do? I doubt if I'd find any kindred spirits in Hankow, and I'm not sure how Charles..." She trailed off, aware of Daisy's quizzical look, and added, "Perhaps I could write something in Chinese about it?"

"That would be an excellent start and I'll show you what we're already doing... As for preaching to the unconverted, that's something essential, isn't it? At least I think so, for though I deplore the belligerent proselytising of our extreme Christian brethren, I can't admire the resigned quiescence of the Buddhist either. As I said earlier, stands must sometimes be made, and mine is on the right of every Chinese female to walk without pain on her own two feet... But look, there are the men returned already—I've been carried away on my pet subject as usual... Archie, are you showing Mr Grant the view? I suppose time has got itself late again?"

She smiled unrepentantly at the broad, placid-looking grey-haired men ahead, and they all walked back together. The Smalls' dwelling was sparsely furnished, though they did not seem to notice, its only luxury being an extraordinary revolving desk made to special specifications. Divided exactly in two, each half had shelves and cubbyholes and each Small owned half—the revolving mechanism allowing whoever was working there to survey the pleasant view from the window. Their only arguments, Archie joked, occurred when they both wanted to work and look outside at the same time. It seemed to Alice an ideal arrangement, having never before met a married couple who shared their interests so equally. Nor had she ever been in a foreign home where Chinese came and went so freely; the most frequent callers being local merchants with whom Archie dealt direct.

"The whole sytem of foreign trade is wrongly organised here," he told Charles as they sat round the stove after supper. "We behave as if China were a colony like India or Singapore, and we keep our white man's distance—negotiating through compradores and middle-men who hold the whip-hand. Look at Telford and his merry tea-men, they can't speak the language, scarcely even venture beyond the race-course and only survive at all because of the few faithful compradores they've employed since the clipper days. They're cruising along on two illusions: first that the English demand for Chinese tea is going to grow, which it isn't, and second that the Chinese are never going to manage the interior and international trade for themselves—which of course they are. Competition is going to get fiercer and..."

"Oh hush Archie, enough of this mercantile gloom," Daisy interrupted. "Now let me make a suggestion instead—Mr Grant, why don't you and Alice consider starting an agency up here? I'm sure there's plenty of scope, and we know the ropes... I warrant Ichang will be a Treaty Port in a few years, then you'll be in clover, as the Yankees say."

"Oh Charles, why don't we?" Alice pleaded. "Look what a help I could be here, and we'd really become part of the place instead of being stuck in a concession as we are now."

She saw the lines of dogged refusal set on his face; at such moments he looked beleaguered, uncertain, and she did not like what she saw. Looking at him, Archie interposed smoothly, "Come, come, ladies, surely you don't expect Mr Grant to uproot himself from Hankow on the instant. He's only been there a year and he'll want to prove something of what I've said on his own pulses. But bear it in mind, my dear chap, and don't get too much in hock with the Hankow gentlemen. They're cliquey, old-school-tie, stick together sort of thing, and their heyday in tea is over."

But Charles only frowned noncommittally, for he was quite impressed with Tommy Telford for one thing and, for another, as he confirmed in the course of their Ichang stay, the very thought of living permanently as the Smalls did filled him with secret dismay. They seemed to have so little contact with their own kind, so few amusements of any sort. It might be alright for Alice, she was so close to the country anyway, but, by the time they boarded the east-bound steamer, he was rather looking forward to such civilised company and amenities as Hankow could offer, deciding that his first encounter with life beyond the Treaty Ports had been less romantic and more uncomfortable than he had envisaged. The Smalls saw them off, the men shaking hands briskly, the women parting like old friends.

Daisy pressed a parcel into Alice's hands. "Take care of it—my only copy and I want it back eventually. But read, mark, inwardly digest!"

As the snow melted in the distant western ranges, the Yangtze waters were rising and the squatters on the mud-banks were uprooting their bamboo hovels stick by stick; water rats too, their winter holes flooding, were burrowing to higher ground and, higher yet, along the overhanging gorges, men were scurrying in and out of caves collecting saltpetre.

"What's the present?" Charles asked idly, contemplating the men's precarious activities as the steamer chugged away.

Alice stowed it firmly in her reticule. "Oh just a book."

"So I gathered, but whose?"

"Some of Wordsworth's poetry, Daisy loves it and thought I would too."

He nodded dismissively and she slipped to their cabin, unwrapping the volume tenderly, flattered Daisy should entrust her with it. She opened and began to read at random: "What is called the nature of women is the result of enforced suppression... for women have to hide and dissemble most of their mental life from men..." She gasped, seeing the little scene between her and Charles in quite a new light. Why had she lied about this very book? Because she had known instinctively he would not like it, would have questioned her—she could just imagine his teasing indulgence, "Subjection of who? You—an Englishwoman living in the nineteenth century, and with the Married Women's Property Act in full force? What rot, Alice!" She did not feel strong or sure enough to contradict him, but once she had inwardly digested Mr Mill's theories it would be different, she promised herself, as she went to join Charles, wishing that their stay with the Smalls could have been longer.

But it was indeed time to return, for one morning soon afterwards Alice awoke to the sounds of unusual activity along the Bund—and there was the first procession of coolies, each with two brightly-painted chests of freshly-picked tea dangling from poles over their shoulders. They had jogged along for miles from the western hill-plantations, crying, "Ahoi, Ahhoi" all the way in a manner peculiar to their calling.

Later that day, silk-robed Chinese merchants arrived in blue sedan chairs with green lattice blinds and yellow curtains through which they seldom deigned to peep. But the sure signal for the opening of the tea-season came the following evening when steamers from Shanghai and Odessa hove into port, decks a-twinkle with lanterns, holds crammed with lead spars, cotton piece-goods and copper wiring to be all speedily unloaded to make room for the first tea consignments. European, American and Russian tea merchants and hong-clerks hastened ashore bringing transit forms and order books; but the most important passengers were the chahsees. Pallid, thin men mostly, who had spent years of apprenticeship in the art of tea-tasting, they were highly voluble on the subject of "that blasted vegetable" as it was jocularly called, habitually silent on most others, as if the development of such excessively sensitive tastebuds in the single cause had circumscribed their general conversational powers.

For the next month Hankow was its liveliest. Every guest room in Nobs' End was occupied, the old hulks moored along the quay, deserted for much of the year, thrummed with mercantile activity, and every godown was stuffed with tea— Scented Orange or Flowery Pekoe, coarse Congo, Lotus Heart and Autumn Dew. In the shaded godown offices, the solemn chahsees held court, surrounded by rows of white porcelain cups and several spittoons. They scrutinised and sniffed each variety leaf, then, for the crucial testing, sipped each variety of every brew, rolled it about their tongues, squelched it through their teeth, spat it out, and pronounced a verdict that could make or break an upcountry merchant and grower for a year.

In the evenings when the days' sniffing, spitting and selling was over, everyone gathered round the Nobs' End dining tables where the talk was all of tea—its price compared to five years ago, the iniquity of some native middlemen caught cheating in the weighing sheds, the excessive caution of the big London Firms, Twinings and Coope, who usually ordered the bulk of the first crop. After the meal, guests strolled outside to take the air and watch the Yangtze tides heaving magnificently in the moonlight, and many a man breathed a fervent prayer to the stars that the season's crop would bring top prices in London even though the omens were not auspicious. Charles was one of these, standing beside his wife on the Telfords' lawn one evening, wishing that he could afford a fashionable Parisian-style gown like Amelia's for her, and that they had a house grand enough for lavish entertaining on the Telford scale. Looking at Alice, he felt a gush of warm love, wanted desperately to make her happy, marvelled that, in their present straitened circumstances, she put such a brave face on it, and seemed content.

And, in large measure she was, for she understood intuitively that the actual business of trading was more enjoyable than spending the profits thereof. So, for the rest of that summer, after the chahsees and clerks had gone, she remained serene in the having of her own man, keeping the house pleasant for him, lying close to his firm male body every night with no fears for the future. Often they would work together in the office, damp towels round their heads to keep cool, arranging for shipments of tough Hupeh grass-cloth, nutgalls and firecrackers to Shanghai, of dried clams, Shensi rhubarb and tobacco to Nanking and, to Changsha, kerosene lamps and aphrodisiacs made of ground ginseng and labelled "Penetration Hard Powder". The last invariably led Alice into an amused, lustful reverie in which she was again spreadeagled on Lung-kuang's red silk coverlet while he, by the light of a new-fangled kerosene lamp, and fired by the powder . . .

The news from the London tea-sales was not good; it was rumoured that Tommy Telford lost so heavily he cancelled a proposed European tour and certainly Amelia looked more than usually vexed. Grant & Greenwood also lost ground, but it was offset somewhat by some small successes in local trade and bric-à-brac. Though Charles did not admit it, this was mainly due to Alice's directly personal dealings with the merchants and shippers who, though highly suspicious of her at first, soon dubbed her "Number-One-Business-female-devil"; it was a compliment earned by her patient haggling over sums that most foreigners considered too trifling. But haggling was a noisy process, and Amelia Telford, calling at the office one day with a special delivery letter from Shanghai, shuddered as she overheard it. Mrs Grant, she later told Mrs Wilcock, sounded like nothing more nor less than a common Covent Garden market-woman, and she felt bound to mention the matter to Tommy that evening, for such behaviour could not but lower the dignity of all the foreign ladies in Chinese eyes. And what a blessing it would be, Amelia concluded, if little Mrs Grant were to begin a family so that her mind should have a more suitable occupation.

The letter Amelia brought was from Frank announcing his imminent arrival, and just two days later he bounded off the steamer, greeting Alice with his usual enthusiasm. His athletic frame was thickening already, she noticed, for he spent more time at his desk these days, less shaking up his liver with the lads. He had developed an air of rather flamboyant well-being and self-satisfaction, for he was enjoying his present life to the full—good food, drink, sex, the excitement of the racecourse, the accumulation of possessions, babies, hopes for the future. And yet, when Alice looked at him she saw first, as she always did after a period of separation, the frightened blubbering boy whom Eldest Brother kicked, the stocky groom running beside Younger Brother's horse, the sulky lad they had brought out of Hunan. And he too, though not blessed with her vivid recall, did not really see, at first, the young woman in high-necked, smocked blouse, broad-sashed navy skirt who was his married sister, but some smaller, blurred version of the same, who had sobbed and screamed as he once had, been hungry, cold and cowed—he and she despicable runts in the land of the proud Celestials, part of them forever unrescued.

So it was no surprise when he said, as soon as they settled in a double rickshaw, "Han-li visited us recently—it was grand to see him again."

"Han-li—how lovely! Is he still at Foochow? How is the family?"

"Yes, he's doing very well—lecturing in navigation. But there's been a sadness in the house..."

"Oh dear—who?"

"The mother, Hidden Glory, died—just slowly faded away over the months, Han-li said. No specific cause. And just after the funeral Han-fei's fourth daughter was born—ill-omened that one will be."

"Yes, poor mite. And Lung-kuang, how has he taken it?"

"He's quite well—his secondary wife and their two young sons keep him happy." He grinned a trifle lewdly.

"I suppose she must have been in her fifties? Hidden Glory? What a melancholy life, Frank—no one knowing or caring about her right to the end."

"Well, Eldest Brother was very upset, he was her favourite and now he's more ill-tempered than ever. Weng and he

329

often quarrel and Weng keeps threatening to leave..."

Alice thought of the house, the courtyard with the carp in their pond, the flowers in their urns, the hall where Hidden Glory's death tablet would not be added to the proud ancestral row; the same passions and contentments among the same people, only fewer of them as the years went by.

"And Han-li lives in Foochow then?"

"And he's married, though he didn't say much about her. The men never do..."

"Married! Well, it happens to us all. And Little Piece? I've often thought of her recently, is she still at home?"

"He didn't say, but he sees Mei in Canton occasionally."

The Grant & Greenwood establishment, Frank noted, was not in the right part of the concession. "So this is where you are? Jolly fine view of the river, hey?"

"Yes—splendid."

"And business—is it good?" He stopped her in the doorway.

"Could be better, could be worse."

"Well, you need to know exactly what you're doing in these days of increasing competition."

"And you think we don't?" she snapped.

"Now Sis, I didn't say that...But I want you to know first—I've come with a proposition from Father-in-law. A very generous offer I promise you. I can count on your support, can't I?"

"Depends what it is, Frank."

"It's very sound—good for you, good for us. I'm assuring you that in confidence, you know you can trust me..." She nodded tentatively as Charles came thundering down the passage shouting a welcome.

It was not Frank's way to beat about many bushes, and once they had settled on the verandah with their pre-luncheon sherries, he broached the subject.

"Well Charles, I expect you're wondering why I've come?"

"My dear chap," Charles protested, "delighted to see you any time, you don't have to have a special reason."

"Nice of you to say so—but the fact is I've come partly on my father-in-law's account."

"Yuan-wang? Doing very well for himself these days I hear?"

"Yep, on the up and up—and taking me with him, I'm pleased to say. He treats me fairly enough and I've no head for the big deals—that's the Eldest Son's line. But that's what

330

I want to talk about now—they...we...are thinking of expanding up the Yangtze here. The river's going to be thrown wide open in the next decade, everyone says so—limitless trading opportunities right into the interior, up to the Tibetan border maybe."

"Yes—I keep hearing about the marvellous future." Charles was terse.

"Well, the long and short is—Grant & Greenwood already being established here in a fairly small way—he's wondering if you'd like to join up with us, under our joint names, with you as sole agents in these parts? All legally arranged and above board, only we'd have the monopoly with you of course."

Charles brooded. "I should have thought there were enough tea-men here already."

"Oh not tea—that's past its peak. Wang's a wily bird and he swears our tea will lose out to the cheaper Indian stuff. The European barbarians, he says, simply haven't fine enough palates to appreciate the subtle native brews that are delicate as sparrows' tongues—and he may well be right."

"I hope to God he isn't."

"Be that as it may, he's not interested in it, it's native manufactures and bric-à-brac he wants to export with some importing of pig-iron and such."

"Good old muck and truck, hey?"

"But that's just what Archie Small and Mary..." Alice broke in eagerly.

He turned on her icily. "Why don't you go and see if luncheon is ready, Alice? This is very much a business discussion."

"And I'm not part of it?"

"Not really, no."

He turned back to Frank. "So your father-in-law really believes this miscellaneous trade will do better than tea, Frank? But how could I...?"

Fuming, Alice retreated to the kitchen, poured another sherry, grabbed the spoon from Snow Duck and stirred the soup vigorously. Returning to the verandah after a few minutes, she heard Frank saying, "...for you own good, yours and Alice's. Honestly, if it wasn't for your being here and part of the family, so to speak, Pa-in-law would be in like a shot and..."

"But here's Alice to say luncheon is served, I hope?" Charles' smile was bland.

"Yes it is...And what's been decided in the absence of

your business partner, Charles?"

"Nothing. Frank is going to show me some figures after lunch, and figures, you've always admitted, are not your forte..." He took each firmly by the arm. "My dear good young Greenwoods, it's time to eat and I'm going to open a bottle of the best French white I've been saving for a truly appreciative visitor. I want to hear the latest Shanghai gossip, Frank, and I want my dear wife to relax and listen too. We sadly lack for frivolity in these parts and it makes her too serious by half! Come—to the wine..." Determinedly he steered them to the table and the conversation away from any business topic throughout the leisurely meal.

At its conclusion, the men disappeared into the office while Alice, mellowed by the wine, snoozed on the verandah, dreaming lazily that all was bound to be well, and that, with Mr Yuan-wang involved, their fortunes would soon be made. But when they reappeared, it was apparent no such happy conclusion had been reached and the subject was again deliberately avoided during supper. Pleading tiredness after his journey, Frank excused himself early.

"See what you can do, Sis, he's so stupidly suspicious of the idea," he whispered as Alice handed him a night-light in the kitchen.

She grimaced. "He hates me to interfere, as you've seen today, and anything I suggest he always takes as criticism. But I'll try..."

Charles was reading the trade reports Frank had brought and sipping a brandy. She picked up her embroidery, feigning calm till his air of unruffled occupation defeated her. "So you've looked at the figures—the agency terms? What do you think? It seems an excellent idea to me. The tea business is overcrowded and uncertain, you said so yourself."

"Maybe, maybe, but it's well organised and we Brits are all in it together. As for this trash trade, I don't like it."

"But the terms, Charles?"

"Oh fair enough on the surface, I admit—but could I trust them?"

"Not trust Frank—my own brother?"

"Oh, Frank's honest of course—absolutely and transparently so. But is he the innocent being used by Wang to persuade me into this? Remember, Alice, you've often warned me against relying too much on the native traders, saying they'll do a barbarian down any day in favour of their own countrymen... Yet now..."

"But Charles, don't you understand? To Wang, as you

332

insist on calling him, we're not just any old barbarians—I'll spell it out for you: Peachy is Wang's favourite daughter. Through Frank and me she's linked to our firm. Therefore we've become part of his family network—and that, to a Chinese, is crucial. And so, even though we're foreigners, he'd never do us down and we could trust him implicitly because he'd use a different set of rules with us. I'm positive his offer is generous and honourable. He intends to make money of course, but not at our expense, though it could be at the expense of some other Hankow merchants, if they're not sharp enough."

"Ah yes that's the point, isn't it?" He poured himself another brandy. "You want me to go into open partnership with a Chinaman even if it does mean doing the dirty on some of our own."

She realised her mistake. "I'm not suggesting any sort of crookedness, just that we seize this opportunity to expand honestly and accumulate more capital, which we're not doing at present."

"We're honest..."

"Yes, and poor."

They glared at each other. "What do you really know about all this?" He drank moodily. "You're a woman with no head for business and are just being ruled by your emotions as usual. You want this arrangement because Wang is Frank's father-in-law and you're devoted to Frank."

Her tone was icy. "I love Frank of course—but my devotion in this case is to the success of Grant & Greenwood. No, Charles, it's you who's not looking at it logically because you've got a snobbish bias against any sort of alliance with a "native trader" or moving out of tea—after all, it's so much more respectable and jolly isn't it—trailing on the coat-tails of Telford and his merry teamen? That's the truth, isn't it?... Now give me a brandy."

He handed her a very small quantity in a very large glass, and she gulped it. "Now come, dear, let's stop quarrelling and accept the offer. Go into it gradually if you like, talk it over with Wang in Shanghai—would that put your mind at rest?"

"Nothing will put my mind at rest, because I'm simply not going into it, so there!" he snarled. "You're getting too uppity in these business matters, my dear. You spend far too much time in the office as it is, instead of keeping company with the other ladies." He swigged his drink and looked at her with unusual venom. "I suppose it would suit your book to have more natives around the place and you hand-in-glove with them, talking their lingo? Why, you might eventually be able to move me out entirely in favour of Greenwood, Greenwood & Wang Ltd . . . All your childhood dreams come true!"

"Charles—you beast . . . you . . . how dare you suggest that I—oh it's too much!" Her voice broke with angry tears. "You're just a short-sighted fool in business matters and I just want to help you, help us both . . . But alright, have it your own way—you will of course. But if things go wrong after you've refused this offer, don't expect me to help. I'll be too busy playing croquet with the ladies and spending your money on dresses and parties and all the things I don't do now—because we can't really afford them! So be sure to make a fortune for me, won't you?" Tears streaming down her face, she slammed out; he poured another drink, flung himself back in his chair.

The reasons Alice had given for his refusal were right to a point, though she didn't know the extent of his indebtedness to Telford, who had so manoeuvred matters that he could buy him out any day if he chose. Sometimes Charles hated Tommy's chummy bonhomie, his arrogant confidence in his superior business acumen, but he was not going to admit that to Alice. We men have to stick together, Telford had said only the other day—and it's not a good idea to let the little wife have too much to do with business, old chap! Women soon get above themselves and the natives hate doing business with 'em, they don't think it's natural. And Telford was right; Alice had just given more proof of that. From now on, he vowed angrily, he would see that she had enough money to join in all the ladies' entertainments, even if it meant going further into hock.

He swilled the liquid round his glass moodily. Dash it, indebtedness seemed an inevitable part of life in China—like the constant noise, the stinks, the gawping filthy crowds. But more depressing still was the sense of being relegated to the barbarian fringes, a mere interloper in the Celestial scheme of things, without power, privilege or even much knowledge of what was really going on. This, he realised, was just what his family had warned him about. "So you think you'll be a swashbuckling merchant-adventurer do you?" his father had snorted. "Sailing up the Yangtze and making a glittering fortune . . . Well there's no room for that sort of caper in China. Once a barbarian always a barbarian there and you'll end up in some mouldy back-of-beyond concession built on a mud-

bank plagued with dishonest traders and riddled with debt—
you mark my words!"

In the late-night quiet of his sitting-room Charles did mark
his father's words, and a flood of guilty, reluctant nostalgia
overcame him. He thought of Madras, its stately offices, the
orderly, consequential lives of its British administrators; and
he had a sudden painful vision of dear dead Maria in a
sprigged dress, standing on the trim lawn of Government
House during some official function with little Peter beside
her. He would write to Harriet about the boy coming here.
It would give Alice another interest for one thing and com-
pensate for their own lack of children.

Why Alice had not yet conceived they did not know and
found it hard to discuss. Charles, assuming his second wife's
attitude to her marital duties was as unenthusiastic as his
first's, pressed his claims fairly infrequently and with a half-
apologetic briskness that seldom roused her. During the early
months, she had occasionally tried leading him towards some
of the inventive, leisurely, uninhibited ways of pleasuring
that she knew, but her initiatives only embarrassed him. Not
the proper feminine behaviour for an English lady, he felt
sure, and it only served as a reminder of that confession about
her past which he had carefully expunged from his consciousness. And so they soon fell into a mutually acceptable pattern
of polite intercourse that sent Charles quickly to sleep afterwards and left Alice wide-awake, her half-aroused flesh longing for what she had once enjoyed.

The coolness that followed their first bitter quarrel was
not therefore melted in the warmth of the marriage bed, but
instead accentuated by a letter from Daisy Small that arrived
soon after. Now the tea-season was over, Daisy wrote, she
felt sure Alice would have time to consider the Anti-Foot-
binding League and she enclosed pamphlets illustrated with
real-life photographs of bound feet in all their ugly deformity.
Charles shuddered when she showed him. "How disgusting—really, it's too much."

"But just what's needed to shake the matrons of Hankow
out of their apathy, as Daisy says."

"Mrs Small should leave this sort of thing to the missionaries."

"No—that's just the point. As Daisy says, our best chance
is to convince the people on purely humanitarian grounds."

He handed the pamphlets back. "Oh those—my dear
Alice, what about the lepers on the quay with their noses and

fingers falling off, the numbers of baby-girls drowned like kittens or put out for the dogs to chew, the criminals starving in cages and spattered with human ordure—with all that going on around us every day, why worry about bound feet? Your so-called humanitarianism doesn't make sense to the Chinese, you know—they're not even quite human in the way we are."

"Oh don't be absurd, Charles, of course they are. I know and I've lived among them. They've had so many more dreadful things to contend with, that's all. We English didn't behave much better in medieval times till our social reformers came along—and they improved matters eventually, as the League will. Listen to this, apparently Daisy tackled an Ichang magistrate on the subject and he said, 'Yes, poor little mites—they have but five years to run'... Think of that, isn't it awful? One's got to make a stand somewhere, as Daisy says, and she wants me to start a branch of the League here, and distribute these to the foreigners and some Chinese officials and..."

"Daisy says, Daisy says," he mimicked tartly. "Well, Daisy can say what she likes in Ichang, but here she's considered an eccentric busybody if you want to know and I'm not having your name associated with her damn fool league. Amelia Telford's already hinted that your behaviour isn't always up to snuff apparently and..."

"Amelia Telford, Amelia Telford! What do I care about that snobby cow?" Alice snorted shrilly. "Why, Daisy's worth..."

"You'd better care about Amelia's opinion," his voice rose in competition, "I'm enough in hock to her husband. So now you have it, Alice. And no, I'm not giving you any details. All I'm saying is that I absolutely forbid you to get on some ridiculous hobbyhorse that would antagonise the whole settlement."

"That's all you care about it, isn't it, Charles? People's good opinion—and I thought you were an adventurer..."

"I have to care, we live here—this is our livelihood." His tone moderated. "Let's not quarrel again, Alice. Just reflect for a moment, even putting the community's views aside, you know the native officials would be affronted by these pamphlets and, given the present political situation, the last thing we want is to stir up trouble."

That, she knew, was true. For the past few months popular feeling against Westerners' presence in the country had been running high again due to the crisis between the Chinese and the French over the tributary kingdom of Annam where the Vietnamese tribes lived. Bands of Annamese peasants had started a guerrilla war against the French who wanted control of all Cochin China. The conflict, though distant, had aroused China's awareness of its vulnerability to foreign aggression; anti-barbarian tracts were again in circulation; some foreign houses in the Treaty Ports had been stoned. Knowing this, the flood of conviction inspired by Daisy's letter ebbed from her and she mumbled, "Oh I suppose I'll have to wait. Things will quieten down soon."

The subject was not mentioned again and Alice wrote a shamefaced letter to Daisy promising to take action when the political situation improved.

In the meantime it worsened. The French captured two Annamese cities and this prompted anti-barbarian riots down-river at Wuhu. In Hankow, the force of native constabulary detailed to protect the Concession was increased from eight men to twelve, and the foreign men formed a volunteer brigade which met once a week to oil guns stored in the godowns and to inspect barriers which, in any uprising, could be used to block off the settlement from the native city. As there seemed no imminent danger of this however, volunteer meetings were quite convivial, lasting into the early hours; and at breakfast the morning after Charles would assure his wife that she was protected by a fine set of fellows ready to lay down their lives to a man if need be. But by this Alice was politely unimpressed, for the idea of any such eventuality seemed absurd.

However, the unsettled international situation adversely affected trade, several of the foreign merchant houses refused to invest more in the China market, and the upswing that usually began in March simply did not materialise. Even Tommy Telford was worried and eventually he and Charles decided to visit Chiuchiang to investigate possibilities of going onto brick-tea like the Russians—who seemed to do very well with the stuff. Amelia, frightened of being left without male protection, went with them, but Alice stayed behind to "mind the shop" as she put it, and welcome Frank who was coming to inspect the Wang Agency now flourishing in Hankow.

Expecting his arrival the day after Charles' departure, Alice made noodle soup, glazed some sugar plums, ran up to the verandah time and again watching for the steamer from Shanghai. When it had not arrived by lunchtime, she coiled in her basket chair and took up her embroidery. A mist began

to form, clouding water and sky to pearly grey, blurring the
red sun to a stained haze, disembodying the usual river
noises.

"Row her to bite the water-side and make her fast,
    In rain and wind we must always find anchorage,
        When the sun sets, I'll buy a bright cloth for my
woman to wear."

The song of a poling boatman drifted to her through the
mist. For thousands of years, she thought, similar sounds and
songs had rolled over these ancient waters, and bent old
women had stood ankle-deep in the mud fishing. The one
below Alice's verandah now lived in a mat hovel propped
against the factory wall; her little net circled in the air as she
threw it out, and each time she drew it in, a few, flat, oval
fish flapped inside.

Inconsequentially, a verse of Yu Hsiang rolled through
Alice's mind:

"Turning without end,
Heaven and earth shift secretly.
Who is aware of it?"

She remembered the day she had returned to Tientsin
with Uncle Robert and seen a man weaving nets where the
Mission had once been. She got up restlessly, wishing Frank
would come, a sense of foreboding strong in her. At length,
as the sun set and the old woman coiled away her net, she
heard a knock and hurried down in alarm. "Frank—it is you?
Thank goodness—but I didn't see the steamer?"

"Hello, Sis. They're not running, haven't you heard?"

"Heard what?"

"A French naval squadron attacked Foochow three days
ago, bombarding the Celestial Navy and its dockyard out of
existence. Reprisal for the Annamese mess... Shanghai's up
in arms of course and the Chinese have commandeered the
river steamers—going to turn 'em into gunboats overnight
they say. Poor fools haven't a hope, just making the appropriate cries of outrage, as old Ben Smythe put it. He was
coming this way too, so we got berths on a Russian coaster,
and here I am."

"Oh, Frank, how dreadful—here, sit by the stove, Snow
Duck'll bring tea. Every single Chinese ship sunk, you say?"

"Yep—the entire navy, such as it was. Not many lives
lost, but an awful lot of face."

"Oh, how furious the self-strengtheners will be—they've

been calling for the build-up of coastal defences for years. And Han-li, I hope he's alright." She remembered how proudly he had once described those Chinese warships to her—the power of their engines, the Whitworth guns bristling on their decks. Lin, Han-li and thousands like them would be hating the guts of every foreign devil.

"Oh curse the French—what right have they to...?"

"Nothing to do with rights, as Ben says. Just the biggest bullies showing their muscle. 'The ambition of the barbarian nations is long, hard and deep, while the stupidity of our scholar-officials is boundless'—or something like that, in the words of a Chinese minister reported in the paper last week. He's right, this goes to show... Give me a brandy and soda instead of tea, Sis, it was cold on the river and this sort of thing always upsets me. Puts me in a beastly position at home, you can imagine..."

"With all the foreigners toasting the exploits of the victorious Froggies?"

"Exactly." He took the glass. "One reason I determined to get away. There's no danger, just a lot of huffing and puffing—there'll be another peace treaty eventually and the Chinese will get the worst of it, as usual. But it's crippling for trade..."

She sighed, stirring the embers of the stove. "And things are shaky already."

"Really? Well, Charles should have agreed to Pa-in-law's proposition. Our agency here is doing very well. Did you know that feathers—on hats, dresses, boas—are very fashionable in Europe just now? We're exporting them by the hundred-sacksful each week. That's what I admire about old Wang—his eye for the main chance, whereas men like your Charles wouldn't stoop to that sort of thing. Anyway, Sis, I've got to see our compradore Old Cho at the Golden Phoenix. I'll unpack later..."

"But, Frank, you've only just come."

"Well, I expected to be here much earlier, didn't I?"

"Oh don't leave yet, we've not talked for months."

"You're not frightened of the big bad yellow men like the other fluttery ladies surely?" he teased.

"Of course not, but I'm tired of being cooped up in this Concession as if we were in an enemy country. Since this situation, we aren't supposed even to venture into Hankow proper."

"Well, I'm certainly going..."

She faced him in the doorway. "Then take me with you.

I'm bored with behaving myself."

"But people are bound to..."

"That's what I hate about these foreign communities—the spying and tittle-tattle. Where are all the adventures I used to dream about?"

"Oh, you always had high falutin' dreams, Uncut Jade. But tell you what—put on your native togs like you used to, remember? And we'll go in closed chairs..."

She ran to her bedroom and soon emerged in a drab-blue robe, hair tucked under a kerchief, face powdered white, eyebrows black.

He surveyed her. "Not bad—more like an abo than a true Daughter of Han, but never mind."

"Better than you can do with that yellow mop—like an old straw horse-box, Eldest Brother used to say."

"Ah, but to Peachy it's royal gold. By the way, she's going to have another child. And daily prayers are going up for a son this time... You don't seem to be doing much in that line?" he looked at her curiously.

"The doctor says it might be difficult because of—what happened in Hunan I suppose. I didn't give him the details of my miscarriage..."

"Oh dear, I'm sorry, Alice." In the ensuing awkward pause, he said "I've sent Snow Duck for two chairs... Er, have you heard from Mother recently?"

"Yes—she seems quite cheerful. They're receiving more money from wellwishers recently because of the revival going on in England, led by those American evangelists, Moody and Sankey."

Frank sang mockingly, "'Hold the Fort for I am coming', etc, etc... And the children?"

"Adam's settled in school, but poor Sunny's so lonely. Mother's hoping to go on leave with Will and Isabel next year and take her. Stepfather won't leave the Mukden Fort, but she certainly needs a holiday."

Snow Duck arrived with the chairs just then and they jogged off in the gathering dusk—across a hump-bridge, through a small gate in the crenellated wall of the "million-people-city" where China began. Their way lay through the street of the druggists whose gilded signboards proclaimed the efficacy of various herbal aphrodisiacs, of dragons' blood tablets and alligator pills. One shop had a special display of liquid extracted from the gall bladders of recently-executed bandits—an infallible cure for boils. Of more sinister import was a hastily-scrawled poster on a nearby wall: "Death to the dog-faced barbarians of France. They have invaded our western tributaries, destroyed our magnificent war-vessels. Their heads are monstrous, their dispositions fiercer than tiger or wolf, their hearts greedier than snake or hog."

The news of the attack on Foochow had reached the city that afternoon, and the Golden Phoenix was unusually animated as a result. Its rooms, some more secret than others, were all designed for the entertainment of the city's business men. Its portals shone with red lanterns; from its ornate restaurant drifted succulent smells of sizzling pork and fish; across the passage in the Good Fortune Hall gamblers stood tense round tables; and through the lattices of the Flowery Chambers came the pluck and whine of romantic song, the scent of women's bodies; along the passages to the inner courtyard the heavy, bittersweet smell of opium hung in the air.

Old Cho met them in the restaurant. "I wondered if you'd get here," he greeted Frank.

"I got a ride on a Russian coaster. This is my sister, Old Cho, come to dine." He concealed his displeasure under a bland smile that cracked his smooth yellow cheeks.

As they settled at a table, Frank asked, "There are antiforeign posters up, I see—does it mean real trouble, do you think?"

"The filthy French toads," Old Cho spat in disgust. "I wish we could blast them all to searing hell!"

Alice was startled by his violence. "Are you of the antibarbarian faction then?" She was half-joking, but he turned narrow, cold eyes on her.

"I've been of that faction ever since I was a lad, foreign woman. Since the day—and more than two cycles of the Rat have gone by since then—when I first saw one of your godrotting vessels rolling on the waters of our Great River. We all went to watch the big-nosed barbarians step ashore as if they owned Hankow. There was a wily linguist from Canton aboard and we asked who those vulgar monsters were. Men from some tin-pot island beyond the far western horizon, he answered. Their leader was a lord in his country—El-gin was his name. Fat as a pig with good living he was, face red as a turkey-cock's. His boat was in the service of *her* majesty, because these barbarians were ruled by a female, and it was called 'Furious'—Furious!" Old Cho sucked his mouth into a humourless chuckle. "What the hell have they got to be furious about? I asked, being a cocky youngster. How dare they sit out there, all primed and prickly with guns like an angry little wasp—Bzzz, bzzz, we should swat 'em straight under the waters, mister, that's what I said to the interpreter. We, the Sons of Han, *we* should be furious... Well, if we'd taken a stronger line in those days, we might not be in this bleeding mess now, with the French toads overrunning our western tributaries and battering our navy to bits. Cost us millions of taels to build those ships—and I'm so furious my hair is on end under my cap!"

"But you can't keep China closed away from the world forever, you know," Frank protested.

"Why not, why not? Our Imperial dynasties did well for thousands of years without the rest of the world... Yes, yes... bzzz, bzzz—throw all the foreign devils back into the sea, I say."

Frank grinned impishly. "I don't think my Peachy would thank you for that, Old Cho."

He snorted. "Well—I might pull just you out again, if you grow a proper Chinese tail... Ah, here's Mr Shen from Szechuan, I told you about him—the upriver trade and all that..."

He ambled to meet the newcomer, and Frank sighed. "Fancy, Old Cho—he isn't usually so disagreeable, this French business has certainly upset him."

Returning, Old Cho introduced his friend, then turned to Alice, "I fear I'm asking you to leave us now, Mrs Grant. We cannot discuss these things before you—a woman and one whose husband has a rival firm..."

Alice jumped up, flushing. "The mistress of this establishment has agreed to let you await in her private apartment."

Frank pulled an apologetic face and Alice followed a servant across a courtyard and into a dimly lit room. The bittersweet smell of opium enclosed her; a middle-aged woman reclined on a couch smoking, a younger woman was crouched over her, next to a spirit-lamp, plucking a lute and singing in a low sweet voice,

> "You and I in the same boat,
> Long leaves bending in the wind,
> Plucking rushes at the Five Lakes.
> We started at dawn from the orchid island,
> We rested under the elms till noon,

". . . You and I plucking rushes,
    Hadn't plucked a handful when night came."

At the song's end, the singer raised her face to Alice; it was a smooth, beautiful oval in the lamplight but its eyes were sightless. "Who's there?"

"My name is Uncut Jade. They said I could wait here while my brother talks business."

The woman bowed. "Then please sit down, this is the mistress of the Golden Phoenix, but she's dreaming."

Alice sat gingerly on another couch next to a white Pekinese dog and watched as the blind woman took a nut of opium from a box in the table and teased it over the lamp. When it was soft she inserted it in the small silver bowl near the pipe's end. Keeping the bowl over the flame, she handed the mouthpiece to her mistress who drew it into her lungs with one long satisfied breath, then reclined again on her porcelain head-rest. As the blind woman replenished the pipe again, Alice said,

"You have a most melodious voice, may I ask your name?"

"Flowing Spring—because I was found wandering by the river one spring day when I was young. I was so lucky because a kind boat-man brought me here—where I've lived ever since. . . And you? There is something different—you smell strangely?"

Alice chuckled. "You must please excuse me, I'm English and it is the smell of the barbarian, I'm told we all have it."

"Flowing Spring, pretty dear," moaned the woman from the couch, "sing again . . ."

Obediently she took up the lute and began,

"The monk of Szechuan on the heights of Mount Omei,
Comes down westward, under his arm a Lu-yi lute.
He plays for me, fingers brushing the strings,
And the sound is like murmuring pine-trees in ravines,
So with the flowing spring song he recreates my soul."

As the soft voice chanted and the poppy-fumes swirled, Alice felt herself drowsing. "Would you like one?" Flowing Spring was holding a pipe for her and Alice hesitated, her senses remembering a strange dream of long ago, when she lay ill in Grandmother Willow's hut.

Flowing Spring smiled. "Come, take it, Uncut Jade. The flowers of your childhood will bloom again. You will walk through gardens you had forgotten you abandoned and see the shadows of strange bamboos under moons of amber..."

Alice took it, inhaled, swallowed, sucked till the pipe was empty. Flowing Spring inserted another pellet. "Don't worry—this is no adulterated mix, it is pure Benares. You have smoked before, I think?"

"So long ago, I'd almost forgotten."

"Ah but the poppy is patient; it knows how to wait."

In the inert half-light two moths circled slowly above the opium tray with its box of pellets, pipes, water and lamp. The box was pink with a yellow design that flared as intensely as a rape-field in full bloom; the moths were liquid white like water-lilies, but powdery too with blue edges like the lamp flame. Alice watched them, totally relaxed and at peace with all the world. Flowing Spring's lovely face smiled sightlessly down at her as she circled into a landscape where a monk with a lute stood on a green mountain. He beckoned to her, but she knew he was waiting like the poppy and she had not yet met him. Behind the monk she sensed a black dwarf lurking, his mouth full of blood. She could scarcely see him though and he went away behind a flat silver cloud.

When she woke her mouth tasted harshly acrid and her eyelids were too heavy to open. When they eventually did, it was on her familiar bedroom and she remembered how Old Cho had bundled her and Frank into closed chairs late the night before. He had been sodden with wine and pleasure, she with the spell of the ancient poppy. A foolish episode that she must never repeat, she told herself sternly, and it had only happened because Frank had lingered long in the Fragrant Chambers.

The next day the river steamers resumed normal service and Frank, returning to Shanghai, passed Charles and the Telfords returning from Chiuchiang. It had been a thoroughly wasted trip, Charles told Alice gloomily, for no one would consider advancing capital for new ventures in the present tricky international situation.

"We got pelted with mud when we went to the Consul's for supper and old Tommy kept shouting, 'But we're not French froggies you stupid sots, we're true blue British bulldogs!' If they understood, it made no difference—Amelia's hat was knocked off and I know now exactly what mud in your eye feels like!"

"Oh dear, how oafish these mobs are. Did they shout 'kill the barbarians' at you—that's a dreadful sound." She shivered.

"I expect so—luckily we couldn't understand. But they have killed a barbarian elsewhere—the French Consul in Foochow was murdered the night after the attack on the dockyard, and that will worsen the situation—see, here's an account of it."

He handed her a copy of the *Mercury*.

"Oh Charles—no, no it was Félix, Félix Fauré, I knew him in Port Arthur—oh dear oh dear, oh no!" She sat down, reading with blurred eyes how Félix had been dragged from his house, kicked along the street, beaten and stabbed to death. His wife and child had been saved by the authorities just in time. She buried her head in her hands and Charles stroked it comfortingly.

"My dear—I'm so sorry. I'd no idea you knew him, or I'd have broken it gently."

She sniffed. "That doesn't matter, I had to know. But Félix—he was so lively and handsome in the French style... To think that..." Too vividly she conjured that last horror—the pain and humiliation, those flashing eyes ground into the dust, blood soaking the dapper facings of his jacket. She clenched her fists in sad anger; the incident was a hazard of diplomacy of course and Félix dead would, the *Mercury*'s editorial said, prove more useful to the French in subsequent bargaining than Félix alive ever had. The wry wit of the living Félix would have appreciated that.

There was nothing to be done of course. In Hankow the Concession's constabulary was redoubled and some foreigners slept with pistols under their pillows. Alice felt the sense of imprisonment keenly and, with time on her hands, drafted a translation of Mill's treatise on women which she sent to Daisy Small, "in the hope," she wrote, "this will serve to show you I'm not quite lost to the cause of women's various subjections. When this dreadful French business is settled I promise to do something for the League. I feel the worst is over, don't you?"

And indeed it was, for neither side wanted full-scale war. That summer the Chinese signed a treaty by which the French gained suzerainty over Annam, and Li Hung-chang, appointed Associate Controller of the Admiralty, set about re-building the country's shattered naval defences. Trade improved and money flowed back in to Shanghai, but in Hankow there was a tremendous row between foreigners and local officials over the imposition of new customs levies which held up shipments, so to Charles it all seemed one damn thing after another. In September, just as trade really picked up, a junk named White Wings that had always been lucky broke its tow-ropes at the Yellow Cow Rapids and sank with all hands, plus quantities of Grant & Greenwood's dye-stuffs and lead spars. On the same day the news of this disaster arrived, the Shanghai steamer brought a letter from sister Harriet in Madras. Charles whistled through his teeth as he read.

"Good Lord, Alice, they're all coming to see us!"

"What—your family?" Her dismay was unconcealed.

"Yes, I told you Harriet and I have been in correspondence about Peter's future and though I'd like him here, it's more than time he went to school in England. Well, George is due for leave next spring, so they propose taking Peter home with them and..." he read aloud, "... we're hoping to make a Chinese excursion first—to Hong Kong, Shanghai, then up the Yangtze to see you and meet your wife at last. Won't that be exciting dear? By the way...I hope you won't mind if we bring Florence Plowden with us? She's married to George's brother Ian you know, and he's going to be up at the North-West Frontier for months a-railway-building... Quite a pretty creature, a bit flighty—and country-born unfortunately.'"

Alice bridled. "Like me..."

He glanced up. "Oh don't mind that—Harriet's a bit of a snob I'm afraid, but very kindhearted." He continued reading: "'Seems rather cruel to leave Florence alone where she's no relatives, so we're suggesting she share our China trip then return to India when we go Home'..."

He flung down the letter. "All sounds perfectly splendid and well-planned—just like Harriet—but they can't possibly come to this pokey little hole." He prowled about agitatedly.

"Charles, how mean of you—I think it's a sweet place and after all I've done."

"Oh you've done wonders, my dear. But it's not the sort of scale Harriet and George are used to in Madras. And there's simply no space—why, we'll need three more bedrooms."

"But can't we explain that now? Before they confirm their arrangements."

"My dear Alice, Harriet and George have given my son bed and board for about five years—the least I can do is offer them generous house-room here for a holiday."

"Yes dear, of course, I'm sorry. But wouldn't the Telfords help out?"

"It won't do, Alice. I've got to put on a better show than

this. Harriet would be horrified—it would confirm all her worst fears about my coming to China—oh, she'd be so scathing!" He shivered.

"You sound quite frightened of her, she is your sister after all."

"But ten years older and very elder-sisterly, and I want to show them I'm making good in spite of their warnings—even if I'm not." He laughed mirthlessly.

"But we're doing alright in our small way."

"Oh yes, we can afford to pay Snow Duck and hire a buggy occasionally."

"And Harriet would look down her nose at all this?"

"Yes she would—and rightly so, Alice. The fact is, my family's standards are—higher than some, and I won't let them down any further."

"As you have by coming to China and marrying me, I suppose?"

"I never suggested that. All I'm saying is that we must move into a house big enough to accommodate my sister, her husband, my son and this half-sister-in-law, whoever she is. They're not due for months yet and there's time—in fact, I've got an idea already. You remember that house beyond the Telfords' where the Ukranian merchant, Markov, lived?"

"Till his wife died of fever caught from that pestilential swamp behind . . . ?"

"Oh pooh, that was a silly rumour. Anyway, Markov left after the funeral and now I hear he mayn't come back, so the place would be for rent. I'll find out."

A few weeks later the permanence of Markov's departure was confirmed and the Russian Consul half-heartedly cleared the house, leaving behind a worm-eaten table, some tea-chests, and a cracked chandelier dangling from a rusty rod in the hallway. The chandelier was the first thing Alice saw when she and Charles looked the place over, its dusty glimmer only adding to the general air of neglect and melancholy. The rent was higher than Charles could afford, repairs were badly needed and most of the rooms overlooked the dreary swamp behind Nobs' End. But it *was* at that end of the Bund, it had five bedrooms and a large dining-room, so, over-riding his wife's misgivings, Charles took it.

Workmen went in to mend floorboards and leaking windows, but, Alice realised, their knocked-up bits of local furniture, their cheap draperies, even the beloved tiger rug, were going to look small and second-rate in the gloomy, lofty rooms. At the market one day she sold the silver walnut from the Carr loot to buy a heavy sideboard, bedsteads, dressing-tables from the Russian dealers, using, she told Charles, money she had saved in Port Arthur against a rainy day.

And the day they finally moved into the house was very rainy; cold mid-winter rain that crept through the crevices the carpenters had not sealed, and positively poured into the fuel store. Wet wood and charcoal spluttered dully in the unused grates, wind whistled through shutters and on their first evening in residence the chandelier, shaken from its tenuous mooring by the unaccustomed activity, fell and shattered in a thousand fragments.

"What the devil's that?" Charles shouted from the bedroom as the sickening tinkles of glass exploded below. He rushed downstairs till his feet crunched as into breaking ice. Alice snatched a lamp and hurried after him, then stopped with a scream. A long brown and black spotted snake, shaken in turn from its winter retreat under the floorboards, reared its flat head at her from the top stair. Its yellow eyes glittered and its forked tongue flicked out with a hiss.

"Charles—help, quick—there's a snake! Call Snow Duck, quick."

Charles grabbed a walking stick and pounded up the stairs, Snow Duck behind him. He was about to crash the stick down on the creature's head when Snow Duck lunged past and grabbed it by the throat.

Alice shrieked, "Careful, careful—he'll bite you!"

"No killee master, him no bitee . . ." Snow Duck panted as the snake twisted in his grasp, flailing its tail angrily.

"Oh kill it anyway, it's horrible!" Alice moaned.

"No, lady—this is the death snake. Not poisonous, no, but it's an evil spirit snake, always attracted to a house where there's been a death—Here, help me, master, it's getting a grip on me . . ."

Shuddering Charles loosened the scaly length that was binding tightly round the boy's arm; its yellow eyes glittered with greater ferocity.

"I'll get a box and carry it back to the swamp," Snow Duck said, as Alice translated for Charles.

"Damn superstition," he grunted. "Tell him to just get rid of it fast."

Snow Duck ran down the stairs holding the snake from him; at the bottom he skidded on the chandelier glass and fell. The creature thrashed out of his loosened grip and slithered across the floor in a series of horribly tinkling slides.

Charles pounded after it, picked up a chair and crashed it down on the snake's head.

"No, stoppee, stoppee, master," Snow Duck cried, but Charles paid no heed. When he lifted the chair, the death snake was dead, its head mangled to a mash of reptilian flesh and glass. Alice rushed down and helped Snow Duck pick slivers of glass from his shaking hands. "Master makee very bad, very bad. No good house now."

"Oh nonsense boy, it's just an old superstition," Alice snapped, but her voice trembled. "I'll get some ointment. Are you alright, Charles? I'll sweep up—and get rid of that horrid creature outside please."

It took hours to clear the glass fragments from every cranny, and Snow Duck, hands bandaged, sulkily refused to help. The fires would not stay alight and they went to bed tired and cold. Lying next to her sleeping husband, Alice was gripped rigid in a paroxysm of terror. The scene of the evening rolled again and again through her mind: the harsh crash, the yellow eyes glittering, the last glassy slither, Snow Duck's bleeding hands, the snake's mashed head. Beyond it in the dark she seemed to see the face of Mrs Markov who had died of swamp fever—a dark-haired woman with a put-upon, wistful look—the dead one who had attracted the snake to the house. And Alice hated and feared the place from that first night on; it was gloomy, pretentious, costly and withdrawn fom the everyday bustle of the river that had given her such pleasure before. Worse than all this, though, was the coiled shadow of the death snake that had died inside, the death that was still inside waiting.

13

Alice moved round the dining-table checking each place-setting yet again, blowing dust-specks from its polished surface, ears straining for the whistle that would signal the arrival of the steamer with Charles' relatives aboard. She had secretly dreaded this day ever since she learned of their coming and the dread had not lessened because the occasion had been delayed. Harriet had written that a most inconvenient famine struck the southern provinces that spring, just before they were about to leave, and poor George had to organise the distribution of emergency supplies, relief works and the usual botherations that occurred in the *mofussil* when the crops failed and people starved.

It was all a great nuisance because they would miss most of Queen Victoria's Jubilee celebrations in England and were now arriving in Hankow at the very fag-end of August, the Limit of Heat, as the Chinese called it, when the flotsam of the year was stranded in stinking piles on the receding water-line and everyone was plagued with lassitude and mosquitoes. Because of the delay, Harriet wrote that they could spend less than three weeks there, for their passages Home were already booked.

"That long," Charles had moaned. "What on earth can we do with them?"

Alice tried to cheer him. "We can visit the Hills of the East Dragon, there's the September race-meeting and the Telfords' croquet-lawn for Peter."

"Oh Peter's alright, it's the adults..." So they sent for cases of wine and brandy from Shanghai, hired an extra cook, a maid-of-all-work and hoped for the best.

"Snow Duck," Alice called. "Are you sure everything's ready for luncheon?" He came in, sweat rolling down his fat cheeks, looking cross. "That new cook's useless, Missee, more damn trouble than he's worth. I could do it all better myself."

"But there'll be six of us at every meal."

"And my new coat's too tight—like a suit of armour round my middle."

"Please, Snow Duck, don't complain—for my sake—you know Master wants us all to look specially smart."

As he shuffled off, hang-dog, she heard the steamer whistle and her heart plummeted. Her sole wish was to take herself off to the Golden Phoenix, there to receive from Flowing Spring's soft hand a pipe that would very soon reveal the inanity of her worries about servants, place-settings, unknown relatives. For, since her first visit, she had secretly returned there sometimes in the dark winter evenings when Charles was away. Flowing Spring greeted her warmly, only she had to pay for her opium as any customer, and the spending of precious money so illicitly saved her from undue indulgence.

But today escape was impossible. Instead she pinned a new green hat atop her head, drew on new gloves, hurried to the landing-stage. Charles was already there, fussing around the hired buggy. Occasions like this, Alice thought, brought out the most boyish in him—enthusiastic, wanting to please, but lacking resources to do it properly. The steamer was nosing to shore and as Alice came up, Charles waved his hat and cheered.

"There they are—there's Harriet, looking every inch the memsahib."

Alice's sister-in-law came down the gangplank slowly, mindful of her voluminous skirt, her back erect, swept-up hair, greyed by many Indian suns, concealed under a light travelling veil. There was a look of faint disdain on her face which Alice first thought was occasioned by the sight of unpretentious Hankow, but which, she later realised, was as permanent as her other strong features.

"Charles—my dear boy, at last! And Alice—I've wanted to meet you for so long!" Her grey eyes surveyed Alice from head to toe quickly, missing nothing, revealing nothing.

As they embraced, Peter scampered towards Charles who cried, "My, but you've grown tall, lad—where are you shooting up to, hey?"

So like Charles he was, Alice saw, with that boyish charm in its proper boyish place—curly brown hair, freckled face, but with a pensive, withdrawn look characteristic of many Anglo-Indian children. Then came florid, amiable-looking George and clinging to his arm, his sister-in-law Florence, who was slender and held a parasol to shade her delicate skin. So they all stood exchanging pleasantries while coolies shouldered their several trunks, portmanteaux, hat-boxes, and Alice wondered briefly if she had, after all, just taken opium, for the whole scene seemed at one remove. Who were these strangers? Who was she among them? And why did she feel they boded ill?

When they reached the house and Harriet had politely praised the flowers in the hall, Snow Duck hissed quietly to Alice that the new cook had just dropped the best tureen filled with the luncheon consommé. She hurried to the kitchen; the cook was not even repentant; she and Snow Duck guiltily scraped it back into a bowl and hoped for the best. In the dining-room they were sipping sherry, Harriet and Florence on the sofa, the men in the window-alcove.

"Not a major disaster, I hope?" Harriet raised a sympathetic eyebrow.

"No—the cook broke the tureen, but luckily it was empty," she lied gaily.

"Oh cooks are dreadful nowadays, not a patch on my mother's time when they really had the interest of the household at heart."

Alice asked politely, "I expect you've quite a large staff to manage?"

"Not really, let's see..." she counted on her dry, many-ringed fingers. "There's the head bearer, the khitmagar who waits at table, George's valet and my ayah who also does needlework, the dhobi, the mali—that's the gardener..."

"And don't forget the bhisti who carries water, the tailor and outside people like grass-cutters, sweepers and stable boys," Florence chimed in merrily.

"Why, that sounds like a regiment, we can't begin to compare with it in humble Hankow, I fear."

Harriet pursed her lips. "Florence and I were just wondering however you manage—and there doesn't appear to be much to entertain the ladies?"

"No, there isn't really, but," Alice said defiantly, "I was born in the country so I'm used to things as they are."

"Quite so," Harriet sighed gently.

"But once you've been to other parts of the world doesn't it make you feel that China is just too ten-thousand-miles-offee?" Florence trilled.

She was, Alice realised, something of a porcelain beauty, with fair curls, blue eyes, but marred by the pout of her rosebud mouth and rather square jaw.

"I've not yet been abroad, so I don't know." Alice smiled determinedly.

"Not anywhere?—how awful for you."

"And you—you've travelled? I believe you were born in India?"

"Well yes, but I've seen Europe now—London of course, Paris, Rome, Vienna... Ian took me for our honeymoon." She listed the cities with the same air of proud possession as the servants had been counted.

"Well, I'm sure Alice will soon be seeing the world too," Harriet interposed. "I gather you and Charles are planning a European tour—at least I hope so," she lowered her voice, "I told Peter he'd see his father over there before too long, he's counting on it."

"Oh yes, next year perhaps..." Alice spoke confidently, wondering how they could afford such an excursion; such calculations obviously did not enter Harriet's head.

They looked across at Peter, standing quiet beside the men and Harriet said, "He's a very pleasant young creature, more studious than his father. I hope you'll take to him, Alice."

"I'm sure I shall," she replied truthfully as they went to the table. The consommé seemed none the worse for its contact with the kitchen floor, indeed amiable George pronounced it excellent. "Ah," Charles looked at his sister for approval, "my little wife's an excellent housekeeper, not going to be put off by a broken tureen, are you, dear?" He raised a glass vaguely at her. "But things have a habit of breaking in this house. The chandelier in the entrance crashed down the very night we moved in and Frank, that's Alice's brother, broke a whole tray of glasses during a tea-season party, remember, Alice?"

She duly made light of it, but had been furious at the time, for Frank, arriving after a visit to the Golden Phoenix, had been unsteady on his feet.

Harriet leaned forward. "Oh yes, Frank—I must say, Alice, how sorry we were not to see him and his wife—what's her name?—in Shanghai, but everything was so hectic, wasn't it, George?"

"Yes m'dear, no time to see anything much really."

Florence said, "Your brother's married to a Chinese lady, I believe? How fascinating. Has she got those quaint little bound feet?"

"No—her mother's a Manchu and they don't bind, luckily."

"Got quite a bee in your bonnet about footbinding though haven't you, dear?" Charles drew the talk away from his Chinese sister-in-law. "There's a lady in Ichang wants to start a league for abolishing the custom throughout the entire land."

"Rather ambitious, don't you know," George muttered.

"Ah but she's an enthusiast, like a missionary only not one."

Harriet sighed. "Oh these enthusiasts, we have them too—want to change everything that doesn't fit their notions."

Alice felt both cold and hot, thinking of Daisy's fine fervour. "But there are certain things one must condemn on humanitarian grounds surely. I mean take suttee—we outlawed that, are you saying we were wrong to?"

Harriet appraised her like a patient headmistress. "No I'm not. But I believe one meddles with the customs of the country at one's peril. And there's a great gap between binding feet and burning widows."

"Anyway, I've heard the Chinese ladies bind willingly, even though it hurts, to please their menfolk?"

Florence shivered theatrically, glancing at Charles who rose to her look with, "Oh men are brutes aren't they, Florence? I often wonder why you ladies try to please us at all. But as for those hideous hooves called 'golden lilies'—how they can appeal, I don't know."

"*Chacun à son goût* I always say," said George. "Moslem, Buddhist, Sikh, Hindu—*chacun à son goût*...That's not bad, is it, Harriet?"

His wife, a fork of pâté near her lips, gave him the briefest of acknowledgments. The meal progressed slowly, the sun poured unremittingly through the lattices and soon a heavy lassitude fell upon them.

"One misses punkahs so," Harriet gasped, moving the tepid air with a fan.

"The houses here just aren't equipped for them," Charles apologised.

"Well they should be. Really, Alice, will you excuse us. We're so fatigued after the journey, we really must rest, mustn't we, Florence. And we haven't unpacked yet. Do you take a siesta, Alice?"

"Not often. And I must go to the market for another tureen, we're rather short."

"You actually go and buy things there yourself, Alice?" Florence marvelled. "But how adventurous of you—we seldom venture to the native markets, do we, Harriet?"

"Ah well, Alice knows the language and that makes a difference. You're probably good at bargaining, dear?"

"Almost too good," Charles interrupted. "But let me show you upstairs..."

"Oh please don't bother," Harriet yawned. "Just send a housemaid up later, after we've rested."

Alice wondered if she might buy a housemaid along with a tureen; but the visitors would discover the full humbleness of their circumstances sooner or later.

"And are you up to having a look round the godowns, such as they are, George?"

As the men rose, Peter jumped up. "Let me come too, Father!"

"Oh well—not much to see you know."

Alice took his arm. "Why not come to the market with me, Peter? Lots to see there, I can tell you."

He hung back, then seeing the men deep in dull conversation, nodded, "Please, Stepmother Alice."

"Oh dear, I can't bear that word, Peter. It sounds so elderly. Why not call me Aunt? I'm that several times over already. Don't you agree, Charles?"

"Whatever you prefer, dear. Stepmother certainly has a rather sinister ring."

The market-bustle usually lifted Alice's spirits and especially so that afternoon following the dignified somnolence of the dining room where words had to be so carefully weighed. "I'll show you something of the real China," she promised, leading Peter down narrow alleys where strips of matting sun-blinds stretched from opposite roofs so that business was conducted in a curiously dappled twilight. In the streets of the idol-makers she showed him the straw, cloth and tinsel models of possessions and animals that were bought only for burning as funeral offerings.

"It's better than burning the widows themselves, isn't it?" he asked solemnly and she hugged him for that.

In the streets of lacquerers, the smells were resinous with jungles of oiled-paper umbrellas hung for sale; nearby, in the street of the potters, Alice haggled over tureens while Peter watched a barber shave the front of a coolie's head. On the way back, they passed the street of fortune-tellers where elderly bearded men kept caged birds trained to pick out lucky cards. Alice paused. "Would you like to try one?"

He shrank back. "No—I'd only be unlucky."

"But what makes you think so?"

"I usually am, that's all."

"Oh come Peter, just think how lucky you are here and now. I always try to remember that about myself."

"But I'm not. I'm just being sent to England though I'd much rather stay with you and Father. I like it here—the people laugh a lot, don't they? More than Indians."

"Peter, I'm absolutely delighted you like China, but you must go to an English school for a while—then you can come here to live with us if you like."

"It will be years and years." He stared moodily at the fortune cards. "And I might never get back."

"Oh nonsense—let's see, how old are you?"

"Nearly thirteen."

She winced, remembering the raw pains of that age when every year seemed eternity. "Let's try your luck anyway." She turned to one of the fortune-tellers.

He opened the cage and a yellow skinny bird hopped among the cards, beady eyes flicking as it lifted the edge of one card repeatedly. Its owner picked it up.

"Very good—mountains of golden fortune for the boy."

Alice snatched it from him. "Dog of a liar...It's a long-long-delay card—grey years ahead." And then in English, "Come, Peter, let's get back."

"It wasn't good was it?" he asked as they hurried away.

"Not good, not bad, a nothing card."

He spoke with conviction. "I told you—I'm not lucky."

The ladies had revived when they returned; Alice put a fixed smile on her face and surpervised supper. When bed-time eventually came she was too exhausted even for customary finger-crossing as she passed the top stair. In the bedroom, Charles was unbuttoning his shirt. "All going rather well so far, don't you think, dear? And that Florence Plowden's a bit of an enchantress, I must say."

"Really?"

"Oh I suppose she's the kind of woman who appeals more to men than other women. But don't worry, I've my little resident enchantress, haven't I? And I'm sure Harriet approves of you." He hugged her and she smiled wearily.

Certainly Florence had looked most fetching at supper in a low-cut gown, her fair curls perfectly arranged in an intricate style that Alice could never manage.

"I'm not surprised she was the one to catch old Ian, though," Charles continued, removing his trousers. "Several ladies tried, but he's one of those chaps who talks, lives, breathes railways and he never even noticed."

"Rather dull for Florence. But I wonder what his attraction was?"

"He's got a good position, good prospects, and perhaps Florence has changed him. She's the sort to get under a man's skin."

"Quite."

"You don't like her, do you?" He kissed her as they climbed into bed.

"Not much, admittedly. But I quite like the others and Peter's a splendid little fellow, Charles, and so well-behaved."

"I imagine he's had to be with Harriet around." He began fondling her breast till she said wearily, "Oh Charles, I'm so tired, it's been a wearing day..."

He obediently desisted. "Yes, we must get some sleep—picnic to the Yellow Crane Tower tomorrow, isn't it?"

The Yellow Crane Tower was famous for its bright green roof and the view from the hill on which it stood. Its main feature was the mighty flood of the tributary river Han, opaque yellow in the sunshine, dotted with brown and red junk-sails, flowing to meet the Yangtze. A thick heat haze hung over the pullulating cities of the plains, foetid smells of human ordure rose from the cultivated paddies below, mingled with the more sickening stench from the decaying corpses of girl-babies left to rot in the tower's purple shadows. Florence wrinkled her pretty nose, and Harriet's disdainful expression lengthened.

"Might as well start back, hey?" Charles glanced at the time, calculating that the awkward before-supper hours could be filled with the return journey. He and George set off downhill, heedless of Florence's plaint for an escorting arm. Politely, Alice waited for her.

"Really—it's alright for gentlemen, but one's skirts get so torn and dirty they drag one down!" Pouting, she hoisted her skirt over the prickly undergrowth, holding her fashionable boater in place with the other hand. "My brother was just the same when we were young—off he'd stride in his strong boots and then laugh at me for being a slowcoach. I used to get so cross."

"I didn't realise you had a brother, Florence?" Idly, Alice watched a striped lizard run under a stone.

"Oh, I don't now, he's dead. He was a sort of explorer, quite useless at anything sensible. He'd take off into the Himalayas for months, leaving me in Calcutta with my old aunt, which wasn't at all amusing... There's my skirt caught again, bother..."

Alice helped her free it, saying sympathetically. "Oh I know how it is with brothers, they always seem to do as they like and get away with it!"

"And the annoying thing was, he was supposed to look after me, being several years older. Our parents died when I was a baby, you see. Oh I'll leave you well provided for if anything happens to me, he'd say as he went off on another mountain climb."

"What happened then?"

"The fourth time he went on an expedition—about twelve years ago now I suppose, he just didn't come back, and didn't leave me any better off either. Worse in fact, because Stewart was my aunt's favourite and once he was dead, she didn't even pretend to care for me..." She sighed—oh, those long, dull hours spent in Aunt's stuffy parlour making pin-cushions for the next charitable fancy fair. While Alice, leading the way down the path, suddenly seemed to see the bright gravel coming up to meet her, for the ground ahead threatened to lurch entirely out of place.

"You never learned what happened to your brother Stewart then?"

"Eventually yes, we were notified by the consular authorities that he died of fever in some remote spot in West China."

Alice's lips were stiff, a prickling sensation in her scalp. "Stewart?—I seem to have heard—What was his name, not Plowden of course?"

"Stewart Carr—oh this awful path, at last we're nearly

down. Whoever would choose to be a mountaineer, such a stupid occupation!" Her laugh tinkled out as they joined the others waiting at the bottom. Alice stood, numb-cold in the hot sun; already the words, the moments for confession were slipping away; absolute confession—now or never. Her mind refused the full implications of such a totally unexpected dramatic challenge; if she could just turn the clock back that little space—see the lizard run under the stone again, not ask about Florence's brother, have time to think. But she was bound, doomed, to have learned the truth soon, the black hand of divine retribution had clawed down on her out of the blue sky and she shuddered.

"Whatever's the matter, Alice?" Harriet looked concerned. "You look quite pale—are you feeling ill?"

Charles put an arm round her waist. "You do look peaky, dear, not like you... Here stand in the shade for a minute." She did so, knowing the decision had been made. Charles fetched her a parasol from the buggy.

"Is she—er—perhaps in a certain condition?" Harriet whispered to him.

He paused. "Well I'm not aware—but this could be an early sign, yes."

Rather to her surprise, Alice did not have to make any further explanations; Charles tucked her into the buggy and they drove quickly home, not seeming to mind her silence. That evening, pronouncing herself recovered, she joined the party on the verandah before supper. She found it impossible to keep her eyes off Florence, summoning back to her reluctant consciousness the face of the dying man in the Inn of the Five Tiger Pass, the girl in the sepia photograph. Poor little Flossie—Stewart had died feeling guilty about her; Alice should have told her that.

"You were talking about your brother this afternoon, Florence?" She sipped a sherry. "Did you ever hear any more details?"

"Oh, the whole expedition died one way or another—Stewart last of all. Such a waste of young men, and I was miserable for ages afterwards. But Stewart was like that—reckless, never caring much about others."

"I'm sure he cared for you really, Florence. Brothers do, in their fashion. And at least all is well with you now?"

She pouted. "I suppose so—but Ian's so often away and thinks of nothing but railways."

"Not when he's with his charming wife, I'm sure," Charles said gallantly.

"Even then quite a lot—though I do what I can to distract him!"

"Lucky fellow," he murmured and Alice, overhearing, thought it would serve her right if her husband fell madly in love with "poor Flossie".

"Florence was telling me earlier that her brother died on an expedition, Charles, did you know?" She tortured herself relentlessly.

"Yes, Ian told me I remember—they went to Ladakh, didn't they? Rum part of the world. I met a chap who'd been to Leh once—absolutely priest-ridden he said, thousands of those filthy lamas wandering about the place carrying prayer-wheels and muttering something that sounded like 'Oh mother pat me tum'."

Florence giggled. "But what were they really saying?"

"'Om mani padme hum' I suppose, it's the universal Buddhist prayer meaning 'Oh Jewel in the Lotus O'." Alice explained.

"How clever of you, Alice—but I like the English version best."

"And so do I—let's see what cook has for our tums tonight." Charles steered her towards the table, giving Alice the chance for another sherry to steady her nerves.

After preliminary discussion of the continuing difficulties with the troublesome Dacoits in Burma, the dinner conversation again turned to India, for the visitors had scant interest in China, and Harriet was determined to remind her brother of all he was missing by living here.

"You should have joined us in Simla last summer, Charles—a splendid season, wasn't it, George? The Dufferins have improved the general tone immensely, so much more fun than that earnest Lord Ripon who was always grumbling about the 'frivolities of hill-station life'. But dear 'Lady D.'—Marchioness of Dufferin and Ava you know—is quite charming, with three delightful daughters. And Lord Beresford is still Military Secretary, such a witty man—organising everyone for picnics, hunting trips, fancy-dress parties—a mad whirl, wasn't it, George? You'd have loved it, Charles—and Alice too, I'm sure."

"The hill monkeys used to swing on my bedroom verandah in the early mornings, Father," Peter added, "and tap on the window. And I had a pony and went up Jakko, and sometimes wished you were there."

Charles laughed off the little silence with, "Well when I've made my fortune here, we'll come and spend a summer in Simla with you, Harriet, promise. You'd like that wouldn't you, Alice? Alice, did you hear...?"

"Yes dear, sorry, it would be lovely... Have some more chocolate pudding, Florence?"

"Oh no, Alice, thank you, I'm sure you're determined to make me quite fat." She preened her slim shape.

"Oh you need have no fear in that direction, I'm sure nothing could spoil your lovely figure," Alice said sweetly, and Florence was a little puzzled by such compliments from one who, being female and of a similar age, she could only regard as a rival for any man's attentions. Alice was very lucky to have such a handsome, pleasant husband, but she seemed to take him very much for granted. It would do her good, Florence thought spitefully, if Charles were to be a tiny bit distracted from his habitual marital bliss; he was undoubtedly susceptible to feminine charms; indeed most gentlemen were, she had discovered. She tossed her fair curls in the lamplight and saw that Charles noticed, though he was again discussing the dreary subject of Indian politics with George.

Alice, pleading a headache, soon slipped unobtrusively away. Alone in her room, she paced about, holding a clenched fist to her mouth. She went to the window; a moonless night, low mist over the swamp, distant mutter of water, boats at anchor; just as usual, yet all changed. In fact, she comforted herself, she was no more nor less deserving of punishment today than yesterday; but yesterday she had not known her victim. How could she have borne the knowledge of her crime so lightly for so long? Truly it had bothered her conscience but little and since her marriage she had scarcely thought of it. Oh, she was even more wicked than she had realised before—was she really the unredeemed creature that Stepfather thought her? Would it have been better or worse if she had liked Florence? But she could not like her, even though she had wronged her. She was vain, shallow and capable, Alice suspected, of considerable hysterical vindictiveness if the truth came out. If only she had never come here... but that was Fate. She shivered. Was the guilty remorse she now suffered sufficient punishment, or did worse things coil in wait?

She unearthed her reticule from the wardrobe, took out the three remaining pieces of loot: a perfume bottle, the amber ring, the musical box. Carr's ravaged face and pleading eyes came to the very forefront of her vision; she had heartlessly betrayed the last wish of a dying man, and a surge of self-disgust overcame all other emotions. She picked up a pamphlet recently delivered by the China Religious Tract Society and read: "Sin is Satan's work; forgiveness is God's great prerogative and most glorious act. But our God is a jealous God, jealous of the honours of mercy as well as of His Holiness. Let us fear to sin against so holy a God, but let us also fear His Wrath, lest we provoke Him by doubting His infinite Mercy."

Heavy words she had heard so often in the past: fear, jealousy, wrath. She was surely doomed. The paper slipped from her fingers and in its place came an ordinary Chinese proverb: "Only watch how the flowers bloom, how the flowers fade. Say not this man is right, that man is wrong." At that, and with a surge of her usual resilience, she made ready for bed, having decided to ameliorate her crimes by contriving to give something to Florence without letting her suspect the truth.

"Harriet, Florence—such a strange thing in the market this morning..." Alice joined the two ladies who were putting new trims on their ball-gowns in readiness for the first of several farewell functions being held by the Telfords, who were about to leave China for good.

Tea prices were even more depressed this season, which had led to a spate of suicides among the Chinese merchants, bankruptcies among the foreign, and Tommy decided it was time to leave the field open for younger men. Amelia had become quite cheerful thinking of promenades by the sea at Eastbourne, where they planned to settle, knowing that never again would she have to watch the filthy river-tides rising so rudely over the croquet lawn.

Harriet raised a politely inquiring face as Alice tripped up, holding out three rings of amber and gold.

"Look at these—from my pet jeweller in Plum Street. He bought them from a pedlar who said one of them's worth a great deal more than the other two, but no one seems to know which. They're quite similar, aren't they? So Harriet, here's one for you, and yours, Florence, and I'm keeping the third. We'll see which one is really good."

Florence slipped hers on, regarding it disdainfully. "Oh I'm sure it won't be mine!"

"Well, promise to get it valued anyway—it's a gamble and I wanted to share it with you."

Harriet laughed. "But what if mine turns out to be valuable? I'd feel quite guilty, Alice."

"Oh no, you mustn't—it would be just luck and you should keep it."

Florence told Charles about the little transaction that evening and, in bed later, he tartly inquired of his wife why she felt they had money to throw about on amber rings. "I wanted to give Harriet something nice without making it obvious, she's been so good to Peter—I think she's got the valuable one," Alice explained, thinking how tangled webs of deception became. Oh if only their visitors would leave so she could gradually resume that state of relative contentment which had been customary before their arrival.

The halfway point of their stay was marked by the Telfords' party, held after the last race-meeting; it would be quite dismal, people kept saying, not to see Tommy and Amelia in the grandstand anymore. For Tommy was such a lucky card and generous too, and Amelia was—irreplaceable. Nevertheless, by Calcutta standards their parties were quite provincial, Florence privately decided, rather like functions in the Indian *mofussil*. Feeling unaccountably chilled, she drew her Kashmiri shawl closer, looking round the Telfords' crowded drawing-room. Not a single army officer to flirt with; even the remotest Indian outpost could furnish that. Hiding a shiver, she went to join Charles and Alice, guessing that their conversation, with Customs man Wilcock and his wife, would be quite uninteresting.

"Ah Florence, there you are..." Charles drew her into the group. "We were grumbling about our local missionary enthusiasts again."

"Government keeps 'em well under control in India I believe, Mrs Plowden?" boomed Wilcock. "And quite right too. A letter in the China Herald recently suggested the whole missionary system is simply a charitable scheme for keeping lowly-qualified professional persons from Europe and America in overseas employment—strong words, but I sometimes feel inclined to agree."

Alice murmured, "But many of them are very sincere, Mr Wilcock, and feel a genuine call. They're not just looking for work, I'm sure."

"Maybe not. But the Call can be remarkably intermittent I may say, considering the time some of them spend resting and recuperating in pleasant seaside resorts."

"But that again depends on the individual—my mother, for instance, has just gone Home with my elder brother and family, and it's her first proper leave for twelve years."

"Ah yes, Mrs Grant, I'd forgotten you come of missionary stock, or I wouldn't have spoken so freely."

At this the group uncomfortably dispersed, leaving Alice

to reflect that one of many disadvantages of her missionary connection was having to justify her way of life in their company, yet feeling obliged to defend them in their absence. By now Charles and Florence were talking animatedly and, resolving not to interrupt, she wandered over to the piano where Amelia was playing operatic airs, her guests standing around humming nostalgically and exchanging reminiscences of operatic performances in London and Vienna. Having no ear for European music, Alice went to the window, tracing, in her mind's eye, the course of the moonlit Yangtze southward through the lakes and into Hunan. One could go from this very quay to Changsha by water. How old was Lung-kuang now? The chrysanthemums would be blooming in the courtyards, the owls hooting in the park beyond—how many nights she had heard them—and in the kitchen quarters the servants might be singing their weary, after-dark songs.

Charles found her there, leaning against a curtain, a slightly forlorn figure in a slightly faded dress of delphinium blue; she did not look happy, he thought, but it was no time to wonder why. "Alice—I fear we must leave at once. Poor Florence isn't feeling well, touch of Chinese liver perhaps."

Relieved to be off, Alice collected her cloak and they all went home, where Florence was put to bed and dosed with quantities of curative camomile tea. But in the morning her condition was noticeably worse; the Russian doctor came, prescribed quinine pills for fever. By the following day Florence was delirious and the doctor, suddenly concerned, prescribed his special fever mix of barley water with eight grains of sal-ammoniac and three of aconite every four hours. By the fourth day the fever was at its height and the doctor shook his head, pronouncing it definitely malarial, of the type quite common at this season when the swamp was at its pestilential worst; Mrs Markov, the merchant's wife, had died of it in this very house, he reminded Charles gloomily.

Alice had long since remembered both that and the snake on the stairs as she sat for hours by Florence's bed, dabbing her brow with lavender water and watching her body feebly tossing, her eyes wandering frightened and stricken as her dead brother's once had. In anguished panic the scenes of the inn rolled repeatedly before Alice's inward eye; her leaving him during his last night on earth, the anguished cries she had pretended not to hear. Oh, she had been young and raw at the time—but that was not really sufficient excuse.

"Do take some rest now, dear," Harriet crept into the dim,

sick-smelling room. "Snow Duck has some hot supper for you. I'll sit with her."

"No, I'd rather stay, I'm not in the least hungry."

Harriet sighed and sat down opposite, lips pursed with worry. It was all so very sad and provoking—their homeward passages were booked from Shanghai in less than a week. Harriet had never thought much of silly little Florence—perhaps if she died tonight, they could just, decently, make the boat? But if she did not? She shook herself from this outrageous wish and dabbed the patient's head guiltily. "You mustn't get too upset, Alice—you should look after yourself, particularly at a time like this you know..." It was half a question, but Alice ignored it. "After all, George and I realise things aren't easy for you here. It's proving a struggle to make ends meet, isn't it? We always guessed that, but Charles would try. His judgment isn't always—well, he's easily led, or misled, as I'm sure you've discovered. Not that he isn't a most delightful man..."

"Yes, I suppose...his judgment, yes...." Alice trailed off, her spirits, already low, sank further for this was not what she wanted to hear just now about her husband who was supposed to protect and guide her—leading her into adventure and perhaps fortune. She knew there was some truth in it, but continued defiantly, "Oh we manage—the business is growing gradually."

"I'm sure, dear, and you've a good head for it, I can tell. You'll help Charles in the right direction. Maria used to—in her quiet fashion she usually had the last word. So I just want to remind you, dear, if this venture does prove impossible, there's always a welcome for you in India."

"Thank you, Harriet," Alice tried to sound grateful, but her heart sank at the idea of such a fate: she a minor mensahib in Madras; Charles in some dull office. A sense of being trapped yet again overcame her as there came a gasp from the bed.

"Where's Ian?" Florence muttered feverishly. "Why isn't he with me? He's never here when...oh dear, is that you, Harriet? Where's Ian?" Tears oozed from her glassy eyes, and Harriet wiped them away.

"There, there, dear, Ian'll be with you soon, don't worry, we're looking after you."

Florence's eyes focused on Alice. "Who's she? Oh yes, Alice—but where's Stewart? He's never here either..." She sank back on the pillow and Alice shivered uncontrollably.

"Alice, you're looking quite ill—I insist you go and eat some supper at once."

Alice stood up, clutching the bed quilt in distress, "Harriet, I...I..."

"What is it, dear?" Harriet's face showed the smooth, absent concern of a worthy headmistress.

"Nothing—yes, I must be hungry." Downstairs Alice fell into exhausted sleep by the fire and was thus spared the last few hours of crisis when the doctor, summoned in the early hours, announced that the worst of the fever was past and that, if given careful nursing, Florence would eventually recover. The verdict, though most welcome of course, put Harriet and George in a great dilemma, only resolved by Alice's insistence that they stick to their travelling plans, for she would be quite delighted to undertake the task of restoring Florence to full health.

"It's extremely good of you, Alice," Harriet's dry hand clasped hers as they stood on the quay the next day. "I feel quite dreadful leaving you with such a burden—for I fear Florence won't be an easy patient."

"Well, just as soon as she's fit enough to travel you must arrange for her to return to India, Charles," George added. "Any expenses we'll meet of course. I've written telling Ian what's happened and I'm sure he'll drag himself away from his engines for a while in the circumstances...We can go aboard now, Harriet...Now, now, Peter, be a little man..."

Peter, his head buried in his father's chest, did not feel in the least manly just then and the mouth he raised for a farewell kiss quivered. "I'm not lucky you know, Father," he said thickly. "It might be ages and ages before I see you again."

"Oh nonsense, son, we're coming to England next year, aren't we, Alice? And we'll take you on a European tour—promise." Charles pushed him up the gangplank. "Mind you get on well at school now."

Harriet put a protective arm on his shoulder and they mounted together. Yet another parting; another increasing distance as the ship, whistle blowing, pulled into the main current. Alice, hating to see Peter's receding figure, squeezed Charles' hand. "We must manage to go Home next year, it would be such a treat for Peter—and me."

"Oh we will. Things are looking up and now Tommy's going there'll be more room for the rest of us. He's a bit of a monopolist, you know."

She glanced at him. "I'm glad you realise it. But you owe him money, don't you—and now he's leaving...?"

"Don't worry your little head about that, I'll sort that out, you just concentrate on getting Florence better as soon as possible."

And, in a spirit of dogged penitence, Alice did. She was not a nurse by temperament and, as Harriet suspected, Florence was not an easy patient. In due course, she managed to totter to the drawing-room and her rosebud mouth resumed its habitual pout, made more woebegotten by her present misfortune. Alice, having sold the last perfume bottle in the cause, stuffed her with beef tea, arrowroot and calves' foot jelly ordered specially from Shanghai, kept every fire in the house roaring for her comfort, listened with all the tolerance she could muster to Florence's tales of the various gentlemen admirers whose hearts she had once captured.

"But weren't you tempted to accept his offer?" Alice asked one afternoon, after the story of some particularly dashing and ardent suitor.

"Oh yes, and he was such fun—but absolutely penniless, dear. And I'd been too long·scrimping and saving every anna in my mean old aunt's house. I was so tired of genteel poverty as they call it—no, I wasn't going to marry a man like that. Whereas Ian has good prospects, and good family background as you see. Quite honestly," she leaned forward confidentially, "I sometimes wonder if I'd have married him if I'd had money of my own—but what else could I do? Only Ian's always so wrapped up in his railways—he even snores like a steam-engine!" She laughed bitterly. And Alice sighed, for there seemed no end to the twists in the screw of her guilt. "Keep mum about that, won't you?" Florence continued. "Ian's not so bad as husbands go, only not as handsome and amusing as your Charles...."

It was lightly said, but Florence's attraction to Charles was quite apparent. When he returned home in the evenings her face immediately brightened, she shook off her hunched dejection, lifting soft, wistful, blue eyes to his.

"Oh Charles, there you are. What dreary weather, isn't it? And I fear I've been dreary too, haven't I, Alice? Now you must play the gallant gentleman and cheer us both up!"

Usually at this juncture, Alice went to help with the tea, while Charles warmed himself by the fire, telling Florence the small annoyances of his day while she clucked in sympathy. As he did so he felt the closeness of her frail and feminine dishevelment, while she was equally aware of the masculine pulse of his body standing over her. Sometimes she leaned forward carelessly so that her flimsy robes of convalescence loosened to reveal the swell of her breasts, sometimes he would shift his leg casually against hers, keeping it there, hard-limbed against her softness. And Alice, returning with the tea, noted their quick readjustments of posture, and tightened her jaw in pained resolution. Oh, it served her right. Let them flirt if they wished; they deserved the pleasure, she the pain. Florence had suffered unknowingly at her hands; let her suffer knowingly at Florence's.

And this thought was uppermost in her mind on the day that Charles, coming to take her tea-tray, said, "Florence has been telling me of Ian's letter—excellent news, isn't it? He'll be back in Calcutta to meet her well before Christmas."

Florence tossed her curls. "And you'll be rid of me at last, Charles! For Alice thinks I should leave in two weeks."

"Rid of you? Why that's not what I meant at all, Florence. Indeed I was just thinking—before you go—I've to make a short business trip to Ichang. So why don't we all go? At least you'd see a bit more of the country beyond this dreary hole and the upriver gorges are magnificent. Then you could transship straight down to Shanghai. What do you think, Alice?"

"Why it's a splendid idea, and the fresh air would buck you up no end, Florence."

Florence was already looking excited at the prospect when Charles' next words added another spark: "Of course it's a bit risky leaving the new compradore here to deal with everything alone but..."

"Oh but there's no real need for me to go too, Charles. I've been before. No, I'll stay and mind the shop—but it would do you the world of good, Florence," Alice added persuasively. Not that Florence needed much persuasion at the thought of days alone with Charles. "But I'm not sure it's quite proper...?" she looked coquettish. "I mean people might imagine..."

"What people? No one here to know even and the Smalls at Ichang aren't that small-minded are they, Charles?"

"Heavens no, and we'll be either on the steamer or staying with them... Well Alice, if you really think...?"

"Yes you two go." She was firm. "And when you change ships here on the way down I'll bring the rest of your luggage to the quay and see the roses in your cheeks again, Florence."

"Alice, you're an angel, really!" Florence smiled in genuine gratitude and Alice, bending over the teapot, thought that the vengeful gods must now be satisfied. What if Florence and her husband did flirt and kiss a little in the secrecy of their cabins? No harm would come of it, and she would never seek to know, for her only consuming desire was to see the last of those fair tossing curls at the earliest possible moment.

The weather was unusually clement for November when Alice waved goodbye to Charles and Florence sailing away upriver. Light-heartedly she watched them out of sight, then went for a long walk—along the Bund, into the native city, out towards the Pagoda Hill; but on the way her buoyancy evaporated. She had optimistically assumed that once Florence's burdensome presence was removed, all would be as before. Instead she was filled with disquiet, still fretted by the unconsidered, long-term results of her youthful dishonesty, still beset with superstitious fear at the odd coincidence that had brought it so closely home to her. And somehow the visitors had seemed to diminish Charles as well as herself. She remembered what Harriet had said of him, how often he had seemed unsure of himself—rather weak and vacillating, though she was reluctant to frame the words.

Like most men, Alice decided drearily, Charles simply wanted money and social standing and if he got them they would simply move to a larger house, perhaps in Shanghai, eventually even to Eastbourne in the footsteps of the Telfords. Their house, she noticed as she came back, was firmly shuttered, its croquet lawn quite gone to pot—how Florence had turned up her pert nose at it, explaining that croquet was dreadfully old-fashioned these days when everyone was playing lawn-tennis.

Alice turned in her own gate, reminding herself the house was now free of that presence, so why did the future still seem lack-lustre? Before leaving, Charles told her that Harriet had thought her pregnant, and was obviously disappointed to learn she was not. It seemed another failure for them both. And that led to a sudden undiminished ache for Lin. How he would scorn the conventionality of her present life after so much fine talk about the regeneration of all China! Were he to see her now, standing in this empty drawing-room, he would consider himself well rid of her. But what was he doing? Certainly the self-strengtheners had not produced a new dawn. The Manchus were still securely in control, the barbarians ever more aggressive. Perhaps Lin too found himself relegated to some confining backwater? That thought depressed her more than any, for she drew inspiration from his glowing, if distanced, enthusiasm and could not bear to doubt it.

As darkness fell the house closed round her with its customary sad chill, the death snake not banished from the stair. It was long since she had been there alone, and, after a solitary supper, the resolution that had kept the one tempting thought at bay snapped. Donning her blue robe and padded winter jacket she bade Snow Duck call a chair; soon after, she received from Flowing Spring's hand the first flaring pipe of oblivion, drawing its smoke deeply into her. The price of pure Benares opium was going up, Flowing Spring told her the next morning when she paid her surprisingly large bill. Merchants were blaming it on the depression in tea, but were probably just making more profit for themselves.

"That's what your husband should go into if he wants to make money," she smiled innocently. "There'd be ways of selling to us direct, without middle-men."

At the time Alice rejected the suggestion out of hand, but it returned to her later when she sat in the office studying the firm's accounts that Charles usually kept locked away. Plainly the business was in a worse state than he had admitted, partly because of a large loan recently repaid to Tommy Telford. Alice felt angry as the ledgers revealed many misjudgments he had not told her about, and she knew it was because he would not trust the trading instincts of a mere woman. But the fact was—hers were keener than his. Damn him, she thought, when he returns I shall tackle him about this.

Restlessly she prowled about the godown, sniffing its multifarious odours, touching its strange substances, trying to recapture the glamour it had once held for her. But now it seemed no more than a messy shed full of absurd things. She had often been told that the Chinese devoted more energy to the pursuit of wealth than any other people, but was it not also true of foreigners here, whose main aims were either to save money or souls? Well, she could not share either of these passions. Back in the office, she slammed the drawer savagely shut on the ledgers—no, let Charles get himself out of this mess, he had already spurned her help. Instead, when he returned, she would at last throw herself wholeheartedly into the work of Daisy's league.

Having made that decision, time hung heavily on her hands and two days before Charles was due back she gave herself one last escape to the Golden Phoenix. It was particularly busy that evening and Flowing Spring was so in demand that Alice received her pipes from lesser hands. The state of disembodied calm was as always, but in the middle of the night she woke and vomited violently. There was a rustle of skirts and the blind woman was at her side.

"Oh dear, Uncut Jade—the girl must have given you inferior mud, not knowing you are a valued customer. I'm so sorry. It won't happen again, I promise... I'll get you a chair, you must go home and sleep for hours—it's dirty stuff you've been given." Solicitously she helped the groaning Alice outside; the freezing night air bit through her clothes like a ravening dog and the bearer's lantern exploded inside her skull like a firecracker. Dumped at her front door, she took what seemed hours actually to get herself inside as the handle slipped from her grasp. Upstairs she stared in the mirror at her dishevelled hair, bloodshot eyes, her mouth sour as a clogged drain, and then huddled miserably into bed, vowing that, from that moment on, the poppy would wait for her in vain.

The torpor into which she pitched seemed endless, but it was only a few hours before she was roused by an urgent thudding. Pale light seeped through the curtains and the sound that she imagined to be inside her head was a pounding on the front door. She lay fearful, calling for Snow Duck, but he slept behind the kitchen and would not hear. Who could it be at such an early hour? Groaning, she tottered downstairs and opened the door, blinking up into a familiar face.

"Daisy—why what time is it?" Mrs Small looked distressed, Alice thought vaguely, and a wave of guilt swamped her. "I'll do something about the League—really, I've just decided to."

"Tush, my dear Alice, it's not that..." Daisy came hesitantly indoors. "You don't look well, dear, is anything—already—wrong?"

"No, no a touch of fever I think... I'm still half asleep. But is it really you? I'm not dreaming, am I?"

"No dear... no it's really me, but..." Daisy's voice trailed away as she unpinned her hat, turned to face her, then her courage temporarily failed. "Before I explain why I've come, could I beg a cup of tea, dear? I've been sitting on the deck of a salt junk all night and I'm frozen stiff."

In the kitchen Alice struggled as if from a remote distance to light the stove, put the kettle on; only then did she realise the oddity of Daisy's appearance, and called out, "But haven't you seen Charles and Florence? They went up to Ichang last week."

There was no reply and in sudden apprehension she ran along the passage.

"Daisy—Daisy...Charles and Florence? Haven't you seen them? Has anything happened?"

Daisy met her at the door, caught her in her arms and half-carried her to the sofa. "There, there, dear...sit down. Oh my poor Alice, I've the most dreadful news—you must prepare yourself..." She paused, staring pityingly at Alice's fearful face. "They...they're...they were both drowned, in the rapids above Ichang. They would go—just a little excursion really, but dangerous at this time of year when the waters are low—all the rocks and shoals and..."

Alice began to scream, she put her hands over her ears so as not to hear herself so plainly, and screamed and screamed. Her mind, first opium-dulled, now enflamed with anguish and disbelief, seemed to be splitting, parting at its very seams. Daisy dabbed at her eyes, tried to rock her like a baby; Alice wished she was a baby.

Snow Duck rushed in, twisting his pigtail round his head, and Daisy told him her news. Hearing the words said again and in Chinese, seeing his fat face collapse into woe, Alice howled the more as the actuality of it penetrated even more. The kettle boiled over and Snow Duck made tea which Daisy sipped gratefully, until Alice groaned and vomited on the carpet. Daisy, distressed, sent Snow Duck for the doctor and Alice, her throat stripped raw with the cheap opium, the vomiting and the screaming, could eventually only gasp piteously, hating to face the silence that would fall if she quietened. "But tell me everything..." She clutched Daisy's hand. "How did it happen? How could it have—just like that? In the rapids you say?"

"It must have been quite quickly over...for them both. They stayed with us, of course, but Florence so wanted to venture upriver a little, it would be exciting, she said, her last chance to see more of the country. Archie warned them of the dangers but—oh my dear, I'm so very very sorry, such a stupid, stupid accident...Anyway, to humour her really, Charles agreed."

"So he wouldn't have gone if she hadn't been there?"

"Well...no, but you can't really blame...he was just being kindhearted and she wanted a little adventure..."

Alice began to scream again, rending the membranes of her throat.

"Hush, dear, calm yourself a little, please... They went in one of old Chin-ling's boats, just for two days, intending to return in time for the downriver steamer. But then they didn't turn up," Daisy dabbed her own eyes. "And we were just getting anxious when Chin-ling and his captain arrived with the terrible news."

"Not everyone was drowned then?"

"No, the tow-ropes broke at the Sorceress Gorge and the boat went out of control, bashing downstream against the rocks. The decks were awash and the captain advised them to jump for the shore, which was quite close. Florence jumped—but not far enough and she was not strong enough to fight the current and got carried away instantly. Charles and one of the crew went to her rescue and all three were drowned in those fearsome whirlpools below the rapids."

"And the rest of the crew?"

"Struggled ashore—and the boat sank."

"So if Florence hadn't been there..." Alice shrieked at her again and Daisy began again.

"But you can't really blame..."

"No I can't blame Florence... not Charles—it's me, me to blame..." She thrust her face into Daisy's, whimpering, "Me, I'm the criminal, the murderer, I killed my husband, I killed them both..."

"You—Alice, my dear, that's madness, madness. Why, you had nothing whatever to do with it..."

"I did, I did..." Alice rushed out into the hall pointing up the stairs. "There—see, the death snake, it's been there all the time waiting, waiting for me, knowing I had to make it all happen... aagh!" She spun round in a shivering arc of terror, and fell, scrabbling the tiles with her hands.

Daisy rushed to her. "Alice... my dear dear girl, there's nothing there—no snake, no nothing... please calm yourself."

As she tried to lift her, the door opened and Snow Duck rushed in with the doctor. They carried her up to bed thrashing wildly and the doctor mixed a sedative.

"Now, Mrs Grant... take this... hush now..."

Daisy held her head while she swallowed, the room spun again and Alice fell back listening to the concerned voices receding. But she must not let things recede yet, and she held doggedly on to her distress till Daisy crept back into the room.

. "Daisy, you must listen—I'm not mad to think it was this way—I must tell you everything please, or I shall never rest...come here..." Her fingers closed over Daisy's wrist and she pulled her down by the bed.

The first actual telling of her long-ago encounter with Stewart Carr was a great relief even in her agony and in spite of its eventual consequences.

"And now," Alice concluded, "how can I ever face life with this burden? For if I hadn't felt so ashamed, so guilt-ridden about Florence, I'd never have let them go off together like that. They were having a mild flirtation, weren't they? It doesn't matter now, but I knew she'd enjoy the trip better without me, and I was so tortured about her...Oh Daisy, Daisy, I've killed my husband and ruined my life—oh I wish I were dead too!"

"My poor, poor dear, you mustn't talk like that for an instant." Daisy, shaken but in control smoothed her hair. "Now you must listen quietly to me. You're making far too many assumptions, jumping to conclusions—can you not see, even in your present distressed state, that causes and effects are more complex than this? My dear, how can I put it simply—our whole lives are made up of a series of 'ifs' and 'buts' and 'if onlys', and it is simply not given to us to make sense of them or of our place in the universe. Certainly you behaved dishonestly by telling no one of the Carr loot— remember though it *was* loot, his theft before yours—and I can see that this coming of Florence into your life years after would seem a fateful coincidence. But there are many other imponderables—of accident, timing, people's feelings, sheer bad luck, over which you'd no control. Clearly you never wished Florence any harm and you must never, ever blame yourself for this tragedy."

"But they were having a little flirtation, weren't they, and if..."

Daisy pursed her lips. "There you go—if. Well, if the rapids hadn't been specially treacherous all would have been well. You can't persuade me that the state of the rapids at the Sorceress Gorge the other day was directly connected to an incident that occurred at the Inn of the Five Tiger Pass twelve years ago!"

"No—but perhaps to bring home to me..."

"Come, Alice, you're getting above yourself. Nature may

sometimes be relentless and cruel, but not personally vindictive—your theory would suggest an arm of justice longer and more avenging than even the devoutest missionary would wish!" She smiled gently. "When you were young and were in fairly desperate straits you kept what didn't belong to you. That is really the beginning and end of the matter."

"But if I'd confessed as soon as I discovered who Florence was..."

Daisy sighed. "Here we are again, faced with the tantalising 'would have beens' of our lives! You won't puzzle them out today, Alice, I've been trying for years and expect to carry on doing so..." She had lowered her voice, for the sedative was at last taking effect and Alice sank into hours of feverish, troubled slumber.

For the next week Alice lay inert trying to absorb the shock of her bereavement and, in her stronger moments, writing sad letters to relatives containing the news. Daisy, understanding, treated her like an invalid, offering tempting morsels and sympathy, reading the sonorously comforting lines of Wordsworth to her on grey afternoons. The care of her fell wholly to Daisy, for Eliza and William were in England, while Robert, recently out of the Army, was on a tour of the Middle East with Mary.

Frank hurried to Hankow when he heard the news and begged Alice to return to Shanghai with him, but the thought of Treaty-Port life depressed her unutterably and she chose instead to return to Ichang with the Smalls. And this, to Daisy, seemed part of an inevitable pattern, for had she not first seen this gifted young woman as her heiress apparent? Was it not now up to Daisy to mould one so unexpectedly and tragically bereft towards a newly fruitful, thoughtful future?

Archie Small arrived to help with the process of clearing up; all the assets of Grant & Greenwood were sold to pay outstanding debts and Alice, practically penniless, kept only the firm's seals in Mandarin and English. That Christmas at Ichang passed Alice by almost unnoticed. Cards from Home with scenes of coaching inns stood about on the Smalls' tables and on Christmas Day the few resident foreigners gathered for a service with the Belgian priests and nuns. Throughout it Alice sat numb, beset with memories of that jolly Shanghai Christmas five years before when Charles had been so winningly, appealingly alive.

How she had under-rated him, she castigated herself,

when he had been so anxious to make her happy and comfortable! Why had she often been so critical of him? Achingly she wished for him back that she might make amends, but the ache was not only on her own behalf but on his—for the years of life he had counted on. Daisy, knowing there was no short cut through bereavement, simply let her huddle for hours in their sitting-room, which she left only to walk up the hill, from which she could look down at the waters of the Great River that had drowned her husband. Sometimes as she stood there, came the chant of the monks in the nearby monastery and, attracted by the sound, she would walk to its entrance and stand in the shadows of the cypresses listening.

One afternoon, greatly daring, she opened the wooden door and quietly slipped inside. Shaven-headed priests in patched gowns were shuffling in procession round the interior of a dim hall, their cast-down eyes showing no awareness of her presence. The leaders were sounding drums, bells, gongs in a ding-dong rhythm, the air was heavy with incense burning on the altar at the far end, where a dusty-gilt Buddha sat, surrounded by tutelary gods.

"We pay homage to all the Buddhas of the present and all the Buddhas of the future . . . we pay homage to the Buddhas of the past . . ." This repeated chorus Alice eventually deciphered, though the mumbled verses eluded her. After a timeless monotony of repeated sound had washed over her, each priest genuflected before the altar and disappeared through a door behind. Alice stayed on, chilly and disappointed. They must have seen her—would no one acknowledge her unspoken need? As she reluctantly prepared to leave a monk appeared through another door and bowed at her.

"The Reverend Abbot will see you now."

"But I . . . I have no appointment."

"It is not always necessary."

She followed him into a cell-sized room where an elderly man robed in black sat reading in a high-backed chair. As she approached, he gestured to a cushion on the floor. She bowed and sat. "Reverend Abbot, I must apologise for . . ."

"It is alright, you don't have to explain yourself. The foreign woman who lives in the old temple told me of you—she said you might come here one day."

Alice smiled at the thought of Daisy's warm caring. "Then you won't mind if I come again?"

"As you wish, but what could you be seeking here?"

"I hardly know—my spirit is so heavy. I suppose I'm

wondering about the meaning of this place—of your faith, of the Zen?"

It was half a question and he sighed gently. "Our Master tells us that to seek the truth of Zen is like looking for an ox when you are riding on the back of it. Has no one explained that to you?"

She shook her head dumbly and an unhurried silence fell. At length she said, "Would you let me come and stay here for a while in your guest-room as travellers sometimes do?"

"But who are you? You are not a traveller?"

"Yes I am—I think I always have been and always will be."

The answer pleased him, but he hesitated. "You are a woman and this is a monastery. It would be irregular."

"But I'm a barbarian woman and therefore the irregularity is not relevant."

He chuckled. "Or the two irregularities cancel each other out?"

"That's it—and make the way smooth." She smiled back boldly. "I've a little money to pay for my keep," she added, knowing the poverty of monks.

"You may come for a while, only don't rush about seeking enlightenment in every corner. If you stop looking, stop talking, stop thinking, there is nothing you may not eventually understand."

"I do not understand you, Reverend," she murmured sadly.

He clicked his beads in sudden impatience. "It is the message of a poem by Seng Ts'an, read it, even if its meaning is beyond you. The guest-room will be ready for you tomorrow and for one hour each day an acolyte will try and teach you a little something. We're quite strict here and live sparsely. Won't that worry you? For I believe you barbarians thrive on the oily fats and fleshes of animals?" He wrinkled his nose.

"In my youth I lived long on rice-gruel and vegetables. Now food is tasteless to me."

He nodded satisfied, waving a dismissive hand.

She had spoken confidently to the Abbot, but when, overriding the Smalls' misgivings, she moved into the monastery she soon found her constitution quite unaccustomed to its frugal regime. The meagre diet sapped her low vitality and the chill cell gave her a feverish cold so that, instead of being lulled into meditative oblivion by the monks' prayers, she had to concentrate on the stifling of disruptive coughs.

And the meaning of the place eluded her, as the acolyte Fa-yen, who came to her every day warned her from the start. He was quite young with a long bony head and hooded eyes; sitting cross-legged before her, usually concealing the contemptuous outrage he felt both for this instrusive female presence and his order to speak with it, he slammed between them a thick book entitled *Platform Sermons containing the Doctrine given out by Hui-neng, the Great Teacher Sixth Patriach, at Tai-fan Ssu*. This was usually sufficient to reduce Alice to that silence in which he hoped to pass their obligatory hour, but occasionally she tried to question him:

"You believe in the Buddha, don't you?" she asked one afternoon. "Will you not try to explain it—him—to me?"

His eyes flipped wide for a second. "What is not the Buddha?"

"I don't understand you."

"The Buddha is to be made within the self-nature and is not to be sought outside the Body."

"But how do I...one, begin to see the self-nature?"

"It is by the discipline of Zen."

"Which you are learning?"

He shook his head. "If you wish to learn Zen, Zen is neither in sitting cross-legged nor in lying down."

"Then we are wasting time here, doing this?"

He bowed his head in silent assent and she asked him to leave. But the next day she tried again. "Can't you explain a little more?"

"The simplest text I know," he replied, "is that of a lamp and its light. As there is a lamp, there is light; if no lamp, no light. When you have understood the Oneness of those two you will have taken the first small step towards emancipation."

"Emancipation?" The word, with its connotation of social subjugations, surprised her. "From what?"

"From thought into thoughtlessness, from form into formlessness—in essence, from the realm of opposites in which we customarily live."

She considered this. "But are these not merely emptiness, non-being?"

"No indeed. Emptiness is not merely negative, it is always within us, not grasping, it is the other half of suchness. Suchness and emptiness make a whole."

He rose to leave and she caught at his robe. "But this suchness—what does that word mean?"

For answer he banged his fist on the wall. "The stone in

the wall, the air in the sky, the crack in the ice, the pain in the heart—these things have the original nature of suchness. In the deep mystery of things as they are we are released from our relatedness to them."

After he had gone, Alice would sit cross-legged, chilled, over-whelmed sometimes by the sense of having fallen down a rabbit-hole and eaten from that side of the mushroom which made her bigger than all the creatures around, so that figures and scenes from her past scuttled through her mind in a series of distant miniatures. So large was she that the two ends of the rabbit-hole seemed almost united—a bright lamp and its light. But the euphoria of this mood was easily shattered and more often she sat looking at the wall, seeing nothing but wall, unable even faintly to discern the meaning of Fa-yen's words. For she possessed an inborn reluctance to contemplate turning herself inside out for the start of that strange journey between subjective and objective which had to do with the meaning of this place.

Nevertheless the monastery was, in some fashion, balm to her troubled spirit. As the weather warmed, she strolled through its groves, taking pleasure again in the dark green of cypresses, translucent pinks and whites of sunlit blossoms against a spring sky. Daisy visited her often, bringing fruit, buns, news of the outside whether she wished to eat and hear or not.

"Alice will come back to us soon," she told Archie confidently. "But I must admire her perseverance. She's not cut out for the contemplative life, but she'll have to understand this for herself."

"Get her involved in the League," he suggested, "it will give her a practical purpose, something outside herself."

But Daisy shook her head. "In her present state she's not interested in native women's feet."

He shrugged, bowing as usual to her womanly intuition, and merely commenting that something was sure to turn up for Alice soon.

Alice, waiting half-consciously for some sign of resolution, lacked Archie's conviction. Her mind, extended or perhaps obfuscated by grief and her spartan monasticism, played with unaccustomed metaphysical speculations and when the sparse doctrines of Zen proved impenetrable, she turned for help to her favourite Taoist poet, Chuang-tse. It was he who had once dreamed of being a butterfly, fluttering about on a summer's day and conscious only of his butterfly happiness. When he awoke he no longer knew if he was a man dreaming he was a butterfly or a butterfly dreaming he was a man.

"Between a man and a butterfly there is necessarily a distinction. The transition is called the transformation of material things," the poet had written. Alice looked at her cell-wall for a while, then took from her bundle of possessions, the only book she had brought with her. And there were Tweedledum and Tweedledee in the dark green wood and the Red King snoring in his red nightcap—dreaming of Alice. Tweedledee said, "'And if he left off dreaming about you, where do you suppose you'd be?' he demanded of her, and 'Where I am now of course,' she replied. 'Not you,' Tweedledee retorted contemptuously. "You'd be nowhere, why you're only a sort of thing in his dream.'"

Also contained in Alice's bundle was a small mirror into which, shunning all vanity, she had not looked since her arrival at the monastery. She looked now, startled to see how thin and wan she had become, understanding suddenly why Daisy worried about her. And then her musings on the nature of reality led her to a rather frightening idea: that there was someone somewhere dreaming about her—staring pale-faced in a mirror, in a cell in a monastery on a peak at Ichang overlooking the River Yangtze in the spring of the year 1888. Just as Lewis Carroll dreamed Alice in Wonderland (or as the Red King did?) or as Chuang-tse dreamed he was a butterfly. But perhaps, her scalp prickled, there was someone else on the other side of the mirror into which she stared so fiercely, who was dreaming them all?

She got up and banged her fist against the wall as Fa-yen had done, then she put the mirror and book away, knowing that, in some instinctive way, there had been a moment of mind-flower-opening as the Zen masters put it, but that it was time to leave the dark green wood, for she had gone in as far as she could.

And the next day Daisy brought a letter from Frank. William, the family and Eliza were en route for Shanghai, he wrote, and Robert and Mary soon due back also. "Robert asks anxiously after you," Frank wrote, "saying that if you're not out of that monastery by the time he arrives, we'll get up another posse and come to drag you back to civilization as you once did for me... He means it, you know, so please come away, Sis, and save us the trouble!"

She frowned angrily at the vision of the three men marching into the monastery, grave and heavy with a sense of duty. She toyed with the idea of running away before they came, throwing herself entirely on the mercy of the country that had never yet let her down. Or perhaps she should become a Buddhist nun? And she giggled at the thought of their horrified faces as she met them in black robes with shaven head. But these were merely wild ideas and the period of retreat was clearly over. The following day she bade a grateful farewell to the Abbot and left, knowing, as she closed the monastery door for the last time, that she had made no more ripple on its contemplative life than a fly lighting on the Yangtze below. But, like a fly, she carried away with her a draught that gave her strength to travel further.

When Mrs Charles Grant, dressed in a sombre grey, disembarked from the Yangtze steamer at Shanghai, she stored her few belongings in the Customs Shed for later collection and took a rickshaw to the Grand Hotel. Luncheon was being served, the dining-room was completely filled and she steeled herself against the cold eyes of the head waiter who did not approve of young women who walked and ate alone. It was, she told herself firmly, something to get used to.

"I'll wait for a table," she told him, "and please bring me a glass of white wine on the verandah."

She sat, sipped wine, flipped idly through a copy of the *Shanghai Mercury*. The names caught her eye at once—on the passenger list of arrivals from England yesterday: Mrs Edward Blake, Mr and Mrs W. Greenwood, Charlotte, Joel, Polly and Thomas Greenwood. She gasped with pained pleasure at that last—so another Thomas Greenwood was born to tread the soil of the Celestial Empire as his grandfather had. She longed to hold the baby in her arms, to see if she could puzzle out any likeness to her father's looks. She glanced at the paper again, its date, 18th May, a reminder that her thirtieth birthday was nearly upon her, and she recalled the words of a Sung poet, "At the age of thirty my renown is small as dust raised by the feet of galloping deer." Never mind; she was not seeking renown.

Leaning back, basking in the sun, she decided to celebrate the arrival of the new Thomas Greenwood and her approaching birthday with more wine instead of lunch. As the drink warmed her, she suddenly recalled with the vividness of yesterday rather than twelve years ago, that spring day when she had first seen Shanghai. How she, Robert and Major Cartwright had drunk champagne in this very hotel, how afterwards, bubbly with it, she had rashly inquired of Robert why the Chinese did not throw every barbarian into the sea and get on with their own celestial business? She smiled, thinking there was much she did not know then that she now knew—and much else presumably, which she did not yet know but one day might, if she lived long enough. She thought dispassionately of Lin, wondered where he was, what he still had to teach her. For she realised that she badly wanted to live in spite of everything—to find that out and much else besides.

When she paid the bill she realised she had but a few taels left in all the world. An almost penniless widow, she thought, without home or children, owner only of a sable-lined jacket, some books, a few clothes, and a long-ago stolen musical box. And yet, as she left the hotel, her feet were winged with the reckless buoyancy of those who travel the world lightly. Spring flowers glowed in the gardens and a merry crowd of American globetrotters just arrived in the mysterious Orient for the first time off the steamship *Mississippi* were bowling along in rickshaws, clutching their hats and calling gaily to each other. The sight made Alice feel mature and wise, but in a way that enhanced the serenity of her mood.

As she walked up the driveway of Frank's villa she heard his voice calling to a servant at the back of the house. In the stable courtyard she saw her brother bent earnestly over the raised hoof of a racing pony. Unobserved, she paused, feeling the years slide away from her even further until the grown man before her was a lad again, a groom with a grubby kerchief twisted round his head standing beside Han-li's horse in the courtyard of the Chu, and she a skivvy in faded blue cotton with a broom in her hand. The bottom and top of the rabbit-hole came together.

"Frank," she said softly.

He looked up and rushed to her with his arms outstretched. "Sis—it's you, at last. We've all been so worried about you. Oh my dear, how are you?" He crushed her to him in a great bear-hug.

"But surely you didn't worry, Frank? You knew I'd be alright, didn't you, *really?*"

He gave her a rare look of love, admiration and understanding. "Yes, Uncut Jade—I knew you'd be alright *really.*"

He linked arms with her, she smiled and they walked into the house.

THE END

ONCE IS NOT ENOUGH
by Jacqueline Susann

Jacqueline Susann follows her enormous successes *Valley of the Dolls, The Love Machine,* and *Every Night, Josephine!* with a story so touching and so exciting in its twists of character relationships, that it will not only captivate her millions of devoted readers but will win her many new admirers.

A novel of love and innocence in a world where everything goes.

0   552   10029   3   £1.95

DOLORES
by Jacqueline Susann

Jacqueline Susann's last book...

is the tragic, intense story of Dolores Ryan, the beautiful young widow of an assassinated American President. Elegant, fashionable and proud in her grief, she was her country's ideal tragic figure and they loved her. Although she lived a very private life, everyone assumed she had millions in the bank. Only Dolores herself knew that she had been left too poor to sustain her extravagant tastes, and too lonely to be fulfilled as a woman. What she needed most was money and men...

0   552   10538   4   £1.25

A SELECTED LIST
OF CORGI TITLES

While every effort is made to keep prices low, it is sometimes necessary to increase prices at short notice. Corgi Books reserve the right to show new retail prices on covers which may differ from those previously advertised in the text or elsewhere.

The prices shown below were correct at the time of going to press. (May '82)

All these books are available at your book shop or newsagent, or can be ordered direct from the publisher. Just tick the titles you want and fill in the form below.

CORGI BOOKS, Cash Sales Department, P.O. Box 11, Falmouth, Cornwall.

Please send cheque or postal order, no currency.

Please allow cost of book(s) plus the following for postage and packing:

U.K. Customers—Allow 45p for the first book, 20p for the second book and 14p for each additional book ordered, to a maximum charge of £1.63.

B.F.P.O. and Eire—Allow 45p for the first book, 20p for the second book plus 14p per copy for the next 7 books, thereafter 8p per book.

Overseas Customers—Allow 75p for the first book and 21p per copy for each additional book.

NAME (Block Letters) ....

ADDRESS ....

....

"AN OFF-BEAT PANORAMIC NOVEL
ABOUT THE YOUNG DAUGHTER OF ENGLISH
MISSIONARIES WHO IS CAPTURED DURING
A MASSACRE AND SPENDS YEARS IN
CAPTIVITY. HER ATTEMPT TO ADJUST TO A
CONVENTIONAL LIFE AFTER HER
ESCAPE MAKES ABSORBING READING."
Western Daily Press

'HIGHLY INFORMATIVE'
Financial Times

'HIGHLY CONVINCING ...
DRAMATICALLY EXCITING
Norwich Mercury

'A SPLENDID READ ... COMPULSIVE'
Hong Kong Standard

'PAT BARR'S BOOK DEALS WITH THE LIFE OF A
FICTIONAL CHARACTER. ALICE GREENWOOD,
WHOSE FAMILY IS MASSACRED DURING AN
ANTI-FOREIGN RIOT IN CHINA. SHE IS
CARRIED OFF AND SOLD INTO SLAVERY. THE
NOVEL RECOUNTS HER EFFORTS TO GET
BACK TO HER OWN PEOPLE – AND MORE
INTERESTINGLY, THE SUSPICION WITH WHICH
SHE WAS TREATED BY HER FELLOW
EUROPEANS ON HER RELEASE.

THE AUTHOR HAS A GREAT FEEL FOR CHINA,
WHICH SHOWS ALL THE WAY THROUGH.'
Tribune